WEIRD

HEROES

ILLUSTRATED FANTASY AND SCIENCE FICTION BY SOME OF THE BEST WRITERS AND ARTISTS IN THE FIELD. AN ENTERTAINING AND ORIGINAL FANTASY EXPERIENCE!

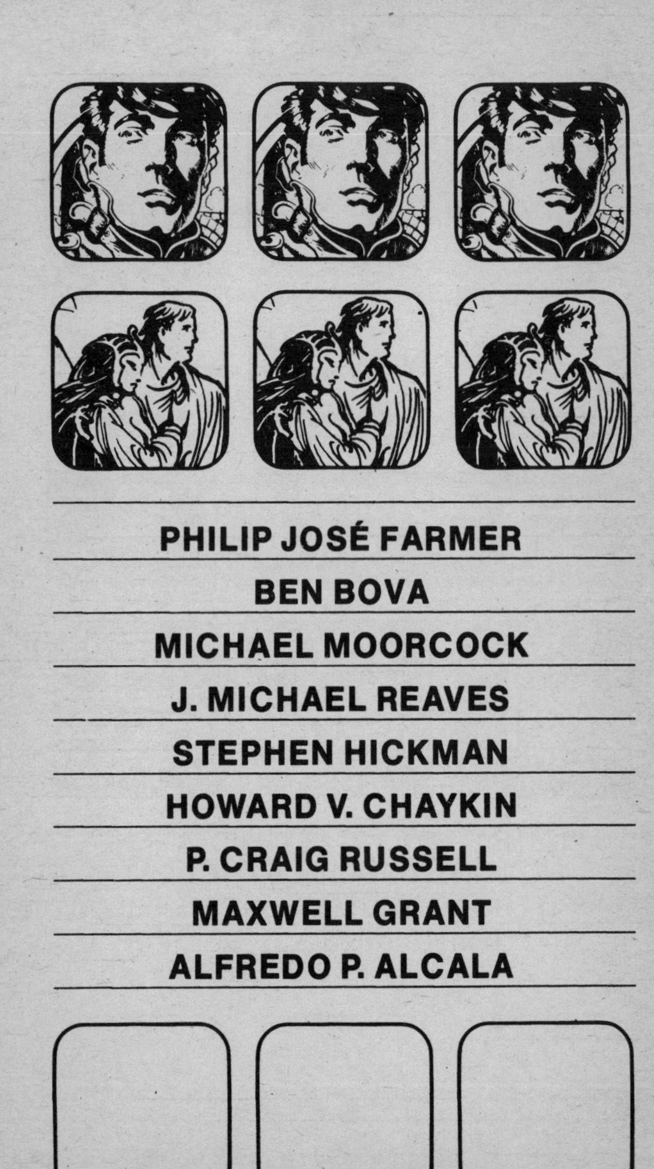
PHILIP JOSÉ FARMER
BEN BOVA
MICHAEL MOORCOCK
J. MICHAEL REAVES
STEPHEN HICKMAN
HOWARD V. CHAYKIN
P. CRAIG RUSSELL
MAXWELL GRANT
ALFREDO P. ALCALA

WEIRD HEROES

VOLUME EIGHT

BYRON PREISS, EDITOR

HBJ

A JOVE/HBJ BOOK

BYRON PREISS VISUAL PUBLICATIONS, INC.

This book is dedicated to Mrs. Jessie King.

Letters of comment are welcomed. Please address mail to WEIRD HEROES EIGHT c/o Byron Preiss Visual Publications, Inc., 680 Fifth Ave., New York City 10019.

Jove/HBJ Books Edition Published November, 1977

ISBN 0-515-04257-9

Library of Congress Catalog Card Number: 77-80705

Printed in the United States of America

Jove/HBJ Books are published by Jove Publications, Inc. (Harcourt Brace Jovanovich, Inc.). Its trademarks are registered in the United States Patent Office.

For information on dramatic and translation rights address:
The Sterling Lord Agency, 660 Madison Avenue, New York City

For information on British Edition rights, address Jove/HBJ Books

Typography and Production by Anthony Basile

Cover painting by Stephen Hickman

Cover Logo by Richard Nebiolo

INTRODUCTION

BYRON PREISS

It is ten p.m. in New York City. Outside, a rather inky black night has little to say to the huge stack of *Weird Heroes* paper next to my typewriter. Unless I open a window, of course, and let a late Spring gust blow one year of work to the winds.

I'd rather not.

In the theatres of the moment, *Star Wars* is setting some sort of post-Jaws attendance record with its space operatic adventures of Han (is-it-really-thirteen-years-since-Napoleon) Solo and Luke Skywalker. The gossip media have the Farrah faucet going full blast and in the back pages of the *New York Post*, *Howard the Duck* leaps forth. The radio sends us *Foreigner*, a heavy rock band intent on saying they're at war with the world and willing to sell 500,000 records to prove it. Nonetheless, they have a nice beat.

It is most obviously a grand time for that keeper of the fads, American popular culture. McDonalds, ABC-TV, prefabricated row houses and throw-away razor blades are landmarks of the late seventies.

Thus, it is with much caution—and much integrity—that we release this eighth volume of a series consciously devoted to popular fiction.

Since it's first volume, *Weird Heroes* has been devoted to giving back "to heroic fiction its thrilling sense of adventure and entertainment—the heartbeat of the old pulps." Yet at the same time, we wanted to experiment. To present stories that were not cliches, that expanded the form of heroic fiction and

avoided the morass of trashy sex and violence too often associated with the adventure genre.

If we've succeeded, if we've entertained you and made you remember the art and stories within, then our writers and artists have fulfilled the goals of the series. If we've given you some popular culture that is new, that is re-approachable and rewarding the second time around, then *Weird Heroes* has expanded the old "pulp" medium and made another place for innovative heroic literature in modern fiction.

If we've taken you to another environment or put you in the center of an adventure, then we say "Thanks".

As the second anthology in our record cycle of publication, *Weird Heroes 8* provides new and classic work by two of the most radical members of the s.f. community. Moorcock and Farmer, known for over fifty fantasy works, are represented here in the company of artists Howard Chaykin and Alfredo Alcala.

Artists Russell and Hickman come to us by way of the comics and paperback painting respectively. Craig, an illustrator with a recent history of Art Nouveau influences, takes his new attachment to Japanese linear art a step further with three new plates for Ben Bova's *Floodtide*, the second installment in the Analog editor's fantasy. Hickman, who produced our cover and seven interior plates for J. Michael Reaves' Kamus duet, is a member of the Wrightson-Kaluta-Trumbo-Sams-Jones-Hickman-Vess conspiracy of illustrators and painters who plan to take over a large portion of the fantasy art scene. They've come around to doing a lot of that already. Down home boys from the South, they share an admiration for such popular American artists as N.C. Wyeth and Howard Pyle. The Kamus drawings you find within are an interesting view of Hickman's linear approach to a painted subject. Both the cover and the plates are evocative of Kamus' milieu in their own ways.

The Kamus of Kadizar stories by J. Michael Reaves are *fantasy* fantasy. Entertainment from start to denouement, they take you to a sensational environment, where Raymond Chandler mannerisms come head on with exotic backstreets and musty alien jails. Reaves has an endearing premise here, a convincing backdrop and some characters that will entertain you in the grand fantasy style.

Throughout the book, there's a host of interesting graphics, introductions and afterwords.

Weird Heroes is meant to be an adventure. Have fun!

See you in the back.

—Byron Preiss
New York June 1977

A note of thanks here to our behind-the-scenes collaborators—Bill Green, a terrific copy editor: Mary Traina and Syd Kahn, patient production people; Basile Associates, a graphic house that takes pains to meet specifications in a rare and appreciated manner; Jeanne Glass, a supportive and understanding editor; Mike Winn, prince of publicity; and Joan Brandt, author's rep. with a terrific accent.

12 SEWARD

76 KAMUS

140 ORION 2

178 KAMUS 2

226 ROBESON

MOORCOCK

CHAYKIN

REAVES

HICKMAN

BOVA

RUSSELL

REAVES

HICKMAN

GRANT

ALCALA

SEWARD

MICHAEL
MOORCOCK

THE DEEP FIX

HOWARD CHAYKIN

INTRODUCTION

Moorcock and Chaykin—the names bring up pictures of stories—adventures on distant worlds, filled with loner-heroes mingling in exotic locales. Surrealistic, sexual, weaving noble tapestries of fantasy and science fiction, Moorcock and Chaykin met for the first time in 1976. A professional admiration turned personal and when the former returned to his native England, he had a new friend. Now, for the first time, since their meeting, Chaykin and Moorcock team up on a fantasy classic.

As Michael will explain in depth in his afterword, *The Deep Fix* was an important step in the development of non-linear, experimental science fiction. Its hero, Seward, is almost a non-hero and his adventures are almost non-adventures, but just when you're asking yourself *what's happening*, Moorcock pulls another card out of the deck and takes you along for the remainder of the trick.

Perhaps one of the weirdest pieces we've published, *The Deep Fix* is a puzzler. If you can read it in one sitting, you can take your brain out for lunch.

Michael Moorcock, by way of short introduction, is one of the most respected fantasists of the 20th century. His *Jerry Cornelius* stories play with time as if it was a character in a story and his assorted short fictions have been reprinted internationally. Moorcock's interests run the gamut from graphic stories to rock and roll, with which he has been intimately involved. He resides in England.

Howard Chaykin, a native of New York City, is an innovative graphic storyteller and illustrator best-known for his thirties-vintage heroes (*Dominic Fortune* and *The Scorpion*) and his space operatic adventures (*Cody Starbuck, Iron Wolf* and *Monarch Starstalker*).

Citing influences from Toth to Forbes to Silverman, Chaykin has brought to the comics medium sophisticated illustration and design. His technique has earned him a lucrative original art market.

Chaykin's recent work has included a strip about Jewish bears in New York bars, a full-color graphic science fiction novel and the adaptation of George Lucas' film, *Star Wars* to comics.

With Byron Preiss Visual Publications, Inc., he has illustrated two rather obscure but interesting detective strips for *National Lampoon—Nick and Nick* and *Hard-Boiled Dick*.

He currently resides in Manhattan.

THE DEEP FIX
by Michael Moorcock

ONE

Quickening sounds in the early dusk. Beat of hearts, surge of blood.

Seward turned his head on the bed and looked toward the window. They were coming again. He raised his drug-wasted body and lowered his feet to the floor. He felt nausea sweep up and through him. Dizzily, he stumbled toward the window, parted the blind, and stared out over the white ruins.

The sea splashed far away, down by the harbour, and the mob was again rushing through the broken streets toward the Research Lab. They were raggedly dressed and raggedly organized, their faces were thin and contorted with madness, but they were numerous.

Seward decided to activate the Towers once more. He walked shakily to the steel-lined room on his left. He reached out a grey, trembling hand and flicked down three switches on a bank of hundreds. Light blinked on the board above the switches. Seward walked over to the monitor-computer and spoke to it. His voice was harsh, tired, and cracking.

"Green 9/7—O Frequency. RED 8/5—B Frequency." He didn't bother with the other Towers. Two were enough to deal with the mob outside. Two wouldn't harm anybody too badly.

He walked back into the other room and parted the blind again. He saw the mob pause and look toward the roof where the Towers GREEN 9/7 and RED 8/5 were already beginning to spin. Once their gaze had been fixed on the Towers, they couldn't get it away. A few saw their companions look up and these automatically shut their eyes and dropped to the ground. But the others were now held completely rigid.

One by one, then many at a time, those who stared at the Towers began to jerk and thresh, eyes rolling, foaming at the mouth, screaming (he heard their screams faintly)—exhibiting every sign of an advanced epileptic fit.

Seward leaned against the wall feeling sick. Outside, those who'd escaped were crawling around and inching down the street on their bellies. Then, eyes averted from the Towers,

they rose to their feet and began to run away through the ruins.

"Saved again," he thought bitterly.

What was the point? Could he bring himself to go on activating the Towers every time? Wouldn't there come a day when he would let the mob get into the laboratory, search him out, kill him, smash his equipment? He deserved it, after all. The world was in ruins because of him, because of the Towers and the other Hallucinomats which he'd perfected. The mob wanted its revenge. It was fair.

Yet, while he lived, there might be a way of saving something from the wreckage he had made of mankind's minds. The mobs were not seriously hurt by the Towers. It had been the other machines which had created the real damage. Machines like the Paramats, Schizomats, Engramoscopes, even Michelson's Stroboscope Type 8. A range of instruments which had been designed to help the world and had, instead, virtually destroyed civilization.

The memory was all too clear. He wished it wasn't. Having lost track of time almost from the beginning of the disaster, he had no idea how long this had been going on. A year, maybe? His life had become divided into two sections: drug-stimulated working-period; exhausted, troubled, tranquillized sleeping-period. Sometimes, when the mobs saw the inactive Towers and charged toward the laboratory, he had to protect himself. He had learned to sense the coming of a mob. They never came individually. Mob hysteria had become the universal condition of mankind—for all except Seward who had created it.

Hallucinomatics, neural stimulators, mechanical psycho-simulatory devices, hallucinogenic drugs and machines, all had been developed to perfection at the Hampton Research Laboratory under the brilliant direction of Prof. Lee W. Seward (33), psychophysicist extraordinary, one of the youngest pioneers in the field of hallucinogenic research.

Better for the world if he hadn't been, thought Seward wearily as he lowered his worn-out body into the chair and stared at the table full of notebooks and loose sheets of paper on which he'd been working ever since the result of Experiment Restoration.

Experiment Restoration. A fine name. Fine ideals to inspire it. Fine brains to make it. But something had gone wrong.

Originally developed to help in the work of curing mental disorders of all kinds, whether slight or extreme, the Hallucinomats had been an extension on the old hallucinogenic drugs such as $C0_2$, mescalin, and lysergic acid derivatives. Their immediate ancestor was the stroboscope and machines like it. The stroboscope, spinning rapidly, flashing brightly colored patterns into the eyes of a subject, often inducing epilepsy or a similar disorder; the research of Burroughs and his followers into the early types of crude hallucinomats, had all helped to contribute to a better understanding of mental disorders.

But, as research continued, so did the incidence of mental illness rise rapidly throughout the world.

The Hampton Research Laboratory and others like it were formed to combat that rise with what had hitherto been considered near-useless experiments in the field of Hallucinomatics. Seward who had been stressing the potential importance of his chosen field since university, came into his own. He was made Director of the Hampton Lab.

People had earlier thought of Seward as a crank and of the Hallucinomats as being at best toys and at worse "madness machines," irresponsibly created by a madman.

But psychiatrists specially trained to work with them, had found them invaluable aids to their studies of mental disorders. It had become possible for a trained psychiatrist to induce in himself a temporary state of mental abnormality by use of these machines. Thus he was better able to understand and help his patients. By different methods—light, sound-waves, simulated brain-waves, and so on—the machines created the symptoms of dozens of basic abnormalities and thousands of permutations. They became an essential part of modern psychiatry.

The result: hundreds and hundreds of patients, hitherto virtually incurable, had been cured completely.

But the birth-rate was rising even faster than had been predicted in the middle part of the century. And mental illness rose faster than the birth-rate. Hundreds of cases could be cured. But there were millions to be cured. There was no mass-treatment for mental illness.

Not yet.

Work at the Hampton Research Lab became a frantic race to get ahead of the increase. Nobody slept much as, in the great big world outside, individual victims of mental illness

turned into groups of—the world had only recently forgotten the old world and now remembered it again—*maniacs*.

An overcrowded, over-pressured world, living on its nerves, cracked up.

The majority of people, of course, did not succumb to total madness. But those who did became a terrible problem.

Governments, threatened by anarchy, were forced to re-institute the cruel, old laws in order to combat the threat. All over the world, prisons, hospitals, mental homes, institutions of many kinds, were all turned into Bedlams. This hardly solved the problem. Soon, if the rise continued, the sane would be in a minority.

A dark tide of madness, far worse even than that which had swept Europe in the Middle Ages, threatened to submerge civilization.

Work at the Hampton Research Laboratory speeded up and speeded up—and members of the team began to crack. Not all these cases were noticeable to the overworked men who remained sane. They were too busy with their frantic experiments.

Only Lee Seward and a small group of assistants kept going, making increasing use of stimulant-drugs and depressant-drugs to do so.

But, now that Seward thought back, they had not been sane, they had not remained cool and efficient any more than the others. They had seemed to, that was all. Perhaps the drugs had deceived them.

The fact was, they had panicked—though the signs of panic had been hidden, even to themselves, under the disciplined guise of sober thinking.

Their work on tranquilizing machines had not kept up with their perfection of stimulatory devices. This was because they had had to study the reasons for mental abnormalities before they could devise machines for curing them.

Soon, they decided, the whole world would be mad, well before they could perfect their tranquillomatic machines. They could see no way of speeding up this work any more.

Seward was the first to put it to his team. He remembered his words.

"Gentlemen, as you know, our work on Hallucinomats for the actual *curing* of mental disorders is going too slowly. There

is no sign of our perfecting such machines in the near future. I have an alternative proposal."

The alternative proposal had been Experiment Restoration. The title, now Seward thought about it, had been euphemistic. It should have been called Experiment Diversion. The existing Hallucinomats would be set up throughout the world and used to induce *passive* disorders in the minds of the greater part of the human race. The cooperation of national governments and the World Council was sought and given. The machines were set up secretly at key points all over the globe.

They began to "send" the depressive symptoms of various disorders. They worked. People became quiet and passive. A large number went into catatonic states. Others—a great many others, who were potentially inclined to melancholia, manic-depression, certain kinds of schizophrenia—committed suicide. Rivers became clogged with corpses, roads awash with the blood and flesh of those who'd thrown themselves in front of cars. Every time a plane or rocket was seen in the sky, people expected to see at least one body falling from it. Often, whole cargoes of people were killed by the suicide of a captain, driver, or pilot of a vehicle.

Even Seward had not suspected the extent of the potential suicides. He was shocked. So was his team.

So were the World Council and the national governments. They told Seward and his team to turn-off their machines and reverse the damage they had done, as much as possible.

Seward had warned them of the possible result of doing this. He had been ignored. His machines had been confiscated and the World Council had put untrained or ill-trained operators on them. This was one of the last acts of the World Council. It was one of the last rational—however ill-judged—acts the world knew.

The real disaster had come about when the bungling operators that the World Council had chosen set the Hallucinomats to send the full effects of the conditions they'd originally been designed to produce. The operators may have been fools—they were probably mad themselves to do what they did. Seward couldn't know. Most of them had been killed by bands of psychopathic murderers who killed their victims

by the hundreds in weird and horrible rites which seemed to mirror those of prehistory—or those of the insane South American cultures before the Spaniards.

Chaos had come swiftly—the chaos that now existed.

Seward and his three remaining assistants had protected themselves the only way they could, by erecting the stroboscopic Towers on the roof of the laboratory building. This kept the mobs off. But it did not help their consciences. One by one Seward's assistants had committed suicide.

Only Seward, keeping himself alive on a series of ever-more-potent drugs, somehow retained his sanity. And, he thought ironically, this sanity was only comparative.

A hypodermic syringe lay on the table and beside it a small bottle marked M-A 19—Mescalin-Andrenol Nineteen—a drug hitherto only tested on animals, never on human beings. But all the other drugs he had used to keep himself going had either run out or now had poor effects. The M-A 19 was his last hope of being able to continue his work on the Tranquillomats he needed to perfect and thus rectify his mistake in the only way he could.

As he reached for the bottle and the hypodermic, he thought coolly that, now he looked back, the whole world had been suffering from insanity well before he had even considered Experiment Restoration. The decision to make the experiment had been just another symptom of the world-disease. Something like it would have happened sooner or later, whether by natural or artificial means. It wasn't really his fault. He had been nothing much more than fate's tool.

But logic didn't help. In a way it *was* his fault. By now, with an efficient team, he might have been able to have constructed a few experimental Tranquillomats, at least.

"Now, I've got to do it alone," he thought as he pulled up his trouser leg and sought a vein he could use in his clammy, gray flesh. He had long since given up dabbing the area with anaesthetic. He found a blue vein, depressed the plunger of the needle, and sat back in his chair to await results.

TWO

They came suddenly and were drastic.

His brain and body exploded in a torrent of mingled ecstasy

and pain which surged through him. Waves of pale light flickered. Rich darkness followed. He rode a ferris-wheel of erupting sensations and emotions. He fell down a never-ending slope of obsidian rock surrounded by clouds of green, purple, yellow, black. The rock vanished, but he continued to fall.

Then there was the smell of disease and corruption in his nostrils, but even that passed and he was standing up.

World of phosphorescence drifting like golden spheres into black night. Green, blue, red explosions. Towers rotate slowly. Towers Advance. Towers Recede. Advance. Recede. Vanish.

Flickering world of phosphorescent tears falling into the timeless, spaceless wastes of Nowhere. World of Misery. World of Antagonism. World of Guilt. Guilt—guilt—guilt . . .

World of hateful wonder.

Heart throbbing, mind thudding, body shuddering as M-A 19 flowed up the infinity of the spine. Shot into back-brain, shot into mid-brain, shot into fore-brain.

EXPLOSION ALL CENTRES!

No-mind—No-body—No-where.

Dying waves of light danced out of his eyes and away through the dark world. Everything was dying. Cells, sinews, nerves, synapses—all crumbling. Tears of light, fading fading.

Brilliant rockets streaking into the sky, exploding all together and sending their multicolored globes of light—balls on a Xmas Tree—balls on a great tree—x-mass—drifting slowly earthwards.

Ahead of him was a tall, blocky building constructed of huge chunks of yellowed granite, like a fortress. Black mist swirled around it and across the bleak, horizonless nightscape.

This was no normal hallucinatory experience. Seward felt the ground under his feet, the warm air on his face, the half-familiar smells. He had no doubt that he had entered another world.

But where was it? How had he got here?

Who had brought him here?

The answer might lie in the fortress ahead. He began to walk toward it. Gravity seemed lighter, for he walked with greater ease than normal and was soon standing looking up at the huge green metallic door. He bunched his fist and rapped on it.

Echoes boomed through numerous corridors and were ab-

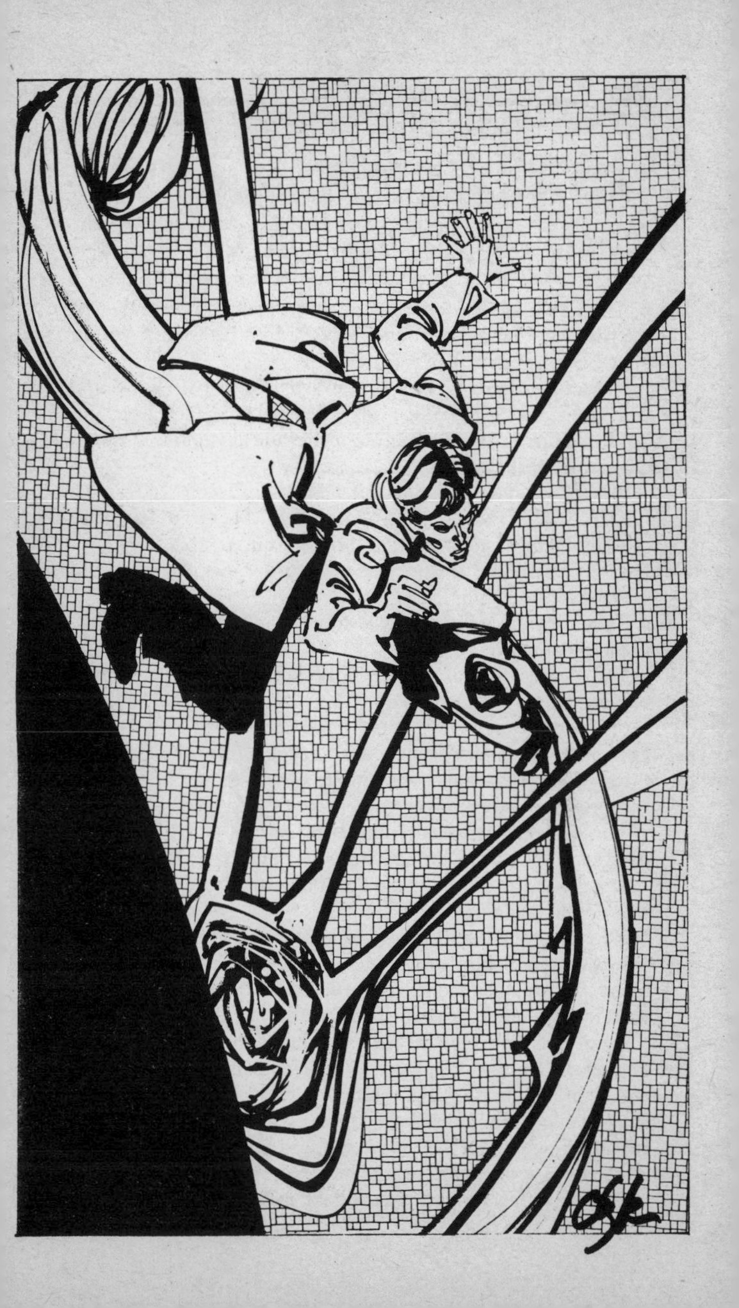

sorbed in the heart of the fortress.

Seward waited as the door was slowly opened.

A man who so closely resembled the Laughing Cavalier of the painting that he must have modeled his beard and clothes on it, bowed slightly and said:

"Welcome home, Professor Seward. We've been expecting you."

The bizarrely dressed man stepped aside and allowed him to pass into a dark corridor.

"Expecting me," said Seward. "How?"

The Cavalier replied good-humoredly: "That's not for me to explain. Here we go—through this door and up this corridor." He opened the door and turned into another corridor and Seward followed him.

They opened innumerable doors and walked along innumerable corridors.

The complexities of the corridors seemed somehow familiar to Seward. He felt disturbed by them, but the possibility of an explanation overrode his qualms and he willingly followed the Laughing Cavalier deeper and deeper into the fortress, through the twists and turns until they arrived at a door which was probably very close to the center of the fortress.

The Cavalier knocked confidently on the door, but spoke deferentially. "Professor Seward is here at last, sir."

A light, cultured voice said from the other side of the door· "Good. Send him in."

This door opened so slowly that it seemed to Seward that he was watching a film slowed-down to a fraction of its proper speed. When it had opened sufficiently to let him enter, he went into the room beyond. The Cavalier didn't follow him.

It only occurred to him then that he might be in some kind of mental institution, which would explain the fortresslike nature of the building and the man dressed up like the Laughing Cavalier. But, if so, how had he got here—unless he had collapsed and order had been restored sufficiently for someone to have come and collected him. No, the idea was weak.

The room he entered was full of rich, dark colors. Satin

screens and hangings obscured much of it. The ceiling was not visible. Neither was the source of the rather dim light. In the center of the room stood a dais, raised perhaps a foot from the floor. On the dais was an old leather armchair.

In the armchair sat a naked man with a cool, blue skin.

He stood up as Seward entered. He smiled charmingly and stepped off the dais, advancing toward Seward with his right hand extended.

"Good to see you, old boy!" he said heartily.

Dazed, Seward clasped the offered hand and felt his whole arm tingle as if it had had a mild electric shock. The man's strange flesh was firm, but seemed to itch under Seward's palm.

The man was short—little over five feet tall. His eyebrows met in the center and his shiny black hair grew to a widow's peak.

Also, he had no navel.

"I'm glad you could get here, Seward," he said, walking back to his dais and sitting in the armchair. He rested his head in one hand, his elbow on the arm of the chair.

Seward did not like to appear ungracious, but he was worried and mystified. "I don't know where this place is," he said. "I don't even know how I got here—unless . . ."

"Ah, yes—the drug. M-A 19, isn't it? That helped, doubtless. We've been trying to get in touch with you for ages, old boy."

"I've got work to do—back there," Seward said obsessionally. "I'm sorry, but I want to get back as soon as I can. What do you want?"

The Man Without a Navel sighed. "I'm sorry, too, Seward. But we can't let you go yet. There's something I'd like to ask you—a favour. That was why we were hoping you'd come."

"What's your problem?" Seward's sense of unreality, never very strong here for, in spite of the world's bizarre appearance, it seemed familiar, was growing weaker. If he could help the man and get back to continue his research, he would.

"Well," smiled the Man Without a Navel, "it's really your problem as much as ours. You see," he shrugged diffidently,

"we want your world destroyed."

"What!" Now something was clear at last. This man and his kind did belong to another world—whether in space, time or different dimensions—and they were enemies of Earth. "You can't expect me to help you do that!" He laughed. "You *are* joking."

The Man Without a Navel shook his head seriously. "Afraid not, old boy."

"That's why you want me here—you've seen the chaos in the world and you want to take advantage of it—you want me to be a—fifth columnist."

"Ah, you remember the old term, eh? Yes, I suppose that is what I mean. I want you to be our agent. Those machines of yours could be modified to make those who are left turn against each other even more than at present. Eh?"

"You must be very stupid if you think I'll do that," Seward said tiredly. "I can't help you. I'm trying to help *them*." Was he trapped here for good? He said weakly: "You've got to let me go back."

"Not as easy as that, old boy. I—and my friends—want to enter your world, but we can't until you've pumped up your machines to such a pitch that the entire world is maddened and destroys itself, d'you see?"

"Certainly," exclaimed Seward. "But I'm having no part of it!"

Again the Man Without a Navel smiled, slowly, "You"ll weaken soon enough, old boy."

"Don't be so sure," Seward said defiantly. "I've had plenty of chances of giving up—back there. I could have weakened. But I didn't."

"Ah, but you've forgotten the new factor, Seward."

"What's that?"

"The M-A 19."

"What do you mean?"

"You'll know soon enough."

"Look—I want to get out of this place. You can't keep me—there's no point—I won't agree to your plan. Where is this world anyway—?"

"Knowing that depends on you, old boy." The man's tone was mocking. "Entirely on you. A lot depends on you,

Seward."

"I know."

The Man Without a Navel lifted his head and called: "Brother Sebastian, are you available." He glanced back at Seward with an ironical smile. "Brother Sebastian may be of some help."

Seward saw the wall-hangings on the other side of the room move. Then, from behind a screen on which was painted a weird, surrealistic scene, a tall, cowled figure emerged, face in shadow, hands folded in sleeves. A monk.

"Yes sir," said the monk in a cold, malicious voice.

"Brother Sebastian, Professor Seward here is not quite as ready to comply with our wishes as we had hoped. Can you influence him in any way?"

"Possibly, sir." Now the tone held a note of anticipation.

"Good. Professor Seward, will you go with Brother Sebastian?"

"No." Seward had thought the room contained only one door—the one he'd entered through. But now there was a chance of there being more doors—other than the one through which the cowled monk had come. The two men didn't seem to hear his negative reply. They remained where they were, not moving. "No," he said again, his voice rising. "What right have you to do this?"

"Rights? A strange question." The monk chuckled to himself. It was a sound like ice tumbling into a cold glass.

"Yes—rights. You must have some sort of organization here. Therefore you must have a ruler—or government. I demand to be taken to someone in authority."

"But I am in authority here, old boy," purred the blue-skinned man. "And—in a sense—so are you. If you agreed with my suggestion, you could hold tremendous power. Tremendous."

"I don't want to discuss that again." Seward began to walk toward the wall-hangings. They merely watched him—the monk with his face in shadow—the Man Without a Navel with a supercilious smile on his thin lips. He walked around a screen, parted the hangings—and there they were on the other side. He went through the hangings. This was some carefully planned trick—an illusion—deliberately intended to confuse

him. He was used to such methods, even though he didn't understand how they'd worked this one. He said: "Clever—but tricks of this kind won't make me weaken."

"What on earth d'you mean, Seward, old man? Now, I wonder if you'll accompany Brother Sebastian here. I have an awful lot of work to catch up on."

"All right," Seward said. "All right, I will." Perhaps on the way to wherever the monk was going, he would find an opportunity to escape.

The monk turned and Seward followed him. He did not look at the Man Without a Navel as he passed his ridiculous dias, with its ridiculous leather armchair.

They passed through a narrow doorway behind a curtain and were once again in the complex series of passages. The tall monk—now he was close to him, Seward estimated his height at about six feet, seven inches—seemed to flow along in front of him. He began to dawdle. The monk didn't look back. Seward increased the distance between them. Still, the monk didn't appear to notice.

Seward turned and ran.

They had met nobody on their journey through the corridors. He hoped he could find a door leading out of the fortress before someone spotted him. There was no cry from behind him.

But as he ran, the passages got darker and darker until he was careering through pitch darkness, sweating, panting, and beginning to panic. He kept blundering into damp walls and running on.

It was only much later that he began to realize he was running in a circle that was getting tighter and tighter until he was doing little more than spinning round, like a top. He stopped, then.

These people evidently had more powers than he had suspected. Possibly they had some means of shifting the position of the corridor walls, following his movements by means of hidden TV cameras or something like them. Simply because there were no visible signs of an advanced technology didn't mean that they did not possess one. They obviously did. How

else could they have got him from his own world to this?

He took a pace forward. Did he sense the walls drawing back? He wasn't sure. The whole thing reminded him vaguely of *The Pit and The Pendulum.*

He strode forward a number of paces and saw a light ahead of him. He walked toward it, turned into a dimly lit corridor.

The monk was waiting for him.

"We missed each other, Professor Seward. I see you managed to precede me." The monk's face was still invisible, secret in its cowl. As secret as his cold mocking, malevolent voice. "We are almost there, now," said the monk.

Seward stepped toward him, hoping to see his face, but it was impossible. The monk glided past him. "Follow me, please."

For the moment, until he could work out how the fortress worked, Seward decided to accompany the monk.

They came to a heavy, iron-studded door—quite unlike any of the other doors.

They walked into a low-ceilinged chamber. It was very hot. Smoke hung in the still air of the room. It poured from a glowing brazier at the extreme end. Two men stood by the brazier.

One of them was a thin man with a huge, bulging stomach over which his long, narrow hands were folded. He had a shaggy mane of dirty white hair, his cheeks were sunken and his nose extremely pointed. He seemed toothless and his puckered lips were shaped in a senseless smile—like the smile of a madman Seward had once had to experiment on. He wore a stained white jacket buttoned over his grotesque paunch. On his legs were loose khaki trousers.

His companion was also thin, though lacking the stomach. He was taller and had the face of a mournful bloodhound, with sparse, highly greased, black hair that covered his bony head like a skull-cap. He stared into the brazier, not looking up as Brother Sebastian led Seward into the room and closed the door.

The thin man with the stomach, however, pranced forward, his hands still clasped on his paunch, and bowed to them both.

"Work for us, Brother Sebastian?" he said, nodding at Seward.

"We require a straightforward 'Yes,' " Brother Sebastian said. "You have merely to ask the question 'Will You?' If he replies, 'No,' you are to continue. If he replies 'Yes,' you are to cease and inform me immediately."

"Very well, Brother. Rely on us."

"I hope I can." The monk chuckled again. "You are now in the charge of these men, professor. If you decide you want to help us, after all you have only to say 'Yes.' Is that clear?"

Seward began to tremble with horror. He had suddenly realized what this place was.

"Now look here," he said. "You can't . . ."

He walked toward the monk who had turned and was opening the door. He grasped the man's shoulder. His hand seemed to clutch a delicate, bird-like structure. "Hey! I don't think you're a man at all. What *are* you?"

"A man or a mouse," chuckled the monk as the two grotesque creatures leapt forward suddenly and twisted Seward's arms behind him. Seward kicked back at them with his heels, squirmed in their grasp, but he might have been held by steel bands. He shouted incoherently at the monk as he shut the door behind him with a whisk of his habit.

The pair flung him on to the damp, hot stones of the floor. It smelt awful. He rolled over and sat up. They stood over him. The hound-faced man had his arms folded. The thin man with the stomach had his long hands on his paunch again. They seemed to rest there whenever he was not actually using them. It was the latter who smiled with his twisting, puckered lips, cocking his head to one side.

"What do *you* think, Mr Morl?" he asked his companion.

"I don't know, Mr Hand. After you." The hound-faced man spoke in a melancholy whisper.

"I would suggest Treatment H. Simple to operate, less work for us, a tried and trusty operation which works with most and will probably work with this gentleman."

Seward scrambled up and tried to push past them, making for the door. Again they seized him expertly and dragged him

back. He felt the rough touch of rope on his wrists and the pain as a knot was tightened. He shouted, more in anger than agony, more in terror than either.

They were going to torture him. He knew it.

When they had tied his hands, they took the rope and tied his ankles. They twisted the rope up around his calves and under his legs. They made a halter of the rest and looped it over his neck so that he had to bend almost double if he was not to strangle.

Then they sat him on a chair.

Mr Hand removed his hands from his paunch, reached up above Seward's head, and turned on the tap.

The first drop of water fell directly on the centre of his head some five minutes later.

Twenty-seven drops of water later, Seward was raving and screaming. Yet every time he tried to jerk his head away, the halter threatened to strangle him and the jolly Mr Hand and the mournful Mr Morl were there to straighten him up again.

Thirty drops of water after that, Seward's brain began to throb and he opened his eyes to see that the chamber had vanished.

In its place was a huge comet, a fireball dominating the sky, rushing directly toward him. He backed away from it and there were no more ropes on his hands or feet. He was free.

He began to run. He leapt into the air and stayed there. He was swimming through the air.

Ecstasy ran up his spine like a flickering fire, touched his back-brain, touched his mid-brain, touched his fore-brain.

EXPLOSION ALL CENTRES!

He was standing one flower among many, in a bed of tall lupins and roses which waved in a gentle wind. He pulled his roots free and began to walk.

He walked into the Lab Control Room.

Everything was normal except that gravity seemed a little heavy. Everything was as he'd left it.

He saw that he had left the Towers rotating. He went into the room he used as a bedroom and workroom. He parted the blind and looked out into the night. There was a big, full moon hanging in the deep, blue sky over the ruins of Hampton. He saw its light reflected in the far-away sea. A few bodies still lay

prone near the lab. He went back into the Control Room and switched off the towers.

Returning to the bedroom he looked at the card table he had his notes on. They were undisturbed. Neatly, side by side near a large, tattered notebook, lay a half-full ampoule of M-A 19 and a hypodermic syringe. He picked up the ampoule and threw it in a corner. It did not break but rolled around on the floor for a few seconds.

He sat down.

His whole body ached.

He picked up a sheaf of his more recent notes. He wrote everything down that came into his head on the subject of Tranquillomats; it helped him think better and made sure that his drugged mind and body did not hamper him as much as they might have done if he had simply relied on his memory.

He looked at his wrists. They carried the marks of the rope. Evidently the transition from the other world to his own involved leaving anything in the other world behind. He was glad. If he hadn't, he'd have had a hell of a job getting himself untied. He shuddered—a mob might have reached the lab before he could get free and activate the Towers.

He tried hard to forget the questions flooding through his mind. Where had he been? Who were the people? What did they really want? How far could they keep a check on him? How did the M-A 19 work to aid his transport into the other world? Could they get at him here?

He decided they couldn't get at him, otherwise they might have tried earlier. Somehow it was the M-A 19 in his brain which allowed them to get hold of him. Well, that was simple—no more M-A 19.

With a feeling of relief, he forced himself to concentrate on his notes.

Out of the confusion, something seemed to be developing, but he had to work at great speed—greater speed than previously, perhaps, for he daren't use the M-A 19 again and there was nothing else left of much good.

His brain cleared as he once again got interested in his notes. He worked for two hours, making fresh notes, equations, checking his knowledge against the stack of earlier research notes by the wall near his camp bed.

Dawn was coming as he realized suddenly that he was suffering from thirst. His throat was bone dry, so was his mouth and lips. He got up and his legs felt weak. He staggered, almost knocking over the chair. With a great effort he righted it and, leaning for support on the bed, got himself to the hand-basin. It was filled by a tank near the roof and he had used it sparsely. But this time he didn't care. He stuck his head under the tap and drank the stale water greedily. It did no good. His whole body now seemed cold, his skin tight, his heart thumping heavily against his ribs. His head was aching horribly and his breathing increased.

He went and lay down on the bed, hoping the feeling would leave him.

It got worse. He needed something to cure himself.

"What?" he asked.

"M-A 19," he answered.

NO!

But—Yes, yes, yes. All he needed was a small shot of the drug and he would be all right. He knew it.

And with knowing that, he realized something else.

He was hooked.

The drug was habit-forming.

THREE

He found the half-full M-A 19 ampoule under the bed where it had rolled. He found the needle on the table where he had left it, buried under his notes. He found a vein in his forearm and shot himself full. There was no thought to Seward's action. There was just craving and the chance of satisfying that craving.

The M-A 19 began to swim leisurely through his veins, drifting up his spine—

It hit his brain with a powerful explosion.

He was walking through a world of phosphorescent rain, leaping over large purple rocks that welcomed his feet, drew them down towards them. All was agony and startling Now.

No-time, no-space, just the throbbing voice in the air above him. It was talking to him.

DOOM, Seward. DOOM, Seward. DOOM, Seward.

"Seward is doomed!" he laughed. "Seward is betrayed!"

Towers Advance. Towers Recede. Towers Rotate at Normal Speed.

Carnival Aktion. All Carnivals to Explode.

Up into the back-brain, into the mid-brain, on to the fore-brain.

EXPLOSION ALL CENTRES!

He was back in the torture-chamber, though standing up. In the corner near the brazier the grotesque pair were muttering to one another. Mr. Hand darted him an angry glance, his lips drawn over his gums in an expression of outrage.

"Hello, Seward," said the Man Without a Navel behind him. "So you're back."

"Back," said Seward heavily. "What more do you want?"

"Only your All, Seward, old man. I remember a time in Dartford before the war . . ."

"Which war?"

"Your war, Seward. You were too young to share any other. You don't remember *that* war. You weren't born. Leave it to those who *do*, Seward."

Seward turned. "My war?" He looked with disgust at the Man Without a Navel; at his reptilian blue skin and his warm-cold, dark-light, good-evil eyes. At his small yet well-formed body.

The Man Without a Navel smiled. "*Our* war, then, old man. I won't quibble."

"You made me do it. I think that somehow you made me suggest Experiment Restoration!"

"I said we won't quibble, Seward," said the man in an authoritative tone. Then, more conversationally: "I remember a time in Dartford before the war, when you sat in your armchair—one rather like mine—at your brother-in-law's house. Remember what you said, old man?"

Seward remembered well. "If," he quoted, "if I had a button and could press it and destroy the entire universe and myself

with it, I would. For no reason other than boredom."

"Very good, Seward. You have an excellent memory."

"Is that all you're going on? Something I said out of frustration because nobody was recognizing my work?" He paused as he realized something else. "You know all about me, don't you?" he said bitterly. There seemed to be nothing he didn't know. On the other hand Seward knew nothing of the man. Nothing of his world. Nothing of where it was in space and time. It was a world of insanity, of bizarre contrasts. "*How* do you know all this?"

"Inside information, Seward, old boy."

"You're mad!"

The Man Without a Navel returned to his earlier topic. "Are you bored now, Seward?"

"Bored? No. Tired, yes."

"Bored, no—tired, yes. Very good, Seward. You got here later than expected. What kept you?" The man laughed.

"I kept me. I held off taking M-A 19 for as long as I could."

"But you came to us in the end, eh? Good man, Seward."

"You knew the M-A 19 was habit-forming? You knew I'd have to take it, come back here?"

"Naturally."

He said pleadingly: "Let me go for God's sake! You've made me. Made me . . ."

"Your dearest wish almost come true, Seward. Isn't that what you wanted? I made you come close to destroying the world? Is that it?"

"So you *did* somehow influence Experiment Restoration!"

"It's possible. But you haven't done very well either way. The world is in shambles. You can't reverse that. Kill it off. Let's start fresh, Seward. Forget your experiments with the Tranquillomats and help us."

"No."

The Man Without a Navel shrugged. "We'll see, old boy."

He looked at the mumbling men in the corner. "Morl—Hand—take Professor Seward to his room. I don't want any mistakes this time. I'm going to take him out of your hands. Obviously we need subtler minds put on the problem."

The pair came forward and grabbed Seward. The Man Without a Navel opened the door and they went through it first, forcing Seward ahead of them.

He was too demoralized to resist much, this time. Demoralized by the fact that he was hooked on M-A 19. What did the junkies call it? The Habit. He had the Habit. Demoralized by his inability to understand the whereabouts or nature of the world he was on. Demoralized by the fact that the Man Without a Navel seemed to know everything about his personal life on Earth? Demoralized that he had fallen into the man's trap. Who had developed M-A 19? He couldn't remember. Perhaps the Man Without a Navel had planted it? He supposed it might be possible.

He was pushed along another series of corridors, arrived at another door. The Man Without a Navel came up behind them and unlocked the door.

Seward was shoved into the room. It was narrow and low—coffinlike.

"We'll be sending someone along to see you in a little while, Seward," said the man lightly. The door was slammed.

Seward lay in pitch blackness.

He began to sob.

Later, he heard a noise outside. A stealthy noise of creeping feet. He shuddered. What was the torture going to be this time?

He heard a scraping and a muffled rattle. The door opened.

Against the light from the passage, Seward saw the man clearly. He was a big, fat Negro in a gray suit. He wore a flowing, rainbow-colored tie. He was grinning.

Seward liked the man instinctively. But he no longer trusted his instinct. "What do you want?" he said suspiciously.

The huge Negro raised his finger to his lips. "Ssshh," he whispered. "I'm going to try to get you out of here."

"An old Secret Police trick on my world," said Seward. "I'm not falling for that."

"It's no trick, son. Even if it is, what can you lose?"

"Nothing." Seward got up.

The big man put his arm around Seward's shoulders. Seward felt comfortable in the grip, though normally he disliked such gestures.

"Now, son, we go real quietly and we go as fast as we can. Come on."

Softly, the big man began to tiptoe along the corridor. Seward was sure that TV cameras, or whatever they were, were following him, that the Man Without a Navel, the monk, the two torturers, the Laughing Cavalier, were all waiting somewhere to seize him.

But, very quickly, the Negro had reached a small wooden door and was drawing a bolt. He patted Seward's shoulder and held the door open for him. "Through you go, son. Make for the red car."

It was morning. In the sky hung a golden sun, twice the size of Earth's. There was a vast expanse of lifeless rocks in all directions, broken only by a white road which stretched into the distance. On the road, close to Seward, was parked a car something like a Cadillac. It was fire-red and bore the registration plates YOU 000. Whoever these people were, Seward decided, they were originally from Earth—all except the Man Without a Navel, perhaps. Possibly this was his world and the others had been brought from Earth, like him.

He walked towards the car. The air was cold and fresh. He stood by the convertible and looked back. The Negro was running over the rock towards him. He dashed round the car and got into the driver's seat. Seward got in beside him.

The Negro started the car, put it into gear, and shoved his foot down hard on the accelerator pedal. The car jerked away and had reached top speed in seconds.

At the wheel, the Negro relaxed. "Glad that went smoothly. I didn't expect to get away with it so easily, son. You're Seward, aren't you?"

"Yes. You seem to be as well-informed as the others."

"I guess so." The Negro took a pack of cigarettes from his short pocket. "Smoke?"

"No, thanks," said Seward. "That's one habit I don't have."

The Negro looked back over his shoulder. The expanse of rock seemed never-ending, though in the distance the fortress was disappearing. He flipped a cigarette out of the pack and put it between his lips. He unclipped the car's lighter and put it to the tip of the cigarette. He inhaled and put the lighter back. The cigarette between his lips, he returned his other hand to the wheel.

He said: "They were going to send the Vampire to you. It's lucky I reached you in time."

"It could be," said Seward. "Who are you? What part do you play in this?"

"Let's just say I'm a friend of yours and an enemy of your enemies. The name's Farlowe."

"Well, I trust you, Farlowe—though God knows why."

Farlowe grinned. "Why not? I don't want your world destroyed any more than you do. It doesn't much matter, I guess, but if there's a chance of restoring it, then you ought to try."

"Then you're from my world originally, is that it?"

"In a manner of speaking, son," said Farlowe.

Very much later, the rock gave way to pleasant, flat countryside with trees, fields and little cottages peaceful under the vast sky. In the distance, Seward saw herds of cattle and sheep, the occasional horse. It reminded him of the countryside of his childhood, all clear and fresh and sharp with the clarity that only a child's eye can bring to a scene before it is obscured and tainted by the impressions of adulthood. Soon the flat country was behind them and they were going through an area of low, green hills, the huge sun flooding the scene with its soft, golden light. There were no clouds in the pale blue sky.

The big car sped smoothly along and Seward in the comfortable companionship of Farlowe, began to relax a little. He felt almost happy, would have felt happy if it had not been for the nagging knowledge that somehow he had to get back and continue his work. It was not merely a question of restoring sanity to the world, now—he had also to thwart whatever plans were in the mind of the Man Without a Navel.

After a long silence, Seward asked a direct question. "Farlowe, where is this world? What are we doing here?"

Farlowe's answer was vague. He stared ahead at the road. "Don't ask me that, son. I don't rightly know."

"But you live here."

"So do you."

"No—I only come here when—when . . ."

"When what?"

But Seward couldn't raise the courage to admit about the drug to Farlowe. Instead he said: "Does M-A 19 mean anything to you?"

"Nope."

So Farlowe hadn't come here because of the drug. Seward said: "But you said you were from my world originally."

"Only in a manner of speaking." Farlowe changed gears as the road curved steeply up a hill. It rose gently above the idyllic countryside below.

Seward changed his line of questioning: "Isn't there any sort of organization here—no government. What's the name of this country?"

Farlowe shrugged. "It's just a place—no government. The people in the fortress run most things. Everybody's scared of them.

"I don't blame them. Who's the Vampire you mentioned?"

"He works for the Man."

"What is he?"

"Why—a vampire, naturally," said Farlowe in surprise.

The sun had started to set and the whole countryside was bathed in red-gold light. The car continued to climb the long hill.

Farlowe said: "I'm taking you to some friends. You ought to be fairly safe there. Then maybe we can work out a way of getting you back."

Seward felt better. At least Farlowe had given him some direct information.

As the car reached the top of the hill and began to descend Seward got a view of an odd and disturbing sight. The sun was like a flat, round, red disc—yet only half of it was above the

horizon. *The line of the horizon evenly intersected the sun's disc!* It was some sort of mirage—yet so convincing that Seward looked away, staring instead at the black smoke which he could now see rolling across the valley below. He said nothing to Farlowe.

"How much further?" he asked later as the car came to the bottom of the hill. Black night had come, moonless, and the car's headlights blazed.

"A long way yet, I'm afraid, son," said Farlowe. "You cold?"

"No."

"We'll be hitting a few signs of civilization soon. You tired?"

"No—why?"

"We could put up at a motel or something. I guess we could eat anyway."

Ahead, Seward saw a few lights. He couldn't make out where they came from. Farlowe began to slow down. "We'll risk it," he said. He pulled in toward the lights and Seward saw that it was a line of fuel pumps. Behind the pumps was a single storey building, very long and built entirely of timber by the look of it. Farlowe drove in between the pumps and the building. A man in overalls, the top half of his face shadowed by the peak of his cap, came into sight. Farlowe got out of the car with a signal to Seward to do the same. The Negro handed his keys to the attendant. "Fill her full and give her a quick check."

Could this be Earth? Seward wondered. Earth in the future—or possibly an Earth of a different space/time continuum. That was the likeliest explanation for this unlikely world. The contrast between recognizable, everyday things and the grotesqueries of the fortress was strange—yet it could be explained easily if these people had contact with his world. That would explain how they had things like cars and fuel stations and no apparent organization necessary for producing them. Somehow, perhaps, they just—*stole* them?

He followed Farlowe into the long building. He could see through the wide windows that it was some kind of restaurant.

There was a long, clean counter and a few people seated at tables at the far end. All had their backs to him.

He and Farlowe sat down on stools. Close to them was the largest pinball machine Seward had ever seen. Its lights were flashing and its balls were clattering, though there was no one operating it. The colored lights flashed series of numbers at him until his eyes lost focus and he had to turn away.

A woman was standing behind the counter now. Most of her face was covered by a yashmak.

"What do you want to eat, son?" said Farlowe, turning to him.

"Oh, anything."

Farlowe ordered sandwiches and coffee. When the woman had gone to get their order, Seward whispered: "Why's she wearing that thing?"

Farlowe pointed at a sign Seward hadn't noticed before. It read THE HAREM HAVEN. "It's their gimmick," said Farlowe.

Seward looked back at the pinball machine. The lights had stopped flashing, the balls had stopped clattering. But above it suddenly appeared a huge pair of disembodied eyes. He gasped.

Distantly, he heard his name being repeated over and over again. "Seward. Seward. Seward. Seward . . ."

He couldn't tell where the voice was coming from. He glanced up at the ceiling. Not from there. The voice stopped. He looked back at the pinball machine. The eyes had vanished. His panic returned. He got off his stool.

"I'll wait for you in the car, Farlowe."

Farlowe looked surprised. "What's the matter, son?"

"Nothing—it's okay—I'll wait in the car."

Farlowe shrugged.

Seward went out into the night. The attendant had gone but the car was waiting for him. He opened the door and climbed in.

What did the eyes mean? Were the people in the fortress following him in some way. Suddenly an explanation for most of the questions bothering him sprang into his mind. Of course—telepathy. They were probably telepaths. That was how they knew so much about him. That could be how they knew of his world and could influence events there—they might never go there in person. This comforted him a little,

though he realized that getting out of this situation was going to be even more difficult than he'd thought.

He looked through the windows and saw Farlowe's big body perched on its stool. The other people in the cafe were still sitting with their backs to him. He realized that there was something familiar about them.

He saw Farlowe get up and walk towards the door. He came out and got into the car, slamming the door after him. He leaned back in his seat and handed Seward a sandwich. "You seem worked up, son," he said. "You'd better eat this."

Seward took the sandwich. He was staring at the backs of the other customers again. He frowned.

Farlowe started the car and they moved towards the road. Then Seward realized who the men reminded him of. He craned his head back in the hope of seeing their faces, but it was too late. They had reminded him of his dead assistants—the men who'd committed suicide.

They roared through the dimly seen towns—all towers and angles. There seemed to be nobody about. Dawn came up and they still sped on. Seward realized that Farlowe must have a tremendous vitality, for he didn't seem to tire at all. Also, perhaps, he was motivated by a desire to get as far away from the fortress as possible.

They stopped twice to refuel and Farlowe bought more sandwiches and coffee which they had as they drove.

In the late afternoon Farlowe said: "Almost there."

They passed through a pleasant village. It was somehow alien, although very similar to a small English village. It had an oddly foreign look which was hard to place. Farlowe pulled in at what seemed to be the gates of a large public park. He looked up at the sun. "Just made it," he said. "Wait in the park—someone will come to collect you."

"You're leaving me?"

"Yes. I don't think they know where you are. They'll look but, with luck, they won't look around here. Out you get, son. Into the park."

"Who do I wait for?"

"You'll know her when she comes."

"Her?" He got out and closed the door. He stood on the pavement watching as, with a cheerful wave, Farlowe drove off. He felt a tremendous sense of loss then, as if his only hope had been taken away.

Gloomily, he turned and walked through the park gates.

FOUR

As he walked between low hedges along a gravel path, he realized that this park, like so many things in this world, contrasted with the village it served. It was completely familiar just like a park on his own world.

It was like a grey, hazy winter's afternoon, with the brittle interwoven skeletons of trees black and sharp against the cold sky. Birds perched on trees and bushes, or flew noisily into the silent air.

Evergreens crowded upon the leaf-strewn grass. Cry of sparrows. Peacocks, necks craned forward, dived towards scattered bread. Silver birch, larch, elm, monkey-puzzle trees, and swaying white ferms, each one like an ostrich feather stuck in the earth. A huge, ancient, nameless trunk from which, at the top, grew an expanse of soft, yellow fungus; the trunk itself looking like a Gothic cliff, full of caves and dark windows. A gray and brown pigeon perched motionless on the slender branches of a young birch. Peacock chicks the size of hens pecked with concentration at the grass.

Mellow, nostalgic smell of winter; distant sounds of children playing; lost black dog looking for master; red disc of sun in the cool, darkening sky. The light was sharp and yet soft, peaceful. A path led into the distance towards a flight of wide stone steps, at the top of which was the curving entrance to an arbor, browns, blacks and yellows of sapless branches and fading leaves.

From the arbor a girl appeared and began to descend the steps with quick, graceful movements. She stopped when she reached the path. She looked at him. She had long, blonde hair and wore a white dress with a full skirt. She was about seventeen.

The peace of the park was suddenly interrupted by children rushing from nowhere toward the peacocks, laughing and shouting. Some of the boys saw the tree trunk and made for it.

Others stood looking upwards at the sun as it sank in the cold air. They seemed not to see either Seward or the girl. Seward looked at her. Did he recognize her? It wasn't possible. Yet she, too, gave him a look of recognition, smiled shyly at him and ran towards him. She reached him, stood on tiptoe and gave him a light kiss on the cheek.

"Hello, Lee."

"Hello. Have you come to find me?"

"I've been looking for you a long time."

"Farlowe sent a message ahead?"

She took his hand. "Come on. Where have you been, Lee?"

This was a question he couldn't answer. He let her lead him back up the steps, through the arbor. Between the branches he glanced a garden and a pool. "Come on," she said. "Let's see what's for dinner. Mother's looking forward to meeting you."

He no longer questioned how these strange people all seemed to know his name. It was still possible that all of them were taking part in the conspiracy against him.

At the end of the arbor was a house, several stories high. It was a pleasant house with a blue and white door. She led him up the path and into a hallway. It was shining with dark polished wood and brass plates on the walls. From a room at the end he smelled spicy cooking. She went first and opened the door at the end. "Mother—Lee Seward's here. Can we come in?"

"Of course." The voice was warm, husky, full of humor. They went into the room and Seward saw a woman of about forty, very well preserved, tall, large-boned with a fine-featured face and smiling mouth. Her eyes also smiled. Her sleeves were rolled up and she put the lid back on a pan on the stove.

"How do you do, Professor Seward. Mr. Farlowe's told us about you. You're in trouble, I hear."

"How do you do, Mrs—"

"Call me Martha. Has Sally introduced herself?"

"No," Sally laughed. "I forgot. I'm Sally, Lee."

Her mother gave a mock frown. "I suppose you've been calling our guest by his first name, as usual. Do you mind, Professor?"

"Not at all." He was thinking how attractive they both were, in their different ways. The young, fresh girl and her

warm, intelligent mother. He had always enjoyed the company of women, but never so much, he realized, as now. They seemed to complement one another. In their presence he felt safe, at ease. Now he realized why Farlowe had chosen them to hide him. Whatever the facts, he would *feel* safe here.

Martha was saying: "Dinner won't be long."

"It smells good."

"Probably smells better than it tastes," she laughed. "Go into the lounge with Sally. Sally, fix Professor Seward a drink."

"Call me Lee," said Seward, a little uncomfortably. He had never cared much for his first name. He preferred his middle name, William, but not many others did.

"Come on, Lee," she took his hand and led him out of the kitchen. "We'll see what there is." They went into a small, well-lighted lounge. The furniture, like the whole house, had a look that was half-familiar, half-alien—obviously the product of a slightly different race. Perhaps they deliberately imitated Earth culture, without quite succeeding. Sally still gripped his hand. Her hand was warm and her skin smooth. He made to drop it, but, involuntarily, squeezed it gently before she took it away to deal with the drink. She gave him another shy smile. He felt that she was as attracted to him as he to her. "What's it going to be?" she asked him.

"Oh, anything," he said, sitting down on a comfortable sofa. She poured him a dry martini and brought it over. Then she sat demurely down beside him and watched him drink it. Her eyes sparkled with a mixture of sauciness and innocence which he found extremely appealing. He looked around the room.

"How did Farlowe get his message to you?" he asked.

"He came the other day. Said he was going to try to get into the fortress and help you. Farlowe's always flitting about. I think the people at the fortress have a price on his head or something. It's exciting isn't it."

"You can say that again," Seward said feelingly.

"Why are they after you?"

"They want me to help them destroy the world I come from.

Do you know anything about it?"

"Earth, isn't it?"

"Yes." Was he going to get straightforward answers at last?

"I know it's very closely connected with ours and that some of us want to escape from here and go to your world."

"Why?" he asked eagerly.

She shook her head. Her long, fine hair waved with the motion. "I don't really know. Something about their being trapped here—something like that. Farlowe said something about you being a 'key' to their release. They can only do what they want to do with your agreement."

"But I could agree and then break my word!"

"I don't think you could—but honestly, I don't know any more. I've probably got it wrong. Do you like me, Lee?"

He was startled by the directness of her question. "Yes," he said, "very much."

"Farlowe said you would. Good, isn't it?"

"Why—yes, Farlowe knows a lot."

"That's why he works against *them*."

Martha came in. "Almost ready," she smiled. "I think I'll have a quick one before I start serving. How are you feeling Lee, after your ride?"

"Fine," he said, "fine." He had never been in a position like this one—with two women either of whom was extremely attractive for almost opposite reasons.

"We were discussing why the people at the fortress wanted my help," he said, turning the conversation back the way he felt it ought to go if he was ever going to get off this world and back to his own and his work.

"Farlowe said something about it."

"Yes, Sally told me. Does Farlowe belong to some sort of underground organization?"

"Underground? Why, yes, in a way he does."

"Aren't they strong enough to fight the Man Without a Navel and his friends?"

"Farlowe says they're strong enough, but divided over what should be done and how."

"I see. That's fairly common amongst such groups, I believe."

"Yes."

"What part do you play?"

"None, really. Farlowe asked me to put you up—that's all." She sipped her drink, her eyes smiling directly into his. He drained his glass.

"Shall we eat?" she said. "Sally, take Lee in to the diningroom."

The girl got up and, somewhat possessively Seward thought, linked her arm in his. Her young body against his was distracting. He felt a little warm. She took him in. The table was laid for supper. Three chairs and three places. The sun had set and candles burned on the table in brass candelabras. She unlinked her arm and pulled out one of the chairs.

"You sit here, Lee—at the head of the table." She grinned. Then she leaned forward as he sat down. "Hope mummy isn't boring you."

He was surprised. "Why should she?"

Martha came in with three covered dishes on a tray. "This may not have turned out quite right, Lee. Never does when you're trying hard."

"I'm sure it'll be fine," he smiled. The two women sat down on either side of him. Martha served him. It was some sort of goulash with vegetables. He took his napkin and put it on his lap.

As they began to eat, Martha said: "How is it?"

"Fine," he said. It was very good. Apart from the feeling that some kind of rivalry for his attentions existed between mother and daughter the air of normality in the house was comforting. Here, he might be able to do some constructive thinking about his predicament.

When the meal was over, Martha said, "It's time for bed, Sally. Say good night to Lee."

She pouted. "Oh, it's not fair."

"Yes it is," she said firmly. "You can see Lee in the morning. He's had a long journey."

"All right." She smiled at Seward. "Sleep well, Lee."

"I think I will," he said.

Martha chuckled after Sally had gone. "Would you like a drink before you go to bed?" She spoke softly.

"Love one," he said.

They went into the other room. He sat down on the sofa as she mixed the drinks. She brought them over and sat down next to him as her daughter had done earlier.

"Tell me everything that's been happening. It sounds so exciting."

He knew at once he could tell her all he wanted to, that she would listen and be sympathetic. "It's terrifying, really," he began, half apologetically. He began to talk, beginning with what had happened on Earth. She listened.

"I even wondered if this was a dream-world—a figment of my imagination," he finished, "but I had to reject that when I went back to my own. I had rope marks on my wrists—my hair was soaking wet. You don't get that in a dream!"

"I hope not," she smiled. "We're different here, Lee, obviously. Our life doesn't have the—the *shape* that yours has. We haven't much direction, no real desires. We just—well—*exist*. It's as if we're waiting for something to happen. As if—" she paused and seemed to be looking down deep into herself. "Put it this way—Farlowe thinks you're the key figure in some development that's happening here. Supposing—supposing we were some kind of—of experiment . . ."

"Experiment? How do you mean?"

"Well, from what you say, the people at the fortress have an advanced science that we don't know about. Supposing our parents, say, had been kidnapped from your world and—made to think—what's the word—"

"Conditioned?"

"Yes, conditioned to think they were natives of this world. We'd have grown up knowing nothing different. Maybe the Man Without a Navel is a member of an alien race—a scientist of some kind in charge of the experiment."

"But why should they make such a complicated experiment?"

"So they could study us, I suppose."

Seward marvelled at her deductive powers. She had come to a much firmer theory that he had. But then he thought, she might subconsciously *know* the truth. Everyone knew much more than they knew, as it were. For instance, it was pretty

certain that the secret of the tranquillomat was locked somewhere down in his unconscious if only he could get at it. Her explanation was logical and worth thinking about.

"You may be right," he said. "If so, it's something to go on. But it doesn't stop my reliance on the drug—or the fact that the Man and his helpers are probably telepathic and are at this moment looking for me."

She nodded. "Could there be an *antidote* for the drug?"

"Unlikely. Drugs like that don't really need antidotes—they're not like poisons. There must be some way of getting at the people in the fortress—some way of putting a stop to their plans. What about an organized revolution? What has Farlowe tried to do?"

"Nothing much. The people aren't easy to organize. We haven't much to do with one another. Farlowe was probably hoping you could help—think of something he hasn't. Maybe one of those machines you mentioned would work against the fortress people?"

"No, I don't think so. Anyway, the Hallucinomats are too big to move from one place to another by hand—let alone from one world to another."

"And you haven't been able to build a tranquillomat yet?"

"No—we have a lot of experimental machines lying around at the lab—that's what I'm trying to do at the moment. If I could make one that works it would solve part of my problem—it would save my world and perhaps even save yours, if you *are* in a state of conditioning."

"It sounds reasonable," she dropped her eyes and looked at her drink. She held the glass balanced on her knees which were pressed closely together, nearly touching him. "But," she said, "they're going to catch you sooner or later. They're very powerful. They're sure to catch you. Then they'll make you agree to their idea."

"Why are you so certain?"

"I know them."

He let that go. She said: "Another drink?" and got up.

"Yes please." He got up, too, and extended his glass, then went closer to her. She put bottle and glass on the table and looked into his face. There was compassion, mystery, tenderness in her large, dark eyes. He smelled her perfume, warm, pleasant. He put his arms around her and kissed her.

"My room," she said. They went upstairs.

Later that night, feeling strangely revitalized, he left the bed and the sleeping Martha and went and stood beside the window overlooking the silent park. He felt cold and he picked up his shirt and trousers, put them on. He sighed. He felt his mind clear and his body relax. He must work out a way of travelling from this world to his own at will—that might put a stop to the plans of the Man Without a Navel.

He turned guiltily as he heard the door open. Sally was standing there. She wore a long, white, flowing nightdress.

"Lee! I came to tell mummy—what are you doing in here?" Her eyes were horrified, accusing him. Martha sat up suddenly.

"Sally—what's the matter!"

Lee stepped forward. "Listen, Sally. Don't—"

Sally shrugged, but tears had come to her eyes. "I thought you wanted *me*! Now I know—I shouldn't have brought you here. Farlowe said—"

"What did Farlowe say?"

"He said you'd want to marry me!"

"But that's ridiculous. How could he say that? I'm a stranger here. You were to hide me from the fortress people, that's all."

But she had only picked up one word. "Ridiculous. Yes, I suppose it is, when my own mother . . ."

"Sally—you'd better go to bed. We'll discuss it in the morning," said Martha softly. "What was it you came in about?"

Sally laughed theatrically. "It doesn't matter now." She slammed the door.

Seward looked at Martha. "I'm sorry, Martha."

"It wasn't your fault—or mine. Sally's romantic and young."

"And jealous," Seward sat down on the bed. The feeling of comfort, of companionship, of bringing some order out of chaos—it had all faded. "Look, Martha, I can't stay here "

"You're running away?"

"If you like—but—well—the two of you—I'm in the middle."

"I guessed that. No, you'd better stay. We'll work something out."

"Okay." He got up, sighing heavily. "I think I'll go for a walk in the park—it may help me to think. I'd just reached the stage where I was getting somewhere. Thanks for that, anyway, Martha."

She smiled. "Don't worry, Lee. I'll have everything running smoothly again by tomorrow."

He didn't doubt it. She was a remarkable woman.

He put on his socks and shoes, opened the door, and went out on to the landing. Moonlight entered through a tall, slender window at the end. He went down the two flights of stairs and out of the front door. He turned into the lane and entered the arbour. In the cool of the night, he once again was able to begin some constructive thinking.

While he was on this world, he would not waste his time, he would keep trying to discover the necessary modifications to make the Tranquillomats workable.

He wandered through the arbour, keeping any thoughts of the two women out of his mind. He turned into another section of the arbour he hadn't noticed before. The turnings became numerous but he was scarcely aware of them. It was probably some sort of child's maze.

He paused as he came to a bench. He sat down and folded his arms in front of him, concentrating on his problem.

Much later he heard a sound to his right and looked up.

A man he didn't know was standing there, grinning at him.

Seward noticed at once that the man had overlong canines, that he smelt of damp earth and decay. He wore a black, polo-neck pullover and black, stained trousers. His face was waxen and very pale.

"I've been looking for you for ages, Professor Seward," said the Vampire.

FIVE

Seward got up and faced the horrible creature. The Vampire continued to smile. He didn't move. Seward felt revulsion.

"It's been a long journey," said the Vampire in a sibilant voice like the sound of a frigid wind blowing through dead boughs. "I had intended to visit you at the fortress, but when I got to your room you had left. I was disappointed."

"Doubtless," said Seward. "Well, you've had a wasted journey. I'm not going back there until I'm ready."

"That doesn't interest me."

"What does?" Seward tried to stop himself from trembling.

The Vampire put his hands into his pockets. "Only you."

"Get away from here. You're outnumbered—I have friends?" But he knew that his tone was completely unconvincing.

The Vampire hissed his amusement. "They can't do much, Seward."

"What are you—some sort of android made to frighten people?"

"No." The Vampire took a pace forward.

Suddenly he stopped as a voice came faintly from somewhere in the maze.

"Lee! Lee! Where are you?"

It was Sally's voice.

"Stay away, Sally!" Lee called.

"But I was going to warn you. I saw the Vampire from the window. He's somewhere in the park."

"I know. Go home!"

"I'm sorry about the scene, Lee. I wanted to apologize. It was childish."

"It doesn't matter." He looked at the Vampire. He was standing in a relaxed position, hands in pockets, smiling. "Go home, Sally!"

"She won't, you know," whispered the Vampire.

Her voice was closer. "Lee, I must talk to you."

He screamed: "Sally—the Vampire's here. Go home. Warn your mother, not me. Get some help if you can—but go home!"

Now he saw her enter the part of the maze he was in. She gasped as she saw them. He was between her and the Vampire.

"Sally—do what I told you."

But the Vampire's cold eyes widened and he took one hand out of his pocket and crooked a finger. "Come here, Sally."

She began to walk forward.

He turned to the Vampire. "What do you want?"

"Only a little blood—yours, perhaps—or the young lady's."

"Damn you. Get away. Go back, Sally." She didn't seem to hear him.

He daren't touch the cold body, the earth-damp clothes. He stepped directly between the girl and the Vampire.

He felt sick, but he reached out his hands and shoved at the creature's body. Flesh yielded, but bone did not. The Vampire held his ground, smiling, staring beyond Seward at the girl.

Seward shoved again and suddenly the creature's arms clamped around him and the grinning, fanged face darted towards his. The thing's breath disgusted him. He struggled, but could not break the Vampire's grasp.

A cold mouth touched his neck. He yelled and kicked. He felt a tiny pricking against his throat. Sally screamed. He heard her turn and run and felt a fraction of relief.

He punched with both fists as hard as he could into the creature's solar plexus. It worked. The Vampire groaned and let go. Seward was disgusted to see that its fangs dripped with blood.

His blood.

Now rage helped him. He chopped at the Vampire's throat. It gasped, tottered, and fell in a sprawl of loose limbs to the ground.

He rolled the Vampire over. He tried to remember what he'd read about legendary vampires. Not much. Something about a stake through its heart. Well, that was out.

But the thought that struck him most was that he had fought one of the fortress people—and had won. It was possible to beat them!

He walked purposefully through the maze. It wasn't as tortuous as he'd supposed. Soon he emerged at the arbour entrance near the house. He saw Sally and Martha running towards him. Behind them, another figure lumbered. Farlowe. He had got here fast.

"Seward," he shouted. "They said the Vampire had got you!"

"I got him," said Seward as they came up and stopped.

"What?"

"I beat him."

"But—that's impossible."

Seward shrugged. He felt elated. "Evidently, it's possible," he said. "I knocked him out. He seems to be dead—but I suppose you never know with vampires."

Farlowe was astonished. "I believe you," he said, "but it's fantastic. How did you do it?"

"I got frightened and then angry," said Seward simply. "Maybe you've been overawed by these people too long."

"It seems like it," Farlowe admitted. "Let's go and have a look at him. Sally and Martha had better stay behind."

Seward led him back through the maze. The Vampire was still where he'd fallen. Farlowe touched the corpse with his foot.

"That's the Vampire all right." He grinned. "I knew we had a winner in you, son. What are you going to do now?"

"I'm going straight back to the fortress and get this worked out once and for all. Martha gave me an idea yesterday evening and she may well be right. I'm going to try and find out anyway."

"Better not be overconfident, son."

"Better than being overcautious."

"Maybe," Farlowe agreed doubtfully. "What's this idea Martha gave you?"

"It's really her idea, complete. Let her explain. She's an intelligent woman—and she's bothered to think about this problem from scratch. I'd advise you to do the same."

"I'll hear what it is, first. Let's deal with the Vampire and then get back to the house."

"I'll leave the Vampire to you. I want to use your car."

"Why?"

"To go back to the fortress."

"Don't be a fool. Wait until we've got some help."

"I can't wait that long, Farlowe. I've got other work to do back on my own world."

"Okay," Farlowe shrugged.

Farlowe faded.

The maze began to fade.

Explosions in the brain.

Vertigo.

Sickness.

His head ached and he could not breathe. He yelled, but he had no voice. Multicoloured explosions in front of his eyes. He was whirling round and round, spinning rapidly. Then he felt a new surface dragging at his feet. He closed his eyes and stumbled against something. He fell onto something soft.

It was his camp bed. He was back in his laboratory.

Seward wasted no time wondering what had happened. He knew more or less. Possibly his encounter with the Vampire had sent him back—the exertion or—of course—the creature had drawn some of his blood. Maybe that was it. He felt the pricking sensation, still. He went to the mirror near the wash-stand. He could just see the little marks in his neck. Further proof that wherever that world was it was as real as the one he was in now.

He went to the table and picked up his notes, then walked into the other room. In one section was a long bench. On it, in various stages of dismantling, were the machines that he had been working on, the Tranquillomats that somehow just didn't work. He picked up one of the smallest and checked its batteries, its lenses, and its sonic agitator. The idea with this one was to use a combination of light and sound to agitate certain dormant cells in the brain. Long since, psychophysicists had realized that mental abnormality had a chemical as well as a mental cause. Just as a patient with a psychosomatic illness produced all the biological symptoms of whatever disease he thought he had, so did chemistry play a part in brain disorders. Whether the change in the brain cells came first or afterwards they weren't sure. But the fact was that the cells could be agitated and the mind, by a mixture of hypnosis and conditioning, could be made to work normally. But it was a long step from knowing this and being able to use the information in the construction of Tranquillomats.

Seward began to work on the machine. He felt he was on the right track, at least.

But how long could he keep going before his need for the drug destroyed his will?

He kept going some five hours before his withdrawal symptoms got the better of him.

He staggered towards one of the drug-drawers and fumbled out an ampoule of M-A 19. He staggered into his bedroom and reached for the needle on the table.

He filled the syringe. He filled his veins. He filled his brain with a series of explosions which blew him clean out of his own world into the other.

Fire flew up his spine. Ignited back-brain, ignited mid-brain, ignited fore-brain. Ignited all centres.

EXPLOSION ALL CENTRES!

This time the transition was brief. He was standing in the part of the maze where he'd been when he'd left. The Vampire's corpse was gone. Farlowe had gone, also. He experienced a feeling of acute frustration that he couldn't continue with his work on KLTM-8—the Tranquillomat he'd been modifying when his craving for the M-A 19 took over.

But there was something to do here, too.

He left the maze and walked towards the house. It was dawn and very cold. Farlowe's car was parked there. He noticed the licence number. It seemed different. It now said YOU 009. Maybe he'd mistaken the last digit for a zero last time he'd looked.

The door was ajar. Farlowe and Martha were standing in the hall.

They looked surprised when he walked in.

"I thought the Vampire was peculiar, son," said Farlowe. "But yours was the best vanishing act I've ever seen."

"Martha will explain that, too," Seward said, not looking at her. "Has she told you her theory?"

"Yes, it sounds feasible." He spoke slowly, looking at the floor. He looked up. "We got rid of the Vampire. Burned him up. He burns well."

"That's one out of the way, at least," said Seward. "How many others are there at the fortress?"

Farlowe shook his head. "Not sure. How many did you see?"

"The Man Without a Navel, a character called Brother Sebastian who wears a cowl and probably isn't human either, two pleasant gentlemen called Mr Morl and Mr Hand—and a man in fancy dress whose name I don't know."

"There are one or two more," Farlowe said. "But it's not their numbers we've got to worry about—it's their power!"

"I think maybe it's over-rated," Seward said.

"You may be right, son."

"I'm going to find out."

"You still want my car?"

"Yes. If you want to follow up behind with whatever help you can gather, do that."

"I will." Farlowe glanced at Martha. "What do you think, Martha?"

"I think he may succeed," she said. "Good luck, Lee." She smiled at him in a way that made him want to stay.

"Right," said Seward. "I'm going. Hope to see you there."

"I may be wrong, Lee," she said warningly. "It was only an idea."

"It's the best one I've heard. Goodbye."

He went out of his house and climbed into the car.

SIX

The road was white, the sky was blue, the car was red, and the countryside was green. Yet there was less clarity about the scenery than Seward remembered. Perhaps it was because he no longer had the relaxing company of Farlowe, because his mind was working furiously and his emotions at full blast.

Whoever had designed the set-up on his world had done it well, but had missed certain details. Seward realized that one of the "alien" aspects of the world was that everything was just a little too new. Even Farlowe's car looked as if it had just been driven off the production line.

By the early afternoon he was beginning to feel tired and some of his original impetus had flagged. He decided to move in to the side of the road and rest for a short time, stretch his legs. He stopped the car and got out.

He walked over to the other side of the road. It was on a hillside and he could look down over a wide, shallow valley. A river gleamed in the distance, there were cottages and livestock in the fields. He couldn't see the horizon. Far away he saw a great bank of reddish-looking clouds that seemed to swirl and seethe like a restless ocean. For all the *signs* of habitation, the countryside had taken on a desolate quality as if it had been abandoned. He could not believe that there were people living in the cottages and tending the livestock. The whole thing looked like the set for a film. Or a play—a complicated play devised by the Man Without a Navel and his friends—a play in which the fate of a world—possibly two worlds—was at stake.

How soon would the play resolve itself? he wondered as he turned back towards the car.

A woman was standing by the car. She must have come down the hill while he was looking at the valley. She had long, jet black hair and big, dark eyes. Her skin was tanned dark gold. She had full, extraordinarily sensuous lips. She wore a well-tailored red suit, a black blouse, black shoes, and black handbag. She looked rather sheepish. She raised her head to look at him and as she did so a lock of her black hair fell over her eyes. She brushed it back.

"Hello," she said. "Am I lucky!"

"Are you?"

"I hope so. I didn't expect to find a car on the road. You haven't broken down have you?" She asked this last question anxiously.

"No," he said. "I stopped for a rest. How did you get here?"

She pointed up the hill. "There's a little track up there—a cattle-track, I suppose. My car skidded and went into a tree. It's a wreck."

"I'll have a look at it for you."

She shook her head. "There's no point—it's a write-off. Can you give me a lift?"

"Where are you going?" he said unwillingly.

"Well, it's about sixty miles that way," she pointed in the direction he was going. "A small town."

It wouldn't take long to drive sixty miles on a road as clear as this with no apparent speed-limit. He scratched his head doubtfully. The woman was a diversion he hadn't expected and, in a way, resented. But she was very attractive. He

couldn't refuse her. He hadn't seen any cart-tracks leading off the road. This, as far as he knew, was the only one, but it was possible he hadn't noticed since he didn't know this world. Also, he decided, the woman evidently wasn't involved in the struggle between the fortress people and Farlowe's friends. She was probably just one of the conditioned, living out her life completely unaware of where she was and why. He might be able to get some information out of her.

"Get in," he said.

"Oh, thanks." She got in, seeming rather deliberately to show him a lot of leg. He opened his door and slid under the wheel. She sat uncomfortably close to him. He started the engine and moved the car out on to the road again.

"I'm a stranger here," he began conversationally. "What about you?"

"Not me—I've lived hereabouts all my life. Where do you come from—stranger?"

He smiled. "A long way away."

"Are they all as good looking as you?" It was trite, but it worked. He felt flattered.

"Not any more," he said. That was true. Maniacs never looked very good. But this wasn't the way he wanted the conversation to go, however nice the direction. He said: "You're not very heavily populated around here. I haven't seen another car, or another person for that matter, since I set off this morning."

"It does get boring," she said. She smiled at him. That and her full body, her musky scent, and her closeness, made him breathe more heavily than he would have liked. One thing about this world—the women were considerably less inhibited than on his own. It was a difference in population, perhaps. In an overcrowded world your social behavior must be more rigid, out of necessity.

He kept his hands firmly on the wheel and his eyes on the road, convinced that if he didn't he'd lose control of himself and the car. The result might be some sort of femme fatality. His attraction towards Sally and Martha had not been wholly sexual. Yet he had never felt such purely animal attraction as

this woman radiated. Maybe, he decided, she didn't know it. He glanced at her. Then again, maybe she did.

It said a lot for a woman if she could take his mind so completely off his various problems.

"My name's Magdalen," she smiled. "A bit of a mouthful. What's yours?"

It was a relief to find someone here who didn't already know his name. He rejected the unliked Lee and said: "Bill—Bill Ward."

"Short and sweet," she said. "Not like mine."

He grunted vaguely, consciously fighting the emotions rising in him. There was a word for them. A simple word—short and sweet—lust. He rather liked it. He'd been somewhat repressed on his home world and had kept a tight censorship on his feelings. Here it was obviously different.

A little later, he gave in. He stopped the car and kissed her. He was surprised by the ease with which he did it. He forgot about the Tranquillomats, about the M-A 19, about the fortress. He forgot about everything except her, and that was maybe why he did what he did.

It was as if he was drawn into yet another world—a private world where only he and she had any existence. An enclosed world consisting only of their desire and their need to satisfy it.

Afterwards he felt gloomy, regretful, and guilty. He started the car savagely. He knew he shouldn't blame her, but he did. He'd wasted time. Minutes were valuable, even seconds. He'd wasted hours.

Beside him she took a headscarf from her bag and tied it over her hair. "You're in a hurry."

He pressed the accelerator as far down as he could.

"What's the problem?" she shouted as the engine thudded noisily.

"I've wasted too much time already. I'll drop you off wherever it is you want."

"Oh, fine. Just one of those things, eh?"

"I suppose so. It was my fault, I shouldn't have picked you up in the first place."

She laughed. It wasn't a nice laugh. It was a mocking laugh and it seemed to punch him in the stomach.

"Okay," he said, "okay."

He switched on the headlamps as dusk became night. There was no mileometer on the dashboard, so he didn't know how far they'd travelled, but he was sure it was more than sixty miles.

"Where is this town?" he said.

"Not much further." Her voice softened. "I'm sorry, Bill. But what *is* the matter?"

Something was wrong. He couldn't place it. He put it down to his own anger.

"You may not know it," he said, "but I suspect that nearly all the people living here are being deceived. Do you know the fortress?"

"You mean that big building on the rock wastes?"

"That's it. Well, there's a group of people there who are duping you and the rest in some way. They want to destroy practically the whole of the human race by a particularly nasty method—and they want me to do it for them."

"What's that?"

Briefly, he explained.

Again, she laughed. "By the sound of it, you're a fool to fight this Man Without a Navel and his friends. You ought to throw in your lot with them. You could be top man."

"Aren't you angry?" he said in surprise. "Don't you believe me?"

"Certainly. I just don't share your attitude. I don't understand you turning down a chance when it's offered. I'd take it. As I said, you could be top man."

"I've already been top man," he said, "in a manner of speaking. On my own world. I don't want that kind of responsibility. All I want to do is save something from the mess I've made of civilization."

"You're a fool, Lee."

That was it. She shouldn't have known him as Lee but as Bill, the name he'd introduced himself by. He stopped the car suddenly and looked at her suspiciously. The truth was dawning on him and it made him feel sick at himself that he could have fallen for her trap.

"You're working for him, aren't you. The Man?"

"You seem to be exhibiting all the symptoms of persecution mania, Seward. You need a good psychiatrist." She spoke coolly and reached into her handbag. "I don't feel safe with you."

"It's mutual," he said. "Get out of the car."

"No," she said quietly. "I think we'll go all the way to the fortress together." She put both hands into her bag. They came out with two things. One was a half bottle of brandy.

The other was a gun.

"Evidently my delay tactics weren't effective enough," she mocked. "I thought they might not be, so I brought these. Get out, yourself, Seward."

"You're going to kill me?"

"Maybe."

"But that isn't what the Man wants, is it?"

She shrugged, waving the gun.

Trembling with anger at his own gullibility and impotence, he got out. He couldn't think clearly.

She got out, too, keeping him covered. "You're a clever man, Seward. You've worked out a lot."

"There are others here who know what I know."

"What do they know?"

"They know about the set-up—about the conditioning."

She came round the car towards him, shaking her head. Still keeping him covered, she put the brandy bottle down on the seat.

He went for the gun.

He acted instinctively, in the knowledge that this was his only chance. He heard the gun go off, but he was forcing her wrist back. He slammed it down on the side of the car. She yelled and dropped it. Then he did what he never thought he could do. He hit her, a short, sharp jab under the chin. She crumpled.

He stood over her, trembling. Then he took her headscarf and tied her limp hands behind her. He dragged her up and dumped her in the back of the car. He leant down and found the gun. He put it in his pocket.

Then he got into the driving seat, still trembling. He felt

something hard under him. It was the brandy bottle. It was what he needed. He unscrewed the cap and took a long drink.

His brain began to explode even as he reached for the ignition.

It seemed to crackle and flare like burning timber. He grabbed the door handle. Maybe if he walked around . . .

He felt his knees buckle as his feet touched the ground. He strained to keep himself upright. He forced himself to move round the car. When he reached the bonnet, the headlamps blared at him, blinded him.

They began to blink rapidly into his eyes. He tried to raise his hands and cover his eyes. He fell sideways, the light still blinking. He felt nausea sweep up and through him. He saw the car's license plate in front of him.

YOU 099

YOU 100

YOU 101

He put out a hand to touch the plate. It seemed normal. Yet the digits were clocking up like the numbers on an adding machine.

Again his brain exploded. A slow, leisurely explosion that subsided and brought a delicious feeling of well-being.

Green clouds like boiled jade, scent of chrysanthemums. Swaying lilies. Bright lines of black and white in front of his eyes. He shut them and opened them again. He was looking up at the blind in his bedroom.

As soon as he realized he was back, Seward jumped off the bed and made for the bench where he'd left the half-finished tranquillomat. He remembered something, felt for the gun he'd taken off the girl. It wasn't there.

But he felt the taste of the brandy in his mouth. Maybe it was as simple as that, he thought. Maybe all he needed to get back was alcohol.

There was sure to be some alcohol in the lab. He searched through cupboards and drawers until he found some in a jar. He filled a vial and corked it. He took off his shirt and taped the vial under his armpit—that way he might be able to transport it from his world to the other one.

Then he got down to work.

Lenses were reassembled, checked. New filters went in and old ones came out. He adjusted the resonators and amplifiers. He was recharging the battery which powered the transistorized circuits, when he sensed the mob outside. He left the little machine on the bench and went to the control board. He flicked three switches down and then, on impulse, flicked them off again. He went back to the bench and unplugged the charger. He took the machine to the window. He drew the blind up.

It was a smaller mob than usual. Evidently some of them had learned their lesson and were now avoiding the laboratory.

Far away, behind them, the sun glinted on a calm sea. He opened the window.

There was one good way of testing his Tranquillomat. He rested it on the sill and switched it to ATTRACT. That was the first necessary stage, to hold the mob's attention. A faint, pleasant humming began to come from the machine. Seward knew that specially shaped and coloured lenses were whirling at the front. The mob looked up towards it, but only those in the center of the group were held. The others dived away, hiding their eyes.

Seward felt his body tightening, growing cold. Part of him began to scream for the M-A 19. He clung to the machine's carrying handles. He turned a dial from Zero to 50. There were 100 units marked on the indicator. The machine was now sending at half-strength. Seward consoled himself that if anything went wrong he could not do any more harm to their ruined minds. It wasn't much of a consolation.

He quickly saw that the combined simulated brainwaves, sonic vibrations, and light patterns were having some effect on their minds. But what was the effect going to be? They were certainly responding. Their bodies were relaxing, their faces were no longer twisted with insanity. But was the Tranquillomat actually doing any constructive good—what it had been designed to do? He upped the output to 75 degrees.

His hands began to tremble. His mouth and throat were tight and dry. He couldn't keep going. He stepped back. His stomach ached. His bones ached. His eyes felt puffy. He began to move towards the half-full ampoule of M-A 19 on the table. He filled

the blunt hypodermic. He found a vein. He was weeping as the explosions hit his brain.

SEVEN

This time it was different.

He saw an army of machines advancing towards him. An army of malevolent hallucinomats. He tried to run, but a thousand electrodes were clamped to his body and he could not move. From nowhere, needles entered his veins. Voices shouted SEWARD! SEWARD! SEWARD! The Hallucinomats advanced, shrilling, blinking, buzzing—*laughing*. The machines were laughing at him.

SEWARD!

Now he saw Farlowe's car's registration plate.

YOU 110

YOU 111

YOU 119

SEWARD!

Y O U !

SEWARD!

His brain was being squeezed. It was contracting, contracting. The voices became distant, the machines began to recede. When they had vanished he saw he was standing in a circular room in the center of which was a low dais. On the dais was a chair. In the chair was the Man Without a Navel. He smiled at Seward.

"Welcome back, old boy," he said.

Brother Sebastian and the woman, Magdalen, stood close to the dais. Magdalen's smile was cool and merciless, seeming to anticipate some new torture that the Man and Brother Sebastian had devised.

But Seward was jubilant. He was sure his little Tranquillomat had got results.

"I think I've done it," he said quietly. "I think I've built a workable Tranquillomat—and, in a way, it's thanks to you. I had to speed my work up to beat you—and I did it!"

They seemed unimpressed.

"Congratulations, Seward," smiled the Man Without a Navel. "But this doesn't alter the situation, you know. Just because you *have* an antidote doesn't mean we have to use it."

Seward reached inside his shirt and felt for the vial taped under his arm. It had gone. Some of his confidence went with the discovery.

Magdalen smiled. "It was kind of you to drink the drugged brandy."

He put his hands in his jacket pocket.

The gun was back there. He grinned.

"What's he smiling at?" Magdalen said nervously.

"I don't know. It doesn't matter. Brother Sebastian, I believe you have finished work on your version of Seward's Hypnomat?"

"I have," said the sighing, cold voice.

"Let's have it in. It is a pity we didn't have it earlier. It would have saved us time—and Seward all his efforts."

The curtains behind them parted and Mr Hand, Mr Morl, and the Laughing Cavalier wheeled in a huge, bizarre machine that seemed to have a casing of highly polished gold, silver, and platinum. There were two sets of lenses in its domed, headlike top. They looked like eyes staring at Seward.

Was this a conditioning machine like the ones they'd probably used on the human populace? Seward thought it was likely. If they got him with that, he'd be finished. He pulled the gun out of his pocket. He aimed it at the right-hand lens and pulled the trigger.

The gun roared and kicked in his hand, but no bullet left the muzzle. Instead there came a stream of small, brightly coloured globes, something like those used in the attraction device on the Tranquillomat. They sped towards the machine, struck it, exploded. The machine buckled and shrilled. It steamed and two discs, like lids, fell across the lenses. The machine rocked backwards and fell over.

The six figures began to converge on him, angrily.

Suddenly, on his left, he saw Farlowe, Martha, and Sally step from behind a screen.

"Help me!" he cried to them.

"We can't!" Farlowe yelled. "Use your initiative, son!"

"Initiative?" He looked down at the gun. The figures were coming closer. The Man Without a Navel smiled slowly. Brother Sebastian tittered. Magdalen gave a low, mocking laugh that seemed—strangely—to be a criticism of his sexual prowess. Mr Morl and Mr Hand retained their mournful and

cheerful expressions respectively. The Laughing Cavalier flung back his head and—laughed. All around them the screens, which had been little more than head-high were lengthening, widening, stretching up and up.

He glanced back. The screens were growing.

He pulled the trigger of the gun. Again it bucked, again it roared—and from the muzzle came a stream of metallic-gray particles which grew into huge flowers. The flowers burst into flame and formed a wall between him and the six.

He peered around him, looking for Farlowe and the others. He couldn't find them. He heard Farlowe's shout: "Good luck, son!" He heard Martha and Sally crying goodbye. "Don't go!" he yelled.

Then he realized he was alone. And the six were beginning to advance again—malevolent, vengeful.

Around him the screens, covered in weird designs that curled and swirled, ever-changing, were beginning to topple inwards. In a moment he would be crushed.

Again he heard his name being called. SEWARD! SEWARD!

Was it Martha's voice? He thought so.

"I'm coming," he shouted, and pulled the trigger again.

The Man Without a Navel, Magdalen, Brother Sebastian, the Laughing Cavalier, Mr Hand and Mr Morl—all screamed in unison and began to back away from him as the gun's muzzle spouted a stream of white fluid which floated into the air.

Still the screens were falling, slowly, slowly.

The white fluid formed a net of millions of delicate strands. It drifted over the heads of the six. It began to descend. They looked up and screamed again.

"Don't, Seward," begged the Man Without a Navel. "Don't, old man—I'll make it worth your while."

Seward watched as the net engulfed them. They struggled and cried and begged.

It did not surprise him much when they began to shrink.

No! *They* weren't shrinking—he was growing. He was growing over the toppling screens. He saw them fold inwards. He looked down and the screens were like cards folding neatly

over the six little figures struggling in the white net. Then, as the screens folded down, the figures were no longer in sight. It got lighter. The screens rolled themselves into a ball.

The ball began to take on a new shape.

It changed colour. And then, there it was—a perfectly formed human skull.

Slowly, horrified, the skull began to gather flesh and flood and muscles to itself. The stuff flowed over it. Features began to appear. Soon, in a state of frantic terror, Seward recognized the face.

It was his own.

His own face, its eyes wide, its lips parted. A tired, stunned, horrified face.

He was back in the laboratory. And he was staring into a mirror.

He stumbled away from the mirror. He saw he wasn't holding a gun in his hand but a hypodermic needle. He looked round the room.

The Tranquillomat was still on the window-sill. He went to the window. There, quietly talking among the ruins below, was a group of sane men and woman. They were still in rags, still gaunt. But they were sane. That was evident. They were saner than they had ever been before.

He called down to them, but they didn't hear him.

Time for that later, he thought. He sat on the bed, feeling dazed and relieved. He dropped the needle to the floor, certain he wouldn't need to use it again.

It was incredible, but he thought he knew where he had been. The final image of his face in the mirror had given him the last clue.

He had been inside his own mind. The M-A 19 was merely a hallucinogenic after all. A powerful one, evidently, if it could give him the illusion of rope-marks on his wrists, bites on his neck, and the rest.

He had escaped into a dream world.

Then he wondered—but why? What good had it done?

He got up and went towards the mirror again.

Then he heard the voice. Martha's voice.

SEWARD! SEWARD! Seward, listen to me!

No, he thought desperately. No, it can't be starting again. There's no need for it.

He ran into the laboratory, closing the door behind him, locking it. He stood there, trembling, waiting for the withdrawal symptoms. They didn't come.

Instead he saw the walls of the laboratory, the silent computers and meters and dials, begin to blur. A light flashed on above his head. The dead banks of instruments suddenly came alive. He sat down in a big chrome, padded chair which had originally been used for the treating of test-subjects.

His gaze was caught by a whirling stroboscope that had appeared from nowhere. Coloured images began to form in front of his eyes. He struggled to get up but he couldn't.

YOU 121

YOU 122

YOU 123

Then the first letter changed to a V.

VOU 127

SEWARD!

His eyelids fell heavily over his eyes.

"Professor Seward." It was Martha's voice. It spoke to someone else. "We may be lucky, Tom. Turn down the volume."

He opened his eyes.

"Martha."

The woman smiled. She was dressed in a white coat and was leaning over the chair. She looked very tired. "I'm not—Martha—Professor Seward. I'm Doctor Kalin. Remember?"

"Doctor Kalin, of course."

His body felt weaker than it had ever felt before. He leaned back in the big chair and sighed. Now he was remembering.

It had been his decision to make the experiment. It had seemed to be the only way of speeding up work on the development of the Tranquillomats. He knew that the secret of a workable machine was imbedded in the deepest level of his unconscious mind. But, however much he tried—hypnosis, symbol-association, word-association—he couldn't get at it.

There was only one way he could think of—a dangerous experiment for him—an experiment which might not work at all. He would be given a deep-conditioning, made to believe that he had brought disaster to the world and must remedy it by devising a Tranquillomat. Things were pretty critical in the world outside, but they weren't as bad as they had conditioned him to believe. Work on the Tranquillomats *was* falling behind—but there had been no widespread disaster, *yet*. It was bound to come unless they could devise some means for mass-cure for the thousands of neurotics and victims of insanity. An antidote for the results of mass-tension.

So, simply, they conditioned him to think his efforts had destroyed civilization. He must devise a working Tranquillomat. They had turned the problem from an intellectual one into a personal one.

The conditioning had apparently worked.

He looked around the laboratory at his assistants. They were all alive, healthy, a bit tired, a bit strained, but they looked relieved.

"How long have I been under?" he asked.

"About fourteen hours. That's twelve hours since the experiment went wrong."

"Went wrong?"

"Why, yes," said Doctor Kalin in surprise. "Nothing was happening. We tried to bring you round—we tried every darned machine and drug in the place—nothing worked. We expected catatonia. At least we've managed to save you. We'll just have to go on using the ordinary methods of research, I suppose." Her voice was tired, disappointed.

Seward frowned. But he *had* got the results. He knew exactly how to construct a working Tranquillomat. He thought back.

"Of course," he said. "I was only conditioned to believe that the world was in ruins and I had done it. There was nothing about—about—the *other* world."

"What other world?" Macpherson, his Chief Assistant, asked the question.

Seward told them. He told them about the Man Without a Navel, the fortress, the corridors, the tortures, the landscapes seen from Farlowe's car, the park, the maze, the Vampire, Magdalen . . . He told them how, in what he now called Con-

dition A, he had believed himself hooked on a drug called M-A 19.

"But we don't have a drug called M-A 19," said Doctor Kalin.

"I know that now. But I didn't know that and it didn't matter. I would have found something to have made the journey into—the other world—a world consisting only in my skull. Call it Condition B, if you like—or Condition X, maybe. The unknown. I found a fairly logical means of making myself *believe* I was entering another world. That was M-A 19. By inventing symbolic characters who were trying to stop me, I made myself work harder. Unconsciously I knew that Condition A was going wrong—so I escaped into Condition B in order to put right the damage. By acting out the drama I was able to clear my mind of its confusion. I had, as I suspected, the secret of the Tranquillomat somewhere down there all the time. Condition A failed to release the secret—Condition B succeeded. I can build you a workable Tranquillomat, don't worry."

"Well," Macpherson grinned. "I've been told to use my imagination in the past—but you *really* used yours!"

"That was the idea, wasn't it? We'd decided it was no good just using drugs to keep us going. We decided to use our drugs and Hallucinomats directly, to condition me to believe that what we feared will happen, *had* happened."

"I'm glad we didn't manage to bring you back to normality, in that case," Doctor Kalin smiled. "You've had a series of classic—if more complicated than usual—nightmares. The Man Without a Navel, as you call him, and his 'allies' symbolized the elements in you that were holding you back from the truth—diverting you. By 'defeating' the Man, you defeated those elements."

"It was a hell of a way to get results," Seward grinned. "But I got them. It was probably the only way. Now we can produce as many Tranquillomats as we need. The problem's over. I've—in all modesty—" he grinned, "saved the world before it needed saving. It's just as well."

"What about your 'helpers,' though," said Doctor Kalin helping him from the chair. He glanced into her intelligent, mature face. He had always liked her.

"Maybe," he smiled, as he walked towards the bench where the experimental Tranquillomats were laid out, "maybe there was quite a bit of wish-fulfilment mixed up in it as well."

"It's funny how you didn't realize that it wasn't real, isn't it?" said Macpherson behind him.

"Why is it funny?" he turned to look at Macpherson's long, worn face. "Who knows what's real, Macpherson. This world? That world? Any other world? I don't feel so adamant about this one, do you?"

"Well . . ." Macpherson said doubtfully. "I mean, you're a trained psychiatrist as well as everything else. You'd think you'd recognize your own symbolic characters."

"I suppose it's possible." Macpherson had missed his point. "All the same," he added, "I wouldn't mind going back there some day. I'd quite enjoy the exploration. And I liked some of the people. Even though they were probably wish-fulfilment figures. Farlowe—father—it's possible." He glanced up as his eye fell on a meter. It consisted of a series of code-letters and three digits. VOU 128 it said now. That was Farlowe's number-plate. His mind had turned the V into a Y. He'd probably discover plenty of other symbols around, which he'd turned into something else in the other world. He still couldn't think of it as a dream world. It had seemed so real. For him, it was still real.

"What about the woman—Martha?" Doctor Kalin said. "You called *me* Martha as you were waking up."

"We'll let that one go for the time being," he grinned. "Come on, we've still got a lot of work to do."

AFTERWORD

I'm glad you're doing *The Deep Fix*. It's a story to which I've got particular sentimental attachment. Though it may not seem it, it was a "breakthrough" in its day (1963, as I recall) and Ted Carnell, then editor of *New Worlds* and *Science Fantasy*, wasn't too sure if he should run it. I wrote it, then, as a "bridge" story between traditional science fiction and what came to be known as "New Wave"—that is, the symbolism was rationalised at the end and interpreted, by means of the drug-dream ending. Later stories, like *The Pleasure Garden of Felipe Sagittarius*, used less rationale, as did the Jerry Cornelius stories. I've always felt that sf was hampered by a need to introduce naturalistic rationalisations for images whose power was often reduced as a result. It was partly why I was always more attracted to the possibilities of fantasy. Since then, of course, I've dispensed with rationalisation in the accepted sense and produced what you might see as "pure" metaphorical or allegorical fiction which has little to do with any other genre. *The Deep Fix* became the name of the band we had for a while in 1974/75 which made the one album *New Worlds Fair*, and it's been the name of a rock band since 1965, when Jerry Cornelius played with it.

The story appeared under the name of James Colvin (the choice of pen name was Ted's—I'd picked James Mendoza (an ancestor) in the last issue of *Science Fantasy* to be edited by Ted. The issue also contained the final *Elric* story (chronologically speaking) and the last of my critical series *Aspects of Fantasy*.

KAMUS

J. MICHAEL REAVES

THE BIG SPELL

STEPHEN HICKMAN

INTRODUCTION

J. Michael Reaves is a very entertaining writer. Very few know that fact because his work has been published nowhere as much as it should. It's one reason why you're getting two Reaves stories between these pages and the back of the book.

Now before anybody starts screaming that we should be running part two of *S.P.V. 166* instead, all we ask is that you write J. Michael a letter. Tell *him* that he should wait a bit longer to get the recognition held back so long. Tell *him* that his prose will eventually get the attention. Tell *him* the reviews will be on their way a bit later. I'm not going to do it. I know Michael. He's big. He works out in a gym. He lifts I.B.M. Selectrics for exercise. He's a talented, experienced writer. They don't fool around, no sir.

Reaves is the author of numerous television shows and his prose has appeared in Terry Carr's respected series of *Universe* anthologies and the *Magazine of F. and S.F.* Illustrator Stephen Hickman is a paperback cover painter for Ace, Jove, and the designer of over a half-dozen t-shirt illustrations.

Together, they form the core of the *Kamus of Kadizhar* fan club.

Kamus, who you're about to meet, is the center of attention in a *fantasy* fantasy. The whole *schmeer*, as we say, just leaks with those marvelous pulp touches—flying dragons, underground paths and attractive, intelligent women. This is an adventure—a trip to a land of intrigue and humor.

Inside you'll meet your first kragor (shades of Wayne Boring) and greet the sound of a huggable phonecub.

Steve's closing illo is an apt bonus.

THE BIG SPELL
A Kamus of Kadizhar Mystery
by J. Michael Reaves

1

My sword needed polishing. The swivel chair creaked as I leaned back and put my sandals on the glass that covered my stone desk. My blade was serving as a paperweight at the moment; it did a poor job of reflecting the amber sunlight. Noon on Ja-Lur is a little brighter than twilight on Earth. I had been thinking about Earth a lot lately; mostly wondering why I had left it to return to the Darkworld. Business wasn't good.

My office was hot and quiet, the oil lamp flame unmoving. Through the narrow window I could see the slums of Thieves' Maze, and beyond that the towers and ships of the Unity Spaceport. If the other wall had a window, there would be a view of Overlord Kirven's palace. I was just as happy that there wasn't.

Dash, my phonecub, was folded like an old wineskin in one corner of his cage. He looked hungry; I knew the look well from my mirror. I squeezed my moneypouch and felt the round outline of one thin dechel. With one dechel I could insult a beggar.

Dash stirred, then unwrapped his two tails and sat up. He perked pointed ears, his black fur bristled, and those solemn silver eyes grew large. I sat up—somebody was calling. The phonecub's small body went lax and his mouth opened.

"Kamus of Kadizhar?"

I didn't recognize the voice, but it belonged to a woman. It had that carefully casual tone that usually means a job. I quit fondling my pouch. "At your service."

"You are the one who solves problems for a fee?"

"I could be an augur or a procurer and do that," I said. "My specialty is investigative work."

"I see." Her voice grew slightly colder. "My name is Valina," she continued, "and I want you to find someone for me."

"My fee is seven hundred dechels a fortnight, Valina," I said. "Plus expenses." No surname and no name of origin

usually meant a slave—I wanted it clear that I didn't work for grain. At least not until that last dechel was spent.

"Fine," she said smoothly. "How do I reach you from the Marketplace?"

"Take the Avenue of Columns west to Manthion Tower. Turn left on Cartrattle Street, right on Whores' Path. I'm in the third room on the second floor of the last building before you reach Thieves' Maze."

She said nothing more. Dash shook his head and yawned. I tossed him the last sweetmeat in a dish on the bookcase, one I'd planned on eating myself, and thought about the call.

A slave with seven hundred dechels? Perhaps she was a front for a wealthy, anonymous master. I glanced around the small chamber I called an office. In one corner was a pile of papers awaiting a filing cabinet from Earth. A chipped wine jug and a few mismatched mugs sat on a wobbly table, flanked by two client's chairs. My trenchcloak hung on the back of the wooden door, and a large section of lath had fallen from the low ceiling. A slight breeze was now bringing ripe scents from the Maze through the window. Not very impressive, but since I was the only private eye on the planet, I couldn't see any reason to be impressive. Valina would have to take me as I was.

* * *

She walked in like she owned the place, and wanted to sell it. She wore a simple slave's tunic of purest black, and a turquoise-inlaid dagger that could open more than letters. Her figure was nice, not outstanding, but her hair definitely was. It was gray, not the gray of age, but a gray like the heart of a cloud that would come to silver even in Ja-Lur's dull sun. It swooped back and curled past her shoulders, making a net that caught an interesting face. A high forehead, small nose, and cheeks that were almost gaunt. Her mouth had a slight curve that didn't remind me of a smile.

Then I saw her eyes.

They were deep and midnight blue, with a look in them as subtle and indescribable as they were unmistakable. If most eyes are mirrors of the soul, then these were still wells reflecting incredible depths. By those eyes I knew she was of the

Blood—a Darklander. Like hunger, I knew the look, and it meant trouble for me. I was a half-breed Darklander, and Darklanders aren't welcome in the Northern Nations. If she sensed the Blood in me, my business could be in jeopardy—along with my life.

"Kamus of Kadizhar?" Valina asked politely. If she knew, she didn't show it.

"We went through introductions once," I said, watching her. "Let's try something new."

"As you wish," Valina said, and smiled. Then she raised both arms in a summoning gesture and, before I could stop her, spoke in Darkland Language. *"Rylah Tobari, ke'n Sorgath!"* The oil lamp guttered and went out. There was a clap of thunder, a billowing of foul, dirt-colored smoke, and I had an uninvited guest.

It stood almost three meters tall, with skin the color of dried blood. It was bald, with pointed ears higher than its crown. The lobes were pointed also. From its shoulderblades rose antlers like the twisted limbs of a hanging tree; they seemed to join with the roiling smoke. Its eyes were yellow against black. It was fanged and taloned and hugely sexed, and it stood in a shaft of dim sunlight from the window, poised on bird-claw feet. It grinned. I didn't. Dash shrieked and tried to crawl into his food dish.

"I think you have the wrong place," I told Valina. "A charlatan lives three houses over in the Maze . . ."

The Darkling laughed. "Creature of a moment," it said, "you have lost your life. Prepare yourself."

"What is this?" I asked. In the dimness they did not see me slip potions from my pouch and mix them by touch. I stared at Valina. "Return this thing to the Dark and let's talk. We might like each other."

Valina smiled again and said, "Since your powers are halved by nature, the Darkling's will be also, to make a fair fight." She spoke a Phrase and the Darkling seemed to dwindle slightly. It looked reproachfully at her and I took advantage of that to cast the compound I had mixed. *"Nithla,"* I cried, *"vorst enyon!"* My pronunciation was terrible, as always. But the fluid ignited in midair nonetheless, and the Darkling blinked as golden smoke mingled with oily brown in the rank breeze from the window. It swung one arm backhanded through the

mist.

"Such a puny spell," it said, in a voice like grating metal. "Did you seriously think it would affect me?"

I shrugged. "Not really, but it was worth a try." I took up my sword and stepped from behind the desk, taking care to stay upwind. "What would you have?" I asked.

"Your soul for sustenance."

"Come and get it, then."

At that it howled and leaped forward, its heavy claws digging into the wooden floor. It lifted a chair and flung it at me. I dodged and heard it smash to kindling against the wall. I swung my sword and drew a black line across its thigh. The wound hissed and steamed, and three stony talons just missed the side of my face. The thing had a reach on me. I lightfooted backward to the bookshelf and heaved a bookend at it. The Darkling caught it, crunched it in its mouth, yellow gaze mocking, then stalked forward, casually lifting one end of the heavy stone desk out of the way. That impressed me, the more so since its strength had been halved. Of course, it had to be powerful to survive in direct sunlight. But I was hoping it was not powerful enough to survive without help.

I glanced at Valina. She was watching me, oblivious to the golden wisps drifting toward her.

I dove forward as the Darkling set the desk down, rolled beneath its slash, and tried to hamstring it. It danced back and I saw its leg coming at me, fell back with the kick, but was still knocked breathless into a corner. It leaped to straddle me—

—And I heard Valina cough.

I thrust upward and skewered an obvious target—the Darkling squawked indignantly and jerked away, tottered, and went down with a crash. There was a sigh and Valina collapsed behind me as the compound had its effect. Simultaneously the Darkling, lying in dim sunlight, gave a whinnying cry and turned to dust.

I rolled over and sat up. I felt as if I'd been racked, but fortunately had not been scratched or bitten. I looked at the fragements of the bookend. They were acid-eaten.

I pulled Valina to her feet and sat her in the remaining client's chair. I slapped her once on each cheek, not gently, and let her head loll forward. She took a deep breath and shuddered. "Head down," I said. "Breathe deeply. And don't

move or I'll break your neck."

She believed me. I sat down behind my desk. After a moment she lifted her head and smiled. I wasn't growing fond of that smile. "Very good, Kamus," she said. "Tell me, how did you know I was binding the Darkling to this plane?"

"It made sense. If it had been strong enough to survive direct sunlight on its own, you wouldn't have been able to control it."

She nodded and ran fingers through streamers of hair. "I had to know if you could battle things of the Dark and live."

"You could have asked and saved us both a lot of trouble," I told her. Then I caught the look she was sending across the still-dusty air. "All right," I nodded, "so we're both Darklanders. I won't tell if you won't. Now stand up, turn around and walk out."

Something that looked bad in eyes as blue as hers flashed. I leaned forward. "You wouldn't get past the first syllable." I meant it. I'm not casual about killing as are most people on my world. A private eye should have a basic moral code. But I wasn't about to give her a second shot at me. This lady was dangerous. I had ways of holding her back.

She relaxed, fingertips smoothing her tunic. After a moment she said slowly, "Kamus, I need your help."

"Why should I help you? I've had furniture smashed, the office is filled with Darkling dust, and those potions don't come cheap."

"I'll reimburse you for everything and a considerable amount besides. I only ask that you hear me out, then say whether you will be of help.

"I am late of the entourage of the Lord of Sassoon."

That was supposed to intrigue me. It did. Sassoon was until recently a small seaside province around twenty kilometers northeast of Mariyad. More recently, within the past week, it had become a blighted land with a large crater where the lord's keep had stood. There had been a plague and quite a few dead peasants. The story was that the Keeplord had been a Darklander, had gotten ambitious, and the Darklord had smote him down, along with castle, servants, and the general countryside. It could be true—but if it was, how had Valina escaped?

I unwrapped a stick of imported chewing gum while

watching her. Some private eyes smoke, but that habit isn't popular on the Darkworld—polluting someone else's air is a good way to get dead. I stuck the gum in my cheek and motioned for her to continue.

"Do you know," she asked, "who the 'Brothers Below' are?"

"I've heard the term in the Maze. It's supposed to be another name for the *Kakush*, a sort of legendary oligarchy of criminals that have their fingers in all the illegal and most of the legal businesses in Mariyad."

"It's the only clue I have to finding Kaan—something he said," she said. "If he's learned too much of the Darklore . . ."

I held up a hand. "The beginning," I suggested.

She stroked her cheekbones with those long, ringless fingers. "I'll start before the beginning," she said.

"A man named Edward Boriun came to Ja-Lur from Earth seven years ago. He was not an ambassador from the Unity of Planets; he was a renegade, a scientist who had discovered that some secrets need more than science for their explaining. So he stole a spaceship and sought a world where magic worked.

"He landed in the Black Desert, north of Ja-Agur. He feigned amnesia and became a slave to a local wizard in one of the coastal towns that trade with the Darkland."

"A charlatan?" I asked.

"You used that word before. I'm not familiar with it."

"A Northern term: a human who claims to have Dark powers."

"I see. No, this man was of the Blood. I was part of his household. I watched Boriun as he learned speech and custom—and Language."

That called for a reaction. "An Outworlder learning Language?"

"There is Dark Blood on other worlds," she said. "It is common on Earth still, though Earth has almost left the area of overlapping cosmos that we call the universe of magic. Because of this, the Blooded on Earth can mate with humans and be fruitful, not sterile as they are here."

That made me relax somewhat. Valina had recognized me as of the Blood, just as I had known her—one Darklander can always recognize another. But she knew nothing of my human heritage. Not all matings between Blooded and human are

sterile.

"There are few pure lines left on Earth," she continued. "But in Boriun the Blood ran clean, and he learned—behind my master's back at first, later at his feet."

"And he killed your master," I said.

"Yes," she said calmly. Sweat was collecting along my headband. If what she was telling me was true, if Outlanders were capable of Darklore, than this could be big. Big enough to forget about very quickly.

"My master never suspected. He died unknowing, his soul plucked and flung to Darklings. There were others with power in the village, including me, but Boriun was more powerful. He made himself a Lord. He was arrogant beyond sanity, but the Darklord did not crush him—even when Boriun chose to bring a plague upon the town. One dark night, the wind came roaring with pestilence through the small village. The next morning there was no living soul left, for Boriun had gone north, taking me with him, and all the rest were dead."

Dash was whimpering in his cage. I watched Valina. The depths of Darkness had left her eyes; now they were as flat as her turquoise blade. I went to the wall lamp and relit it—the shadows were getting too thick.

"We crossed the Inland Sea and came to Sassoon, where Boriun took the Keeplord's throne. He was still not satisfied; he continued his studies, searching until at last he found a single Phrase of the *Synulanom*, a spell powerful enough to give him control of all the Northern Nations from the Mountains of Rool to the Eastern Ocean. When he finds the rest of it, he intends to speak it, and with the power gained, he will conquer the kingdoms.

"Then he intends to challenge the Darklord."

I swallowed my gum. "That settles it," I said. "This is out of my league. I've gone up against quite a bit for my fee, but not someone who's crazy enough to challenge the Darklord."

"Don't be foolish," Valina said with a flash of teeth. "Boriun is walking dead—the Darklord will crush him. It's Kaan I'm worried about."

"I'd almost forgotten about him."

"Four months ago two Unity agents, Daniel Tolon of Earth and Kaan Ta'Wyys of Thanare, made planetfall. Boriun caught them entering his Keep. He sentenced Tolon to be a

galleyslave, but offered Kaan a chance to learn and rule by his side. Kaan was also of the Blood; he and Boriun had dabbled together in Darklore, but the evil of it had repelled Kaan. Still, they were linked, and so Kaan had sensed Boriun's plans to conquer Ja-Lur and had come to stop him.

"He refused Boriun's offer at first, but later decided he would need knowledge as a weapon. So he learned, and he used his new spells to help me escape, last week. I heard the next day that the Keep had been destroyed and that all within it had vanished." She took a deep breath. "I'm afraid for Kaan. I know how easily the Dark secrets can corrupt those of less than pure Blood. I want you to find Kaan for me, Kamus, find him before the Darklord does."

Then she joined me in silence. I picked up a stick of gum and toyed with it, ran a finger along the flat of my blade, and in general pretended to think about it. I'd already thought about it, and I knew I didn't want to touch this case with a ten-foot battlelance. All I wanted was to break it to Valina in a way that would avoid more unpleasantness.

"What makes you think the destruction wasn't the Darklord's move?"

"If Kaan were dead, I would know it," Valina said flatly. I didn't argue with that; they were both of the Blood.

"But I've tried to contact him through the Dark," she added, "with no luck."

"Any idea where Boriun and Kaan have gone?"

She shook her head. "It couldn't be far; Boriun wanted to start his rule in this nation of Adelan. I have nothing but that cryptic phrase that Kaan whispered to me just before I escaped. He did not have time to tell me more."

I looked at her. She had told me the whole story without so much as a hair losing its place. Her eyes were still flat, oddly lacking. "Why do you want to find Kaan so badly?" I asked.

"Because I love him," Valina said coolly. "I thought that was understood."

"Not by me. You could have been reciting a history lesson."

That was my second mistake of the day. Valina's eyes suddenly got very nasty—so nasty that I gripped my sword in case she was thinking of another test. She wasn't. Rising, she pulled seven large gold coins from her moneypouch and tossed them on my desk. They cracked the glass deskcover.

"You'd better know something in three days," she said, each word cold as a snake's kiss. Then she turned and left, quickly, before I could tell her I had no intention of taking the case.

I looked at the cracked glass and the shambles the Darkling had left. Seven hundred dechels to start me on a case involving Outworlders and Darklanders, a case that could bring both the Unity of Planets and the Darklord himself down on me.

I sighed, swept the coins into my hand, pulled out a sheet of parchment, and began an expense account, starting with the bookend.

2

I fed Dash and told him to take any messages. Then I took the quick route to the Unity Spaceport, through the heart of Thieves' Maze. Dank Lane was a street I usually avoided, but I wanted to reach the Spaceport before Customs closed. I still had no intention of getting involved in this case to any great degree; I merely intended to give Valina an idea of where to look for her Outworld lover. I wasn't going to invade any sorcerer's citadel to carry him out—that was definitely not in the league of a half-breed Darklander who could barely keep the few spells he knew from backfiring.

Dank Lane was narrow and high-walled—the slender strip of sky above was dark, dark blue with a smear of honey to the west. Mariyad traffic grew thick toward the streets near the Spaceport, and Outworlders foolish enough to enter the Maze were fair game and easy marks. This deep in the Maze, however, few bothered to keep up appearances. Cripples sauntered by me with crutches slung over their shoulders, on their way to beg at the gates. Blind men eyed me suspiciously. I didn't fit—I wasn't burly enough for a footpad nor tattered enough for a beggar. Were the lane less crowded, I would have had trouble. But too many thieves spoil the taking, so I thought myself safe.

Until I noticed that I was being followed.

Suppertime in the Maze; I could smell lentils, boiled meat and cheap wine. Dank Lane twisted between rickety, gap-boarded houses, jammed together and piled at overhung angles. Railless stairways hung like gray cobwebs down high brick walls that made night out of evening. At times the lane

was almost ankle-deep in cess, save for a narrow path of foot-polished cobbles at the center. Not everyone bothered to keep their feet dry. The one following me didn't—I noticed him trying not to be noticed, dodging from one clot of people to the next. I studied him from the corner of my gaze: a small, stooped figure in rags the color of wormwood. No threat by himself, but if he were in league with others . . .

Then I caught another glimpse, and noticed the familiar cadence to his limp. A motley group passed between us and I ducked for the shadow of a doorway. As he passed I put out an arm and grabbed his grime-stiff cloak, regretting the probability of fleas, and pulled him in.

"What news, Ratbag?" I asked him.

He squealed, of course, and stared at me. His eyes were stitched with red and set barely wide enough for a nose the shape of a cornerstone. Scabs and burst purple veins littered his face. "Kamus!" His voice was as shrill as a cart axle. "I wanted to warn you—I—"

"Of course you did." I shoved that last dechel between his crusty teeth to stop their chattering. "You always have my welfare at heart. Who you selling out this time?"

He spat the coin into a blacklined palm and stopped shivering. "No gossip. Word is that someone is looking for you—a savage, it's told. A skin-clad Outlander with murder on his breath. He's sure been told where to find you by now."

I looked at him suspiciously. "This out of the kindness of your heart, Ratbag?"

"You always pay top for news of the Maze, Kamus." He glanced pointedly at the dechel.

"That's all I've got right now. You'll get more next time." I thrust Ratbag and his urine-sharp smell away from me, and watched him scuttle into alley dimness. Then I headed for the Maze exit, holding my breath like a man in a slaughterhouse.

I couldn't recall offending any savages lately.

* * *

The Spaceport was a kilometer from the city wall, surrounded by knee-high savannah grass. It was small, not over an acre in size, and the only one permitted on the Darkworld by the Darklord. Though he rarely spoke to anyone on the planet, the

Darklord had his ways of issuing edicts. After several attempts at building other spaceports in other major cities had been foiled by foundation collapse, spontaneous human combustion, and other setbacks, the Unity of Planets had decided to be content with the one outside Mariyad.

Once I stepped from grass to plasticrete and passed the sleek, gleaming weapon detectors, I was considered subject to Unity law. Once inside the boundary the little Darklore I was capable of would not work, just as technological devices did not work outside—again, the Darklord's policy.

I entered a public gate guarded by two crewcut Earthlings wearing the form-fitting white uniforms of the Unity Service. Muscular knuckles gripped rayguns as I passed. They looked as if they wanted me to try something just to relieve their boredom.

I walked down the wide white concourse toward the Terminex. The Unity symbol—twenty melded golden globes with a ring about the whole—shone over the rising doors. Past the low roof, against a purple sky, a polished silver globe of a ship descended toward its berth without a sound.

A few Outworlders, all bipedal and dioxidiferous, were busy behind ticket counters as I entered the large hexigonical chamber. The only nonmilitary entity was something green and webbed, dozing in an air-chair. I crossed the resilient cream-colored floor, had my sword taken from me at the weaponcheck counter, and floated up a tube to Customs and Acculturation. I always felt uneasy in the Spaceport. Everything was hushed and whispered, and the creak of my leather trappings and empty scabbard made me feel like an easy target. I reminded myself that I was, after all, a private eye, and private eyes are supposed to feel out of place everywhere. It didn't help.

An information-retrieval robot waited behind the Customs counter. It was a dull-gray cylinder the size of a crystal ball pedestal, with a sensor screen delicate as a spiderweb on top. A function light eyed me as I leaned on the imitation marble counter and popped my gum.

The robot whirred and said, "*Sssp.* May I help you, sir? I must warn you that there has been a dysfunction in my primary-unit continuity circuits within the past seventeen minutes. This may interfere with optimum performance and

efficiency. *Kzzzt.*"

I sighed. "Customs information, month of Telander, local calendar. I need a list of those Outworlders entering Ja-Lur during that period."

"This information is restricted to Beta-Twelve Unity personnel or Ja-Lurians of comparable author-*click*-author-*click*-authority. *Nnnn.*" The function light flickered and the robot said politely, "*Ssssp.* May I help you, sir? I must warn you . . ." and went through the entire speech again.

"Ah—I'm Sergeant Sumak of the Mariyad garrison, here on City business," I told it. "I just showed you my papers. On authority of Overlord Kirven Saculas, I request a list of Outworld entries during the month of Telander."

"I regret I must request to see your papers again, sir." Its light blinked again and it added, "*Nik-nik.*" I waited a moment, then demanded, "Well?"

"Your papers, Sergeant?"

"I've showed them to you twice, Darkbegotten! That does it. I'll tell the Overlord of the Unity's lack of cooperation and violation of treaty immediately!" I turned and started for the tube.

"My apologies, sir. The list." It gurgled and a small cassette dropped from an aperture onto the counter. I pouched it and headed for the reading room as the robot blinked and asked if it could help me again.

* * *

It was quite late by the time I reached the Market-place. The crowd had thinned—a few baggy-robed crones pinched pears at fruitstands, some beggars and street musicians whined each in their own way for alms. Streetwalkers whispered silkily as they walked. The usual.

I went into the Blue Lotus Tavern and took a high-backed graywood corner booth, away from the sound of ale slopping from tankards and the smell of old barracks jokes. Quite a few Guardsmen hung around the Blue Lotus. I usually overheard interesting things there. They might not have anything to do with whatever case I was on, but they were interesting.

Slave girls danced, bells tinkling, in each of the tavern's corners. A eunuch and a panderer were harmonizing badly at the

bar. I ordered a stew—the scents of the kitchen had reminded me how hungry I was. It would be my first good meal in several days.

I sat there and thought about what the cassette had told me. *Daniel Tolon, Earth Citizen, Age 34, Height 1.5m, Weight 85.7kg, Blood Type O. Occupation: Freelance trader (perishables). Arrived 0900, Twelfthday, Seventhmonth, U.Y. 25.* His visa had been optioned to Own-Risk upon planetfall, which meant he was free to leave Mariyad and the Northern Nations, and if he died as a result he got an unmarked grave (if lucky) and his family a short condolence form. The form was marked sent as of a week previous, as he had not been heard from since planetfall. So much for Daniel Tolon.

But there had been no listing of a Kaan Ta'Wyys of the planet Thanare. He had forged his name . . . which meant he wanted no one to know of his coming to Ja-Lur, not even his next-of-kin. Which was interesting.

I had some sour wine and thought about Valina. I would have liked explanations of some things, such as what her relationship to Boriun had been—though I could guess that rather easily. And I could not help wondering how Boriun planned to challenge the Darklord. It was quite a jump from deposing a Keeplord to overthrowing the mysterious man tacitly acknowledged by most as being beyond challenge, even with the uncertain help of the *Synulanom*. The more powerful a spell, the harder it is to remember and speak the words that make it up. The *Synulanom* must have been lost hundreds of years ago—perhaps even banned by the Darklord.

The serving girl set a tureen full of stew in front of me and I shelved speculation. The Darklord could wait; I was ravenous. I picked up my spoon—and a hand slightly smaller than a saddle came down on my wrist.

My eyes followed the hand up an arm an ogre would have envied, and I was staring at a tanned, impassive face. Looming over my table was a character out of place even in the melting pot of Mariyad: almost as tall as a Darkling I'd met recently and seeming two axe-hafts across the shoulders. He was coffee-colored and naked save for a loincloth of spotted junglecat hide. A totem-tattoo of the same beast was over his left breast. He was covered with scars and missing most of his right ear; his eyes had an obsidian color and expression, and

his hair, also black, was a long mane bound by a leather thong. He wore leather armguards as well, scuffed with bowstring marks. I figured him for a barbarian. I'm not a detective for nothing.

"Kamus of Kadizhar?" His voice was pitched lower than a quake. He didn't wait for an answer. "Come." He hoisted me away from my stew. I grabbed the booth with my free hand. "I'm eating," I said. "Interrupting a meal isn't civilized."

One corner of his mouth lifted slightly; I expected to hear it creak. "I'm not civilized," he said.

"You're not someone I want to know, either. Go slay a dragon or something and let me finish my stew."

The corner lifted a bit more. It would be a half-smile in a hundred years or so. The arms at my wrist flexed slightly; my feet left the floor and suddenly I felt like I was on the rack. I gasped, let go, and staggered toward him. The tavern had grown fairly quiet. Guardsmen nudged each other and pointed, grinning.

"Will you come?" the barbarian asked quietly. "Or be carried?"

Since chances were good that this was the savage about whom Ratbag had warned me, it seemed suicidal to leave the tavern with him. So I shouted at the guardsmen: "What's it come to when a citizen can't even have a meal in peace!" One guardsman there was more drunk than the others. "Outlander pig!" he bellowed, "to dare annoy a taxpayer!" and drew sword. He was a very large Guardsman, also very drunk, and surrounded by drunken friends who urged him on. None of that helped—the barbarian took the edge of the Guardsman's blade on his leather armguard at just the right angle to deflect it without injury; it shaved hairs from his arm. Then one massive sandaled foot caught the Guardsman in the stomach and sent him across the tavern like a crossbow bolt, to splinter a table and die coughing blood.

The barbarian released me. "Fight," he told me, and unsheathed a broadsword that looked as long as a rafter beam.

I wasn't on the barbarian's side, but that made little difference—the killing of their comrade had brought the rest of the Guardsmen to attack both of us with a sotted roar. Slaves and dancers vanished with the ease of long practice. A Guardsman made a blind-drunk thrust at me; I parried it with

a chair, grabbed the tureen of stew, and threw it in his face. Wine pitchers shattered mirrors and windows, tables were overturned, tapestries rent, and patrons slashed while I headed toward the door. Silos the tavern owner crouched behind the bar with a look of weary resignation—this was probably the third fight in a fortnight. And Guardsmen never pay for damages—one of the advantages of being a Guardsman.

I retreated before a relatively concerted attack by three more of them, kicked a table in their faces, and dove for the door. Everyone was fighting indiscriminately by now, guardsmen and outraged civilians. If I didn't get out of there fast I would be forced to kill someone, which I didn't want to do. The barbarian wasn't bothered by such scruples; I could see him fighting head-and-shoulders above the crowd. It would have given me a hernia just to lift that broadsword, but he swung it singlehandedly, mowing down Guardsmen right and left.

Just as I reached the door it swung open and a captain rushed in, sword ready. Behind him were five or more men. The captain thrust at me, and I barely had time to draw sword and parry. I brought the flat of my blade down on his neck—he bent double and I stepped on his back and went out the window. I landed, rolled to my feet, and leaped. A swordslash whistled beneath my sandals as I scrambled up the steep-shingled roof and leaped across the alley to the next building. I ran rooftops for several blocks before pausing to remove my identifying trenchcloak. Then I dropped to the pavement.

I was on Cobbleweave Street, a good distance from the Blue Lotus, and I was in trouble. I had probably been recognized, and I had attacked a captain of the Guard—at least, that's how it would be reported. My first day on a case usually goes better than that.

Whoever that idiot of a barbarian was, he had probably ruined my career in Mariyad. Most of the Guard knew me and had little love for me—this would be all they would need to put me underground. I started back to my office. I had a friend at the Garrison; a lieutenant named Sanris. Perhaps he could help me, somehow . . .

I turned a corner and a grip gentle as a sea serpent's asked me into a recessed doorway.

"You fight well," the barbarian said.

I simply stared at him.

"Follow me," he said, and turned toward the street, his grip on my arm like a lead tourniquet. I pulled my dagger and he flicked it from my hand as if it were a toothpick. I spoke three Words and he staggered, looked vaguely ill, then straightened and shook off the effects of the spell. He turned to face me and shifted his grip from my arm to my neck. There was a battlefield roar of blood in my ears, and the street darkness about me broke into bright colors and ran into blackness.

3

There was a chariot race being held in my head. I was glad I hadn't eaten the stew—I would have lost it. My body was one solid ache—even my hair hurt. I blinked, and candlelight seared my eyes.

"He's awake." The barbarian's gravelly voice.

"You shouldn't have been so rough, Ult." Another voice, much lighter but still male, with a curious accent.

"He used Darklore. He comes from beyond the Black Desert." The usual barbarian paranoia for anything that smacked of horns. Every Darklander has a pickled human heart personally autographed by the Darklord and a penchant for sacrificing virgins. I had never been south of the Inland Sea and I'd never sacrificed any virgins, at least not in that way. I didn't correct him, however, it being all I could do at the moment to squint my eyes and make out two forms standing over me. I concentrated on the smaller one, and eventually it developed a face.

It was a lean face, with long, straw-colored hair and pain lines too new to look at home. He was recently tanned, the skin along his hairline still peeling. There were pouches of weariness around eyes the same storm-gray of Valina's hair. He wore a slave's tunic of light brown. The hints of whip-welts laced his upper arms and shoulders.

He squatted beside me, looking concerned. "Kamus, I apologize. I merely told Ult to fetch you . . . I should have made it clear he was to bring you in one piece."

"What do you want?" I croaked.

He grinned uncomfortably. "I want to hire you to find somebody."

That struck me as funny, too. I might have laughed if my throat hadn't been in pain.

He offered me some wine; it went down as gentle as lava and stunned my stomach. Then he taught me how to stand again. My tunnel vision widened and I saw we were in a small, stifling garret room with one round, unglazed window, gray-curtained with spiderwebs. Two pallets lay at opposite ends of the room. The feeble dawnlight and the single candle showed me that the wooden walls were rotten and termite-gnawed, and the floor sagged dangerously under the barbarian's wide stance. Faintly below I could hear the scrabbling of rat through grain, and I could smell the toasty scent through various other reeks, not the least of which was barbarian body odor. This was a warehouse attic, and they had been here for some time.

"My name is Danian," the straw-haired one said. "That's all you need know—and that we're willing to pay you this." He handed me a moneypouch that I almost couldn't lift. The leather bulged with a myriad tiny flat planes; I tugged open the drawstrings and tipped precious stones into my hand. They caught the dim light and played joyously with it. I was meeting quite a few rich slaves.

"They're all yours," Danian said. "Enough to relocate you anywhere in the Northern Nations and keep you fed for years to come. And all you have to do for them is find someone."

I looked over his shoulder at Ult. "You can keep them if you'll spit him over a slow fire instead," I suggested.

The big man made a sound like an avalanche and started toward me. Danian whirled, put both hands against the massive chest, and snapped, "No, Ult! Back!" He looked like he was trying to hold up a toppling tree. "We need his help!" Ult subsided slowly, glaring.

"That wasn't bright," Danian told me.

"If I was bright, I wouldn't be here. Thanks to your brass-brained friend, what little business I had in Mariyad is no doubt ruined. You think I feel like helping you now? Why didn't you just come to my office earlier and ask?"

"There are people looking for me," Danian said.

"Considering your friend's manners, that's understandable. Look, pretending for a moment that I'll help you, I still don't know nearly enough. I don't know what your interest is in this person, or what you intend to do with him—"

"Her," Danian said.

"Whatever. I expect honesty from my client. I give him honesty in return. Those are the terms I work by."

"These are our terms," Danian replied. He put a hand on his sword hilt. Now I was being threatened. "You really don't have a choice. You know Mariyad much better than we do—both of us are foreigners. We need to find a woman named Valina, and you're going to help us."

"Valina," I said. Things began to connect.

"I say kill him," Ult suggested. "You can't trust Darklanders." He pulled his sword halfway clear.

I kept a pensive look while I checked out Danian again; the hints of whip marks, the recent tan, and his outrageous accent, which I now realized was Outworld. Things were definitely beginning to connect. I pulled out a stick of chewing gum, slid it into my mouth, rolled up the foil, and snapped it into a spiderweb. "Tell me about this Valina," I said.

He told me. It wasn't news. She was a slave from a northern province who had escaped from her master with important knowledge. Her master wanted her back, and had sent Danian and Ult to fetch.

"Bring her to us, or tell us where she is, in a day's time. Once we have Valina, you'll have this." Danian held up the pouch again.

"One day," I answered. "It will take longer than that just to find a lead, unless I'm luckier than I've ever been before. And what about the Guardsmen? How can I hunt while I'm being hunted?"

Danian shrugged. "I didn't say it would be easy."

I raised my hands helplessly. "Considering the alternative, what can I say? I'll try."

"Excellent," Danian said, and smiled. "Tomorrow dawn we'll meet you at the intersection of Butcher and Mace Streets, in the heart of the Maze. I'm sure you'll have good news."

Ult smiled also, and popped one massive knuckle. It sounded like a neck turned too far the wrong way.

I started to leave. "Wait," Danian said, and before I could turn he flipped a blindfold over my eyes. "We have to take precautions," he said as he led me down a flight of rickety wooden stairs. "You understand."

He opened a door and we stepped out into morning coolness.

I smelled damp alley garbage. Danian led me down twisting streets; I was in Thieves' Maze, no doubt of it. After much doubling back and path crossing, we stopped.

"Remember," Danian said, "Butcher and Mace, tomorrow at dawn," and I felt him start to unknot the blindfold. Then there was a shout from one side and the sudden rush of booted feet; Danian's hands tore away from my head and I heard a broken curse. I reached up to rip the blindfold away, but a fist against my cheekbone sent me stumbling into the wall.

"Take them!" someone shouted. There was the heavy steel sound of swords sliding from scabbards.

The rough brick tore the blindfold free. I was sprawled by a low wall. Ten Guardsmen had surrounded Ult and Danian, who stood back to back under a wooden balcony. Ult swung a two-handed massive stroke that slammed into one Guardsman's armor hard enough to knock him off his feet. Danian handled his smaller blade awkwardly, trusting Ult's gigantic swaths to protect him as well.

I saw all of this in an instant as two Guardsmen pulled me to my feet and pinned my arms. I was headed for the gibbet anyway, so: *Dammi gwil, sinald pai!"* I shouted. It was supposed to stiffen the Guardsmen's leather cuirasses and leggings, immobilizing them. Evidently I mispronounced something, because the balcony above Ult and Danian abruptly collapsed with a rending of wood and a shattering of pottery. Ult pushed Danian free and himself dived to safety, but I saw five Guardsmen caught beneath the debris. One of the two holding me clapped a hand over my mouth and they dragged me around the corner while Ult hoisted Danian over the low wall and leaped after him.

I was dragged through a low, skull-leering gate and out of the Maze onto Blackmark Street. Ahead was a barred Guardwagon into which I was tossed. A filthy rag was stuffed in my mouth and one Guardsman lashed the beasts into a clattering gallop down the street. I lay twisted with the other guardsman's sword poised over me in hay stinking from the blood of prisoners who had previously tried to escape. So I didn't move, save for bouncing about as the wagon careened on. I didn't even turn my head. I knew all too well that we were headed for the City Garrison and the dungeon. I had been there before.

* * *

Captain Thoras had sandy hair; the sands of the Black Desert. Every time I saw him it was sweat-damp, even in winter. I had seen him much too often. He had eyes as kind as pit vipers and a habit of baring his teeth as he talked. It was hard to feel confident around him. He was a large man, starting with his bones and including, according to the wenches at the Blue Lotus Tavern, not quite everything else. Thoras was also one of the few Guardsmen I knew who had a mind of any dimension. His hobby was collecting antiques and curiosities, and I had just been added to the list.

At the moment, he was sitting in a wide, high-backed chair in a narrow, high-ceilinged room. There were some barred windows, a stone desk bigger than mine, a mangy phonecub in a dirty cage, and little else. When I shifted my feet the room echoed. The oil lamps had been put out. I was sitting on a small stool surrounded by three Guardsmen who held torches over my head. I was sweating. I was supposed to.

Thoras had his scuffed boots on the desk. He balanced a chipped dish on one knee, on which were some lonesome, sharp chicken ribs, ivory-clean. A row of red knuckles next to his mouth hid most of a chicken leg, which he was polishing to match the ribs. I watched those last bits of fowl vanish, swallowing in time. My stomach was growling, but I couldn't have eaten even if Thoras had tossed me a bone. My arms were manacled and a bronze clasp covered my face from nose to throat.

Thoras eyed the bone and belched at it. "Kamus," he said, in a voice his children probably thought was jolly, "I don't understand your continuing antagonism toward the Guard. Haven't we bent over our swords to be nice to you? When you returned from Earth with your crazy idea of becoming some sort of mercenary for private hire, we let you do it. And though we've crossed purposes once or twice, I've never had you on the rack."

He began to beat out a slow tempo with the leg bone against the heel of his hand. "But now . . . as if attacking Captain Sarya wasn't enough—though privately I wish you'd killed the crystal-sniffer—you've shown yourself to be a Darklander,

and proven it by hurting five good men. Not to mention helping that murdering barbarian and his friend to escape." Thoras shook his head. "Bad, very bad. But because I like you, Kamus—or did before you showed your true colors—I'll let you speak your side." He waved the bone at the three torchbearers. One of them released the clamp while the other two pricked my throat with daggers.

"If you try to speak Language," Thoras cautioned me, "they'll cut out your voicebox. Now—tell me about it."

I told him how the fight in the Blue Lotus had come about. "The savage took me back to his friend, who offered me jewels to take a case for them. They weren't giving me much choice, so I agreed. Then your men attacked us."

"At which time you called upon the Dark and injured five of them," Thoras said. His voice had lost its jolly.

I took a deep breath. "I'm only half-Dark, Thoras. My mother was human; she was . . . raped on Shadownight by an exile from the Darkland." The words came hard—I felt as if I was insulting my mother by telling Thoras how I had been conceived. "So my powers are uncertain. I was trying to bring down the barbarian and his friend when I shouted that spell. It backfired."

Thoras stared at me. "A half-breed Darklander," he murmured. "Like Mondrogan the Clever, I suppose, of old legend. Well, Mondrogan supposedly made up for his lack of power by his wits, which is more than you've done." He slapped the bone against the desk as though it were a gavel. "You spoke Language, that makes you a Darklander, and that means you die."

I was afraid he would look at it that way. Now my only hope was to gain some time by playing on Northern superstition. "Killing a Darklander can have serious consequences, Thoras."

The man with the clasp slapped it over my face hastily, before I could try any kind of deathcurse. Thoras nodded at my words, setting the dish carefully on his desk. He kept playing with that bone; it was beginning to bother me.

"Should I slay you by force of arm, your spirit will haunt me by day; should I slay you by force of nature, your spirit will haunt me by night," he said, quoting an ancient saying. "Still, I understand there are ways to deal with your kind." He posed

the bone between two fingers. "I could ruin your eyes, ears, and sense of smell by delicately using a sharp-filed dead man's bone, and thus render your spirit senseless and harmless. Or I could have you buried alive beneath another's grave, so that your spirit would be unable to pass the body above you." He pulled his lips back from his teeth and snapped the bone in half. "Just to be on the safe side, I think we'll do both of these, and burn your cadaver to boot. Sentence will be carried out at dawn, between day and night." He gestured and they pulled me to my feet. "Find him a cell, below window level but not deep enough for him to call any subterranean gaunts or the like. Keep him gagged, but do him no violence—if a drop of his blood touches you or your weapons, you're in for a lifetime of ill luck. Take him away. Tomorrow dawn he dies."

It didn't look like I would be keeping my appointment with Danian and Ult. I wasn't sure if I had the power to return and haunt anyone after death or not; I had never given it much thought. But I would certainly make an effort as far as Thoras was concerned.

Two of the Guardsmen hustled me from his presence and along the dingy, bare corridors of the Garrison. We went down an iron stairwell that coiled in the center of the building, its lower depths lost in blackness. A clammy breeze hushed about us as we descended. The Guardsmen said nothing. The only sound was the flat clanging of their boots against iron as we hurried to meet the rising echoes.

There were no grinning death's heads over the dungeon gate, no signs to the effect of *Abandon All Hope, et cetera.* None were needed. Beyond the gate, recessed iron-bound wooden doors lined a chamber, dimly lit by two guttering torches.

"Here's an empty one," one of the Guardsmen said, pushing the door open. They led me into the cell respectfully, and left me there.

It was shadownight-black inside, save for faint phosphorescent tracings of slime on the ceiling which illuminated nothing. I shifted my shoulders experimentally. The manacles binding my arms were locked just above my elbows, preventing me from slipping my arms over my legs in a contortionist trick. I tried scraping the back of my mouth-clasp along the stone wall. No good. I backed up to the door and explored it with

my fingers. Cold iron, moldy wood. But one of the iron strips near the bottom stood away from the wood.

I lay down and worked my head into position. My neck was in knots of agony by the time I hooked the lock on the strip and tugged. The clasp unsnapped and the thing fell away from my face with a dull clank. I lay on the slick, damp floor, exhausted; I had fought for my life three times within the past two days on nothing but wine and chewing gum. After a while I began to shiver, and I dragged myself to my feet.

I could speak Language now—for what that was worth. The Guardsmen had taken from me the potions I carried which enhanced and stabilized my badly spoken spells. Without them I might turn myself into a frog. Possibly I could summon up a Darkling powerful enough to free me from the dungeon—but one that powerful I would be unable to control. They would burn and bury a mindless, soulless moron at dawn.

I leaned against the wall and thought about it.

That door, despite its mold and rust, was strong, as were the walls. There was a good chance of backlash from any spell powerful enough to shatter them. But a door was only as strong as its latch. I crouched before the lock and began to speak.

I could not gesture with my hands behind my back. The Words sounded garbled and unfamiliar as I spoke them. My foot slipped once, and I lost the cadence. Still, at the end of the spell I could smell the thin tang of newly rusted metal.

I stood and hurled myself against the iron-bound wood. The door creaked, but did not give. I ruined my other shoulder, and this time the lock gave way. I stumbled out into the corridor.

My arms were still manacled, but I managed to reach through the bars of the gate and unlatch it. Now all I had to do was fight my way through the entire armed Garrison with my hands tied behind my back. Simple. I put a foot on the stairs, intending to have a cautious look. As I did so, I heard the stairwell echo dimly to a tread far above. I hurried back into the chamber, pulled the two torches from their niches with my teeth and doused them in a slimy puddle. Then I closed the door of my cell and hid in the corridor just outside the chamber. I hoped there wasn't more than one coming. The strain of the past few hours was starting to make itself felt. I leaned against

the wall until a wave of dizziness passed.

Yellow, flickering light began to illuminate the stairwell. After a moment, a single Guardsman came into view, his face in shadow. He paused at the chamber entrance, then stepped in cautiously. He stopped at my cell, sword unsheathed.

I slipped into the chamber behind him and opened my mouth to shout a spell. He heard me and turned quickly, and I saw his face. I swallowed the first Words of the spell, grinned instead, and said, "Hello, Sanris."

4

Sanris of Taleiday and I had been friends for over a year, ever since my first case, in which I'd saved him from being eaten by the giant rat of Solipta. Solipta was a crazed nobleman who had invented a growth serum. Since then, Sanris had been my inside man at the Garrison, and we had helped each other professionally and personally many times.

He was far too intelligent to be a Guardsman, and claimed he only kept the job because it attracted women. In that area, he was certainly enjoying his work. He liked taking risks if the stakes warranted it, and was not above taking graft; still, he was by far the most honest Guardsman I knew. I trusted him.

He led me out of the dungeon by a secret passage that functioned as an escape route for the guards in the event prisoners ever got out of control. That accomplished, I was hidden in the house of one of his many lady friends. This one was a rich and more-than-slightly-kinky noblewoman who lived at the north end of Mariyad. She put me in a bed that felt like a cloud and was bigger than my office. I slept the rest of that day and most of the night, and woke up ready to eat my sandals. I didn't have to; I was served a seven-course breakfast, and milady made it clear that the feast need not stop there if I so desired. I declined, not because she was Sanris's lover—he wouldn't have minded—but because I needed all my energy for something else.

After she left, I closed the heavy fur curtains, rolled up the plush and flammable rug, and started work. Sanris had returned my possessions, including my potion pouch. I mixed compounds and ignited them, and eventually sat in the center of a circle surrounded by flames that ran the gamut of the

spectrum. I started to chant softly.

The dark room grew darker, until I seemed to be floating in the middle of space. As I chanted, the flames began to elongate, becoming thin, glowing lines that wavered and joined over my head like a cage of living fire. It sounds spectacular, but it was really one of the simpler spells, which was why I didn't make any mistakes as I sent my Call out to Valina.

It took some time to get an answer. I kept wondering what milady would think if she stuck her head in to see if I'd changed my mind. The sight would probably make her more determined than ever to get me into her bed. Northern women had certain myths about Darkland men.

I had almost given up, when suddenly the lines of color shattered soundlessly, then whirled together into a fiery wheel that blurred and became Valina's face. The image faded away below her shoulders, but it looked like she was naked.

I hope I'm not interrupting anything, I said.

She shook those beautiful gray curls and looked at me thoughtfully. *This must be important*, she replied, *for you to call through Darkness to me.*

It would have saved me a lot of trouble if you had left the name of your phonecub; but you're right, Valina, this is *important. I'm off the case.* I saw her nostrils flare and her eyes blaze. I spoke quickly to prevent any interruption. *I have some information for you, and once I give it, we're quits. You can pick up your seven hundred dechels at Pallas the Moneyholder's. He's open until sundown. Don't bother threatening me, Valina, because it won't work. You couldn't possibly hand me more trouble than I'm in already. The Guard knows I'm a Darklander, and they've sentenced me to death. I'll be lucky if I can save myself, let alone help you.*

You incredibly clumsy dolt! she broke in, her telepathic voice seething. *You bungler! By Ja-Agur, I ought to—*

Your sympathy's appreciated, I replied. Now here's the information: Daniel Tolon, the Earthling, is looking for you. He's calling himself Danian. He has a fistful of jewels and a large, unfriendly barbarian named Ult to persuade people to talk about you. I gave him no leads. Now it's up to you.

Valina was silent for several seconds. The last time she spoke, her voice was acid fire; this time it was pure ice: *Hiring you was quite probably the biggest error I've made in this entire affair,*

Kamus. I only wish I had the time to make you regret your incompetence. You've wasted valuable time, led my enemies upon me, and given me nothing helpful.

Maybe I'm not coming through clearly, I said. *They found me. I didn't find them. They're waiting for me to meet them with information about you—an appointment I have no intention of keeping. I'm going to be quite busy with my own problems for some time.*

She wasn't listening. *Kaan could be anywhere in Adelan by now. Could be anywhere . . . but how to . . . the* Kakush . . .

She broke the connection with an impatient gesture. The room returned to normal darkness. I drew the curtains and opened the windows, then lay back down and brooded.

Her last thoughts had been fragmentary, and obviously not directed at me. It takes concentration to keep private thoughts separate in a telepathic conversation. She had made her feelings quite clear in the thoughts that had been meant for me, however. And she was right—I had bungled. I had made few moves worthy of my profession. I had become overwhelmed by the rapid sequence of events, and things had gotten completely out of control. But I couldn't think of a way to remedy it. I'd be lucky if I thought of a way to save my life.

Sanris arrived later, bringing Dash with him, and we split a bottle of wine. I noticed him watching me from behind his drinking mug. He had been subtly studying me since the rescue. I pushed my hair back from my forehead and said, "No horns, Sanris."

He grinned and emptied his mug. "I don't know much about sorcery or about Darklanders, Kamus. I'll confess it frightened me when I heard you were one of them. But I know you, and I'd trust you if you told me you were Jann-Togah, son of the Darklord, himself. If you say the spell you used on those men wasn't meant to hurt them, I accept that. Still, I'm glad I knew none of them personally."

"I had no intention of wounding them." I felt badly about those five; it wasn't the first time my incomplete abilities had caused others harm. For better or for worse, however, I had the Blood in me. A Darklander can no more resist using Darklore than a human can resist using any of his five senses.

I cracked a chei nut on my swordhilt and asked, "What does the Guard know about the *Kakush?*"

"The Maze Lords? The nefarious Brothers Below?" He chuckled. "Periodically some pompous undersecretary from the palace issues memos ordering a full-scale investigation of them, and then someone else countermands it as a waste of time. If you want my personal opinion, with the slipshod, graft-ridden way this city is run, even Overlord Kirven could be one of the Brothers Below."

"Do you believe the *Kakush* has a criminal elite that influences city government?"

"I believe it's possible. Why?"

I didn't answer. "The Brothers Below" was a phrase Kaan had told Valina just before her escape from Sassoon. And she had mentioned the *Kakush* just before breaking contact with me earlier. *How did they figure into this case?* I wondered, then remembered that I wasn't on the case anymore. There were other things on my mind.

"I've got to figure out some way to get myself reinstated as a citizen, Sanris."

"There is no way," Sanris said. "The Blood is anathema in Mariyad, Kamus, and you know it. When the Overlord hears of this, there won't be anyplace for you to hide in the entire nation of Adelan. You've got to go west; Vanastas, maybe, or Hestia. I have a friend on the balloon-boat lines who can smuggle you out. You can join one of the crystal caravans that cross the Nonule Hills. No one will suspect you in that company; crystal runners have all sorts of strange people with them."

"Thanks," I said. "But I don't want to leave Mariyad. If only—"

Dash leaped to his feet abruptly and began lashing his tails frantically against the cage bars. "Kamus! Kamus!" There was no mistaking the shrill voice that came from the phonecub's mouth, just as there was no denying the panic in it.

"Ratbag! What's wrong!"

"Kamus, I saw him kill Gallian! The hooded man—he spoke three words, and Gallian's skin shriveled and broke, and blood—"

"Ratbag, calm down! Where are you?"

"At a public phonecub in the Rusty Sword Tavern, in the Maze. Kamus, I'm scared. There's Darklore in the Maze . . ."

"Just stay where you are," I ordered him. "I'll be right

there."

"All right, Kamus." The reedy voice sounded relieved. Dash shook himself as the connection broke and chittered for a sweetmeat. I gave him the nut I'd cracked and looked at Sanris.

"The Rusty Sword," I said. "It's a sleazy dive in the heart of the Maze." I buckled on my swordbelt.

"You're not thinking of going there?"

"Ratbag is a ferret, I admit, but he's always dealt fairly with me." I was out the door by this time, tossing words over my shoulder. "If he's in trouble, he deserves my help."

"You're insane," Sanris told me, following at a run. "If Thora gets his hands on you again—"

"That's *my* worry. You stay here."

"If you haven't any more sense than to go bulling into the Maze in search of a flea-ridden crystal-sniffer, you at least need eyes behind you."

We stopped arguing at the street. I hailed a passing carriage. "The Skull Gate," I said. "And hurry."

We ran from there. Fortunately it was early morning, and most of the Maze's inhabitants were still asleep or hung over, else our obvious urgency would have brought trouble. When we reached the Rusty Sword, however, there was no sign of Ratbag. The tavern was not even open, and wouldn't be for another three hours. All around us were the crowded, tumble-down buildings of the Maze, standing only because they had no place to fall. There were few people in the street, other than a few bodies in doorways It was as tranquil a scene as the Maze had to offer.

"You see," Sanris said. "He's played you for a fool."

I examined the phonecub in its cage outside the tavern. No clues there. "Who is Gallian? Or was, rather."

Sanris thought. "Possibly Gallian of Port Rizh, a merchant who fronts for much drug traffic. Quite a few guardsmen are on the take from him, in various ways. But why would he be a Darklander target?"

I shrugged. "Is there any proof Gallian was connected with the *Kaukush*?"

"Rumors only, just as there are rumors about every unscrupulous businessman and politician in Mariyad."

"Well, let's go look for Gallian, then," I said.

"This is folly," Sanris said sadly, but he followed me.

Gallian did not live in the Maze, of course, but he transacted some of the shadier aspects of his business within its boundaries. It was here that Ratbag must have seen him. There was a huge crowd about the building when we got there, however, and it included a number of Guardsmen. I saw Thoras bending over a mass of bloody pulp that bore a faint resemblance to a human being. The crowd was becoming unruly at the presence of the Guard in their domain. There was no way I could learn anything here, not with Thoras and his men about. It seemed that everywhere I turned in this case, I ran into a stone wall.

We faded back quickly into the Maze, walking slowly down Dragonpock toward Blackmark. After a few blocks Sanris said, "Kamus, it must be obvious to you now that this is too big for you. Darklanders, Outworlders, the *Kakush* . . . even if you weren't a hunted man in Mariyad, you'll only have your head handed to you if you persist in unraveling this. Take my advice: Get out of Mariyad."

He was right, and we both knew it. This was a case that Mondrogan and Beowulf together would back away from. I sighed. "What time does your friend's balloon-boat leave?"

"In time for you to pack some belongings and food." He put an arm across my shoulders. "I will miss you, my friend."

I would miss him, too. And my work, and this city. I didn't want to leave Mariyad. For all of its corruption and cruelty, it fascinated me. But Sanris was correct—I was in over my head. Nothing I had worked on before had ever come close to this.

We were approaching an intersection; suddenly, on the other street, two unmistakable figures came into view. I recognized them at the same time they recognized me. The four of us stopped. Ult saw Sanris and his hand went for that broadsword again. "Betrayal!" he growled to Danian. Danian stopped him with a gesture, and they approached us slowly.

"Do we fight?" Sanris asked softly.

"Are you kidding? I've seen Ult in action. He'd make basket cases out of us. We'll try talking first, then running."

They stopped out of reach of our swords but within easy reach of Ult's. "You're late, Kamus," Danian said.

"I've been busy. A little matter of escaping from the Garrison."

Danian nodded. "And so you have no news. I thought so. Well, despite our fugitive stature, Ult and I are honest men. I feel it was our fault you were captured, and we owe you for that." He handed me another pouch, smaller than the first one he had tempted me with. "A portion of the jewels, to make up for the trouble we've caused you. If you run across any information and want to let us know, Silos at the Blue Lotus will put you in touch with us. Good luck, Kamus." He turned and walked away. Ult gave me a final superstitious glower and followed. I stood tossing the bag from hand to hand, watching them disappear around a corner.

"Finally a bit of good luck," Sanris observed. "If that pouch really is full of jewels, you've got enough wealth to see you safely through your relocation."

"Let's get out of the Maze," I said.

It wasn't easy; Guardsmen were all over the place, and we had several narrow escapes. I could not return to my office or home to pack, of course—the Guard had both under surveillance. Sanris persuaded a few ladies to shop for some traveling needs while I lay low until time for the balloon-boat to leave.

I felt uneasy about Ratbag; he had seen something he wasn't supposed to, and the mysterious hooded Darklander he spoke of might be after him. Sanris promised to look for him after I was safely out of town. I was feeling rather heavily indebted to Sanris.

Finally everything was ready at the balloon-boat port. I was hidden in a special room on the top floor of one of Mariyad's largest brothels; the owner was another of Sanris's friends. The room was an overdressed, fetish-filled chamber replete with leering, well-endowed statues, a tiled ceiling mosaic depicting one hundred and one different positions, and red drapes hung in vulva folds. There was also an enormous waterbed; this last had been an Earthling suggestion. It was made from the rubbery skin of a giant sea slug.

Sanris entered. "I'll not be able to see you off," he told me. "There's a rumor that you've been seen by the docks, and Thoras wants every man available at that end of the city."

"Who started the rumor?" I asked. He grinned. "The men need exercise on occasion." He gripped my hand. "Good luck and good-bye, Kamus. May we meet again some day. There's a

eunuch downstairs named Yesh who will take you to the balloon-boat port. He can handle anything up to and including Ult."

"You'll be hearing from me, Sanris."

He turned toward the door, and I started to get off the bed.

The attack came totally without warning. There was a loud crackling noise all about us, and the red draperies suddenly writhed and turned black, like flower petals on fire. Darkness descended with a rush before we could even draw swords. The walls and floor of the room seemed to fall away, to sink and stretch in a strange new perspective. I grabbed Sanris's arm and pulled him onto the shaking waterbed. There was a feeling of rushing upward, as though the outer edges of the room were streaming away from us, as though we were erupting toward the ceiling. But there was no ceiling above us—only darkness.

"Salan mach torrad!" I shouted. The spell worked somewhat; the dreadful soundless rushing slowed a bit. Sanris crouched on the bed next to me, sword drawn, trying not to be affected by the apparently bottomless depths that now surrounded us.

"Don't panic!" I told him. "It's only an illusion, to disorient us!" Actually, I wasn't sure. I had never seen a spell like this before.

Sanris pointed upward. "Kamus, look!" The blackness overhead, an inverted bowl of night, was cracking. Veins of red and yellow shattered over the surface, like tinted lightning. Bolts of fire began to crackle toward us. I smelled ozone. It was no illusion, that was for sure.

I shouted another spell which slowed our ascent again, but not as much or for as long this time. Fire bolts were hissing all about us now; the ruptured sky was very near. The furs and silks were already smoldering, bits of them dropping like meteors into the blackness below. The thunder and crackling was deafening. I couldn't hear the spells I was shouting. Sanris grabbed me and pulled me across the quaking bed, and a fire bolt struck near where I had been, burning a hole in the bedskin and releasing a cloud of steam. It also gave me an idea.

"The water!" I shouted. "Of course!" I gripped the waterbed frame and shouted: *"Tilye maldaz, bol!"* In response a geyser of water erupted from the center of the bed and poured

upward into the raw heart of the fire. Sanris stared, wide-eyed. The bed should have been emptied in an instant, but the spell kept the jet of water pumping thousands of liters at the fire. We wrapped ourselves in furs to keep from being blistered by clouds of steam. But it was working—the bolts were weakening, and our rate of ascent was slowing as well. The spell wasn't broken yet, however. I fumbled potions from my pouch, mixed them as best I could—I would need all the help I could get to break this one. Incense mingled with steam as I chanted. The thunder grew muffled and distant. The steam had a reddish tinge now, but we felt no heat. The darkness was fading—I could see hints of the walls about us. I flashed a grin at Sanris, gave him a thumbs-up sign. He wasn't familiar with the Earthly gesture, but he could see the spell was fading. He grinned and sat up, letting the blanket slip from his shoulders.

And then one final bolt of fire stabbed through the steam and enveloped him, turning his flesh and clothes into an explosion of cinders, freezing his grin into the leer of a naked skull. A cloud of greasy smoke mingled with water vapor as his bodily fluids evaporated. The skeleton hung together for a moment, then clattered into a pile.

An instant, one horrified instant, was all I had to see his death. Then the lights went out. There was a moment of whirling vertigo, and when I opened my eyes I was back in the boudoir. The room was undisturbed, tranquil. The draperies were unburned. Only two things kept it from being a dream: the empty and ruined waterbed I sprawled upon, and the baked bones that had been my friend, Sanris of Taleiday.

5

I went back to the Maze.

It was evening of the day after Sanris died. After leaving the brothel I had gone back to my home, and by a combination of spells and luck had gotten past the Guardsmen and inside. I found my few volumes on Darklore still where they were hidden, and some research provided me with a disguise spell. It was only effective at night—Ja-Lur's dim sunlight would evaporate it. But it took me past Guard patrols and back to the Maze.

Before I left the brothel, I had made another Call to Valina.

There was no answer.

From what I had seen of Valina's powers, she wasn't capable of such an attack as the one in the brothel. But if she had found the missing phrases of the *Synulanom*, she might have used them to supplement her Darklore and so form such a spell. Given the power, the motivation to attack was certainly there.

But there was another possibility to be considered: Edward Boriun. He probably had the power, but what was his motivation?

Once in the Maze I started some elementary detective work. If I'd done that three days before, it might have saved a life. Now I had the feeling it would cost more lives before I was through.

I dropped the disguise spell at first, as there were no Guard patrols in the Maze at nighttime. After a few hours, however, I spotted someone following me. I spoke the spell and left him watching a tavern while I walked out in front of him to continue my search. It didn't take very long. I made a few threats, bruised my knuckles once, and soon had a trail that led me to a hidden chamber in the basement of a gambling house. In the chamber was a strawtick mattress that stank of offal, and crouched on the mattress was Ratbag, and he stank of fear.

I dissolved my disguise and entered, closed the door, and stood with my back against it.

"Kamus, I had to run. That hooded man, the Darklander—he's after me, I know it. I saw him kill Gallian without a torch, just words that made the blood burst from his pores." Ratbag was shivering convulsively. His skin looked even more jaundiced than usual in the glow of the single oil lamp.

"Calm down," I said. "If a Darklander wanted you dead, you'd be dead by now. You help me and I'll protect you."

"Why should I trust you?" he whined. "You're a Darklander, too, they say."

"But that's exactly why you should trust me, Ratbag. Who better to keep you safe from Darkness? Listen to me. What do you know about the *Kakush*?"

"Not to talk about them, that's what I know. They got eyes and ears everywhere. They own the Maze, and a good deal of the city, too. Cross them and you wake up dead."

"Do you work for them?"

"Everybody works for them, Kamus, whether they know it or not. Out of ten things you buy in a day, eight of them bring money to the *Kakush*—Brothers Below."

"Was Gallian of Port Rizh one of them?"

"I think so," he said, his teeth chattering.

"Do you know where and when they meet?"

"Kamus, *please* . . . I'd sooner take my chances with Darklanders than the *Kakush*—"

I put my hand under his pointed wet chin and lifted him to his feet. "That's just what you're doing. Ratbag, I've no time for your paranoia. *Do you know where and when they meet?*"

His shivering had increased to the proportions of a seizure, but he managed to say, "I delivered a message there once . . ."

"Very good." I changed the subject before he lapsed into catatonia. "Now about this Darklander . . ."

"He—he was slight-built, that's all I can say. I couldn't see his face, just his hand when he spelled. A small, pale hand, like a child's."

"A child's . . . "Did he wear rings?"

"No, not a one."

"Did you notice anything else? Any glimpse of his face, or hair?"

"Hair—I did see a curl of hair under the hood. Gray, it was. He must've been a little old man."

"No doubt," I said. "Now, there's just one more thing you can do for me, Ratbag." I put my hand firmly on his shoulder. "Take me to the *Kakush*."

It took some time and the promise of a handful of jewels to persuade him. He followed me back to the tavern, where the lad who had been tailing me—a thin Maze urchin—was still waiting for me to exit. I watched him, judged his price, then came up behind him and caught him by the neck, slapping a few dechels into his palm.

"Who's paying you to follow me?" I asked him.

"Two men, sir, if it's pleasin'. A giant in skins and a—"

"Good enough. You carry a message to the smaller of the two. Tell him to stop wasting time this way and meet with me at the Rusty Sword tavern in one hour Got that?"

He got it. Off he scurried, sniffling.

Ratbag looked at me. "I've never seen you like this, Kamus. You're all orders and threats. What's happened?"

I didn't answer him. I started for the Rusty Sword.

Valina's search for Kaan was somehow tied up with the *Kakush*, and she had been wandering around the Maze in hood and cloak, attacking possible members. Her temper wasn't serving her well; spelling the blood out of people isn't the best way to keep a low profile. I thought I knew why she was looking for the Brothers Below. If I was right, and I survived, I might be one step closer to seeking justice for Sanris's death.

We waited in a secluded booth for them. The Rusty Sword was a much dingier place than the Blue Lotus. It boasted one bored dancing wench, and most of the customers were under the tables. I spent my time reassuring Ratbag, and getting him just drunk enough to be brave.

At last Danian and Ult joined us. Ult squeezed his bulk between bench and table and aimed a dirk-sized finger at me, saying, "I've got protection against your spells." He was wearing a necklace of kallith blubs, the smell of which was supposed to repel Darklanders. It was one superstition that worked; kallith bulbs repel anything with a nose, except barbarians.

"Keep him quiet," I told Danian, "and listen. I know you're really Danial Tolon of Earth. I know you're a Unity security agent, and that you came to Ja-Lur with Kaan Ta'Wyys to find Edward Boriun. I know you're looking for Valina now in hopes she can put you back on Boriun's trail. Well, I'm looking for her, too. She's directly or indirectly responsible for the death of a friend. I propose we join forces."

"And why should I trust you?" he asked.

"Because it's easier than playing stupid games of tag in the Maze. I'll admit I wasn't entirely honest with you, when we first met, by not admitting I knew Valina. But you weren't honest in your reasons for wanting her. These games get us nowhere. I'll find her, with or without your help. What's it to be?"

Ult, for once, kept his mouth shut as Daniel Tolon considered. "What's your plan?" he asked.

"Are you with me?"

"We are."

"We're going to invade the inner sanctum of the *Kakush*," I told them.

* * *

Torchlight glimmered in rainbows from stagnant, greasy puddles. The jagged skyline of the Maze rose against the golden lights of downtown Mariyad to the north and the harsh white light of the Spaceport to the south. Ratbag led us down an alley and into a narrow passageway between two buildings. He stopped at a boarded door, counted off paces, and knelt to hook his fingers under a large flagstone in the center of the passageway. He pulled and it pivoted from over a hole black as blindness.

Ratbag looked at me. "Don't make me go down there with you, Kamus," he pleaded. He was in bad shape. Terror was part of his life, but he had had a lot lately even by Maze standards. "All right," I said. I paid him the jewels he'd earned and he ran like a spider. "Good luck, Kamus," came floating back on the thick night air.

"You're not worried about betrayal?" Ult asked.

"You have betrayal on the brain. As long as his pouch jingles, Ratbag's trustworthy."

"I hope so," Tolon said.

We started down. We descended by means of niches carved in the rock wall. I had no way to measure the distance; the pivoting flagstone had closed above us, leaving us in total darkness. But it must have been at least a hundred meters before my sandals touched bottom.

Once down, I dared not make any kind of light. Ult led us, using his barbarians's keen of smell and hearing. We followed a twisting corridor for quite some time without encountering branches or forks. Then at last we came to another pivoting section of stone, this one at the end of the corridor. Ult pushed it open a crack, and light made us blink. When our eyes were adjusted, we went through the revolving door.

We were in another corridor, large, with an arched ceiling. The light came from oil lamps set at intervals. A steady breeze kept the air in motion. We followed the breeze. There were doors set in the walls, most of which were locked; the few that weren't showed only sparsely furnished living quarters. It was like being in an underground hotel. We saw no one.

I had disguised Tolon and myself with a spell when we entered the lighted corridor. There wasn't much I could do for Ult—the spell only changed features and gait and did nothing for size. He wouldn't have stood for a spell being put on him,

anyway. Tolon and I looked like typical Maze cutpurses, which hopefully were a relatively common sight in this underworld.

We came to a fork in the corridor, and Ult stopped. "We're out of the Maze by now," he whispered. "We must be under downtown Mariyad—I'd say the Marketplace, or the Garrison."

"And not a sign of a soul," Tolon said. "A place this size wouldn't be completely deserted."

"Listen!" Ult said sharply. Faintly, behind us, was the sound of several sets of footsteps.

The lamps in the left-hand fork had been doused for some reason, so we chose the right hand. "Let's find an empty room and wait for them to pass," I said, trying doors, all of which were locked.

"Can't you cover us with some sort of invisibility spell?" Tolon asked.

I shook my head. "It would take too long, even if I got it right." I tried another door, which opened. I looked in cautiously—it appeared to be a large auditorium, with other doors at the far end. "In here!" They followed me and I shut the door.

That was a mistake. The footsteps grew louder, until they were right outside the door, and then stopped. We drew swords as we hurried toward the other doors. They were flung open when we were halfway there, and in rushed at least twenty swordsmen, while behind us entered ten more.

"It appears that we were herded into a trap," Tolon said.

I nodded. I had anticipated as much; the *Kakush* probably had this procedure down pat. But they would not expect a small-time Maze beggar to use Darklore. I had a spell rehearsed for just this occasion. As the swordsmen closed in on us, I opened my mouth to shout it—and something, probably a dagger thrown hilt-first, hit me at the base of the skull. I saw the floor coming my way, but didn't feel it hit.

* * *

Again my head felt like ice giants were using it for a game of handball. Again there were faces hovering over me as I opened my eyes, this time quite a few of them. Faces and knives . . . I

was surrounded by men who held blades next to my body.

I recognized many as influential and respected businessmen and officeholders; others I had seen in the Maze, dressed in filthy rags. The *Kakush* was present, in all its subterranean glory.

Then one more face moved before my eyes: a flat, cold face with snake eyes and black hair. *Captain Thoras*, commander of the Mariyad Garrison.

The *Kakush* ran Mariyad, no doubt about it.

Thoras bared his teeth in his version of a smile. "Kamus, you're as much a half-wit as a half-breed." He recognized me, of course; my disguise spell had vanished when I lost consciousness.

I looked about me—I was strapped to a cot in a small chamber. The crowd kept me from seeing if Tolon and Ult were there, too. There was no gag to prevent me from speaking Language—just those thirty-odd knives all an inch from my skin.

"So tell me," Thoras continued, sitting on the edge of the bunk and tickling my nose with a dagger, "to what do we owe this visit?"

"You should know," I said. "That parchment of Darklore is yours, isn't it?"

He leaned back, eyes wide. Murmurs of surprise came from the assembly. "How did you know that?" Thoras asked.

"It makes sense," I said. "You're an avid collector of strange and esoteric things. Furthermore, when you sentenced me, I noticed that you had an uncommon knowledge of Darklanders. Those two interests made you the natural one to buy such a curiosity if it was offered to you."

He nodded. "I'm impressed. Yes, I acquired the parchment from a Southern trader some months ago. On the chance that it was something important, I donated it to the *Kakush*. We hoped that we would somehow, someday, be able to translate it."

"Why didn't you tell me about it when you had me?" I asked. "I could have told you if it was more than just a grocery list."

Most of them laughed. "Hand a possibly dangerous spell to a Darklander?" Thoras said. "That stupid we're not, Kamus. No, we've managed to obtain some Darklore books, and we

have the parchment partially translated. It is a spell, isn't it?"

I sighed and nodded. "It's part of something called the *Synulanom*. But even if you translate it, Thoras, what good is it to you? You'd need someone of the Blood to get results."

"It's a bargaining point. You're the second Darklander it's lured here. Someone wants it badly, and might be willing to pay quite a bit for it."

The *second* Darklander—so they had managed to catch Valina . . . either that, or someone entirely new had entered the picture. I hoped not. "You've got hold of something big," I told Thoras. "Too big. If you advertise possession of the *Synulanom*, you'll attract the attention of someone who wants it badly, sure enough. But he doesn't have to bargain. What he wants, he takes."

That put a chill on the party. People looked at each other in apprehension. "The Darklord," someone murmured.

"That's it," I agreed. It was the best way to convince them what a tiger they had by the tail. It made an impression, judging by the worried whispers now circulating.

"Quiet!" Thoras bellowed. "You all knew tampering with Darkness was risky!" He turned to me again. "If it's the Darklord who wants this *Synulanom*, then so be it. He's not a god and we'll deal with him if we have to. And we can. You're looking at the *Kakush*; the real rulers of Mariyad and all Adelan. We can resist any pressure he puts on us."

"Enough of this," someone else said—I recognized him as Oreus Bodag, Chief Adjutant to the Prime Minister. "We have nothing to gain from bragging, Thoras. Dispose of him, and let's get on with the translation."

Thoras grudgingly agreed to this, and fitted me again with bronze mouth-clasp and manacles. Then he led me through the crowd and down a series of corridors. At last we came through another revolving wall section and into a chamber that looked vaguely familiar. After a moment, I knew why: it was similar to the cell chamber I had been in before as Thoras's quest. We were in the Garrison dungeon, on the bottom level. No wonder Thoras hadn't wanted me imprisoned too deeply before. The *Kakush* were using the lowest levels of the Garrison for their own purposes!

As he pushed me into an empty cell, I caught a glimpse of Valina, also gagged, and Daniel Tolon, in separate cells.

Thoras slammed the door shut.

"This time, Kamus," he said, "I promise you'll die at dawn. Slowly."

After he had gone, Tolon called my name. "Ult fought his way free and escaped," he said. "Do you want to know how they caught us?" He sounded disgusted. "They smelled that damned kallith bulb necklace he was wearing. The superstitious idiot." He coughed, then continued. "Maybe you've wondered how he came to be with me, Kamus. I suppose you know that Boriun sentenced me to one of his galleys on the Eastern Ocean. Ult was my oar-partner. We led a slave revolt and took over the galley. I saved his life during the revolt. We sailed north, and on an island we found an ancient shipwreck and a chest full of jewels. The rest of the slaves are now living high in other countries, but Ult insisted on helping me find Kaan. He's as faithful as a hound. And about as intelligent."

He sighed. "Kaan's probably long dead by now. I don't know why he insisted on trying to stop Boriun himself, instead of telling the Unity. I didn't even know what he intended until after planetfall." He laughed shortly. "I thought it was a vacation."

I could see Valina through the grids in the cell doors. I was grateful for her mouth-clasp, considering the glare she sent my way. She was obviously blaming me for this, which was no surprise, as she had been blaming me for everything so far. I watched her, wondering if she was the one who had attacked me and killed Sanris. Had she gained access to the *Synulanom* just long enough to send that spell my way? It didn't look like I was going to find out.

I examined my cell, but there was nothing that suggested an escape plan. It seemed as if I could only wait for morning, and death. But I hadn't entirely given up hope. I had known Thoras for some time; he was as fond of torture as a cat. He would have to come back and taunt me some more.

He did. After a few hours he returned to my cell, carrying a large, brittle scroll. I stared at it as he unrolled it and held it up, grinning. It had to be the fragment of the *Synulanom*. One end was frayed, as though a piece had been torn off.

In the doorway leading to the stairwell, a shadow moved. I kept my eyes on the scroll.

"It's translated," Thoras said. "Except for one key Phrase, it's complete—and with that Phrase, it could make some Darklander ruler over all the Northern Nations, and grant power beyond compare. I just wanted you to rest assured, Kamus, that we'll put it to good use."

The shadow in the doorway moved into the torchlight and became Ult, with a dagger in his hand. He took two long steps and was behind Thoras. Thoras quit talking; a second mouth across the throat doesn't make anyone more talkative.

"Ult!" Tolon cried.

A second shadow, scarcely as tall as Ult's waist, turned out to be Ratbag. He deftly picked the locks of our cells and then picked my mouth-clasp and manacles, chattering an explanation as he did so. "It was Ult's idea," he said, his eyes darting everywhere for more of the Brothers Below. "He found me and told me what had happened. He made me—I mean, I volunteered to help. I told him that the Garrison was over the *Kakush* underworld. We picked a fight with some guards—" he had to gulp and close his eyes at this memory— "—and got ourselves thrown in the dungeon."

I looked at him closely. His pupils were pinpoints, and his skin was flushed. He was packed with dream crystals. It had been a hard night for Ratbag.

"Ult," I said, as I picked up the *Synulanom*, "I've underestimated you."

"I didn't do it for you," he growled as he tore the lock off Tolon's cell.

Ratbag opened Valina's cell and saw her dark cloak and hood. He let out a squeal like steam escaping and hid behind me. I looked at Valina. "We'll have to work together to get out of here," I told her. "Agreed?"

She nodded, slowly.

"Pick her locks, Ratbag. She won't hurt you."

"What do we do now?" Tolon asked.

"Now we get out of Mariyad," I said. "Our lives won't be worth a dechel if we don't."

"We still don't know where to look for Boriun and Kaan," Valina said.

"True. But we have this," I said, holding up the *Synulanom*. "And I think it's going to be our ticket to them."

6

With my abilities backing up Valina's, we had no problems sneaking out through the Garrison and across town to the balloon-boat port. Ratbag did not go with us. He hadn't been seen aiding us, he said, and he wanted to keep it that way. I couldn't blame him.

Valina did not speak to me any more than was necessary during our esçape, which suited me. I still wasn't at all sure how to react to her presence. She was my prime suspect for the murder of Sanris, but she was also my client. I wished I had had a chance while in the underground to ask how long she had been locked up with metal around her mouth; that would have helped. If she had been caught by the *Kakush* before the attack on Sanris and me, she would have an alibi. I could ask her, of course, but she would be smart enough to lie if it wasn't true.

As the amber sun rose, we caught a northbound balloon-boat. My plan was to stop close to the ruins of Sassoon, which was now a thriving tourist attraction, and look for clues. I would follow any I found, wherever I had to, to find out who killed Sanris. And I would keep a close eye on Valina while I did so.

The balloon-boat lines of Mariyad were the best in the Northern Nations. Each craft was supported by four balloons over twenty meters wide, and pulled by teams of twenty kragors, flying reptiles of a breed similar to those used by the Flying Guards. They were built of light, strong emsam wood, and carefully ballasted to provide stability even in high winds. They were capable of carrying over thirty passengers at once.

I stood at the stern, watching Mariyad and the coast fall away behind. The farmlands and patches of forest were still misty with morning fog. The purple sky looked like a deep, still lake, and it was easy to want to somehow fall upward into it, to lose myself in it. I wasn't happy with the way things had turned out. My best friend was dead, and I was in exile. Not the best foundation for a good reputation as a private eye. I hoped milady would give Dash a good home.

Daniel Tolon came to stand beside me. He took up the lifeline every passenger wears while on deck and clipped it to the wooden railing, contemplating the view.

"You're from Kadizhar . . . where is that?" he asked me.

"An island in the middle of the Inland Sea. Both the Northern and Southern Nations have owned it since I was born there; it spends most of its time being occupied. At the moment, it's autonomous."

He stared westward at the distant Nonule Hills, a band of darker purple against the sky. "This is a strange world," he said. "Lovely, in a dreaming, bemused sort of way. I have the feeling it's very, very old."

I shrugged. "What world isn't?"

"Thanare, for one. It's a terriformed colony world. A hundred years ago it had a poisonous atmosphere and a decaying astroid belt that kept dropping meteors on it. Then the Unity made a paradise of it. You should see it. I don't know how anyone born there could ever want to leave."

The next line was obviously mine. "Kaan Ta'Wyys did."

Tolon sighed. "Yes. Yes, he did. I don't know why. I've been his closest friend in the Unity Service for seven years, and I've never known what motivates him. He didn't enjoy being an agent, never talked about his reasons for joining. Yet he was a good agent, better than me—he's saved my life many times. But he had no pride in his work, no love for it." He was silent for awhile, then said, "He's AWOL here. That's why I haven't reported what's happened . . . why I'm trying to find him myself. Once I get him off this world, maybe I can find a way to keep him from being court-martialed . . . I owe him that much." He looked at me. "Do you know what I mean?"

"Close enough. I owe some things myself. A friend of mine died because I took this case."

"I'm sorry to hear that."

"He was trying to get me safely out of Mariyad. His reasons weren't completely altruistic, I'm sure. He was a Guardsman, and crooked, though not as much as most. His commander—the one Ult killed—was a Maze Lord, one of the Brothers Below, and my friend must have known it. You should have heard him trying to talk me into a balloon-boat. He died trying."

"People do strange things for friendship," Tolon said.

I felt the outline of the scroll sewed into the lining of my trenchcloak. "They do for a fact," I agreed. I unclipped my lifeline and went forward.

I found Valina the only one inside the cabin, on a bunk, asleep. I watched her for a moment, then laid down on the next bunk, hands behind my head, staring at the ceiling. She claimed to be motivated by love, and yet she was the coldest, hardest woman I'd ever met. If only I had some idea of what went on inside her head. Of course, her coldness and hardness didn't mean she wasn't capable of love, any more than it would keep some poor fool like Kaan Ta'Wyys from loving her, if he did.

If he did . . .

Right about then, she landed on my chest.

My lungs collapsed, and the world went red. Through a roaring in my ears. I could hear Valina speaking Language, and knew I wouldn't live past the final Word. I kicked out at her with both legs, and it felt like my ankles were tied to my insides with a very short cord. But it kept her from completing the spell. I rolled over on top of her, trying to keep her occupied while I wrestled air back into my lungs. She wriggled out from underneath me and grabbed my trenchcloak, pulling it off my shoulders fast enough to spin me around on the floor. Somehow I got my legs in a straight line between my head and the floor and pushed; I half-leaped, half-collapsed on her. She had torn open the lining and found the fragment of the *Synulanom*. She was hissing, and her eyes looked like two flat, blue stones. I slapped her, hard. It did no good. She started to toss another spell my way; I wrapped part of the cloak around her head, and spoke first.

"Dulemeen ghoor, tas zule gen!"

It was a simple sleep order; I hadn't time for anything fancy. But instead of putting her out, it put her in a trance—she stood relaxed, eyes open and empty. I went over the Words again, mentally. I had pronounced them correctly. Which meant that my spell had combined with . . . another.

Valina's motivation. It had been staring me in the face every time I saw her. Her eyes; the flat look that came and went. She was ensorcelled, under a geas, and had been since I first met her.

But I didn't have a chance to question her. Now that our fight was over, I could hear shouting from outside, on the deck. I looked out one of the windows; a batwinged shape carrying a rider flicked past. I ran up the steps to the deck, and

saw the sky filled with Flying Guardsmen on kragors. Two of them had already landed on the wide forward deck, folding their wings and diving under the curve of the balloons, then breaking their fall at the last moment by flapping their wings. It was a dangerous and difficult maneuver. I saw Ult come charging around the corner of the cabin, brandishing his pigsticker. The wind from another landing knocked him sprawling. He almost went over the side. One of the kragors casually brought the knobbed end of its tail down on Ult's head, and the barbarian was out of the fight.

Passengers were running and screaming. The cold air from the kragors' wings buffeted us, and their hoarse croaking made it hard to think. Another kragor landed, and the wind flung an old merchant off the deck; he dropped with a thin scream toward the ground, three thousand meters below.

Valina had followed me to the deck. She stood behind me, watching everything impassively. I pulled my sword, and one of the kragors stretched out a sickle-shaped head split with gleaming teeth and snapped the blade with a bite.

"*Dammi gwil, sinald pai!*" I shouted. The spell worked this time; unfortunately, it worked on me and Tolon, who had just arrived from the rear deck. Our tunics and leggings stiffened until we could move only with great difficulty.

"Don't you know any other spells?" Tolon asked me.

There were four kragors and riders on deck, now. The Flying Guardsmen, small, incredibly strong men bred for their job, all wore black tunics. "No one moves!" one of them shouted. A crewman didn't listen—he tried to jump one of the Guardsmen. The small man knocked him completely across the deck and over the side with a casual backhand blow. One of the Guardsmen circling the balloon-boat put a crossbow bolt into the deck at another crewman's feet as a warning.

The Guardsmen spoke again, pointing at Valina, Tolon, and me. "You three—mount behind my men." Tolon and I did so, moving with dreamlike slowness. Two Guardsmen slung Ult's bound, unconscious body across one of the kragors' humps, and another fetched Valina from the cabin.

"Don't bother trying any more Darklore," he added. "As you can see, we're protected. Your spells will only backfire." I was glad that at least I had gotten the words right this time.

We were strapped into the second seats of the saddles. The

kragors fell away from the deck, caught the cold air under their wings, and flew toward the west. The balloon-boat disappeared quickly behind us. We flew over forests that gave way to rough, uneven ground that rose toward the Nonule Hills. Occasionally, below us, I could see flashes of deep, irridescent green, much brighter than the dull foliage; the flashes moved like large, quick amoebas. I don't know what they were; there's still a lot of this world I haven't seen. I also saw a rare water sloth in a small lake—a huge furry island with teeth. It would have been a nice ride if I hadn't been so worried about my destination.

The Guardsman I rode with said nothing. We had only one nasty moment, when Ult woke up and insisted on trying to kill his Guardsman and himself in some sort of dramatic escape attempt. My captor circled in close, drawing a bead with his crossbow. I solved the problem by speaking the few Words that put the barbarian to sleep again. This was no time for heroics.

We flew for over an hour, turning north and following the hills. They grew rockier and more inaccessible, and soon we were flying over a landscape that looked like it had been hacked with an axe. The hills were mountainous now, with steep cliffs and narrow passes. We went through a final pass so narrow that the tips of the kragors' wings almost touched the walls. It opened into a cloud valley; we dropped through the gray mists, and I saw what had to be our destination: a black basalt spire in the center of the valley. It had towers and parapets after a fashion, all roughly blasted from the rock; it looked like a sand castle made by a retarded ice giant. Surrounding it at the base were crude huts and livestock pens, and a few hectares of tilled land.

We spiraled to a landing on the flat surface of the tallest tower. The rock was no more than ten meters across, with stairs leading down into the center. It was wet and slippery, scraping the bottom of the clouds, and strong gusts of wind blew from all directions. I was never happier to be taken inside an enemy fortress.

The inside was done in Basic Cavern, with bare rock walls and ceilings, lit by Dark-activated potions that would burn eternally. We passed a few servants, also dressed in black. Everything was black—the interior decorator must have been

a blind man.

Valina was still in her trance, but Ult had regained consciousness and was occupying most of the Guardsmen's attention. Eventually we were deposited in the most comfortable cell I'd seen during this case; a large room with a window cut in the rock wall, draped with tapestries and cured skins. There was a thick rug and soft, feather-stuffed couches and chairs. There was also a table with a meal set for four, which Ult promptly ate.

Tolon and I sat down to wait. "This is Boriun's citadel," he told me. "I recognized some of the servants . . . and the color scheme, of course. Congratulations to us; we made it." He snorted. "I wonder if Kaan is still alive. Not that it matters now, I guess."

"We still live!" Ult said, with his mouth full.

"Oh, shut up," Tolon replied tiredly.

The door opened. A tall man with a red mane of hair entered. He was dressed in black robes that made his pale skin look almost sickly. His face was serene, and his green eyes had that Darkland look in them. He wore no weapons. He nodded to each of us with a faint smile.

"Boriun," Tolon said, using the name like a curse.

Ult said nothing; he just picked up a hambone from the table.

"Don't be foolish," Boriun warned. "I could turn that into a tricorn snake, and you'd be dead in a second."

Ult dropped the bone hastily. The red-haired man inclined his head toward Valina's blank stare. "Even colder than usual, I see. You appear to be in a sort of thrall, my dear. *Pansa mach tas zule.*" Valina shuddered, and new depths suddenly appeared in her open eyes. She was even less happy to see him than Tolon and Ult were.

He turned to me. "Kamus of Kadizhar, I presume. You are the one I want to talk to."

I stood up. "I've been wanting to talk to you, too."

"I knew it!" Ult said. "Dogs of the same leather stick together."

Ignoring that, the red-haired man addressed me, "As Daniel said, my name is Edward Boriun."

"You can make them believe that if you want," I said, "but don't try to play it on me. You're Boriun's acolyte, Kaan

Ta'Wyys, and you can drop the disguise spell any time."

He looked at me in surprise, then threw back his head and laughed. He spoke three Words, and his face wavered like rippling water, to be replaced by thinner, sharper features, blue eyes, and pale green hair. Kaan stopped laughing and grinned at me.

"You *are* astute," he said.

"Kaan!" Valina was on her feet and in his arms in an instant, or tried to be. He did not respond to her embrace, except to pat her lightly on the shoulders once and then let his hands fall to his side. "You should have told me!" she said accusingly. "You defeated Boriun! That means we've won! I've brought the *Synulanom*, and together we can rule all of the North, we can challenge the Darklord himself!"

"Ah, yes, the *Synulanom*," Kaan said, turning toward me. "I believe the sword-wielding sleuth has it, am I correct?" He held out his hand. "It would be useless to resist, of course."

I ignored his hand. "You've kept a close watch on her," I said.

"She had an important task," Kaan replied, "although she didn't know it. He gestured impatiently with his outstretched hand, which I continued to ignore. I clasped my hands behind my back and started a slow stroll around the room.

"Find the *Kakush*, steal the *Synulanom*, and return to Sassoon. That was the geas you laid on her, right?" I kept my eyes on Valina. Kaan did not. She looked from him to me.

"Kaan?" she said, uncertainly.

Kaan folded his arms and smiled. "You fascinate me, Kamus, truly you do," he said. "How did you guess I had killed Boriun and taken his place?"

"I didn't, until just before your men captured us. That was when I saw the spell you put on Valina. You had learned somehow that the Maze Lords had the *Synulanom*, but you couldn't escape Boriun with the missing Phrase to search for it. So you helped Valina to escape, gave her money, and commanded her to find the *Synulanom*."

I wasn't looking at Valina either, now. I hated to put her through this, but she would learn soon enough. The sooner she became Kaan's enemy, the better it might be for us.

"Maybe Boriun caught on, or maybe an opportunity presented itself—I don't know," I continued. "But your battle

with him took place the next day, and caused the destruction of Sassoon Keep."

"Enough of this," Kaan said. "The scroll, Kamus, if you please."

I stopped across the room from him and pulled it from the lining of my trenchcloak. "You underestimated the power of her love for you," I said to Kaan. "She searched for this under your gaes, thinking it was her her idea, intending to bring it back to liberate you and rule beside you. But to increase her chances of finding you, she hired me."

Kaan snapped his fingers. *"G'nai!"* he snapped. The *Synulanom* leaped from my grasp and slapped into his hand. "You will regret forcing me to do that," he told me softly.

"When she hired me," I said, "the first thing I did was go to the Spaceport and check the entry records. I found Tolon's, but not yours. Which meant you'd entered under an alias. Why? Because you had no intentions of leaving. Tolon told me you were unhappy with the Unity Service. Valina told me you were linked with Boriun because you had studied Darklore together offplanet. You knew what he was doing, and you came to stop him.

"But only because you intended to take his place."

Kaan turned toward the door. "You're a witty and erudite conversationalist, Kamus, but I really have no more time for this."

I glanced at Valina. There was agony in her eyes, but she still did not quite believe. I gave it one last try. I told Kaan, "Valina wanted to find you before the Darklore had a chance to corrupt you; not everyone of less than pure Blood can handle it. You couldn't; you had been corrupted years before. You used her as a tool to find the *Synulanom*. And now she knows it."

"Kaan!" This time it was a cry of pain. She rushed toward him again; I wasn't sure whether she meant to embrace or attack him this time. The move wasn't completed; Kaan paralyzed her with a Phrase, then turned to me.

He chuckled. "Very good, Kamus. Excellent, in spots. You would have made a good detective, I think. Pity . . ."

"Kaan." Tolon stood up. "You're saying he's right?"

"For the most part, Daniel. I was bored with the Service, with risking my life for low pay. I'd helped depose enough

tyrants on various worlds to wonder what being one might be like. Now I'm on the verge of finding out, and no one will depose me, I guarantee you that. The Darklord would never ask the Unity for help, and he can't stand alone against a unified North."

The pain in Tolon's face was as great as that in Valina's. He took a single step toward Kaan.

"Now, don't make me paralyze you, too," Kaan warned. "You'll all be my guests for a short while. I might need some experimental subjects to test various aspects of the *Synulanom*, and servants are hard to find out here." He turned toward the doorway. "If you'll excuse me, I have a date with destiny."

"One last thing," I said. He raised an eyebrow at me. "I still don't know if it was you or Valina that killed my friend Sanris of Taleiday. It doesn't matter. If she did it, it was while she was spellbound by you, so I hold you responsible."

Kaan looked puzzled. "Whatever are you talking about?"

"You attacked me two nights ago in a Mariyad brothel with some sort of fancy brimstone spell, to scare me off the case. Don't try to deny it."

"I'm afraid I'll have to. You were wrong on some parts of your deductions, Kamus; you're a bit too eager to make up facts when you don't have enough evidence. Boriun destroyed Sassoon to cover his tracks, not in battle with me; I didn't know enough to safely challenge him then. In fact, our battle took place only two nights ago."

"Wait a minute. Are you saying you were fighting a Dark duel with Boriun when Sanris and I were attacked?"

"It certainly appears that way."

"I don't believe it," I said.

Kaan shrugged. "Suit yourself. But think it through, Kamus: Why should I try to scare you off the case? From what I could tell by watching Valina, you were already off the case—in fact, you made a considerable point of having never taken it. If you hadn't seemed like such a bungler—though I admit you have more talent than I thought—I would have wanted you *on* the case. I *wanted* Valina to find me." He smiled then and left.

I spoke a spell to release Valina from her paralysis. She collapsed into one of the chairs, sobbing. The room was very quiet. Tolon sat looking at his hands, and Ult watched him in

concern. I had nothing to say to any of them.

Kaan's alibi made perfect sense. There was no reason for him to have been behind the attack in the brothel. Which meant that I was going to die without knowing who had killed Sanris.

* * *

I stood at the window and stared at the ground below. The clouds filtered the already-dim sunlight, making it always evening in the valley. I could see a few peasants' fires, like orange dots. The only way out of this chamber was through the window, and I didn't know any spells that would grow wings on me. Not that it made any difference. Even if we did escape from Kaan's citadel, where did that leave us? In a mountain wilderness, hundreds of kilometers from the nearest city. And very soon, Kaan would begin his reading of the *Synulanom* which would change the world, and not for the better.

A Flying Guardsman passed by the window. He had been circling the spire at this level for the past few minutes, evidently with orders to keep an eye on the window. Kaan was taking no chances. We were going to die here; it was that simple. There was no way out.

That was the way I had felt in Mariyad, and it had taken the death of a friend to snap me out of it. I couldn't let myself sink into hopelessness again. Ult's philosophy, simplistic as it was, was right. I looked at him, then out the window at the passing Guardsman on his kragor.

"There's a way out," I said. The only problem was, it was certain suicide.

"What did you say?" Tolon asked.

"I said there's a way out of here, just maybe. I'm going to try it. If it works, I'll have us out of this room. If it doesn't, I'll be dead, which might not be such a bad idea either."

"What are you talking about?" Ult demanded.

I told him.

"You're insane," Tolon said.

"Granted," I said, "but I'm going to try it. I'll need your help, Valina."

She did not answer. She sat on a corner of the couch, hug-

ging herself, rocking slightly back and forth. I crossed the room and pulled her to her feet.

"Remember me, Valina? Have you forgotten how much fun it was?" Then I slapped her. She drew back, her blank face filled with shock. "You—"

"That's better. Show a little life. After all, it's only the end of love, not the end of the world."

"You have no right to—"

"I have *every* right to. I'm about to risk my neck for you, so show some interest." Then I led her to the window. The Flying Guardsman passed by again.

"Let me get this straight," Tolon said. "Ult is going to throw you out the window and you're going to try to land on the kragor?"

"It's impossible," Ult said. "He's going too fast. And if you managed to do it, the Guardsman could still rip you in half. Those little men are strong."

"Under normal circumstances, yes. Now, here's my plan: When he comes around again, Valina will recite a spell to slow down the reaction of both the kragor and the Guardsman. When he comes around after that, Ult will give me a leg out the window and I'll jump him. If I'm lucky, I'll take him by surprise."

Valina nodded, slowly. "It might work . . ."

"It has to work. You can't get his attention long enough to enthrall him but you should be able to slow him down. Get ready; he'll be coming by again soon."

The Flying Guardsman passed the window again, and Valina started chanting. We waited. I was poised across the room, and Ult stood by the window, hands formed in a stirrup. Tolon watched from the other side.

"Here he comes!" he said. "Ready . . . Now!"

I ran, leaped, put one foot in Ult's hands and felt him launch me like a stone from a catapult out the window. The ground far below blurred past. I did a mid-air flip and came down, feet first, into the second seat of the saddle just as the small man started to turn slowly toward me. The sudden weight caused the kragor to squawk and drop several meters, which didn't help his confusion. I pulled the Guardsman's dagger from its sheath and had its point to his ribs and my arm around his neck by the time his eyes got wide.

We were parallel to a balcony. "Land your beast there," I told him, pointing. I spoke slowly so that he could understand me; to him, the rest of the world was accelerated. He had no time to think about a counterattack; the kragor was down before he fully realized what had happened. I put him out with the pommel of his dagger then. I was taking no chances; he could have torn off my arm and beaten me to death with it. I shooed the kragor back into the sky with its unconscious cargo. The saddlebelt would keep him safe. I wished I had the time for a reaction of fear and nausea to what I had just been through as I ran back down the corridor to the door. In a moment, Valina, Tolon, and Ult were free.

Ult gripped my shoulder like a tree grips the soil. "That was a brave gamble, Darklander. I'm impressed."

"Thanks." I pried his fingers loose. "Do you mind? I'll need all the circulation I can get."

"How do we find him?" Tolon asked.

"I don't know," I admitted. "But we'd better hurry, before—" And then I stopped, and stared at Valina. She stared back. "Yes, I feel it, too," she said.

There was no way to describe it: a soundless, vibration-less tension that charged our minds. Kaan was beginning his recital of the *Synulanom*, and we could feel it in our blood, by our Blood.

"We can find him now," I told Tolon. Valina and I started running, pulled like iron toward a lodestone. Tolon and Ult followed, down those bare, black corridors. We didn't meet any servants or guards; they had probably all taken a holiday while their master became ruler of the North. The feeling grew stronger as we approached the center of the spire. I ran until the walls looked red instead of black. If Kaan finished speaking the *Synulanom*, there would be no reversing it. I could hear the Words echoing now.

We rounded a corner. Ahead of us was a barred door. Tolon passed me, and suddenly the floor beneath him opened up—a pivoting stone, like the one that led to the *Kakush* underground. His cry echoed for a moment before the stone pivoted back into place. I was going too fast to stop, so I jumped it. Ult stopped by bracing his arms against the corridor walls, and used his body to stop Valina. "Daniel!" he shouted, pounding at the floor with his fists. The trapdoor would not open.

"Daniel!"

"There's no time, Ult!" I shouted. "Break down this door before Kaan finishes his spell!"

Ult felt the trapdoor and hurled himself at the wood. The latch held, but the hinges splintered, and we tumbled inside.

We were in a large chamber, filled with statues of Darklings, altars, and burning incense in holders. Kaan stood at an altar near the far wall, in front of a door. The *Synulanom* was before him, illuminated by a single candle, and I could see that it had been joined with another piece of parchment. It had been made whole; the missing Phrase had been added.

He saw us, and his expression would have frightened a Darkling. It didn't frighten Ult; the barbarian ran toward him, bare hands outstretched. Kaan kept chanting, his voice filling the room with pounding, echoing Words. He gestured without losing a syllable, and a whirling cloud of amber smoke appeared, condensing into a scorpion three meters long. Ult tried to stop, slipped on a rug, and sailed beneath the monster on his back. It struck at him with its stinger and missed. Ult leaped to his feet and began throwing statues at it, which bounced off its exoskeleton.

I threw the dagger at Kaan—it curved around him and hit the floor behind him. "Valina!" I shouted. "Do something!"

She stared at Kaan. "I—can't . . ." she whispered. Her love had shackled her better than any spell could.

"Great," I said, as Kaan turned toward me.

He didn't have to stop reciting. He could use the Words of the *Synulanom* to cast spells at me by gestures alone. But he had to keep glancing at the parchment; the more powerful the spell, the harder it is to remember and pronounce. His divided attention was the only thing that kept me alive. I was shouting the most powerful spells I knew, and the thunder of his voice drowned them. The Phrases were the only sound in the universe.

"DAMATH UMAL RANIBAR PAI K'CHEN,
SHILYEH CTHUL TAND MACH SORBAEN . . ."

I could *see* the spells he cast—the air was so charged with force and so full of incense particles that the spells were visible as brilliant bolts and waves streaming from his hands. That

helped me avoid them, but not for long. He hurled a latticework of green, glowing bands that wrapped themselves around me, pinning my arms. He was nearing the final Phrase now; I could feel it. The room crackled with energy as Kaan lifted his hand to hurl the bolt that would finish me. His fingers glowed crimson, and I tried one last trick. As he looked again at the scroll I chanted the simple disguise spell both he and I had used before. Kaan looked up again, saw the face I had taken—and faltered. The thunder of his recital faded. He had lost the cadence!

And in that single moment of weakness, before he could recover and before I could press my hopeless advantage, the pulsing energy in the room combined in a blinding rainbow flash and vanished. Suddenly, everything was quiet, and the smell of ozone mingled with incense was all that was left of the battle. Kaan stood with arms outstretched, mouth open and eyes empty. He swayed and then collapsed on the altar, knocking over the burning candle. It rolled across the surface until it hit the scroll. There was a thin crackling as the dry parchment began to smolder.

A Flying Guardsman's dagger was now planted between Kaan's shoulderblades. I looked beyond it, at Daniel Tolon framed in the open door behind the altar.

Valina began to sob quietly as the small fire flared and then burned out.

Tolon kept his eyes on the dagger. "There were passages under the floor," he said. "Stairs. I followed the sound of the fighting." He looked at me. "You have my face," he said in dull wonderment.

I spoke the words that dissolved the disguise spell. Then I heard a step behind me and turned quickly. There stood Ult, bloody, disheveled, and grinning. He held the huge, knob-shaped end of the scorpion's tail in one hand, the stinger still dripping. "I think I'll make a helmet out of it," he said proudly.

I shook my head. "It'll turn to dust when sunlight hits it," I told him. "It's made of Darkness." Ult dropped it quickly and kicked it away from him.

I held my fingers against the vein in Kaan's neck, just to be sure. He was dead. I wondered if it had been a moment of concern that made him hesitate when he saw his former partner

standing before him, or only surprise.

"I knew who I was killing, Kamus," Tolon said pleadingly.

Valina was still crying for something that had never been. I looked at the body of Kaan Ta'Wyys, lying in the ashes of the *Synulanom*.

"I wonder if you did," I said to Tolon.

* * *

I went back to Mariyad. I knew it wasn't a bright move, but I had my reasons.

We had no trouble leaving the deserted citadel. I put a docility spell on four kragors and they carried us southeast to Port Rizh; from there we caught a balloon-boat and arrived in Mariyad by evening of the next day.

I said good-bye to Daniel Tolon at the Spaceport. He had decided to report that Kaan Ta'Wyys had died trying to prevent Edward Boriun's takeover attempt. I suppose it made him feel better.

Ult was going west, as there was a rumor of a war among the Plains tribes, and fighters might be needed. He shook my hand in farewell, almost taking some of my fingers with him. By jumping out of a window onto a flying kragor I had earned his respect and friendship. That, and a major miracle, would put my life back the way it was before he ruined my dinner at the Blue Lotus.

As for Valina . . .

"I'm going north," she told me. "The cold and the snow may be a kind of cure for the pain. And the further I get from the Darkland, perhaps the less I'll feel like a Darklander. I hope so."

I said I hoped so, too, for her sake, although we both knew it wouldn't work. She would only feel more of an outcast. But maybe she needed that, for a time.

"You do believe that I had nothing to do with your friend's death?" she asked me.

"That's the only part of this case that's unsolved," I admitted. "But I have a theory that I don't like."

"And it is?"

"Now that Kaan and Boriun are ruled out, there's only one other I know of who has the power to cast such a spell."

"The Darklord," Valina breathed. "But that's absurd! Why would he want to scare you off the case?"

"He wouldn't. But Kaan's reading the *Synulanom* was a good reason to keep me *on* the case. And what better way to keep me on than to give me a reason to seek revenge?"

"But if he were going to interfere, why didn't he simply kill Kaan?"

"Who knows the Darklord's motives? Like I said, it's only a theory. It'll need a lot of proof, which I'm not likely to find."

I watched her balloon-boat leave, then used my disguise spell to go to Pallas the Moneyholder's and pick up my fee. I found Dash still at milady's, and collected a few other things that I'd need for my trip west.

The last thing I did was go to the graveyard. where I paid my respects to a slab with Sanris's bones buried beneath it.

I still intended to avenge my friend, but it would have to wait awhile now. I needed to make a new life before I could think about devoting it to Sanris's memory. I was fairly sure that Sanris would think it a stupid way to spend one's time, seeking absolution from a pile of bones. I half-thought so myself. But even if Sanris's life hadn't had any particular meaning beyond wenching and wassail, his death still deserved meaning. Or at least justice.

I was the only private eye on the planet, and I couldn't let anyone cross me, not even the Darklord. Valina had said that Darkness corrupts those of less than pure Blood. I had known that for years. But there were ways to prevent it. My job was more than just a job—it was my way of keeping the Darkness at bay. A private eye must have a basic moral code.

I suddenly realized that the night was almost gone. I had stood brooding too long over Sanris's grave; the sun was rising. The balloon-boat port was halfway across Mariyad, and my disguise would disappear in sunlight. I ran for the street, pulling my hood up. There wasn't a carriage in sight. The first faint rays of the sun touched me, and I felt the disguise spell evaporate. And to make matters worse, a trio of Guardsmen came around the corner just then and spotted me.

Before I could shout a spell and run, they recognized me. One of them nodded curtly. Another, a young private I had seen at the Blue Lotus, said, pleasantly, "Hello, Kamus, how's business?" Then they passed me and continued down the

street.

I stood staring. Surely by now every Guardsman knew I was wanted. I started walking, slowly. I saw other Guardsmen; none of them tried to arrest or attack me. I went to my office. Sanris had told me it had been ransacked by the Guard. If so, there was no sign of it now. This was no trick of the Guard's, I was sure; they weren't subtle enough for that. Either I was going crazy, or—

—that major miracle had happened.

It had. I visited my old haunts, the Blue Lotus, the Maze, over the next few days. Ratbag had no memory of helping me invade the stronghold of the *Kakush*. Beggars and businessmen whom I remembered as being Maze Lords brushed past me without a sign of recognition. I even visited the Garrison; Thoras was indeed dead, but evidently I had nothing to do with it. Somehow, all knowledge of my participation in the events of the past few days had been erased. My business in Mariyad was as healthy as ever, for what that was worth.

It was the proof I needed. Only the Darklord could have spelled the memory out of so many people. He had made it safe for me to stay in Mariyad, and I had no idea why.

Evidently, he had some sort of plan. But I had plans, too, and they didn't include being part of his plans. The Darklord had killed Sanris, casually, and ripped my life apart, and now, just as casually, he had helped to put it back together. I couldn't let him continue manipulating me—but how was I going to stop him?

I had no idea. But one thing was certain: I couldn't be his pawn. I had to have free will, to make my own decisions, to solve cases on my own. A private eye can't be a puppet. It's bad for business.

Some day, I would have to explain that to the Darklord.

ORION 2

BEN BOVA

FLOODTIDE

CRAIG RUSSELL

FLOODTIDE
by Ben Bova

I awoke.

My eyes opened and showed me a blue sky, bright with sunlight and puffy white clouds. The memory of searing agony and death faded from my mind.

"I live," I heard myself say, my voice hushed and calm. "I am Orion and I am still alive."

Sitting up, I saw that I was resting on the cool grass of a broad, open meadow that sloped gently down toward a distant river. The grass was long and wild and matted; no blade had ever cut it. Rocks and boulders jutted from the green; no one had ever cleared them away. Down by the river a line of trees swayed in the warm wind, rising up from a tangle of low foliage that hugged the riverbank.

I looked down at myself. My garments were a simple kilt made of hides and a leather vest. A braided belt around my waist held a small knife.

Closing my eyes for a moment, I tried to puzzle out where I was. Obviously I had traveled back through time again. First I had been sent from my own era some fifty thousand years back to the so-called twentieth century. Or so Ormazd, the Golden One, had told me. Now I had been sent even further back.

I had left the twentieth century in a blaze of nuclear fury, sacrificing my body to fiery death inside a fusion reactor to thwart Ahriman's plan for destroying the whole human race. But where was I now? What age was this?

In a single step I had gone from the hell of tortured atoms inside the nuclear fusion reactor to this calm, grassy meadow. Frowning with concentration, I forced myself to recall that step. Sweat beaded my face and trickled down my ribs as I sank down on the grass, oblivious to the sun and wind and sweet-smelling earth around me, and forced my mind to visualize my step through time.

Everything blacked out around me. Gradually I began to see myself moving across a dark emptiness, a void of cold and blackness where time itself does not exist, where all the flow of events from moment to moment is frozen in an eternally static, soul-chilling temporal vacuum. I saw myself as if in slow mo-

tion, propelled through that black, frozen void. But there were stars etched solemnly, unblinkingly, against that darkness. I saw their pattern shift abruptly as the void gave way to this sun-warmed morning.

Fifteen thousand years. Opening my eyes again, feeling the life-giving rays of the sun on my chilled body, I knew that I had traveled another fifteen thousand years back, to a time before the beginnings of human civilization. The first cities had not yet been started, nor the first villages. The Pyramids of Egypt were still a hundred centuries or more in the future. Glacial ice sheets two miles thick still covered much of the world.

Yet here it was springtime. I must be far south of the ice, I reasoned. Insects buzzed and scurried through the grass. Birds swooped overhead.

And I knew one other thing. I had not come here voluntarily, of my own free will. I wouldn't know how to, even if I tried. I had been sent, propelled, driven to this time and place by Ormazd. Because somewhere near here dwelt Ahriman, the dark one, the destroyer who seeks the annihilation of the entire human race.

I am Orion. My task is to find Ahriman. I would not have been sent here if he were not nearby. I am to search out the Dark One, through all the eons of time, and destroy him before he succeeds in destroying humankind. For this purpose was I sent from my own time, more alone than any man has ever been in the history of the world, robbed even of my memories: to seek, to find, to die if necessary, and to seek again and die again as often as I must to stop Ahriman.

But why this time and place, in the peaceful morning of humankind's existence? What damage could Ahriman do here?

With a shrug, I got to my feet and looked around. I saw that I would begin to find the answers to my questions soon enough. Coming over the grassy ridge a half-mile to my right, silhouetted against the bright sky, was a line of thirty-four people.

Without moving I watched as they headed my way. They were slender, fair of skin, their hair reddish and wild and long.

Their clothes were hides, like mine. They were caked with dirt and I could smell their sweat as they drew closer.

Their leader spotted me and stopped their march so abruptly that the children, back toward the end of the line, bumped into their elders and jostled them. I almost laughed.

For several long moments they did nothing but gape at me. My eyesight is far beyond normal. I could see the puzzled, even frightened, expressions on their faces. Hands fingered stone knives and long, knobby-shafted spears. Even the women were armed, and some of the bigger children carried sticks and clubs.

A hunting tribe. Out of the dawn of human history. Shaggy-haired, unkempt, hungry-slim, and wary of a stranger.

The man in the lead had raised his hand to stop the tribe's march, and it still hung poised in the air as he stared at me. The young woman beside him said something. I could see her lips move, but couldn't catch what she was saying because the wind was blowing away from them.

The leader turned and pointed to two men, further up their line. They looked at each other in the classic *Who—me?* manner, then started walking slowly—very slowly—down the grassy slope toward me, hefting their long spears as they approached. The others gathered around their leader in a ragged semicircle, ready to charge at me or run back over the crest of the ridge.

The pair approaching me were teenagers. Thy were beardless, although their coppery hair was shoulder-length and matted. Every muscle and tendon in their arms and torsos was rigid with tension. Their knuckles were white as they held their spears. Their lean, hollow-cheeked faces were too young to look truly fierce, but they certainly lacked nothing in grimness.

I held both my hands out, open, palms up. The universal sign of peace. At least they could see that I had no weapons in my hands.

They halted a good ten yards from me. Close enough to drive a thrown spear clean through my body, if I were slow enough to let that happen.

"Who are you?" asked the one on my left, in a quavery, cracking adolescent's voice.

Somehow I wasn't surprised that I understood their

language. Ormazd had programmed so many things into my brain; why not a primitive tongue that had not been spoken for millennia?

"I am called Orion," I answered.

"What are you doing here?" asked the other one, his voice a bit deeper, but equally shaky. He held his spear aloft, ready to throw it, as he spoke.

I kept my hands outstretched from my body. I knew that I could break their spears, and both their bodies, too, anytime I chose to. But I doubted that I could handle all the rest of the tribe if they decided to attack me *en masse*.

"I come from far away," I said. "I have traveled a long, long time." *No lie*, I told myself. "I am a stranger in your land and seek your help and protection."

"Traveled?" the second one snapped. "Alone? You travel alone?"

"Yes."

He shook his head vehemently. "No one can travel alone. The beasts would kill you, or the spirits of the dead. You are lying."

"No, it's true. I have traveled alone."

"You belong to another tribe. They are hiding nearby, waiting to ambush us."

"I have no tribe. That is why I want to join your tribe. I am weary of being alone. I seek your friendship."

They glanced at each other, then looked back at me.

"You cannot be of our tribe," the deep-voiced one said. "Who is your mother? Who is your father? They are not of our tribe. *You* are not of our tribe."

So that was the situation. You were born into the tribe or you were an outsider, a danger, a threat. Maybe you could marry into the tribe, but I even began to wonder about that.

"I know I am not of your tribe, but I would like to stay with you. I can help you. I am a good hunter. My name means 'hunter.' "

Their jaws fell at that.

"Yes," I said. "Orion means 'hunter.' What are your names? What do they mean?"

They both started yelling and brandishing their spears. I could see their pupils dilating with rage and fear, sweat sheening their bodies, the veins in their necks and foreheads throb-

bing furiously.

Beyond them, the whole tribe came to alert and began hurrying down the slope toward us. The two teenagers were edging closer to me, leveling their spears and working up the courage to begin using them on me.

I made a very quick, very human decision. I turned and ran. I had no desire to frighten them further, or to risk being swarmed under and chopped to bloody pulp by their stone-tipped weapons. So I ran.

They threw a few spears, which I easily dodged. They chased after me, but their speed was nowhere near mine. In less than a minute I was beyond the range of their spears. Their leader sent a relay of eight men to take off after me, but their endurance was pitifully short. I jogged down toward the river, crashed through the underbrush, and stayed among the foliage and trees, where it was cooler. By midafternoon all their runners were on the ground, panting and exhausted. I went along at a steady pace for another hour, then splashed into the river to refresh myself.

By nightfall I had figured out what had upset them. Primitive tribes are naturally very wary of strangers, and they also feel that a man's name carried his soul or strength with it. To give your name to a stranger is to invite witchcraft or death, rather like giving your fingernail clippings to a voodoo priestess. I should have known that from the outset. Now I had terrified them and made them triply afraid of me.

As the sun set behind a row of rocky hills across the river, and the sky flamed into achingly beautiful reds and purples, I picked out a soft mossy spot among the trees for my night's sleep. I usually need only a few hours of rest, but I felt physically tired and even more weary mentally.

Then the far-off roar of a hunting cat echoed through the darkening air. With a reluctant glance at the soft moss, I climbed the biggest tree I could find and settled down in a hard wooden notch to spend the night. I fell asleep immediately.

Ormazd came to me in my sleep.

It was not a dream, it was a purposeful communication. I saw him shining against the darkness of night, his golden hair glowing with light, his face smiling yet somehow neither happy nor glad.

"You have found the tribe." It was neither a question nor an

acknowledgement of success. His robes were golden. He was seated—but on what, I could not see.

"Yes, I found them," I reported. "But I frightened them and they chased me away."

"You will gain their trust. You must."

"I already know how to do that. But why? What is so important about this gaggle of primitives?"

"The Dark One seeks to destroy them. We must counter him."

"But what would Ahriman gain from wiping out a tribe of thirty-some Stone Age nomads? How would that affect human history?"

Ormazd eyed me disdainfully. "What matter is that to you? Your appointed task is to kill Ahriman. *He* is stalking this tribe; therefore, *you* will use the tribe as bait to stalk Ahriman. What could be simpler?"

"But why me?" I demanded. "Why have I been taken from my own time and programmed to kill Ahriman? Why can't you do it yourself? Why must I die when I don't even understand . . ."

"You do *not* understand!" Ormazd's voice was suddenly thunder, and the brightness radiating from him became almost too painful to look at. "You are the chosen instrument for the salvation of the human race. Ask no pointless questions, but do as you must."

"I have a right to know who I am and why I am being made to do this," I insisted, even though Ormazd's blazing eyes felt as hot as the nuclear fires that had killed my body fifteen thousand years in the future.

"You doubt me?" It wasn't a question, it was a threat.

"I accept you. But that's different from *knowing*. I had a life of my own once, didn't I? If I have to die . . ."

"You have already died and been reborn in another time. You will die again . . ."

"No!" I still felt the pain of death.

"Yes. You must die if you wish to step through time. Even if for no other reason than to return to your own time and the friends and family of your original life, you must die. There is no way to move through time, except by death."

I heard myself ask, "Is it true that your race . . . killed all of Ahriman's race, except for him? When was the War? What

happened?"

"That you must learn for yourself," Ormazd said, his image beginning to fade before my eyes. He added, "And for me."

I was stunned. "No, wait! You mean you don't know what happened? You don't know what your race did to his?"

But he was only a pinpoint of light now, dwindling into the all-engulfing blackness. I heard his voice whispering from far, far away:

"Why do you think my race is not the same as yours, Orion? Are we not brothers?"

I realized I was staring at the dark night sky. Pinpoints of stars looked back at me from the unfathomable depths of space. I looked for the constellations of Orion, but found nothing familiar in that sky.

It was a simple matter to get the tribe to accept me. If they would not take me as their equal, then I must join them as their superior.

I had boasted of my hunting abilities. So I began taking game from the countryside and leaving it at their smoldering campfire, while the whole tribe slept. A rabbit or two, at first. Then some fowl I flushed out of the bush and hit with thrown rocks. I fashioned a crude bow and arrow and brought down a young deer.

I watched the tribe every night, from a distance and always from concealment behind rocks or bushes. They were surprised at first, when I started leaving them gifts. Then they became fearful and began posting sentries through the night. I always managed to slip past them and leave my kill near their fire.

Soon enough I was turned into a legend. Orion was eleven feet tall. His eyes darted flame. He could leap across rivers and stop spears in midair just by glancing at them with his fierce countenance. He was a mighty hunter, who could bring down a mastadon singlehandedly (it took the cooperative efforts of several tribes to hunt the really big game).

I chuckled to myself at their stories. And I listened every night to learn the names of each person in the tribe, from Dal their leader to Kralo, the teenager with the cracking voice.

Finally I spent a night and a day of *real* hunting. I had figured out the length of their days' marches and saw the place where they would camp two days hence. In fact, the spot by the river was already blackened by the fires of countless earlier camps.

With my bow and arrow, and a sling I had devised for throwing rocks, I started amassing a huge pile of slain meat for the tribe—rabbits, birds, deer, succulent young boar. I left the food at their intended campsite until it got so high that I had to spend as much time defending the cache from wild dogs and other scavengers as I spent in hunting more game.

The dogs were my only real trouble. They had not yet been tamed to the point where the long symbiosis between man and dog had begun. And they hunted in packs, with much intelligence. I hated to do it, but I had to kill several of them before they learned that my cache of dead game was not to be bothered.

I guarded the pile of meat until I knew the tribe was almost within sight of it. Then, as they cleared the trees they were moving through and came into view of the cache, I hid in the foliage a few hundred yards from their campsite.

They were ecstatic. They had never seen so much food in one place before. They raced to the campsite and gawked at all that meat. Only slowly did their joy begin to turn into awe, and then fear.

From my hiding place in the bushes I could see them start to glance around uneasily.

Dal, their leader, said, "Only Orion could have done this."

"Can it be all for us?" asked Adena. She was also a leader of sorts, but more like a medicine man or shaman than a chief who decided where they would march and where to camp, as Dal did.

I let them settle down as the evening slowly pulled its violet blanket over their grassy campsite. They were wary of taking any of the meat I had left them, and Dal, Adena, and the two oldest men of the tribe discussed the situation in earnest whispers as the darkness deepened.

Just before the first star showed itself, I walked out of my hiding place with my final kill across my shoulders—a fine deer stag.

"Greetings," I called to them out of the gathering shadows.

"It's me . . . Orion."

Now they were victims of their own propaganda. They had puffed up their stories about me so far out of proportion that they seemed terrified of me. None of them moved as I approached their flickering campfire. Their faces were rigid with fear and surprise. Probably expected me to strike them lightning, I suppose.

I dumped the stag's carcass next to the fire, alongside all the other meat.

"Why aren't you eating? I gave you all this food as an offer of friendship."

Adena recovered her wits first. She was as tall as any man in the tribe, almost my height, and almost fearless. "You did all this? Alone?"

Giving her my best smile, I said, "I told you that I was a good hunter. Don't be afraid of me. If you don't want to allow me to join your tribe, then at least let me stay with you for a little while. I can teach you all how to hunt the way I do."

They remained unmoved and unmoving. I could see the conflict warring in their grimy faces. They were scared half out of their wits by me. Yet to be able to hunt down animals like that! It was a tempting offer. Which would it be, I wondered: their fears or their bellies?

Adena stepped closer to me and studied my face in the dancing firelight.

"Are you a man or a spirit?" she asked.

She was as close to being beautiful as any of these people could be. Tall and slender, her body was lithe and strong, yet completely female. Her bare arms and legs were dirty, scratched here and there. A scab covered one knee. Her face—if you could forget the wildly matted, filthy red hair—had good high cheekbones, a small straight nose and firm little chin. Her lips were thin and slightly cold-looking. Her eyes were gray and deep, accustomed to looking beyond the surface of things.

I laughed. "A man," I said. "I'm only a man."

Dal moved up beside her. There were no weapons in his hands, yet he was clearly being protective.

"You look like a man . . . yet . . ."

"I *am* a man," I said.

"Your eyes are strange," he said. "Your hair . . . your face."

Looking at the other tribe members as they stared at me, I

·PLR·

realized what he meant. They all had gray eyes and stringy reddish hair. The men were all bearded; some, like Dal, kept their beards to a fairly short set of ragged chin whiskers. Others, especially the two tribal elders, let their gray beards dangle as long as they wanted to. I wondered if either of them had reached fifty, or ever would.

My eyes are brown, of course. My hair a dark black that tightly curls into short ringlets. My face is smooth; I have never had to shave—a beard simply does not grow on me.

"I'm different from you in some ways, true enough," I admitted. "But I am also the same as you in many ways." Actually, I was an inch or more taller than any of them except Dal, who was almost exactly my height. But I was much heavier than any of them.

"I come from far away," I explained. "All the people of my tribe have eyes like mine. And hair like mine. Many of them are much bigger than I am . . ."

"If they all hunt the way you do," said Adena, with a smile, "they must be very fat."

I laughed. "Some of them are."

"Where is your tribe?" Dal asked. "Why are you alone? Why have you come to us?"

"My tribe is far away . . . so far that I can't find it. I'm alone. I don't know if I can ever find my tribe again. I don't want to spend the rest of my life alone. I don't want to die alone." As I said it, I realized how literally true it all was, and how much I really meant it.

"It is not good for a man to be alone," Adena said, with surprising warmth and understanding in her voice. "Even the mightiest hunter needs a tribe and a family."

Like all humans facing a difficult decision, they finally settled on a compromise. Dal spoke quietly to the two elders of the tribe, then asked the whole group if they would agree to let me stay with them long enough to show them my tricks of hunting. They voted yes to that, almost unanimously. But they insisted that I had to sleep far from their campfire each night. Some of them didn't quite believe that I was not a spirit.

I accepted that; I had to. No one brought up the question of what to do with me *after* I had shown them all my hunting techniques, but I was content to let that remain an open

matter.

Dal and Adena stayed very close to me at all times, as the tribe continued its migration across the springtime landscape. He was still worried that I might be a spy from another tribe. Apparently they met other tribes fairly often on these migration trails, and sometimes fought them, even though there was usually plenty of game and water for everybody. The fights were generally over campsites, and they seldom amounted to much more than throwing rocks and spears at each other. It was rare for anyone to be killed in such skirmishes.

From what I could gather from Dal and the others, several tribes generally lived together in the same area for the summer. They would break up in the autumn and travel their separate ways through the winter, then return to the same meeting grounds the following spring.

Adena's interest in me was purely professional. She wanted to make certain that if I really did turn out to be some sort of demon, she would find out about it before I could do any damage to the tribe.

For weeks I walked with the tribe as we slowly traveled across the springtime landscape of the Pleistocene. I showed them how to track game, how to make bows and arrows, and how to use a sling. I taught them to build spear throwers that extended the range of their favorite hunting weapon. We began to hunt larger game than any single tribe had ever before attempted. I saw nothing as large as a mastodon or mammoth, but we did trap a buffalo in a pit I showed them how to camouflage. It fed the whole tribe for days.

Without astronomical instruments it was impossible to tell exactly where on the face of earth I was. But from the visible constellations—Bootes, Andromeda, Perseus, the Little Dipper, and a strangely lopsided Big Dipper—I concluded that we were somewhere south of the Caucasus Mountains, heading north and west along a trail that the tribe followed every springtime.

In a few weeks we had climbed out of the rolling grasslands, through a cold and mist-filled mountain pass where I could glimpse ice-covered spires of rock far above us, and then out into a dark and gloomy forest. Huge boles of pine and spruce alternated with groves of birch trees. The underbrush was

tangled and thick where sunlight filtered through the grand canopy above us. Dal kept us on a trail that was shadowed and almost bare—easy hiking.

Many things about the tribe surprised me. For example, he young women joined the hunt alongside the men. Small children stayed at camp with the elders. Old women gathered fruits and greens. Everybody else hunted.

Adena was among the best of them all, as fierce and fearless as any mythological hero. And she was faster afoot than most. I saw her chase after a wild boar that had crashed out of some underbrush and scared everybody else into flight. Adena threw her spear at it and let out a blood-curdling yell, and the boar dashed off back into the brush. Picking up her spear, she dashed after it through the trees, never glancing around once to see if anyone was with her. By the time I reached her she had the boar spitted, but it was still very much alive and had just shaken the spear from her grip. I threw myself on its back and slit its throat before its tusks reached her.

We dragged the beast back out of the foliage to the rest of the hunters. We were both splattered with blood and mud, and both laughing.

Dal eyed me more suspiciously than ever as we made our way back to camp that afternoon. But he was no longer worried that I was a spy from another tribe. Nor was he afraid that I was a spirit instead of a man. He was just plain jealous, despite the fact that he had at least three young women pampering his every desire.

That night Adena proclaimed that she was going to perform a blood ritual in honor of slaying the boar. She wanted the tribespeople to allow me to take part in it. They were wary and Dal was vehement: I was an outsider, and only members of the tribe could take part in the ritual.

So I sat alone in the darkness far from their camp that night as their fires blazed wildly and their strange cries split the calm forest darkness. All around me the tree trunks loomed, black and unyielding. For hours I listened to the tribe's screams and howls and I told myself I was glad not to be one of them. And yet . . .

The eerie cries had dwindled to silence and the glow of their fire had sunken to a sullen glower of red among the trees. I was

half asleep when Adena came to me. Even in the darkness I could tell that she was smeared from head to foot with the blood and entrails of the beasts we had killed that day.

"You could not come to the ritual," she said, her voice high and breathless from excitement, "so I have brought the ritual to you."

Part of me was disgusted with her and her primitive blood lust. Part of me was disgusted with myself for taking her in my arms and wallowing in her stench and passion. But still another part of me was as wild and fierce as she was, and for at least a little while I was alone no longer.

Days later we emerged from the brooding forest and entered a region of low, rounded hills where the grass was green and sweet, and wild grains grew in patches here and there. We crossed noisy, splashing streams and small copses of trees. Flowers bloomed. It was a beautiful countryside.

"Soon we'll be at our valley," Dal told me as we walked ahead of the tribe's main body. If he knew about what had happened at the blood ritual back in the forest, he gave no indication of it. And I didn't press the issue. Most likely, what happened at such rituals was not a subject to be discussed or even remembered afterward.

"*Our* valley?" I asked.

He nodded, smiling like a man who was on his way home. "We stay in our valley every summer, with the other tribes of red-haired people. It's a good place. Plenty of water and grain and good hunting. Everyone is happy in our valley."

It *was* a lovely valley. Two days later, as we stood by the bank of a slow, meandering stream that dropped down a series of terraced stone steps into the floor of the valley, I saw why Dal was so happy to be here. The valley was sun-warmed and green. The stream's gentle waterfall ended in a lovely pool, from which the stream continued quietly down the length of the valley, to disappear in a narrow gap between rocky cliffs.

It was a very snug niche in the hills, and very defendable. The only real access to the valley was down the stone terracing of the waterfall; it was slippery, but not at all difficult to get up and down. On all other sides, the hills rose steeply up from the valley floor in cliffs that were at least a hundred feet high.

Dal's tribe was the first one there. The people raced down

the wet stone steps, laughing and happy, to the valley floor. Before the day ended they had felled trees and chased game. By the time the next tribe arrived, a few days later, Dal's people had already set up a primitive settlement of mud-walled huts with tree branches and hides for ceilings. The huts were more underground than above, but to these Stone Age nomads they seemed like palaces.

"We stay here," Dal told me, "until the grain turns to gold. Then we harvest it and carry it with us for the winter. Unless," he frowned, "the snows come before the grain ripens."

And in a flash of understanding I knew why Ahriman was here and what he planned to do.

Ahriman's savage desire was to destroy the whole human race. He was trying to do this by finding the turning points in human history and altering them in a way that would cause the destruction of all humankind. Both he and Ormazd knew that if Ahriman could cause a large enough change in history, the whole fabric of space/time would be warped unbearably, and our continuum of matter and energy would fall in on itself and be destroyed. All the stars and worlds and galaxies and swirling clouds of gas in our interstellar space—all of it would die in a single, vast cataclysm.

To accomplish this, Ahriman sought out the crucial nexus points of human history. I met him first in the twentieth century, when he tried to turn the first controlled nuclear fusion reactor into a titanic lithium bomb that would have triggered a world-shattering nuclear war.

Now, here, fifteen thousand years *before* that nexus, we stood at another vital crossroads of human history. This tribe, this collection of ragged, dirty, wandering hunters, was going to make the transition from hunting to farming. I was going to see the beginning of the Neolithic Revolution, the step that turned humankind from primitive savages to civilized city-builders. And Ahriman was going to try to strangle that development, prevent it from happening.

But how? I could only watch and wait.

Life in the valley was pleasant and easy. The days lengthened into golden summer, but without the oppressive heat and humidity I had known in other times. The grain ripened and grew tall. The nights were cool and wind-tossed. The valley itself had been gouged out by a glacier that had now melted,

leaving only the cold bubbling stream that ran the valley's length as a reminder of its ice. The cliff walls that faced most of the valley were too steep for game to climb, so the tribe's hunting became a simple matter of penning the animals against the cliffs and slaughtering them at their leisure.

I was training the hunters in using the bow, which delighted them—Adena most of all. Dal seemed more concerned with the crops, however, than with hunting. All through the long days of summer he seemed preoccupied, as if some enormous problem were weighing him down. At first I thought he was worried, or even angry, about Adena and me. But there was nothing for him to be worried about. Except for that one blood-crazed night of the ritual, we had not touched each other.

The rest of the tribe was accepting me, gradually. Where first I had been an object of fear, of awe, of legend—now they were looking at me as a strange but no longer scary man. They even let me build a hut close to those of the rest of the tribe.

One afternoon, while Adena was leading a hunting party out toward the far end of the valley, I saw Dal staring soberly at the ripening grain fields. His face had filled out quite a bit, as had his belly. Everyone had gained weight, now that they no longer had to march each day and food was plentiful.

But Dal's face was knotted into such a serious frown that I decided to speak to him, man to man.

"Dal, are you troubled by something I have done?"

He seemed startled, but more by my being beside him than by my words. He turned toward me, squinting slightly into the sun that was at his back.

"What? Something you . . . no, no, not really." Dal shook his head, but there seemed to be very little conviction in either his voice or his gesture.

"I'm going to take a walk," I said, "up to the top of those hills across the valley. Do you want to come with me?"

"Up the cliffs?" Now he looked alarmed. "No one can climb up the cliffs. They're too steep. I've tried. So have many others."

I shrugged. "Let's try it together. Maybe two men can get to the top where one man alone would fail."

He gave me a curious stare. "Why? Why do you want to climb where no man has climbed before?"

"That's just it," I said. "Because no man has done it yet. I want to be the first. I want to see how the world looks when I'm standing in a place where no one has ever stood before."

He scratched his scrubby beard. "It sounds crazy."

"Haven't you ever done something simply because you wanted to do it? Haven't you ever had the desire to do something that no one's done before?"

"No," he said, his gray eyes looking out toward those steep hills, wondering, wondering. "We always do things just the way they have always been done. That's the best way, just as our fathers and their fathers did it."

"But somewhere, sometime, one of them must have done it for the first time. There's a first time for everything."

He looked back at me. "Do you really think we could reach the top?"

"Yes, if we work together."

He turned back toward the hills. They were steep, all right. But even an amateur rockclimber could handle them, and I knew within me that Ormazd had programmed me with much more than an amateur's strength and skill.

Dal broke his gaze away from the hills. He glanced at the golden grain fields nearby as a breeze sent a swaying wave through them. Then he grinned at me.

"Yes," he said. "I want to see what's on the other side of those hills, too!"

We used vines instead of rope, and our bare, travel-hardened feet had to do instead of climbers' boots. But the hills were nowhere near as forbidding as they seemed at first glance. It was a struggle, but we reached the top in about an hour of steady, sweaty work.

The view was worth it.

Dal stood puffing, smiling, wide-eyed as we looked far to the east and saw a glittering sea that stretched on to the distant horizon. Turning south and west we saw mountains rising in rocky splendor until the tops of the farthest ones—almost lost in haze—showed white snowcaps. The tallest of the mountains was a nearly perfect cone, topped with snow, like Fujiyama. I realized, that, like Fuji, it was a slumbering volcano.

"There's so much to see!" Dal shouted. "Look at how small our valley seems from here!"

"It's a big world," I agreed.

We could see Adena's hunting party chasing happily down at the far end of the valley, where the stream disappeared between vertical rock cliffs. The huts of the various tribes were huddled in the middle of the valley, almost lost in the sea of gently waving grain.

Dal stared down into the valley and slowly his face lost its exultant happiness. He began to frown again.

"Dal," I asked again, "is it something that I've done that is worrying you?"

"No . . . not really." He hesitated, then turned to face me. "Well, maybe yes. In a way."

"Is it about Adena?"

"It concerns her, too . . . I've been thinking . . . it would be a good thing for us to stay in this valley. Why should we leave when the snows come? We have plenty of food here. We can live in the caves along the hillsides during the winter and eat what we have saved from the summer's harvest. There would be plenty of game, even in the snow. Why must we travel back along the path that our fathers have traveled?"

So that was it. Despite myself, I could feel my pulse quickening.

"Why did your fathers begin traveling their path?" I asked.

With an impatient wave of his hand, Dal answered, "They followed the game herds when the beasts moved south for the winter. But the herds get smaller every year. And the grain here in the valley gets taller and fuller every summer. We make food from the grain—and even a drink that makes you feel as if you're flying."

Bread and beer, the two staples of Neolithic life. I wondered which of them was more important in Dal's mind.

"But how does this affect Adena?" I asked. "Or me?"

"Adena says it would be wrong to change our fathers' ways," Dal said, looking so unhappy that it was clear he half-agreed with her. "She says the spirits of our fathers would be unhappy if we didn't follow the same trails that they followed every year. She says the grain only grows each year because we have done our fathers' spirits wish. They wouldn't allow the grain to grow if we stayed here all year."

"That's wrong," I said. "The grain grows just as the rain falls and the sun shines. It's all completely natural, and the spirits of your fathers have nothing to do with it."

He didn't seem very encouraged by my botanical knowledge. "Adena loves the hunt. So do all the others. Now that you have shown them how to hunt even better, Adena says we don't need the grain at all."

"Have you spoken to the elders about this? Or to anyone else in the tribe?"

"No. Just to Adena."

It was my turn to hesitate. Should I interfere? Was it part of Ormazd's plan that I help these people take the first step toward agriculture?

Ormazd's plan be damned, I said to myself. *These people are my friends. They have accepted me, despite their fears. They have not left me to wander alone.*

I put a hand on Dal's shoulders. "Talk to the whole tribe. To all the tribes. Tell them what you just told me. And I will show them how the grain grows, how to make it grow even better. The spirits of your fathers will be pleased with your new idea, not angry. I will help them to understand this."

He smiled slowly. "Like you helped me to climb the hill?"

"We helped each other. I could not have climbed up here by myself."

His smile broadened. "All right. I'll speak to all the tribes. Tonight."

It was a strange and fascinating argument, for as long as it lasted.

The tribes gathered around their central fire, in the middle of the makeshift village, after everyone had finished the evening meal. Darkness was falling fast. This was the time when the old men (that is, those over thirty) began telling stories. They would take turns and keep everyone enthralled for hours with tales of wild hunts, strange demons in the dark woods, monsters with forty arms and a hundred legs, dragons and witches.

But this night, Dal stood before the people and told them, with much hemming and hawing, that he thought they should stay in the valley permanently.

Everyone listened patiently without interrupting, although I saw the elders sitting together and shaking their heads, their

gray beards waving from side to side in perfect, stubborn unison.

Finally, Dal said, "And if you want Orion's words about it, he will be glad to tell you. He knows how the grain grows, and many other things that can help us."

Adena jumped to her feet. "Dal, we are not meant to stay in one place. This valley is prepared for us each year by our spirit-fathers. But how can they prepare it if we stay here watching all year long? Everyone knows the spirits don't do their work when people are watching. How can . . ."

That's as far as she got. An explosion of blood-curdling shrieks shattered the night air, and flames seemed to burst out all around us.

Everyone jumped every which way. A spear thudded into the ground near my feet. Screaming and yelling came from everywhere as the people of the tribes ran to their huts, terrified.

But not Dal. "They're burning the grain!" he roared.

I had seen them a moment before he had. Naked men. Warriors from another group, painted with hideous colors on their bodies and faces, throwing spears into the crowd around the campfire and using torches to burn the grain fields.

"Demons!" Adena screamed. And they did look inhuman, the way they were painted, with the firelight flickering off their glistening skins.

A spear whizzed past her head. A trio of the strange warriors dashed into one of the huts. Screams of pain came from inside.

"They're men," I bellowed. "They've come to kill us!"

Before I could even think about it, I was inside my own squallid hut, grabbing my bow and a handful of arrows. I could hear Dal shouting outside, and more of the tribe's people yelling. The first shock of panic was wearing off very quickly.

A painted warrior leaped into my hut. I floored him with a chop to the throat. Over his body I stepped, out into the flame-lit screaming confusion of battle. I notched an arrow and sent it into a warrior. Dal was beside Adena, the two of them battling with spears against four spear-wielding warriors. I knocked one off with an arrow just as Dal ripped a second through the belly with his spear. Adena went down on one knee but

spitted her opponent as he tried to jump on her. By that time I had put an arrow through the neck of the fourth warrior.

In the light of the blazing grain and the campfire, I saw several of our tribespeople on the ground. But there were more of us on our feet, fighting. The strangers were falling back now, throwing torches at our fighters to slow our pursuit.

I sent the last of my arrows after them. Adena gave the shrillest war cry I have ever heard and went charging into the night, straight into the retreating invaders. Dal was half a step behind her. I sprinted madly after the two of them.

They were plunging into a trap, I saw. The warriors who had attacked the village were backing away toward the grain fields, but crouched down there in the smoky shadows were still more warriors, waiting to spring the trap shut. Adena and Dal, with half a dozen of their tribe's young men, were rushing headlong into the trap.

I was coming up from a slightly different angle, and the crouched, waiting warriors didn't notice me for a moment.

That moment was enough. I raced at them. One of the waiting warriors finally saw me, turned, started to raise a warning shout as he pointed his spear at me. I saw it all as if in slow motion. My reflexes were in overdrive. None of them could move fast enough to escape me.

I took the front end of the warrior's spear in one hand and jerked it away from him. In the same motion I kicked him hard enough to send his nasal cartilage into the base of his brain, butted the end of the spear into the second man's windpipe, then swung the spear around to gut the third man in line. The others started to run, but I was on them and within seconds it was over.

I turned to see the other invaders in real flight now, as Dal and the other tribespeople chased after them, blood lust echoing in their victory cries. Adena, blood-smeared and triumphant, stood over the body of a dead warrior. Her gray eyes gleamed in the firelight. I wouldn't want to face her in a fight, no matter how fast my reflexes.

Then a movement in the shadows off to one side caught my attention. Another trap being organized? I moved toward the motion, noting that the fire in the grain field was already dying down, producing more smoke than flame. The grain was ripe and full of moisture; the rains had been light but consistent

enough to keep the grain from becoming tinder-dry.

I pursued the shadowy figure as he retreated. He was difficult to see through the wafting smoke. He seemed to blend in with the darkness.

As I got closer to him he abruptly stopped and turned to face me. I skidded to a halt a few feet in front of him.

Ahriman.

His hulking body loomed before me, his broad, heavy face lost in the shadows. But I could see the dying firelight flickering in his eyes.

"Yes," he whispered hoarsely. "Ahriman."

Before I could react I was knocked off my feet by a tremendous blow that racked every nerve in my body with excruciating pain. Darkness flooded over me.

When I came to, we were deep underground. A natural hiding place for the Dark One.

It was a cave of ice. Cold, glittering, translucent ice surrounded us. The floor and walls were smooth, polished blue-white. The ceiling, high above, was craggy with frozen stalactites. I could see my breath puffing from my open mouth, and I was shivering.

Ahriman was sitting at a curved metal desk that was studded with pushbuttons and control switches along its top. Viewscreens were fixed to the ice wall on one side of the cave. Beyond the desk, behind Ahriman's dark, brooding bulk, stood a dully gleaming metal canister, big enough to hold his body. Its top half was hinged open. Machinery and metal cylinders stood alongside it.

The viewscreens were blank, the machinery unattended. Ahriman sat silently in the massive chair behind his desk, studying me. He was as I had remembered him from fifteen thousands years later: skin the color of ashes, his hair also gray and cropped close around his broad skull, widely space cheekbones, flat nose, lipless mouth, and practically no chin at all. His eyes were red, as though inflamed with anger or pain or perhaps both. Heavy, sloping shoulders and thick, almost gorillalike body. Hands as large as my head, with short, blunt fingers.

He was wearing a skintight suit of metallic fiber, open at the throat. It glittered in the cave's soft lighting. I looked up but could see no lamps, just a glow that seemed to be coming from inside the ice.

"Bioluminescence," he said. His voice was a grating whisper.

I nodded, more to test the throbbing in my head than to agree with him. The pain was receding quickly. Cautiously, I tried shutting down on the pain signals altogether. It worked. I was in full command of my body.

"You recognized me, up there," Ahriman said.

"We have met before," I answered. I realized that I was sitting in a soft, comfortable chair, unfettered in any way. I could move my hands and feet freely. I must have looked rather odd, though: a grime-streaked, hide-covered, half-naked savage sitting in an ultramodern, high-technology office. In a cave of ice.

"When did we meet?" he asked.

"In the twentieth century . . . fifteen thousand years in the future from this time."

He almost smiled. "I see. I haven't been there yet. Obviously you are traveling backward through time to the war, while I am moving foward toward the End."

"But you know me," I said.

"Yes." His fingers clenched into fists. "We met almost half a million years ago, on the ice fields of a place called Vertzsallos."

"Is that when the War happened?"

He shook his massive head. "Earlier. Much earlier. Before the Ice Age."

"A million years ago."

"More or less."

"And you still fight on? You are alone, and yet you still won't let it rest?"

"Ormazd's people destroyed my race. That is why I am alone. That is why I can never let it rest."

I edged slightly forward in my seat. Ahriman noticed, and rested one of his heavy hands on a slim rod that lay on the desktop.

"You have felt the shock of the stunner already. If you try to move further off that chair you will feel it again."

I sat back and tried to relax. "Am I one of Ormazd's people?"

"Yes."

"And the tribe I'm living with?"

"Yes."

"The whole human race?"

"All of what you call *Homo sapiens sapiens*. They are all Ormazd's people."

"Then Ormazd himself is a human being."

"From far in the future. Yes. He is human . . ." And the Dark One made that word, *human*, sound like a curse.

"But what does Dal's tribe have to do with your vengeance? They can't harm you."

His smile was utterly mirthless. "Surely Ormazd has told you that I seek to alter the critical nexus points of human history. What else can one man alone do, when faced with the task of destroying a whole race . . . a whole universe, perhaps."

"But how can one small tribe of wandering hunters affect all of human history?"

"Don't take me for a fool. That tribe is about to make the change from hunting to agriculture. Oh, it will take many generations, of course, but the basic germ of the idea is already in Dal's head. Several other tribes have tried the same thing and failed. Others will try, in the future, and I will see to it that they fail. But this is the crucial point. This is the nexus . . . because Ormazd has sent you here to make certain that your race *does* make the transition from savagery to civilization. Your being here makes this the battleground."

I said nothing.

"If I stop Dal from keeping his tribe in that valley, then your race will never develop agriculture. Instead of going on to build cities and civilization, instead of going into your Neolithic population explosion, you will remain a small, scattered collection of hunting tribes. *With the instinct for war built into you.*"

He stressed that last sentence, savored it, hissed it at me as if it were a challenge.

"It will be an easy matter to get your bloodthirsty tribes to kill each other, given enough time. All I need to do is lead them into collision courses, where two tribes will bump into

each other. Your own savage instincts will do the rest for me."

"But the tribes don't always fight when they meet," I argued. "Just as often, they work together."

"Only when food is plentiful. It won't be if they don't develop agriculture. Already the hunters have thinned out the herds that they live on. Food will be scarce, I promise you."

"There are too many tribes for you to destroy them all. They're spread out all over the globe . . ."

"Not so." He seemed glad of the chance to tell me about it. "Your own ice glaciers have penned your tribes into a comparatively small area . . . here in the Caucasus, in eastern Asia, and in northern and equatorial Africa. No human foot has crossed the glaciers into the Western Hemisphere as yet. And none ever will."

"But they did. By my time the human race had covered the globe and expanded throughout the solar system . . . and out to the stars."

"Yes, but I can change that. I can destroy it, rip apart the structure of space and time. And I will do it right here and now."

"By stopping Dal's tribe . . ."

"His and the others. If I can prevent them from turning to agriculture, then I will have all the time in the world to kill off each of your wandering barbaric tribes. Think of it! Centuries, millennia, eons! It will be a long, delicious feast of killing."

I was listening to him with half my mind. The other half was calculating my chances for jumping at his throat before he could reach that stun-rod.

"In the end, when your primitive blood drinkers have destroyed each other, the wrenching of the time continuum will be so severe that the earth, the sun, the stars themselves will collapse in on themselves. A temporal black hole. At last."

I jumped for him. But the distance was too great. From the expectant leer on his dark face I realized that he had made the same calculation, and placed my chair just far enough away to give him a chance to grab the rod.

The pain was even worse this time. I blacked out.

I awoke to the sound of trickling water. I was resting on hard stone, in utter darkness. It took a long while before the buzzing in my head stopped, even though I exerted every effort to control my whole nervous system and shut off the pain.

When I tried to sit up I bumped my head on more rock. I was in a narrow cleft of stone, left there by Ahriman. Slowly moving my hands to either side, I felt a blank rock wall on my right, and an edge that dropped down into nothingness on my left.

Vision was useless. The trickling water came from overhead. Carefully, I turned over onto my stomach and felt down along the ledge as far as I could. No bottom. I dropped a loose pebble over the edge, then strained my ears to hear it hit something. Not a sound. With a larger rock I tried the same thing. After what seemed like an hour I heard a faint, faint splash. Water down there, far below.

I began crawling forward, not knowing if I were moving in the right direction. But there was nothing else to do.

For hours I inched along, blind as a mole, without knowing where I was heading. No light reached me. No sounds except my own breathing and, gradually, the far-off murmur of running water.

Then I realized the rock was getting warmer. It reminded me of the underground cell Ahriman had trapped me in the first time we had met. But this was a natural cave, not a bubble of trapped energy. The warmth was coming from a natural source. Maybe I was moving deeper underground, rather than toward daylight.

I stopped and tried to think it out. And got nowhere. Then I tried to put myself in Ahriman's place. What was he going to do?

Destroy Dal's tribe, came the answer.

How? I asked myself. The surprise attack by the other tribe had failed. Dal's people would be on guard now. Even Adena, stubborn as she was, would refuse to leave the valley as long as she felt somebody was trying to force them out. The attack would make Dal's people want to stay in their valley and defend it against invaders, that much I knew.

But Ahriman is no fool, I told myself. *He would have foreseen that.*

Then the purpose of the attack must have been to force the tribe to stay in the valley. But that didn't make sense—unless Ahriman was going to destroy the tribe and the valley together!

How? Earthquake? Could he control tectonic forces? I

didn't know. But the answer came to me soon enough: a loud slapping, sloshing noise from below me. A wave was surging through the underground river that flowed down there in the darkness.

"A flood," I said, my voice sounding strangely muffled against the close confines of the rock. "Underground heat to melt underground ice. The stream that runs through the valley will become a runaway flood. They'll never have a chance of getting out."

And neither would I. The water was lapping noisily below me, getting closer, rising up to drown me in this prison of rock.

Having died once, to be reborn, did not make me eager to die again. Ormazd was in control, I knew, but the more I learned about him and his powers, the more I realized his limitations. If he had unlimited power he could deal with Ahriman directly, without the need for me. He had the power to pull me through death and project me into another time and place—once. I had no confidence that he could or would do it again . . . or even that he knew where I was and what I faced.

So the choice before me was to wait for the water to rise up and engulf me or to plunge down into it. Time was vital. If I survived at all, it was important that I get to Dal and Adena to warn them of the flood.

I rolled over the edge of the rock ledge and dropped like one of my tossed stones toward the water. There was plenty of time for me to orient my body feet-downward, the best way to take a really long fall.

The water felt like cement when I finally hit it, and then I was plummeting deep, deep down in ice-black water, every nerve numbed and shocked, no sensory input except a bubbling in my ears.

I bobbed to the surface at last, took a deep, happy breath and half-swam, half-road the current wherever it was leading me. I noticed it was in the direction opposite to the one in which I had been crawling.

After what seemed like hours, my outstretched fingers touched solid rock in front of me. The river dipped into a deeper tunnel, where there was no airspace for me. I had no choice. I filled my lungs and then dove under, letting the current carry me along.

The oxygen in my lungs was soon exhausted, yet the river

still filled its underground tunnel. I began to squeeze oxygen from all the spare cells in my body, consciously shutting down whole muscle systems and organs that I didn't need, such as the digestive tract. I had to keep the circulatory system going and my brain alive. Everything else had to be sacrificed to that, no matter what the consequences.

Even so, I slowed down my heartbeat and turned myself into a virtual catatonic trance state, passively flowing down the underground river. It seemed like months. But finally the darkness around me began to brighten and I floated to the surface of the river.

Air! Real, breathable air. It tasted wonderful.

The river was emptying into a huge cave, turning it into a vast underground cistern. I dragged myself up onto dry ground, every part of my body jangling from lack of circulation. Sunlight filtered through an opening far overhead, I felt too weak to reach it.

For a while there was nothing I could do but lay there on the pebbly dirt and try to recover my strength. Gradually, I forced myself to climb up toward the opening and the daylight.

Once there, I saw that it was a narrow fissure of rock that lay behind one of the drops in the outside stream's many-tiered waterfall. Looking down behind me, I saw that the underground river was filling up the cave I was in, and when it had reached the brim, where I now stood, it would suddenly gush out with a tidal wave of water that would sweep everything in the valley before it.

I staggered out of the cave. The waterfall knocked me to my knees. I crawled over to the edge of the gentle stream, too weak to get to my feet again. Through blurring eyes I saw the valley spread out below me, beautiful, peaceful, vulnerable. I had to get down there to warn them, but I could barely move.

"Look!" came a shout from above and behind me. "It's Orion!"

"He's come back from the dead!"

I blacked out.

Adena's taut, lovely face was staring at me when I opened my eyes again.

"You are alive," she said gravely.

"Yes." My voice was normal. I felt strong again. I glanced toward the doorway of the hut we were in, its only opening. Outside the pink light of dawn was just starting to show.

"Where's Dal? We've got to get out of this valley . . ." I sat up, despite her attempts to push me back onto the pallet of leaves.

She told me swiftly that Dal had been wounded in the final skirmish of the battle, two nights earlier. A rock-tipped spear had gashed his thigh. Nothing serious, but he could not walk until it was healed. *Infection*, I thought, realizing that Adena's primitive medicines were all that we could do for him.

I got up and pushed past her, walking out of the hut. In the early light, I could see that the stream was already broader, noisier, moving faster through the valley. The underground cistern had not yet overflowed, but it could only be a matter of hours now. Far off in the distance I heard a rumble and felt the ground tremble. *Volcano*.

Adena was beside me, and the whole tribe was gathering around me, staring with wide-eyed awe.

It quickly became clear that when I disappeared after the battle, they assumed I had been killed and taken away by spirits. With Dal wounded and me gone, Adena became the tribe's natural leader. She posted lookouts at the top of the waterfall, the only easy access into the valley, to warn the tribes below of any more attempts to invade the valley and raid us.

The lookouts had seen me emerge from behind the waterfall, from inside the rock, from the netherworld, underground. In the awe-filled eyes of these people, I had returned from the dead. They didn't know whether to kneel at my feet or run away from me.

A couple of young men brought Dal out from his hut. His right upper thigh was swathed with leaves bound by thongs and smeared with a gummy-looking poultice. People from the other tribes began to gather around, under the heavy, cloud-laden sky, gaping and staring at me.

"Dal . . . Adena," I said, ignoring the others. "We must leave this valley. Now."

Dal looked bewildered, Adena merely curious.

"Leave? Why? What is . . ."

A roar of thunder shook the ground. But it didn't come from the sky. Angry red flashed on the horizon to the south and west. A volcano was smoldering, preparing to erupt. Ahriman was flexing his muscles.

"Everything in this valley is going to be destroyed," I told them. "There will be a flood that will sweep everything away."

Dal frowned at me. "But the stream has never . . ."

"It will now. We must get out of this valley quickly, before it becomes a deathtrap."

"Up the waterfall steps," Adena said.

"No," I answered. "That's where the flood will start. We'll have to go up the cliffs at the far end of the valley."

Now she looked shocked. "No one can climb those cliffs."

"We can. We must."

Dal looked down at his injured leg. "I can't."

"You will," I said.

They stood there, wavering, uncertain. I raised my voice to the whole crowd of pressing, staring people.

"We are going to leave the valley," I shouted, making my voice as firm and commanding as possible. It echoed off the hillside walls.

The people stirred. They looked at each other, but said nothing. They did not move away.

I pointed toward the stream and warned them of the flood to come. I gestured toward the sullen, red glow on the horizon, where the volcano was still growling. But it was Adena who finally moved them.

"Do as Orion commands," she shouted at last. "He has been in the land of the dead, under the ground, and has returned to warn us. Do not anger him or the spirits of the dead by failing to obey."

This was something they could understand. They started heading for their huts to gather their few meager possessions.

"Wait!" Dal shouted, wincing with pain. "Every man and woman who has worked in the fields to gather grains and roots and berries . . . every one of you take seedlings and fruits. Take a sample of every kind of grain, every fruit, every root and berry and leafy plant. Bring them with you! Carry them along with you, and wherever we go, we will have them to put into the soil. We will make them grow in our new home."

It was my turn to stare. The man had just invented agri-

culture. And I smiled as I realized how these events would be distorted, over the centuries, into mythology.

All that morning the people worked as they had never worked before. The volcano's rumblings frightened them, the sky turned black and deadly, with flashes of lightning to scare them even more. Adena set a team of shaky young men at the base of the waterfall, to make certain no one panicked and tried to get away from the valley in that direction. The waterfall was obviously getting stronger, starting to roar and drown the terraced rocks where it had formerly splashed gently. The stream was rising as it coursed through the valley.

Under Dal's limping direction, most of the people were bent over the crops in the valley floor, gathering seedlings and plantlings.

I led a group of teenagers, the wiriest and most agile youngsters in the valley, to the tough cliff face at the far end of the valley. We scrambled up to the top, roped together like alpinists. Once there, we set up a crude systems of pulleys, using vines and trees. We lowered ourselves down again and signaled that we were ready to start moving people to safety.

Dal and Adena began hustling the people toward us, and we helped them climb, scrabble, grope, inch their way up to the top of the cliff. The elders and the pregnant women got vines slipped under their shoulders and a pair of sturdy, grinning teenagers to help them up to safety. Babies rode on peoples' backs.

We were no more than halfway through the job when the flood burst upon the valley.

The waterfall simply exploded in a mammoth shower of water and steam, hurling rocks halfway down the valley. The cistern had not only reached its overflow point, but heat from the tectonic forces that Ahriman was manipulating had brought the water close to the boiling point.

A wall of white water gushed down the valley, roaring like all the demons of hell let loose at once. Steam hissed off into the dark sky and a hot rain began to fall on us.

The people froze in terror, watching the all-consuming wave hurtle toward us.

"Move, move, move!" I screamed, pushing them up the first few scrabbling steps of the cliff.

They jerked into frantic life, more than a hundred men,

·PCR·

women, and children climbing for their lives. I helped them, Adena and the teenagers helped them. Everyone was scratching his or her way up the face of the rocky cliff. More youngsters were scrambling down from the top, risking their lives without a moment's thought to help the others.

The flood surged toward us, frothing angrily. In glimpses over my shoulder I saw it swirl through the huts of our little village, drown all the grain fields, and reach white, growling fingers closer and closer toward us.

The volcano erupted and the ground shook hard enough to knock people loose from their perches on the cliff wall. They fell, bones broke. There was nothing we could do for them. Now screams of agony and terror were added to the roars of the flood and the volcano.

I found myself at the top, racing along the lip of the cliff, helping people scramble over the edge to safety. The hot rain soaked us all and turned the rock to slippery goo. We fell, we splashed, we struggled, we got up and fell again. But we pulled people to safety. We scrambled and slid partway down the cliff to grab those who couldn't make it on their own and helped them up.

Then I saw Dal, standing alone at the base of the cliff, watching us help the last of the stragglers, his face set into a stubborn mask of self-control. He neither frowned nor shouted for help. He leaned on a gnarled spear shaft, his injured leg resting stiffly against it and watched his people reach safety. Behind him, the raging hot waters of the flood roared and bubbled closer, closer.

With a yell, I grabbed a vine and literally jumped over the cliff's edge. Adena and a couple of the fastest-thinking, quickest-moving teenagers grabbed the end of the vine that was knotted to a young tree and held it tightly for me.

I was halfway down the cliff face when the flood waves smashed into Dal and knocked him sprawling against the rock wall. I let go of the vine and dived into the angry, hissing water after him. The water was frothing hot, almost boiling. It scalded, it blistered me. I automatically turned off the pain receptors in my brain and made a grab for Dal's unconscious body.

I reached him, then swam and pushed myself along the rocks to the loop of vine that the others were dangling from

above. Adena had dropped partway down the rock wall, her hands gripping the lifeline, her face tight with determination.

I got Dal's shoulders through the vine loop as the water roared and bubbled around me. Steam clouded my vision. I felt, rather than saw, Dal's body being hoisted up and away to safety.

The boiling-hot water was dragging me under. All my strength was gone. My last conscious sight was a glimpse of someone standing on a rock in the middle of the flood, heavy arms folded across massive chest, glowering darkly at me: Ahriman.

We've beaten you again, I said to him silently. But I knew there would be another meeting, another time. He still lived, and I would have to live again.

The water surged up and over me. I gave way to pain and death.

KAMUS 2

J. MICHAEL REAVES

THE MALTESE VULCAN

STEPHEN HICKMAN

THE MALTESE VULCAN
A Kamus of Kadizhar Mystery
by J. Michael Reaves

1

Stam, the high priest of the starship *Yith'il*, was annoyed with me. "I am not used to waiting," he said—or rather, the intercom over my head said. I was sitting on a folding seat in a clear oval bubble. The bubble floated in a tankful of murky water, as did Stam. Stam looked like a large, brownish-yellow barbell with two half-flaccid sacs, the smaller containing brain and sensory organs, the larger containing everything else. Three tentacles radiated from the headsac, with a sphincter mouth centered at their base. One tentacle had a prehensible tip and suckers, one was bifurcated to provide an opposable grip, and one had a serrated chitinous claw like a lobster's chela on its end. His eyes were at the ends of a Y-shaped stalk that sprouted above the tentacles.

The murky tank was his private quarters aboard the *Yith'il*, a ship that looked like a fish bowl with tachyonic thrusters. It was compartmentalized by milky crystal walls, and filled with water. Stam's quarters were furnished somewhat better than my room above the Demon's Dance Tavern in Mariyad: a few slimy rocks, some strands of kelp, and a couple of irridescent crab-creatures thrown in for atmosphere. On a rock beside Stam was a control console consisting of several glowing, shell-shaped objects. Occasionally the cephalopod would fondle one with his bifurcated tentacle and the shell would ripple through various colors.

The water was murky because Stam communicated by releasing clouds of ink in various patterns, which were translated into words for me. The patterns that meant he was not happy about waiting were being dispersed by the circulating pump. When they were gone, I said, "I came as soon as I got your call. Security's tight around the Spaceport today; they almost didn't let me on board. Now that I'm here, what can I do for you?"

Stam tickled one of the shells, and a curtain of kelp parted to reveal an inset screen. It lit up with an image that was some-

what distorted by the currents in the chamber; a lean, muscular humanoid about two meters tall, wearing a pair of green trunks. He stood with his arms crossed in a regal pose that was about as unselfconscious as a Darkling learning to knit. Stam turned one eye toward the picture and kept the other on me. More ink stained the water, and the translated words were hushed and reverent. "This," the cephalopod said, "is my god."

A snappy comeback to that seemed inappropriate, so I kept quiet.

Stam stroked the shell again and the picture dissolved into a closeup. The face was lean and aristocratic, with arched cheekbones and even more highly arched eyebrows. He had a widow's peak of blue-black hair that shone like wet fur, and pointed ears. He was amphibious; I could see parallel slits of gills in both sides of his neck, under the jawline. His expression was supercilious, but there was also danger in it. I wouldn't want to meet him in a dark alley. Or on a lighted boulevard.

"You will meet him soon," Stam said. "He is Taqwatkh, the Bringer of Lightning, the Glorious Redemption. It is for him that the Spaceport security has been increased—for reasons which need not concern you, our god has found it necessary to leave our world and grace the Unity of Planets with his presence."

"Great," I said. "And how do I fit in?"

"We have a layover of three days before conditions will be right for tachyonic transposition to Centrex, the Unity homeworld. During this time, I have reason to believe that there will be an assassination attempt on Taqwatkh. I want you to help protect him."

One thing about being the only private eye on the planet—I get all the cases, big and small. This one didn't sound small. Before I could ask questions, however, Stam said, "You must prepare to meet Divinity; Taqwatkh will return soon," and reached for his shells again.

"Wait a minute," I said. "I haven't decided whether or not I'll take the case."

Stam's totally nonhuman face somehow managed to look shocked. "There is no question! Taqwatkh needs protection! He is the Bringer of Lightning, the Glorious—"

"I remember," I said. "But with all due respect, he's not *my*

Bringer of Lightning. And if I'm going to help protect him, I'll have to know a lot more than you've told me so far."

Stam twisted his tentacles into knots. "It was only with the greatest difficulty that I convinced Taqwatkh of your necessity. It is not meet that I should discuss sacred things with an Outworlder and a human."

I didn't mention that I wasn't entirely human. "It's also not meet that I should take a case blindfolded." I watched my words puff like smoke signals of ink from the translator. "Why don't I make it easy on you? I'll tell you what I know—which isn't much—and you can fill in the blanks. I know that you come from a planet called Malta II by its colonists. I've heard that there's been some conflict between the colonists and the cephalopods, and I assume the assassination threat has to do with that. Now I'll ask some questions."

"I could be defenestrated and boiled alive if Taqwatkh learns how I am overstepping my authority."

I folded my arms. "If you want me to work for you, I need facts. Do you fear assassination from the Earth colonists?"

Stam's body rippled nervously. "Yes. The colonists, who inhabit the many archipelagos of our ocean world are members of an old Earthly religious sect known as the Knights of Malta, or Knights Hospitalers. They are best known now for their advances in biology and genetics, but they are also a fanatically religious group. They have made several attempts to convert us by force to Christianity. Since they are colonists from a Unity planet, Taqwatkh is going to Centrex to protest. I believe some of the Knights are fanatical enough to attempt to kill him to prevent this."

"If he's a god, why does he need my protection?"

"Do not confuse our god with theirs, or yours. Our god has the ability to cast bolts of power, to teleport, and to lift great weights, but he is not omnipotent. Like some ancient Earthly gods, he has foibles and faults. Nevertheless, he is our redemption."

I decided never to argue theology with an intelligent octopus. "What makes you think they'll try something while you're on Ja-Lur?"

"While we were landing, a message from Malta II was broadcast to a personal receiver somewhere in the Spaceport. Security personnel were unable to locate the receiver, though

everyone was searched thoroughly. The message was: 'The Vulcan has landed.' "

That meant nothing to me. "So?"

"Vulcan is the name of an ancient Earth deity, a mythological god of fire who forged thunderbolts. I believe it is a code word chosen by the Maltese to describe Taqwatkh and to alert the assassin. We cannot take chances."

"I still don't understand why you need me. Aren't the combined security of the Spaceport and your own personnel enough to—"

"But Taqwatkh refuses to remain on board! He insists on entering Mariyad to pay periodic visits to one Apolgar Zad, a local chemist. For this he should have the protection of someone who knows Mariyad. He refuses to take any guards with him—he leaves the ship incognito."

"I get it. When does he make these little excursions?"

"Usually in the afternoons—he has just left, in fact. You may name your price to protect him."

That did a lot to influence my decision. I was wary of taking this case—if anything happened to this Taqwatkh while he was on the Darkworld, it could cause a serious diplomatic crisis. It wasn't the first potential worldbreaker I had handled, however; if I did it once, I told myself, I could do it again.

"You've got a deal," I said.

Stam unwound his tentacles with a snap that rocked my bubble. "Excellent!" he said. "Now you must meet arrgghhh . . ."

"Who?" I asked. Stam said nothing. His ink slowly dispersed in the current. His eyes stared, and his tentacles floated loosely. From somewhere behind his headsac, red streams began to streak and stain the black clouds.

I pressed the Emergency button.

* * *

Stam was not dead. He had been given a near-fatal dose of niotrinaline, a chemical which caused brain damage in Maltese cephalopods. The blood I had seen came from a burst artery in his headsac. How the niotrinaline had been added to the water filter of Stam's quarters was the subject of considerable controversy over the next few hours. I was cleared of any suspi-

cion immediately; I had been in a bubble of unbreakable plastic, constantly monitored by an automatic life-support.

The doctors at the Spaceport infirmary said Stam would remain in a coma for several days, but, barring complications, he would live. I left the infirmary intending to return to the *Yith'il* and wait for Taqwatkh's return. Though my client was in a coma, I still felt I was on the case, and I wanted to talk to Taqwatkh. His absence during his high priest's mysterious malady had put the entire Spaceport in an uproar. I was on my way back to the ship when Taqwatkh saved me the trouble of waiting for him; as I stepped out of the lift tube toward the slidewalk, something uncomfortably like a small bolt of lightning scorched the pavement too near my feet. I reached to my belt for a sword that was still at the weaponcheck counter as I whirled around. Standing at the top of a ramp was Taqwatkh, who had just proved he deserved his first title. He descended the ramp like a parade and stopped in front of me, arms folded.

"Very impressive," I said. "Is that your whole act?"

He let a sneer lift his lip. "You are Kamus of Kadizhar," he told me.

"That's amazing. Now try this one: I'm thinking of a number between—"

He grabbed the front of my tunic and suddenly I was dangling in the air at the end of an arm like a steel beam. "I will not have this," he said between his teeth.

"Neither will I." I grabbed his arm and swung my legs to the side, then jackknifed them above his head. My tunic ripped, but the unexpected movement overbalanced him, as I had hoped it would; he was incredibly strong, but his mass was little more than mine. We landed in a heap, and I was up first. I was saved from dismemberment by a security team, who respectfully restrained Taqwatkh.

He gestured imperiously and they released him. He had the power of command, no doubt about that; it radiated from him. The security team, who had been hunting for him, now melted back, looked about nervously, and quickly found something else to do. I noticed that several of the team were Mariyad guardsmen, part of a cultural exchange program, according to their badges.

After they left, Taqwatkh said to me, "I will control my

temper,'" in a voice quiet as ten sandcats after a large meal.

"Good of you."

He gave me a look that made me feel like a child with a runaway mouth. He did have power—I could feel the inner strength and confidence, and it almost had me shifting my feet uncomfortably. I kept my eyes on his.

"Stam hired you to protect me," he said. "I tell you that this will not be necessary. I am Taqwatkh. If a god cannot protect himself, he does not deserve the title."

I replied, "Stam hired me with your best interests in mind. The Darkworld isn't a member of the Unity of Planets yet; once you leave the Spaceport, you leave the Unity's protection. Mariyad can be a dangerous city, and a lot of its people don't like Outworlders. I think you could use someone who knows the streets." And I could use that blank check Stam had promised me.

"I am a god," he said slowly. His flat expression could have been painted on his face.

"I'll argue with that later," I said. "Your own high priest admitted you're not omnipotent."

He took a deep, ominious breath. "It is not for my subjects to question my motives, intentions, or whims; I am absolute. How then should an Outworlder and an alien dictate to me? Stam was mistaken. You are not needed."

"Stam is in the infirmary," I reminded him. "Aren't you interested in learning who put him there? I am."

"You—are—not—needed," Taqwatkh repeated. "That is all." He made a slicing gesture with his hand, and teleported away from me. It was the first time I had ever seen it done without the aid of a transposition arch, and it was impressive. He vanished like an edited frame in an old-time movie and simultaneously reappeared at the top of the ramp. It would have been more impressive if he had teleported further than ten meters, and if he hadn't stumbled slightly upon reappearing. He walked away without looking back.

Religions on Ja-Lur include polytheism, monotheism, pantheism, and deism. Many worship the Darklord as a god, but there are also plenty of anthropomorphized animals, masochistic martyrs, and elevated ancestors. Some of the more esoteric deities include Rumulund, the earth god of Rool, best described as forty acres of living land, and Skalos, the spider

god of Niax—every world has at least one spider god.

But I had never thought of any of them as "gods," even though most tried to control the destiny of as many mortals as they could. Although I was a half-breed Darklander with limited supernatural powers, I had a scientific explanation of it all. They weren't "gods." None were. Other universes overlapped ours in places, and they ran by different natural laws—"magic" to us. The "gods" of Ja-Lur and elsewhere were, in my opinion, just other-universal entrepeneurs. But Taqwatkh did not fit even that liberal definition. He was only a humanoid, with limited powers probably no greater than mine. Yet I scrambled for a living providing fixed duels and poisoned goblets, while he was the absolute ruler of a world. Not that I felt like an underachiever; I was satisfied with my life. Usually, anyway. As far as I could see, the only thing that had put Taqwatkh in his position was his powerful personality, and I couldn't even be sure it was that—what was impressive to me might be laughable to a cephalopod. I wondered how Taqwatkh had managed to be the "god" of a species different from himself. Not that it was unusual—most "gods" on Ja-Lur were nonhuman, there was the Cthulhu cult on Earth, and so forth. But I was curious as to how it had happened. I watched Taqwatkh returning to his ship and admitted to myself that I was fascinated by him and his position, though I was less than enchanted with him personally. I wanted to learn more about the Maltese cephalopods and the man they called their god. I also wanted to know who had tried to assassinate Stam, and why. But it didn't look like I would be doing any of these things. Taqwatkh had just taken me off the case.

2

I met Lohvia of House Zad on the afternoon of the next day. The sun was a dark brass smear that could be stared at for minutes without blinking. Shadows were blurred at the edges and black in their hearts. A few stars still glimmered around the edges of the indigo sky. All in all, it was a bright, clear day.

I was walking through the wealthier part of Mariyad, along Taafite Street. Behind low, wide walls broken by ornate gates, beyond cropped grass and sculpted shrubbery were the manses

of shipowners, generals, and statesmen. Even the air was sweeter here, laced with salt from the sea breezes that washed the soot and smoke toward the poorer parts of the city.

There were a few people on the street; noblefolk who walked with the rustle of silk and satin instead of the scrape of coarse cotton and leather. The men wore court daggers slightly larger than nail files and looked uneasily at my sword. I seldom passed through this part of Mariyad. I stopped even less seldom. But I had a reason for being here today. Out of curiosity, and because I had nothing better to do, I had decided to take a look at the house of one Apolgar Zad.

The address surprised me—chemists and apothecaries seldom make the kind of money Taafite Street demanded. When I saw the place, I was even more surprised. The building was in an awkward stage between house and castle, and had more wings than a flock of bloodbirds. Any room in any of the sections would be twice the size of my office. Gables and peaks made the whole thing look like a mountain range with windows.

As I approached the open gate I heard the faint melody of a lute. I stopped just inside the grounds and watched. A woman with long, bright hair was leaning from a window in one wing, listening to a minstrel who sat crosslegged on the grass beneath her. He was a tall, thin lad, on the edge of gangliness, dressed in black and gray. He had a pleasant peasant face, much too full of innocence. He was not singing, only playing light and cheerful notes. As I watched, he bounced to his feet and began skillfully pantomiming a story, using his hands and still keeping the tune on his lute. The lady above smiled at him and clapped her hands, though there was a slightly worried look on her face. Still, it was a nice, pastoral scene, and those don't come often to a private eye. I couldn't tell what story the minstrel was miming, though it seemed to have something to do with Mondrogan the Clever, a legendary hero also supposed to have been a half-breed Darklander, ages ago.

I'd had my look at Apolgar Zad's mountainous mansion, and so I turned to head back to my office on the edge of Thieves' Maze. But just then a heavy oaken door bound with iron opened directly below the window. It didn't open slowly, for all its weight; it flew wide open and smashed against the gray wall, drowning out the minstrel's lute. A small, wiry man

in green tunic and leggings ran out. He had a flying kragor emblazoned on his cuirass. He was slightly over one meter tall, but seemed built of pure fury. He reached the minstrel in three long steps, wrapped a fist in the baggy gray blouse, and lifted him completely into the air. The woman in the window above screamed. The lad, balanced on the small man's fist, kicked and waved, trying to brain his attacker with the lute. The small man seized and crushed it in his free hand.

About this time, I noticed that I was running across the grass toward them. I knew it wasn't a bright move. I didn't need the symbol on his green uniform to tell me that the man was one of Mariyad's elite Flying Guards; his size and strength were clues enough. He was capable of bending my sword into a plowshare, or around my neck. My only chance against him would be to try a spell and hope it worked, but I couldn't do that with witnesses about. I realized all this, but still I ran. I knew how it felt to hang like laundry from someone's upheld fist, and I suspected that the minstrel didn't like it any more than I had.

The Flyer saw me coming, and whatever mayhem he planned was suspended, along with the minstrel. The lady stopped screaming. I came to a stop before them. Everyone waited to see what I would do, including myself.

I didn't draw sword—one of the few smart ideas in me this morning. I expected to see the Flyer's arm begin to tremble—not even a Flying Guard can hold a man heavier than his own weight one-handed in the air for more than a few minutes. But the Flyer's arm remained as stiff as a Guardsman on a three-day leave.

"Why not let him live to learn from his error?" I suggested. "He's only a boy."

The Flyer looked at me and smiled unpleasantly. Then, instead of lowering the minstrel, he simply opened his fist and let him drop, heavily, completing the destruction of his lute. During all of this the lad had remained silent.

The small man somehow managed to look down at me, though his eyes were level with my chest. His expression was two parts anger and one part disdain, but I had been stared down by an expert yesterday; I wasn't bothered. He was as lean as dried meat, this Flyer, with eyes like hot, black cinders. Tension showed in every tight muscle; even his hair seemed

clenched, in tiny black curls.

"Who are you?" he asked.

"Kamus of Kadizhar. I'm an investigative mercenary."

The Flyer nodded. "I've heard of you. The fool who charges a fee to mind other peoples' affairs."

"I wouldn't describe it quite that way . . . let's just say I'm a music lover."

"So am I," retorted the Flyer.

"I liked his playing, before you broke his lute," I went on doggedly. "Why not let me take him to some street corner where people have a poorer taste in tunes?"

"Why should I not kill him? I think it would be a favor to the world of music." He was one of those who won't let go of a joke after snagging it by accident. I was spared any further variations on the theme by the appearance in the doorway of the lady from the window.

"You won't kill him, Xidon," she said. Her words fell on him like stones, and he suddenly looked his height again.

This was my first good look at her. She was an impressive woman; tall and thin, with hair long and full enough to make her blue lace gown seem almost superfluous. A brooch about her neck held the three horns of a tricorn snake against a dark background. Her face was the sort that gives itself fully to whatever emotion possesses it. Such a face can be as smooth and pale and hard as frozen milk, and does its most harm that way.

She reminded me of someone I had known.

Xidon's fury melted like bogmist. He tried to recapture the scene by pointing indignantly at the minstrel, who now sat sadly inspecting the wreckage of his lute, and saying, "Lohvia, the squawling of this begpenny—"

"At the moment," Lohvia said coldly, "he carries much more favor with me than you do." I winced—I couldn't think of a better way to see the poor lad pounded into pemmican. But the Flyer was beaten by now. He said pleadingly, "He should at least learn to play decently before—"

"Leave, Xidon—you're only making matters worse."

His jaw snapped shut and he turned away from her, raked the minstrel with a look that should have left scars, and, ignoring me, pulled a whistle from his beltpouch and blew.

"Your father must hear of your indiscretion," he told her. By that I assumed she was Apolgar Zad's daughter.

"And your commander of yours," she replied, sweetly. The Flyer's hard brown face drained of all expression then, and became an earth-colored mask. Any further words were cut short by the arrival of his kragor, which landed with an explosion of wind that tore at the grass and bushes. Xidon put one hand on the saddle pommel and gave me a look that belonged in a furnace. I was still smiling—now didn't seem like a good time to stop. He vaulted into the saddle and shouted, "Ho!" The kragor lashed its barbed tail, sprang from the ground, caught air beneath his wings, and hurtled away in thunder. In a moment it had vanished into the soot-dark sky; Xidon had at least managed a dramatic exit.

Lohvia paid no attention to his departure. Instead, she went to kneel beside the minstrel.

The lad held his shattered instrument, his lower lip trembling. Lohvia spoke soothingly to him. "I can give you money for a new lute, Niano," she said. "I feel responsible for what happened." He looked at her with a flash of indignation in his eyes, then touched her cheek with the tips of his slender fingers and shook his head.

I watched Lohvia's movements and mannerisms, and remembered someone else.

Niano stood, clutching the remains of the lute. He offered me a grip that was weak, but firm and cool. I said, "Xidon won't forget." It would do no harm for him to be wary. He pointed to himself, then to the sky, and shook his head. He did not intend to forget Xidon, either.

I watched him leave, and decided that I respected Niano. The fact that he was a minstrel did not impress me in itself. The cobbled streets and roaring taverns of Mariyad have always been filled with itinerant singers and poets grubbing a meal for a song or story. Some of them are good; most think they are. Nearly all lead a starveling, hand-over-lute existence, sleeping with vermin more often than with each other. But that never stops new romantics from taking to the road with their songs, usually to die of malnutrition or other stomach disorders, such as swordthrust. Niano was a romantic to the core; that I could tell. But what really impressed me was that he had become a minstrel despite the considerable setback of being mute.

"He plays beautifully," Lohvia said, more to herself than to

me. "He mimes the legends of Mondrogan the Clever with such verve and expertise that words are not necessary." The tone of her voice said that she was in love with this voiceless vagrant, just as Xidon was obviously taken with her. A pretty triangle: no one could have anybody. I was sure Apolgar Zad would as soon see Lohvia wed a Darklander as a penniless minstrel. And Xidon was forbidden by law to marry outside his race. For centuries the Flying Guards were bred selectively to produce a race light and strong enough to ride and control the kragors. He had less chance of her hand than Niano.

I watched her watching Niano, and I tried to decide what it was about her that reminded me so strongly of Thea Morn, an Earthwoman I had once known and loved. Thea had also been tall and blonde, but there the resemblance ended. In subtle ways, however, Lohvia reminded me of her.

It had been a while since I had closely inspected my feelings about Thea's memory, and it was something of a shock to realize that she had been dead long enough now for me to feel only a quiet sadness and, as I watched Lohvia, a kind of enjoyable nostalgia. Part of me was glad that it had finally come to that, and part of me regretted the loss of pain.

Lohvia interrupted my thoughts by turning to me. "Thank you for stopping Xidon," she said. "I'd like to do something to repay you, Kamus."

"You can," I told her. "Invite me in for a few minutes' talk."

She hesitated, then smiled and nodded. She led me inside and into a sitting room hung with tapestries that must have used up five generations of weavers. I wasn't completely sure why I wanted to talk with her, but my reasons had nothing to do with Taqwatkh's visits to her father. I asked her to tell me about herself, and settled back to listen. Lohvia was in her middle twenties, bored with being a rich merchant's daughter and fascinated by the carefree, footloose life she imagined Niano led, which was about what I had expected to hear. I watched her talking, the way she lifted her chin when happy and quirked her lips when exasperated. I listened more to the tone of her voice than her words, and remembered . . .

When a limited cultural exchange program was announced between Earth and Ja-Lur five years ago, I had put in my application along with thousands of others, not really expect-

ing to be one of the few chosen. I had no idea why I was granted a visa—the qualifications were complicated and secret, requiring approval by a quorum of Lords and Overlords, and, according to rumor, the Darklord himself.

While on Earth I traveled, attended special acculturation classes at the finest universities, and in general experienced the luxuries and pains of an advanced civilization. I had to have genetic adjustments to shrink my pupils and protect my skin from the powerful sunlight, but other than that I fit in well on Earth. They had cleaned up the cities a century before, and solar power supplied the population of three billion with everything they needed. It was so peaceful that it didn't take long for me to become bored, and I passed my time reading books about Earth's past. The late nineteenth and early twentieth centuries seemed much more alive and interesting times than the present.

"Of course," Lohvia was saying, "I realize it would be a radical change in my lifestyle to marry Niano. But I think I'm adaptable enough. And he has enough talent to be the court minstrel of Overlord Kirven . . ."

I had met Thea at a luxurious resort in the Iberian States. I asked her if she came here often and she said she owned the resort. Like Lohvia, she was the daughter of a rich man. Thea's father, Strangland Morn, Chairman of the Board of Directors of Intrasolar I.T.A.T.&T., had more millions than the Maze had roaches; it was literally impossible to spend them all. Before he died in a spaceship collision, he had bought each of his seven children thousands of incredibly expensive gifts, including terriformed planetoids complete with gravity generators.

Thea did not hate being rich—she loved it, and although she gave most of her money away to charities, her extravagances were still enough to make me lean heavily toward socialism. Despite my aversion to her unearned wealth, however, I loved her. And she loved me. Her big mistake was trying to show it with money; she spent more on me than the Gross Planetary Product of Centauri IV. We would have breakfast on Luna, brunch on Mars, tiffin on Titan, and dinner on Halley's Comet. Finally, guilt made me call a halt to the high living. I was beginning to feel like a gigolo. I told Thea I wanted to go back to Ja-Lur, to try making it on my own as a private eye.

"I'd be willing to give up my fortune," Lohvia said. "It doesn't mean anything to me. If Niano doesn't become court minstrel, I'd try living on the streets with him . . ."

That was what Thea had told me. She even proposed a trial period for us of roughing it in a dangerous prehistoric wildlife preserve on her planetoid, to see if she could stand the primitive life. She endured the danger and the dirt for two days; then, after a tearful confession that she couldn't take it and didn't want to hold me back, she ran into the Transportal and teleported back to her automated castle on top of the planetoid's highest mountain. I tried to follow her, but the Transportal wouldn't work, leaving me to hike through twenty miles full of saber-tooth tigers, tyrannosauri, and other genetic backbreeds.

"I love him," Lohvia told me, her eyes shining. "And he loves me. So nothing can separate us. Nothing."

When I got back to the castle, I found Thea lying dead before the Transportal. There wasn't a mark on her—evidently a Portal's malfunction had killed her in transit. I carried her up to the highest bedroom tower, which overlooked half the planetoid and strapped her in the bed. Then I put on an air-suit, went down to the underground control complex, and shut off the gravity generators. Instantly the atmosphere, rivers, forests and lakes, exploded into space, forming a beautiful ring of ice around the planetoid. The castle's foundations shook with the quakes, but held. I went back and looked at Thea, now a frozen beauty who would sleep forever in her airless castle. Then I flew back to Earth, caught a spaceship for Ja-Lur the next day, and tried to forget the pain and still remember Thea. It seemed I'd finally begun to . . .

. . . I realized that Lohvia had asked me a question and was waiting politely for an answer. I smiled while replaying the part of my mind that had been listening to her.

"Yes," I replied, "I think true love is a wonderful thing. It happens about as often as a snake wears sandals, but when it does, it's always worth waiting for."

"That's exactly how I feel," she said breathlessly. "And I'm seriously considering running away with Niano. What do you think of that?"

She was everything that age hates youth for: vibrant, innocent, and almost bursting with love. I thought of Niano's per-

formance for her, and the look on her face as she had watched him leaving. They would make quite a couple. I realized I wanted to see in their happiness an echo of what I had had briefly with Thea, but I didn't want to encourage Lohvia to do something that would change her whole life just because it had almost worked for someone else. But wouldn't it be better for her to take such a chance—what could she learn about life, protected in this mansion? I opened my mouth, not sure what I was going to say—and was saved by a young slave woman who entered through some drapes the size of stage curtains. She bowed and said, "You have a visitor, Milady."

"Yes, I do, Janya," Lohvia snapped. "He sits beside me now." She waved her fingers in dismissal, but the slave didn't leave. Instead, she said, "Your pardon, Milady, but there are visitors and visitors, if you take my meaning."

Lohvia turned and stared at her, and all of a sudden she was nervous. She nodded quickly, then turned to me and said, "It seems I must play protocol for a moment, Kamus; please excuse me," and was up in a swirl of silk and out of the room, her thin pale fingers combing at her hair as she left.

The slave—a small lady with brown hair and an almost childish figure—looked at me coolly for a moment, then turned and followed Lohvia.

I leaned back on a couch soft enough to swim in and put my feet on the rim of a plant pot the size of a well. Luxurious as the place was, it couldn't hold a taper to the least of Thea's many mansions. By Darkworld standards, however, it was almost as impressive as Overlord Kirven's palace. I started to wonder about Apolgar Zad—he was obviously an important man in Mariyad, and according to Stam, he had dealings with the heads of another world. I wondered if he was reasonably close to honest, or if he was a member of that obligarchy of crime called the *Kakush*, which some said really ran Mariyad and all of Adelan. I shrugged. It was none of my business. I wasn't on a case here; I was merely indulging myself in what suddenly seemed a not-entirely healthy invocation of the dead. I decided it was time to go. When Lohvia returned I would leave. I had no business casting her and Niano in a remake of my love affair with Thea. They had their own dream to make come true.

Lohvia entered through the drapes then, and I stood. But in-

stead of saying good-bye, I said, "What's wrong?" Because she was obviously very upset. Her hands fought with each other and she didn't meet my eyes as she replied, "Nothing. I must ask you to leave now, Kamus. It's been a pleasure chatting with you." She took my arm and steered me toward the door. I stopped and faced her. "Lohvia, you're not a very good liar."

She let a smile flicker on her lips—it died fast. "Please, Kamus. Believe me, it has nothing to do with Xidon or Niano. But your presence would complicate matters. Please?"

It looked like the only direction left to me was down the hallway and out the door. Once outside, though, I stopped on the lawn and looked back. I had planned to leave anyway, but not under circumstances like these. I didn't have to be a great judge of ladies in distress to know that something was wrong. I reminded myself that this woman was Lohvia of House Zad, not Thea Morn, and decided that I had a firm grip on that. Whatever was going on was none of my business. So I started prowling around the shrubbery that surrounded this wing of the mansion.

Before long I found an open window that let me into a bedroom. The door was open, and I slipped into the hallway and tried to find my way back to the sitting room. In no time at all I was hopelessly lost. At last I heard what I thought was Lohvia's voice at the top of a sweeping marble staircase. By the time I reached the corridor at the top, however, she had stopped talking and I had no idea which way to turn. That problem was solved by approaching footsteps. I hid behind a stuffed horned catamount, near a door. Around the corner came Janya, the slave that had announced Lohvia's visitor. When she passed me, I quickly opened the door beside me and slipped into the room.

I was in a laboratory, full of benches lined with stoneware beakers, retokts, and dishes. I looked around. It was quite impressive. But what impressed me the most was the body lying on the floor, beneath a window.

It wasn't easy to recognize, though I'd seen it alive and happy not an hour ago. It was Niano, the mute minstrel, with his chest and head crushed just like the lute still strung across his broken back.

3

I didn't move. Some half-filled beakers still steaming over just-extinguished candles told me that the laboratory had been used quite recently, which meant someone might return at any time. A shattered container had left a slight dusting of white powder over most of the floor, disturbed by footprints near one workbench. A single set of bare footprints led from the bench to the body, and a set of large, sandaled prints went from the bench to the door. Niano wore sandals, but his feet were too small to have made those prints. It looked like two people were in the room when Niano entered through the window—the barefoot one had killed him and left by the window, while the sandaled one had left by the door through which I had just entered only a moment before.

That was all I could tell without closer examination of the body, but I didn't want to leave my footprints in the dust. So I took some potions from my beltpouch, mixed them, and cast the result—a fine, transparent powder—into the air as I spoke a Phrase of Darkland Language. The powder spread through the air and condensed into a flat layer of mist about the thickness of a fingernail, and settled over everything in the room except Niano and me, clinging to contours and outlines without disturbing anything. I stepped onto it, crossed the room without touching the floor, and bent over Niano.

His blood had not yet begun to clot; another sign that it had just happened. There were no clues as to who had done it, other than the fairly obvious fact that it was someone with superhuman strength; his skull had been caved in by a single blow and his ribcage was splintered, probably from a bearhug. Then I noticed something odd: his tunic over his chest appeared to be slightly burnt.

I stood and looked out the window. It opened onto a large balcony. From there I could see that this side of the mansion was quite close to the outside wall—about twenty meters of lawn separated them.

Directly below me was Janya the slave, approaching a row of rainbow crystal trees that lined the wall. There was no sign of anyone else. Janya glanced up and saw me at the same time that I saw her. She shouted, "What are you doing up there?"

I was in for it now. "You'd better send someone up here," I told her. "There's been a killing." Her eyes grew big, and she ran back inside.

I walked back across the room and spoke the Words that dissolved the protective-shield spell. Then I looked at Niano. The moment I had recognized him, I had put aside the shock and sorrow I had felt—my professional side had taken over. A private eye can't help getting involved at times, but he can't let it interfere with his work. But now the facts had been noted, and now the only things left to think about were Niano, who had lost his life, his music, his stories, and all his chances at love—and Lohvia who had lost him.

I went back into the hallway, closing the laboratory door behind me, and then I heard Lohvia's voice calling my name. I turned and watched her come down the hall, wearing an apprehensive face. Walking with her was Janya, and a man—

That was as far as I got before I realized what he was, and the shock of it almost made me forget what was in the room behind me. He was tall and wiry, deeply tanned, and wore a short kilt of deep red with a sword hanging scabbardless from a strange feathered belt. And he was a Darklander. That in itself was enough to set me back; Darklanders aren't popular north of the Inland Sea. But his nationality by itself wasn't what had me gaping. It takes a Darklander to know a Darklander before a Word of the Language of Spells is spoken; there's a certain sense of recognition, felt by no sense known to humans, that names us to each other. It centers around the eyes, but it has to do with sight the same way color has to do with the shape or texture of an object. I can't describe it, but the strength of it varies with the power of the Darklander. And I had *never* felt such power from anyone of the Blood before. On a scale of one to ten, he was fifteen and I was about negative five.

I scrutinized him as he approached with Lohvia. His hair was long and straight, glossy black, and bound by a single leather thong. His face was lean and full of sharp angles—cheekbones, supraorbitals, and nose all jutted emphatically. His eyes were the color and temperature of the Arctic Sea. In both appearance and attitude, he reminded me of Taqwatkh. He smiled slightly. I didn't say anything. I didn't know who he was, and wasn't sure I wanted to. Another com-

plication was all I needed at this stage.

Lohvia said, "Kamus, Janya said you told her there had been a killing. What do you mean?"

I've had to tell people of death before, and I'll have to again. It's never easy. But I doubted if it would ever be harder than it was this time. I tried to make it as gentle as I could; my words sounded harsh and unfeeling to me. She tried to go into the laboratory, of course. I held her until her strengthh had turned to tears against my chest.

The Darklander watched me through the scene, his smile gone now, his face totally impassive. But somehow, I still had the feeling that he was amused, deep inside.

He turned to Janya. "Call some slaves," he told her. "And Apolgar Zad."

* * *

Apolgar Zad was a tall, thin man, mostly legs, with a short torso and almost no neck. He stalked around the huge, lushly carpeted main hall like a reed-bird through savannah grass, making dour expressions that tugged his long nose from side to side.

The main hall of his mansion was large enough to be a hangar for a Unity spacecruiser, so the five of us weren't crowded. Besides myself, there was Apolgar, Lohvia, the Darklander (who had been introduced to me as Palos of Zaibor), and Captain Olarus of the Mariyad Garrison. Lohvia was very white and still. Palos of Zaibor was enigmatic. Olarus was bored. I could tell he was bored because he had just announced the fact.

Apolgar turned and pointed a carrot-shaped finger at him. "Bored or not," he said in a querulous voice, "I want you to take action on this. Precipitate though she is, my daughter still means much to me, and I will have the liquidation of her friend avenged."

Olarus spread his hands. He was younger than Thoras, the previous Garrison Captain, and even less likeable, if that was possible. His most outstanding feature was that he had no outstanding feature; he wore a crowd face, which was an asset in his work.

"All this fuss over a wastrel so poor he didn't even have a

voice?" he said languidly. "Come, Apolgar. The Guard has better things to do—"

"You have nothing better to do than to react to my wishes," Apolgar Zad told him. "I am not without influence in this city, you know. My daughter has told you who murdered this Nolo—"

"Niano—" Lohvia murmured.

"Quite so, quite so. All that is left for you to do, Captain Olarus, is to arrest the killer."

"Arrest a Flying Guard, one of Mariyad's finest fighting men, on mere suspicion of killing a beggar? Oreus Bodag would have my head! You have no proof, other than the traditional hot temper of the little men—"

"No proof? You say my daughter's hypothesis has no proof? Why, man, have you not listened to his testimony?" and he pointed at me. "The circumstances of the young man's death indicate an attacker possessed of enormous strength. You have admitted that there is room on the laboratory's balcony for a kragor to land. It has been substantiated that this Flyer was jealous of the chemistry between the minstrel and Lohvia. Add to this his volatile, unstable temperament, which you yourself noted, and the equation is complete, the reaction inevitable."

"What about the footprints?" Olarus asked. "The bare prints might possibly be Xidon's, but the sandal imprints must belong to someone else—why, they're large enough to be made by your feet," and he grinned as he looked at Apolgar's huge, ill-shined boots.

Apolgar glared. "I have reached my boiling point," he announced. "I have become saturated with your picayune protests. I say the analysis is correct; all that remains is for you to arrest the offender. I take full responsibility for this action."

Olarus shrugged. "That's different." He stood and straightened his headband. "I'll send several men to the Flyers' barracks—I've a hunch this Xidon won't take kindly to being arrested." He turned and bowed to the Darklander. "An honor, Palos of Zaibor." The Darklander nodded and smiled that faint smile again. I wondered how honored Olarus would feel if he knew he was talking to someone from Ja-Agur. The Garrison Captain bid farewell to Lohvia, then looked at me and said softly, "If this causes me trouble, Kamus, I'll have

your hide stretched between poles."

I smiled. "If this causes you trouble, Olarus, you'll be worrying about your own hide." Olarus scowled and left, wading with difficulty through the rug. After he had gone, I stood and made my good-byes. Apolgar Zad thanked me for my noble efforts on behalf of his daughter. Lohvia thanked me, her voice fragile and ready to shatter; she turned away quickly and left the room. Apolgar started after her saying hurriedly to the rest of us, "Janya will see you out."

Janya watched the curtains swirl into stillness after daughter and father, then turned to Palos and me and said, "Gentlemen?" and made a gesture toward the exit, setting it off with arched eyebrows.

"You seem to take this quite calmly, Janya," remarked Palos of Zaibor, as we walked down the corridor.

"One grows used to emergencies and calamities in Apolgar Zad's house," she said. "As one grows used to strange visitors." Her light voice had more than a touch of sarcasm in it. All Palos did was look at her and smile that slight smile of his, but it took the cockiness out of her. I was fascinated by this Palos. I was fairly familiar with the Who's Who of the Darkland, and I had never heard of anyone by his name with so much raw power. Just walking next to him kept me on overload; it was like standing by a furnace.

"Is murder an everyday thing around here?" I asked her. She looked at me. She had short, brown hair and an elfish-thin face, one that looks all wrong without a smile and mischief in the eyes. Now it looked somber and more than a little scared. It made me slightly angry with this mystery man—who was he that he could cow Lohvia and this slave, anyway?

"No," Janya said. "Murder has never happened before, that I know of." Though she did not look at Palos, I had the impression that last was meant for him.

"At least we know who did it," Palos said, as Janya escorted us to the door.

"Do you really think Xidon did it?" I asked him.

He grinned at me; he had an easy, open grin. It broke the ice of those eyes and made one forget how cold they had been. "Who else could it have been? He certainly had a motive. He flew his kragor to the window, killed the poor lad, and left by the same route."

"What about the footprints?" I asked.

"Well, one set of them had to be yours, of course—the barefoot set. For some reason, you took off your sandals when crossing the room—unless you floated across the balcony."

He was toying with me—he knew I had used a spell to keep my prints out of the dust, and he was pointing out how lucky I was that no one else had mentioned it, such as Olarus. I had forgotten to leave a set of my own footprints—mistakes like that wouldn't help my reputation any.

"It still leaves a number of questions unanswered," I said. "How did Xidon know Niano would be in that room? Why didn't Janya, who must have left the house almost the same time as the killer, hear the kragor's wings?"

"And what was Niano doing there? Doing business with the owner of the sandaled prints? That means someone else knew of the killing." This came from Janya—I was beginning to admire her. Palos obviously wasn't. He flashed her the same grin as he had me, only somehow it was now as chilly as an ice giant's ankle.

"You have quite a curiosity," he said in gentle warning, "for a slave."

Janya did not have time to react to this, because her attention was suddenly distracted by something overhead. She pointed at the purple sky and shouted, "Look!"

We looked—overhead, Xidon was spiraling toward the same wing where he had attacked Niano this morning. I looked at the window and saw Lohvia leaning on the sill, staring at the ground where the minstrel had played for her. The thunder of the kragor's wings made her look up, quickly, as Xidon came in for a landing.

Janya turned and ran back into the mansion. Neither Palos nor I moved as the Flyer landed, the backwash from the wings ripping shrubbery to shreds. Xidon leaped from the saddle, looked at the window, and stopped, confused. Lohvia was no longer there.

"Lohvia?" he called uncertainly.

"*Murderer!*"

She flew at him, fingernails first, through he door he had ruined earlier. Xidon's jaw dropped, but he was quick enough to twist out of her way and let her sprawl into a flowerbed. Palos and I charged to the scene. I had my sword out as Xidon

leaped back into the saddle; I slashed the reins as he tugged them, and he sprawled backward and almost lost his mount. But he recovered, shouted a command, and the beast took off.

Then I saw Palos of Zaibor extend one arm, his fingers crabbed in a Dark gesture. He spoke no Words, but the kragor jerked as though caught by an invisible lasso, and went into a steep dive toward a fandala tree. Xidon somersaulted free in midair and landed running, but I was running, too—I slammed into him and we rolled across the lawn together until we hit the stone base of a statue. I came up on top, my fingers around his throat, and what I felt made me loosen my grip in surprise. He flung me off his chest like an empty tunic and leaped to his feet. The statue beside him was of an ice giant, solid marble and three meters tall, but Xidon ripped it free of its pedestal as though it were made of dandelions, and lifted it above his head to crush me. Fortunately, he was still standing on the soft lawn—the weight of the marble drove him into the ground up to his shoulders. At the same time, Palos knocked the statue from his grip with another gestured spell. Xidon tried to claw his way out of the soft ground, then collapsed as a final spell put him to sleep.

During all the spell-casting, Palos had not used a single syllable of Language. I had seen power like that only once before—when Kaan Ta'Wyys of Thanare was filled with the power of the *Synulanom*, and even he had been speaking the Phrases of that spell. Paols of Zaibor, I concluded, was one powerful Darklander.

So powerful that his Bloodline had to come direct from the Darklord himself.

He helped me to my feet. "Congratulations," he said. "We seem to have saved Captain Olarus the responsibility of catching the murderer."

"This was your idea of a criminal sneaking back to the scene of the crime?" I asked. I dusted myself off, and something tickled my hand; several strands of Xidon's hair had been caught on a ring I was wearing. I pulled them free and was about to cast them away, but reconsidered and put them in my potionpouch.

Palos watched me, with that smile. "Saving hair to build a spell around?" He asked. "I'm surprised at you, Kamus. That's a charlatan's trick."

He had finally openly acknowledged my Blood. I wanted to return the favor by calling him by his real name, but things were by no means settled down at House Zad; slaves were dashing about, helping a hysterical Lohvia and surrounding an unconscious Xidon, and Apolgar Zad was on the scene, shouting orders no one was listening to. I went back into the mansion to find a phonecub and call Olarus. If my hunch was right, the Garrison dungeon would be a good place for Xidon.

I also needed a quiet place to think about the possible reasons why a living legend would be visiting Apolgar Zad. Because with such power as I had just seen, Palos of Zaibor could only be one person: Jann-Togah, the son of the Darklord.

4

There have been almost as many legends of Jann-Togah as there have been of Mondrogan the Clever. How he was exiled by his father from Ja-Agur, the Darkland, for trying to usurp his father's throne, and of his efforts to recross the Inland Sea and break a barrier spell that kept him from his homeland. According to the stories, his power had been halved when he was thrown out, and even at full strength, he had been no match for the Darklord. I didn't want to think about how powerful that would make the Darklord, as I intended—somehow, some way—to make him pay for causing the death of my friend, Sanris of Taleiday, and for trying to run my life and career. True, since he had restored my secret life as a Darklander in Mariyad, I had seen no other evidence of attempts to make me into a puppet. Sometimes I thought that my determination to confront him was overreaction. But I could not shake the conviction that the Darklord wasn't through with me. Being of the Blood, I've found my intuitions usually have some truth in them. Which might explain why I was instantly convinced that Palos of Zaibor was Jann-Togah.

Probably every mental case in Mariyad has at some time claimed to be Jann-Togha, just as they've claimed to be his father. Some of the more aspiring charlatans in the city have put his name on their shingles, and sold enough aphrodisiacs and death potions to retire as a result. I had also met several Darklanders who claimed to be him. I didn't believe them. But

I was convinced that Palos was the real thing.

It was quite late by the time I got back to my rooms above the Demons' Dance Tavern. I had waited for the Guard to come for Xidon, and Lohvia had sat with me and talked about safe, trivial subjects, such as what Earth had been like, and sobbed occasionally on my shoulder.

Though I was tired, I didn't sleep well that night. I kept seeing that brief, happy scene on the lawn between Lohvia and Niano—a happy scene that would never happen again. I finally gave up and waited for dawn to trickle in, then headed for the Unity Spaceport. There I took a lift tube to the infirmary. After filling out hundreds of forms and getting enough paper cuts to warrant a medal, I was allowed to turn over Xidon's hair sample for cell analysis. The analysis would be instantaneous, but they wouldn't get around to doing it for several hours. While I was waiting, I visited Stam's room.

He was conscious and almost recovered. His room was a water-filled chamber with a bed that looked like a cross between a fishnet and an ancient Earthly moonshine still. Several tasteful arrangements of coral sent by concerned acolytes aboard the *Yith'il* were set about the room.

Again, Stam wasn't happy with me. "Why are you not with Taqwatkh, to protect him on his journeys into Mariyad?" His ink signals were hastily formed—they caused static in the airlock's coder translation.

"Take it easy," I advised. "You're not a well cephalopod. Taqwatkh hasn't left yet." I didn't really know if he had or not, and didn't mention to Stam that the Bringer of Lightning didn't want me anywhere near the case—the high priest had enough worries. "I need a few questions answered," I told him, "if I'm to do a good job as a bodyguard. The first and biggest is: exactly why is Taqwatkh going to visit Apolgar Zad? Were they roommates at seminary school, or what?"

Stam was some time in replying; when he did, the answer was evasive. "If Taqwatkh has not seen fit to tell you, perhaps I would be overstepping my authority."

"He'll never know. The information could be important."

"In fact," he signaled slowly, "I do not know why he insists on these visits. There are many matters I am not fit to know—this, evidently, is one of them. I do know that, according to our scriptures, he made a similar pilgrimage to this

planet a thousand years ago, our time. This was long before the Unity was established, of course—just after we had developed space travel under Taqwatkh's guidance."

"Now we're getting somewhere. Do you know if this current trip has anything to do with someone named Jann-Togah?"

"I have heard the name—the exiled son of your mysterious Darklord, is it not? But I have not heard my god mention him."

"How about a Flying Guard named Xidon?"

"No, never."

So I thanked him, told him I was on my way to protect Taqwatkh from the forces of evil, left the water chamber, and stood around pulling my lip. I intended to do my best to protect the Maltese god from any assassination attempts—even if Taqwatkh didn't want me on the case, I considered myself on it for a variety of reasons. I felt Niano's death was somehow connected with Apolgar Zad's dealings with Taqwatkh, and with Jann-Togah, and I knew Lohvia had enough grief without an interplanetary assassination in her front yard. What was the connection between them all? I had no answers, yet, but I decided a good place to start looking would be the Spaceport Library.

* * *

The entire written history of Ja-Lur had been put into an electron-lattice memory cube one centimeter across. I dropped it into a scanner and started reviewing the scrolls written by historians looking back nine hundred years ago, which corresponded to a thousand Maltese years. There was no mention of visitors from the sky or of a lightning-flinging, teleporting alien. That lead blocked, I decided to look into the history of the Knights of Malta.

That cube said that the island of Malta, on Earth, had been ruled by a resurgence of the Knights Hospitalers for almost a hundred years. Their discoveries in genetic manipulation, cloning, and bionics were the most advanced on Earth, and eventually they developed an army of "android angels" (the Seraphim Mark IV class), which, along with the special-effects department of a leading holofilm company, they used to stage a very spectacular second coming. The android "messiah" told

the nations of the world to turn over their leadership to Malta. Religious wars raged over the planet, until the deception was unmasked by a special-missions team of the Roman Catholic Church, acting under the direct orders from the Pope. As a result, the entire population of Malta was banished to Beta Draconis III, or as they renamed it, Malta II.

That was interesting, but it still didn't tell me why Taqwatkh was visiting Apolgar. I had the feeling that information would be the link I was looking for, but I had no idea where to start looking. The entry on the native race of Beta Draconis III, the cephalopods, was quite general and sketchy, and all I learned from it was that they called their world by an ink signal meaning "Globe of Slime and Stench"—the cephalopod equivalent of "Paradise."

So I gave up, and decided to see if I could go to the source of the problems and find any answers. I was fairly sure what Taqwatkh's reaction to my continued interest would be, and I wasn't looking forward to it. But I had reached a deadend.

As I was on my way to the landing plates, however, the P.A. system announced a call for me, from Mariyad. I went back into the Terminex and found a public phonecub—sophisticasted technological devices, such as vidphones, don't work outside the boundary of the Spaceport, by mandate of the Darklord. Nor does magic work inside the Spaceport, but phonecubs operate by telepathy, not magic. I scratched its ear and said, "Kamus of Kadizhar here."

The cub refused to transmit until he was offered a sweetmeat; fortunately, I happened to have one in my pouch. I dropped it into his mouth; he chittered in thanks, then opened his mouth and spoke in Janya's voice.

"Hello, Kamus," she said. "I thought this was where you'd be."

"You're a better detective than I am, today. What is it? Has anything happened at the house?"

"Nothing momentous," she said. "But I'd like to talk to you—I think I can clear up a few things for you."

"And why would you like to do that, Janya? Not that I'm counting the horns on a gift kragor."

"Kamus, being a slave for Apolgar Zad is a better life than most freefolk know. So I'm trying to protect myself, as well as my master and mistress. Apolgar Zad is dealing with

Darklanders."

I counted five for the proper effect, then said slowly, "That makes matters interesting."

"I can make them much more interesting, but not over a phonecub. Darklanders can tap their minds, you know."

I'd never been able to, but I didn't tell her that. "All right, Janya—I'll meet you at the Blue Lotus Tavern at noon." Taqwatkh habitually made his mysterious trips to Apolgar Zad in the afternoon, so there would still be time to get back to him, hopefully. And I had the feeling I could learn more from Janya than from the Bringer of Lightning.

Before I left the Spaceport, however, I checked back with the infirmary. They had finally done the analysis I had requested, and what they told me made a lot of the puzzle clear.

* * *

Janya was sitting in one of the high-backed corner booths of the Blue Lotus, as far away as possible from the ale-guzzling, joke-roaring Guardsmen, slavetraders, and other clientele. I felt guilty about asking her to meet me here—although she was a slave, she was used to much better surroundings, as she had pointed out. To me, the Blue Lotus was practically a second home. I apologized to her and she said, "Kamus, I once made my living bellydancing in a much more disreputable tavern than this one. The only thing I find offensive about this place is the age of the Guardsmen's jokes. But we've better things to talk about." She leaned close to me and said, "Palos of Zaibor is a Darklander."

It was no act to look impressed, even though she was telling me news I already knew. What impressed me was Janya herself. She was as pale and fragile as a crystal tree blossom, but she had a quick mind, a fine and facile wit, and considerable courage. She would make a good ally, I decided, and I ordered us mugs of ale. I described Taqwatkh and asked Janya if she had ever seen him, without telling her who he was.

She nodded with excitement. "That's the other Darklander! Palos wants to abduct him; he's threatened Apolgar with financial ruin unless Apolgar helps him."

"How can Palos cause that?"

"Because he helped Apolgar move up in society years ago,

by supplying him with Black Desert dream-crystals."

So Apolgar had made his fortune by supplying Mariyad with illegal drugs. I pulled out a pack of chewing gum and thrust a stick into my mouth. "You've spent a lot of time listening behind curtains."

"I told you—if Apolgar and Lohvia are ruined, I go back to bellydancing."

"What is Apolgar doing for the 'other Darklander'?"

"I'm not sure; but it concerns some sort of drugs or chemical concoction."

I nodded. "In the laboratory where Niano died."

"Yes."

"Do you know if Palos has ever been in there?"

"Not that I can say. Xidon has—I surprised him lurking about there once."

Things were falling together, but I still needed a stronger motive for Niano's killer. "Who do you think killed Niano, Janya?"

She looked surprised. "Why—Xidon, of course. Who else but a Flying Guard could have mangled him like that?" She sighed. "I miss Niano. He had so much talent. He knew all the tales of Mondrogan, including some that I'd never heard before."

A Guardsman at the bar was talking about the extraordinary strength of the Flying Guard imprisoned in the Garrison dungeon. I kept one ear on him while I said to Janya, "Such as?"

"Never mind that. What about Apolgar's—"

"What were some of the stories Niano told?" I repeated. I'm not sure why I asked—maybe just to keep her occupied while I listened to the Guardsman's tale.

"Well, did you know that Mondrogan once saved . . ."

". . .put him in the strongest cell," the Guardsman told Silos the tavernowner. "Jungan was on duty when that Flyer ripped that solid bronze door from its hinges and crushed poor Jungan beneath it like a scarab . . ."

". . . monster from the sky with the strength of a hundred men, who could cast bolts from his fingers . . ."

". . . burst through the Garrison wall and was gone before . . ."

". . . come to Ja-Lur because his powers were waning, and

there was a certain drug here that could restore them. Mondrogan—"

I slapped the table hard enough to cause whitecaps in my ale. "That's it!" I shouted. Those two stories had suddenly made Niano's murder clear to me, and also told me that I might be too late to prevent Taqwatkh's assassination.

Ignoring the bleary, surprised stares of the tavern's occupants, I grabbed Janya and we ran out. The Marketplace was empty, except for a few pedestrians. "You can never find a carriage when you need one," I growled, and started down the street at a run.

"Kamus, wait!" Janya ran to catch up with me. "What is it? What about—?"

"I don't have time to explain now, Janya. I've got to get to the Spaceport before—"

Just then I noticed a flicker of something at the edge of my vision, and I suddenly had the feeling we were being followed. But I couldn't see anyone behind me who looked suspicious. I kept one eye toward the rear as we hurried through the Marketplace. There were a few old women cackling over hens, one or two panderers, and harlots advertising yards of flesh, but I could see nobody interested in Janya and me. Yet I couldn't escape the feeling that we were being shadowed. I ducked into a dim, unoccupied marketbooth, pulling Janya in after me, and watched the few passersby. No one glanced our way, but the feeling of being watched grew.

"Kamus, what—"

I laid a finger across my lips. And then I saw it, as it slid into the booth, a darker outline against the dimness. It flowed along the wall, elongated by the angles of the wooden booth—a shadow, unattached to a body. Trailing from one heel was a thread of Darkness that ran across the dirt floor and out the door. The shadow hovered near us as Janya pressed her hand against her lips and shrank against me. It was ectoplasm in negative, a Body of Darkness. And I had a good idea who it belonged to.

I unsheathed my sword as it rippled along the gray, ill-fitting slabs of wood. I knew there was nothing I could do against it with unenchanted steel, but I had an image as an ignorant human to maintain. So I swung, uselessly and watched the tip of the blade graze wood fibers and leave the shadow un-

harmed. It raised a shadow blade and swung—the black image left the wall like a ray of night and flickered quite close. Janya controlled herself with an effort that I felt as she pressed against me. I stroked her hair and said, "Don't worry."

"It's Darkness, isn't it, Kamus?"

"I can't imagine what else it could be."

"Well," she said. "I've seen better shadow skits at a childrens' puppet show."

The shadow moved again, and its entire length stood against one wall. Previously, it had been too distorted to recognize—now Janya gasped and said, "That profile—it's Palos!"

His voice spoke inside my head. *Well, Kamus. You and Janya just won't leave well enough alone, will you?*

Since he had contacted me, I could respond without setting up a spell, and without Janya's knowledge that I was communicating with him. *I think you'll be sorry you're delaying me*, I told him, *if you want Taqwatkh's business with Apolgar Zad to be successful. And I think you want that, because I know who you are.*

"Kamus, he's just standing there," Janya whispered. "Shouldn't we try to run?"

"You can't run faster than Darkness," I told her. "Wait—I don't think he'll harm us."

His shadow rippled along the wall away from us like intelligent ink, causing Janya to breathe a sigh of relief. It appeared to cross its legs and lean against the wall with arms folded. *So tell me; who am I, and what do I want with the Maltese god?*

You're Jann-Togah, son of the Darklord, and you want to use Taqwatkh, the Bringer of Lightning, in your campaign against your father.

The shadow nodded. *Very good, Kamus. You just might make a better ally than an enemy.*

I'd make a better ally than Taqwatkh would. His power bolts are running low, aren't they? I don't know anything about the cephalopods' religion, but evidently the bolts are important—they call him the Bringer of Lightning.

His full power is beyond conception, Jann-Togah said. *He is the reason for the cephalopods' advanced civilization. Obviously, an aquatic race would have little heavy industry such as exists on other worlds. It is hard to make fire and, as I understand it, generate electricity underwater. Taqwatkh's power bolts fill*

these needs.

But his power runs low every thousand years, their time, I said. *And he has to come to the Darkworld, where certain chemicals or herbs exist that can pep him up. He must have made quite an impression the last time he dropped in; minstrels are still telling about his battle with Mondrogan the Clever. You knew his reason for being here—as soon as he's up to strength, you intend to use him against your father.*

He won't be up to strength this time, I'm afraid, said Jann-Togah with a sigh. *The secret of the elixir has been lost, and Apolgar has been unable to duplicate it.*

"Kamus!'" Janya said desperately. "Has he got you enthralled? You're just staring at him—"

"It's all right," I assured her. "Somehow, he's talking to me, in my head."

"What's he saying?"

"Quiet—I can't hear." I communicated: *Jann-Togah, Taqwatkh will be of no use to you or anyone if we don't get to him immediately. He's been under threat of assassination since his arrival on Ja-Lur, and I know who the would-be assassin is. He may have already struck.*

Who is it? Jann-Togah demanded.

Xidon.

The Flying Guard who killed the minstrel?

He's not a Flying Guard. The Spaceport infirmary tells me he's a Knight of Malta, genetically altered to resemble a Flyer. He got into the Yith'il *as part of an exchange program with Unity Security, and tried to kill Stam, the high priest. Xidon would have gone after Taqwatkh then, but Taqwatkh was at Apolgar's laboratory. Then he was arrested as Niano's murderer. He's broken out of the Garrison dungeon, and he's on his way to finish his mission. And he'll do it—he's been specially bred to kill Taqwatkh—unless we stop him!*

Jann-Togah's shadow straightened up at this. I could hear him putting the facts together in his mind, just as I had—it didn't take him long. *I'll meet you at the Spaceport,* he snapped. *Get there as fast as you can!* And his shadow vanished.

"Let's go!" I pulled Janya out of the marketbooth.

"But what did Palos say?" she demanded.

"We've even less time now than we did before," I said. "In

fact, you'd better not come—"

"You're going to leave me here without telling me what's happening? Think again, Kamus."

I looked around desperately for a ride, and saw one: trundling down the street in our direction was a racing chariot, its driver half dozing on his feet, holding the reins loosely.

"I hope you don't regret this," I told Janya. "Get ready to move fast," and I pulled two pinches of powders from my pouch and tossed them into the air. I muttered a Phrase—hopefully, too low for Janya to hear—and the powders ignited, causing a burst of crimson light. The two jemlas pulling the chariot reared and then bolted in panic, scattering what few shoppers there were. The charioteer, caught completely by surprise, went axe over armor and into a fruitstand. I grabbed the railing as the cart careened by me and managed to pull myself onto it. I grabbed the reins and pulled, slowing enough for Janya to leap aboard—then I speeded up. The jemlas—much like Earthly horses, except for residual wings and forehead horn, which have caused Earthly mythologists some sleepless nights—broke into full gallop, and we were off. We hurtled out of the Marketplace and headed up the Dragon's Back, a street named for its series of small, regular humps, like a serrated backbone. We hit only the high spots. The chariot wheels screeched, iron rims striking sparks, as I made a right on Blackbrine Street. Astonished faces flickered by. Janya clung to the sides of the chariot, instead of me, as we careened over the cobblestones. I hit a wet patch and the chariot slewed to one side, scattering a group of citizens and a few Guardsmen; the latter shouted for me to stop. I snapped the reins harder.

"Kamus, you're going to be in a lot of trouble," Janya said—one of the great understatements of the year. I didn't answer. We skirted the high wall that surrounds the Maze, roared by the building that held my office, and headed for the West Gate.

The gate detail saw and heard us coming. Fortunately, traffic was light at this hour. Peasants with pushcarts and litter-bearers leaped out of our way. One litter overturned and pitched a fat woman, wearing more silk than a ship wears sailcloth, into a cartful of squealing pigs. I didn't stop. The gate's iron bars began to lower—the wrought emblem of Mariyad, a

Flying Guard astride a kragor, came into view as we rushed toward it. "Hang on!" I shouted to Janya, "And keep down!"

The jemlas were well trained—they didn't slow at all, though the teeth of the gate tore at my hair as we went under it. A few crossbow bolts shattered against the sides of the chariot, and the feathers on one tickled my ear. Then we were on the turnoff that led across the quarter-kilometer of savannah to the Unity Spaceport.

As I approached, I saw a kragor overhead, dropping toward the main entrance of the Spaceport Terminex. Janya saw it too; she grabbed my cloak and cried, "Xidon!" I had had the same idea, and was trying to think of a surreptitious spell that would protect us from aerial attack. But the flying reptile came out of its dive and landed in a green explosion on the grass near the road, I saw that the rider was Jann-Togah.

By this time we had attracted quite a bit of attention. Guardsmen were charging from the West Gate toward us, and Unity soldiers were pouring from the Terminex. Janya and I tumbled from the chariot just in time to be seized by a white-uniformed native of the planet Moran—he was built for seizing, having four arms mounted on a snakelike body.

"Relaxxxx," he said. "I don't know what the idea wassss . . ."

"Arrest Xidon of the Mariyad Guard!" I shouted. "He's going to kill Taqwatkh of Malta II!" but I couldn't make myself heard over the pandemonium. The Mariyad Guardsmen were demanding we be taken into custody, and the Unity soldiers were insisting the matter would have to be decided by their superiors.

Jann-Togah was being held by several soldiers. I saw him make a series of his sign-Language gestures. At first, I noticed no difference in the shouting madness; then I realized that, instead of speaking Adelanese, the Unity soldiers were all talking in their various native tongues. Communication quickly disintegrated. A scuffle between a soldier and a Guardsman broke out, then another. The Moranian released us as someone stumbled into him from behind. Jann-Togah pulled me out of the crowd. "This will keep them busy while we attend to Xidon. Come!"

"Wait a minute! They might kill each other!"

"The confusion spell will not last long. It's your

choice—stay and you'll be arrested."

I caught Janya's hand. "You've got a point," I told Jann-Togah. "Let's go!"

We ran around the Terminex and along the boundary between grass and plasticrete, past the thin, silver force-fence projectors. There was little activity once we passed the hotel and the warehouses; all Spaceport security was at the front gate. The landing field was quiet, with only a few ships on the landing plates. The *Yith'il* was berthed on the near side of the field, about fifty meters from the force-fence. As we caught sight of it, Janya pointed and shouted, "Look! The other Darklander!"

Taqwatkh had just emerged from the ship. He was standing on the high hatch platform, hands on hips. He seemed to be looking for someone.

Jann-Togah pointed also, at a figure crouched on a nearby conveyor ramp. "Xidon," he said. "With a gun."

5

The Maltese Knight was huddled on the arch of the swooping ramp, which stretched in a parabola from a warehouse loading dock and intersected several freight lift tubes. He rested a raygun against the railing, aiming it at Taqwatkh. The beam could puncture a meter of metal.

Which is what it did, because I yelled, "Duck, Taqwatkh!" He turned, startled, as Xidon fired, and a stream of pressurized water shot from the ship's hull. The hull self-sealed as Xidon turned, saw us, and fired. He was above the level of the force-fence, but he had forgotten the Darklord's mandate—prohibiting Outworld science on Ja-Lur, and so the beam reached only the edge of the field and then blinked out a meter short of us. Janya and I ducked reflexively; Jann-Togah slammed his hands against the invisible, unyielding force fence, searching for a way to climb or break through it.

Xidon provided that, with some help from Taqwatkh. Instead of retreating into his ship, the famous Bringer of Lightning decided to take the offensive. He tried to teleport from the *Yith'il* to the closest arc of the ramp, but didn't quite make it—he reappeared in midair and managed to seize the ramp's railing as he fell. The ramp shook, upsetting Xidon's

next shot. The beam drilled into one of the fence projectors; there was a shower of sparks, and the section of the force-fence before us vanished.

Xidon screamed in rage. Jann-Togah staggered forward, recovered, and ran toward the loading docks and the ramp's base. Janya and I followed him. The Darklord's son and I were powerless now, and vulnerable to Xidon's rayblasts. But Xidon was having problems of his own; Taqwatkh was on the ramp and coming toward him.

Several faces belonging to various species had appeared in the ports and hatchways of some of the ships, watching, but no one dared interfere in this battle of titans. Xidon fired at Taqwatkh, but missed; the beam sliced almost completely through the thin, curving metal, causing the ramp to sag dangerously. Taqwatkh leaped over the cut and kept coming. Xidon fired again, and this time the Maltese god managed to deflect the beam with one of his weakened powerbolts. The beam shot off at a tangent and neatly sliced the top from one of the power silos near an Aldebaran cruiser. A well of coruscating energy was exposed; it shimmered in rainbow colors and filled the air with the smell of ozone.

Taqwatkh let fly another bolt, which knocked the gun from Xidon's hand. He expected the Knight to be stunned by it, but Xidon showed no effect—he was genetically immune to Taqwatkh's powerbolts.

Surprise made Taqwatkh hesitate. Xidon leaped forward and crashed into him; both of them tumbled from the swaying ramp. They landed on the cargo deck platform of the Aldebaran cruiser, and there the fight went on.

Xidon braced himself against the ship, tore free one of the hatch doors, and threw it at Taqwatkh, who teleported out of its way. He reappeared behind Xidon and brought both fists down on the small man's neck. Xidon staggered, recovered, and the two grappled again, their blows denting the spacecraft's hull.

Jann-Togah had stopped his ascent of the ramp when they fell from it. I started to run toward the Aldebaran cruiser when Janya shouted, "Here, Kamus!" I turned; she tossed me the raygun which she had caught when Xidon dropped it. I aimed at the cargo deck. The angle from the ground was steep, and I was afraid of hitting Taqwatkh, but I had no choice; Xidon's

strength and his immunity to the powerbolts were giving him the upper hand. Taqwatkh was weakening. I fired, and as I did the entire conveyor ramp sagged again, directly into the path of the beam. The beam sliced through it completely. The partial cut Xidon had made earlier acted like a hinge, and the entire section, with Jann-Togah hanging on, dropped and swung toward the cruiser. Taqwatkh managed to break free of Xidon just as the severed end of the ramp crashed into the platform. The shock broke Jann-Togah's grip and he slid down the ramp, colliding with Xidon and knocking the Knight off the platform. Xidon had time to scream once before he plunged into the open energy silo and was instantly annihilated.

Then there was silence, except for the crackling of the energy silo. Neither Janya nor I moved for a moment. Then Janya said, "Kamus, I hope you're not going to tell me you planned it that way."

I grinned at her and spun the raygun around my finger.

There were shouts in the distance, and I saw a small army come around the warehouses in our direction. "Here comes the Unity," I said. "And they're not happy."

Jann-Togah and Taqwatkh descended to the ground by a lift tube and joined us. Taqwatkh stared at me with his haughty look. "So, detective," he said. "I see you did not heed my order."

"Luckily for you," I told him. I didn't feel like talking to Taqwatkh. I turned to Jann-Togah and said, "You realize that we're guilty of breaking about twenty interstellar laws."

Jann-Togah nodded, and then the Unity surrounded us. An Earthling general, portly and red-faced, was shouting, "Lock 'em up! I'll have 'em all on Devil's Asteroid for this! Illegal entry, unauthorized use of weapons, destruction of Unity property . . ."

"I think not," Jann-Togah said. And somehow his quiet voice doused the shouting completely. Everyone stared at the son of the Darklord and Taqwatkh. Separately, either one had enough sheer presence to cow a regiment—together, I truly think they could have challenged the Darklord himself.

"Do you know who I am?" Taqwatkh asked. The general worked his jaw several times and managed to pump a reply up his throat. "The—the emissary from Beta Draconis III."

"More than emissary—absolute ruler and god. Do you wish

your superiors at Centrex to know that you tried to arrest a visiting deity?"

"Ahem," said the general. "Well. Since you put it that way . . ."

* * *

The four of us were gathered in the airlock chamber before Stam's infirmary room. The high priest had just finished thanking me so effusively that the ink hid him from sight. Taqwatkh had come as close to thanking me as he could, saying, "You have done well in my service, Kamus of Kadizhar." I had said nothing to that. I didn't want to be reminded of it.

I had done my job, all right. I had saved the Bringer of Lightning from assassination. I had been on the wrong side, from the start.

"But tell me, Kamus," Stam asked, "how did Xidon manage to poison my water with niotrinaline? Even if he was part of the security exchange program, they were constantly checked for concealed weapons."

"But Xidon *was* a weapon," I told him. "The Knights of Malta had designed him genetically to kill you and Taqwatkh. His body was capable of manufacturing and secreting niotrinaline. He was amphibious—when I wrestled with him on Apolgar's lawn, I felt the gill slits in his neck. That, and his unusual strength, made me decide to have his hair cells analyzed for a genetic breakdown.

"He might have been planted here years ago, to wait for Taqwatkh's coming. He was undoubtedly under orders to destroy himself once his mission was completed, leaving the blame on Ja-Lur instead of the Knights. But he fell in love with Lohvia, and that ruined his cover."

"It was, of course, easy for you to deduce my reasons for wanting to abduct Taqwatkh," Jann-Togah said. "But how did you know Apolgar Zad was working to restore his powers?"

"I didn't, until almost too late. His first visit to the Darkworld and his battle with Mondrogan the Clever had been preserved in legend and song, instead of historians' scrolls. But Niano was a minstrel, and he knew the legend."

Taqwatkh kept his eyes on me. His face was impassive.

"It all makes sense," Janya said. "Except how Xidon killed Niano. He had the only motive, of course—jealousy. But I'm sure I would have heard his kragor landing on the balcony when I was outside."

"You didn't hear it," I said, "because it didn't land. Because Xidon didn't kill Niano."

Janya looked at me in shock. "But who else could it have been?" she asked. "Who else was strong enough—" and then she stopped. The room became very still. Even Stam's tentacles stopped moving.

I was very tired, very sick of the whole affair by now. I was tired of thinking about why I had done what I had done. But I had to put it into words, now. "Try this," I told them. "Niano was worried about Lohvia. So instead of leaving, he reentered the mansion, perhaps through the same window I used. He wanted to learn what Apolgar was up to. He hid in the laboratory, and was there when Apolgar tried and failed with his latest elixir."

No one said anything. Taqwatkh's expression did not change, but his eyes pinned me to the wall.

"Niano was a minstrel," I repeated. "He knew the legend of Taqwatkh and Mondrogan. Maybe he became excited when he realized it was true, and Apolgar and Taqwatkh heard him. Taqwatkh wanted his presence there a secret; perhaps he was afraid that if his cephalopod followers learned his powers were dying, there would be anarchy on Malta II." I took a deep breath. "He tried to kill Niano with a powerbolt first. His powers were very low, and so the bolt merely burned Niano's chest. So he finished the job by crushing Niano."

Janya said slowly, "I didn't hear him leave—"

I nodded. "Because he teleported from the balcony to the street. The wall was close—even his failing powers were enough to let him escape. Olarus was right; Apolgar left that second set of footprints. He ordered Olarus to arrest Xidon because he wanted to protect Taqwatkh." I turned to him. "You must have promised Apolgar quite a fortune for his help. He was already a wealthy man."

"I am the god of a planet," Taqwatkh said. "It is a simple matter to buy wealthy men." He added, quietly, "I could kill you."

"Your power is fading," Jann-Togah said. "You are dying.

You cannot aid my cause. If you kill Kamus, I will kill you. I have killed others like you before."

"You have no powers in this Spaceport," Taqwatkh retorted. "I am still strong enough to destroy you all. But what difference would it make? Shall a god be punished for the death of a mortal Outworlder? He was an insect—I crushed him. There was no need for Apolgar Zad to blame another to protect me. I am Taqwatkh. Neither the Unity of Planets nor the Overlord of Mariyad could question my act. I am a law unto myself."

"You are dying," I told him. "Your search here is a failure. And when you die, Niano will be avenged," and I tried to believe it as I said it.

Taqwatkh laughed then, a great, bellowing laugh of pure evil. "There are other chemists," he said. "There are other worlds. Long ago, I gave the cephalopods civilization and spaceflight, that they might aid me when the time came for my quest. The search is not over. I will find the ingredients for my elixir; perhaps on Centrex, while I make my protest against those petty colonists." He turned to Stam. "You will be released tomorrow," he said. "And tomorrow we will leave."

Stam had sunk deep into his webbed bed. His translated voice was broken and halting. "My Lord . . . I . . ."

"You do not question."

"I—do not question."

Taqwatkh looked at me again. "You are a creature of a day," he said. "I have watched the stars collapse. What are you to me?"

He left the room.

After a long silence, Stam said to me, "Kamus . . . you must understand . . ."

"I know," I said. "Whatever his faults, he's your Glorious Redemption. Well, good luck."

"I—will see that you are paid whatever you—"

"Forget it," I said. I walked out, followed by Janya and Jann-Togah.

We left the Spaceport without talking. When we reached the road to Mariyad, Jann-Togah stopped. "This is where I leave you," he said. "This plan to regain my homeland has failed me, but there are other plans."

"You've got my vote," I said. "I have a bone to pick with

your father, too."

He smiled slightly. "I know. Tell me, Kamus—you knew Taqwatkh had killed Niano, and yet you helped save him from the assassin's raybeam. Why?"

I had been asking myself that, over and over. I had thought that the only answer was the obvious one: there would have been interstellar repercussions and a possibility of war between the cephalopods and Ja-Lur if Xidon had succeeded. But was that the heart of it? It had been my job to protect Taqwatkh, regardless of how I felt about him personally. But he had countermanded Stam's hiring me, so had it really been my job? It would have been justice to let Xidon kill him, I knew. But Niano would not have wanted revenge at such expense; at least, I hoped not.

There was nothing else I could have done, and yet I felt like I had betrayed Niano and Lohvia. I had wanted to see them happy. Instead of answering Jann-Togah, I turned to Janya and said, "Don't tell Lohvia the truth. Let her think Xidon killed Niano."

"You don't have to tell me that," she said softly.

Jann-Togah said, "I think you are a very sentimental person, Kamus of Kadizhar."

"Is that so? Then tell me, Darklord's son—if you knew that Taqwatkh was useless to your conquest of Ja-Agur, why did you risk your life to save him?"

He had been turning to go, but that got him between the shoulders. He stiffened, turned, and looked at me, eyes full of surprise at himself.

"I'll tell you why," I said. "Because you felt sorry for Taqwatkh. Because he was alone on a pedestal, lonely and frightened. And you know the feeling."

He closed off everything in his face; it became merely a mask of flesh. I had gotten to him, and he did not like it. Janya huddled against me under his gaze. After a long moment, he said simply, "We will surely meet again, Kamus."

Then he turned and started down the road toward the Southlands. Always toward the South, for Jann-Togah. I was as sure as he was that we would meet again—and I wasn't looking forward to it.

Janya locked her arm in mine, and we started back toward Mariyad. My head was full of thoughts about Lohvia and

Niano, about a love that never had a chance. Lohvia was so beautiful, so much like Thea had been.

I looked down at Janya. She was nothing like Thea had been, nothing at all. That made me surprisingly happy.

It was evening; the sun was a lump of molten gold on the horizon. We strolled slowly toward the West Gate. "So tell me," she said. "what does the only private eye on the planet do for relaxation after he solves a case?"

I shrugged. "Well, sometimes I go to the Blue Lotus and watch the dancers."

"How about a private show?" she asked, with a smile.

ROBESON

MAXWELL
GRANT

THE GRANT-ROBESON PAPERS

ALFREDO ALCALA

INTRODUCTION

When this series was initiated in 1975, we sub-titled the books, *A New American Pulp.* In many ways, we still respect that phrase.

Philip Jose Farmer, distinguished chronicler of *Greatheart Silver (W.H. 1,2,6),* has come up with a fantastic pulp find for fans of the old magazines. Complete with new illustrations by noted Filipino cartoonist, artist and painter Alfredo P. Alcala, the *Grant-Robeson Papers* are a remarkable and entertaining group of materials.

Rather than go into details here, Phil's preface covers most of your probable questions. It should be made clear however, that Phil is a pulp historian, the author of Tarzan's biography and expert on most of the heroes of the thirties.

Alfredo Alcala, inker and penciller from many American comics of the past five years, rarely gets to show some of the other facets of his artistic skill. His influences, from Leyendecker to Cornwall to Wyeth have been important factors in his style of painting and tone illustration. He can render effectively in the popular realistic style of the earlier part of this century, as epitomized by Leyendecker. Noted for his compositions and line, Alcala's *oeuvre* is recognized from Asia to Europe.

Both Phil and Alfredo currently reside in the United States.

THE GRANT-ROBESON PAPERS
by Maxwell Grant and Kenneth Robeson

Foreward

Maxwell Grant is famous as the author whose by-line appeared on all but one of the *Shadow* novels. Kenneth Robeson is equally well known for his *Doc Savage* and the *Avenger* series.

The work at hand, Number One of *The Grant-Robeson Papers*, is the first new fiction by Grant since a softcover *Shadow* novel in 1967. "Savage Shadow," however, was written in 1935, four years after the appearance of the first *Shadow* novel. Kent Allard, sometimes known as Lamont Cranston, always known as the Shadow, is not Grant's hero in this tale. Kent Robeson is the protagonist.

In the story by Ken Robeson, to appear in the future, Maxwell Grant is the main character.

Why should these two writers use each other as their heroes? And why should these works, written in 1936, have been unprinted until 1977, forty-one years later?

These stories and others by Grant and Robeson have been in a small safe in a residence on Riverside Drive in Manhattan. Your editor was recently made aware of this when the estate of the late J***** D***, a wealthy manufacturer of safes, was inherited by a cousin, L***** C******. (The names are not revealed because of the wishes of the latter.)

It seems that Mr. D*** was an admirer of the works of Grant and Robeson. One reason for this was that Mr. D*** had been, in the early part of the twentieth century, a fighter against crime whose exploits pioneered the path for Doc Savage and the Shadow—not to mention the Spider.

Mr. D***, a collector in various fields, offered Grant and Robeson a tempting sum to write stories which would be unique items, so unique that only he, aside from the two authors, would know of their existence until after his death. Grant and Robeson were contractually obliged not to mention these stories until after Mr. D***'s death.

Though these two prolifics were busy, they had time enough to write sixteen short stories and novelets for the eccentric

collector. Being good friends, they decided, half-jestingly, half-seriously, to make each other the heroes (sometimes, the antiheroes) of their respective tales.

After the first four stories were written, Mr. D***, who was also a science-fiction buff, asked them if they would transfer the scene of their tales to the future—say, the late 1970s. He was interested in seeing, if he lived long enough, how close their fictions would come to reality.

The two responded to the challenge, but they retained their original heroes. In the stipulated decade, they would have been old men. But the writers arranged for both their protagonists—each other—to travel in time to the '70s. Thus, they were still young vigorous men, able to survive and adapt to the strange conditions of the future. They also agreed to depict a common milieu for their heroes, the same future world.

These "future" tales may appear in the heroic fantasy books of Byron Preiss Visual Publications from time to time. It should be interesting to note how closely these approximate reality while in other respects widely missing the mark.

Mr. D*** also asked that each writer attempt to write in the style of the other. This presented a problem. As the student of the *Savage, Shadow* and *Avenger* epics knows, both experimented with different styles during their careers. Even their concept of their heroes changed somewhat over the years.

The two sometimes wrote in one or another of the other's styles and sometimes tried entirely new styles. Mr. D*** apparently did not object.

SAVAGE SHADOW
by Maxwell Grant

1

There were no shadows here. Yet the white-haired man insisted he saw one. His own.

Kenneth Robeson, on this cold, cloudy December day of 1932, thought the tall, scholarly looking, middle-aged man must be crazy. He felt sorry for the daughter, a tall, beautiful, bronze-haired woman of about twenty-five. They were standing by the ramparts of the observation deck of the 86th floor of the Empire State Building. Robeson didn't know why they had come here to endure the bone-chilling wind. Aside from himself, they were the only people who'd stayed long out of the warm concession and display rooms.

He was up here to get an idea for a story. For a whole series, in fact. He'd spent one of the few coins in his pocket to take the elevators to this floor. He'd hoped that looking down on New York City might inspire him. But all he'd been able to think of was the Depression which gripped everybody except criminals.

The man and woman had come along about ten minutes later. He'd eyed them, especially the woman. She didn't look like a tourist or a newcomer, the only people who ever came up here. Her clothes were what he imagined the smart set would wear. A graduate of Vassar with money of her own. The man looked like a college teacher, since he wore tweeds and his hair was as wild as an orchestra conductor's. Or an absent-minded professor's.

They'd not been interested in the view. Instead, they gesticulated violently at each other. Thinking that something he might overhear could give a spark for a story idea, he'd edged close enough to hear them.

"You must go back, father!"

"Never! I tell you, they're doing evil things to me!"

That was enough. His mental ears were pricking up and Robeson moved even closer toward them. Writers had no shame about eavesdropping.

A minute later, as he tried to make sense out of their

passionate, incoherent dialog, he saw the man jump to one side. He pointed down at the floor and said, "There it is! My shadow!"

His daughter spoke soothingly, though her face showed her distress.

"Now father, there's no shadow there! It's an hallucination. Admit it, you're sick!"

He saw her suddenly stiffen, and he turned to see what she was staring at. Three men had come onto the platform. Two were shorter by four or five inches than his own six-foot-three. They were chunky and dark-faced and wore long, black overcoats and dark fedoras. The third was almost as tall as he, slim, elegantly dressed, and blond. He was quite handsome, though a scar disfigured his left cheek. It could have been made by a knife. Or a saber.

The blond man smiled coldly on seeing the two by the rampart. He said something to his companions. Followed by them, he strode toward the couple.

A few seconds later, two more men came out. They wore dark overcoats, but the caps and the white trousers suggested they were ambulance personnel or hospital attendants. One of them carried a straitjacket.

The white-haired man tried to run. His daughter called out to him to stop. The tall blond gestured to the two thuggish looking men, and they ran after the fugitive.

Things happened fast after that. The white-haired man tripped and fell. The woman screamed. The blond grabbed the father, rolled him over, and tried to remove the father's coat. The two struggled. Then the thugs seized the elderly man and held him while the coat was taken off. One of them, struck by a flailing fist in the nose, howled. He hit the white-haired man in the belly.

Robeson started forward. The woman ran up to the man who'd hit her father and began beating on him with her fists. The blond pulled a hypodermic syringe out of his coat pocket. The woman staggered back, pushed by the man she'd attacked. He was yelling names at her which no gentleman would use in a lady's presence.

Robeson cut his speech off with an uppercut to his chin. Then he fell into a blackness, only vaguely aware that he'd been hit over the head from behind.

2

He awoke flat on his back on the cold concrete. The woman and a cop were looking down at him. His head hurt, but not so much he couldn't get to his feet without help. The father, his three attackers, and the two men with the straitjacket were gone. They'd been replaced by the curious from the 86th floor.

"Sure, me lad," the big cop said in a thick Irish brogue. "Are ye all right?"

"I don't think so," Robeson said. "Otherwise, I'd not have gotten into this mess in the first place."

"The blond gentleman said he's preferring no charges." The cop took a pencil from his pocket and held it, ready to write in his notebook. "I'll need your name, occupation, and address. And your version of the particulars."

Robeson gave it to him. The cop's eyebrows went up when he learned that Robeson was a writer. They ascended as far as they could go on hearing his residence.

"Bleeker Street, is it?" Indicating that anyone who lived in that area was of no consequence.

"Ye should go to a hospital and get checked out, me boy."

"I'll be okay," Ken said. He looked at the woman, whose makeup was smudged with tears. "How about you? Aren't you preferring charges against the man who hit you?"

She shook her head. "No. I'm not hurt. It wouldn't do any good, anyway. Father *had* escaped from a sanitarium. I shouldn't have interfered. But they were so *brutal*!"

"They shouldn't have hit a pretty colleen like you who was just showing a natural concern for her father," the cop said. He put away his notebook. "Ye both should go inside where it's warm and maybe drink a cup of coffee."

Robeson watched him walk away. He said, "I'm sorry about your father. It's none of my business, but . . . is there any way I could help?"

Looking utterly miserable and hopeless, she said, "No. No one can help."

"Well, at least you could tell me what it's all about. Maybe getting it off your chest will help."

He felt the blood rush to his face. Even with the coat on, she looked more than full-bosomed.

"I mean . . ."

She began crying again. In a minute, they were inside, sitting at a table while the waitress was getting their coffee, and she was pouring out her troubles. Despite the pain in the back of his head and the feeling that he should be working out his series ideas, Robeson listened intently. Anyway, what she was telling him could eventually become the basis of a story, even if it didn't inspire him about the project at hand. All was grist for the writer's mill.

She was Patricia Burke. Her father was Professor Winston Burke, a teacher of chemistry and biology at a small upstate New York college. Her mother had died five years ago. Patricia, "Trish" for short, had taken care of the household duties for her father but had managed at the same time to attend classes at Kanyoto College, graduating in 1928. She'd gotten a job at a high school near Kanyoto, commuting to her father's home and taking care of him.

Then the Depression had come, and she lost her job. In 1930 she had gone to Manhattan to work as a bookkeeper for a friend who was managing a chain of beauty parlors. Her father had tried to make her stay at home, and this had led to a quarrel. Though they wrote to each other now and then, she hadn't visited him for a year. He felt that her duty was to be his housekeeper. Moreover, he strongly disapproved of her living alone in the big wicked city. Some of his letters even hinted that he did not believe that she was living alone.

"He's a very moral man," Trish said. "A real churchgoer. He just can't believe that I can resist the temptations of New York City. Which doesn't say much for his trust in me.

"Anyway, about a year ago I got a very excited letter from him. Instead of preaching to me, as he usually did, he told me that he had been experimenting with a chemical compound which, when injected into people, could force them to be moral. He didn't tell me the formula, of course, nor did he explain exactly how people could be made to act like saints.

"It was then that I began to have misgivings about his sanity.

"Six weeks later I got a letter saying that he had gone to see a big industrialist in Utica. This man, Mr. Bierstoss, was also very active in his church. In fact, he owns a radio station most of the programs of which are devoted to spreading the Gospel. You know, sermons, hymn songs, collecting money for mis-

sionaries. Stuff like that.

"Another letter followed. Father was in seventh heaven. Bierstoss was going to finance his experiments. I didn't hear anything from them until a month later. Actually, I didn't hear from him directly. I got a letter from a colleague, Professor Smithton, an old friend of the family. He said that my father had been acting peculiarly lately. I should come right away.

"I got a leave of absence and packed. But before I could get going, Smithton phoned. He said my father'd had a complete breakdown, and he was now in the Restful Meadows sanitarium. That's up in the Catskills. Mr. Bierstoss was paying for the treatment.

"I tried to phone Bierstoss, but I could never get through to him. His secretary said he'd call back, but he never did. So I drove up to the sanitarium.

"Doctor von Adlerdreck met me in his office. He was very nice but firm. My father, he said, was in no condition to have visitors. In fact, he probably wouldn't even recognize me. But he had great hopes that my father would recover completely in time. The doctor said he'd keep me advised. When it was okay for me to visit my father, he'd call me."

Kenneth Robeson gave no sign of his impatience. So far, there was nothing out of the usual in her story. Her father was undoubtedly crazy. He felt sorry for her, but he could do nothing for her. Still . . . maybe he could use her tale as a basis for the first in his series. It would make a socko beginning.

First, however, he had to get his characters outlined, establish their motives, their main purpose. Create a great villain for his hero and his sidekicks to combat.

The big shot at Street & Smith was waiting for him to come up with an idea that would excite him. If he could bring it in within the next three days, and set the big shot on fire with it, he'd be on easy street for a long while—if the series caught on with the public. A novel a month would bring five hundred dollars a month, big money. He could rap out a novel in a week and have plenty of time left to write other stuff, another novel, three or four short stories. Maybe he could bring in fifteen hundred dollars a month. Then, if the series continued to be popular, S & S would raise his rates, and in a year or so he'd be making three thousand a month.

Thirty-six thousand smackolas a year. Wow!

But if he couldn't get an advance within the next three days, he'd be kicked out of his sleazy, cockroach-ridden apartment. And he might have to sell apples on a corner like so many poor devils. Might, God forbid, be in such desperate straits he'd have to hock his typewriter.

He felt himself turn pale at the prospect.

No, he'd starve first.

He came back to his surroundings with a start. Trish Burke was looking at him peculiarly.

"Aren't you listening?"

"Sure. You were saying . . . ?"

"Restful Meadows was supposed to be a high-class sanitarium. I was thankful that Mr. Bierstoss was footing the bills. If it'd been up to me to pay, poor father would have had to go into the county hospital, a real snake pit. But I didn't like the two men that lounged around the doctor's office, doing nothing except making rude remarks and drinking hooch from a flask.

"The doctor was a well-educated man; he'd attended the University of Berlin and a medical school in Vienna. I couldn't understand why those two thugs were around. I questioned him when we were alone for a moment, and he said they were his chief aides. He used them when a patient got violent.

"That seemed rather fishy to me. But I was in a state of grief and shock. So I left. What could I do?

"However, I had found out the names of the two attendants. When I got back, I phoned my cousin, Clyde Burke. He's a reporter for the *New York Classic*."

"A real rag, a notorious example of yellow journalism," Kenneth said.

"Yes, I know. I don't know why Clyde works for it, since he is a very good reporter. Maybe because it doesn't demand much of his time, and he moonlights for other papers. It doesn't matter. Anyway, I asked him about the doctor and the two men with him.

"Clyde said the sanitorium had a good reputation. Von Adlerdreck was said to be a fine doctor, but at one time the FBI had investigated him about his rumored connections with the New York German-American Bunds. But they'd not been able to establish any link.

"However, Clyde was very surprised when I told him the

names of the doctor's two associates. He said they were notorious criminals. Both Antonio 'Chips' Bufalo and Roberto 'Eggs' Ovarizi had been members of a Brooklyn mob. But they'd left town suddenly. Not because of the police. They were pro-Mussolini, and the Italian-American gangsters are violently anti-Mussolini. Il Duce had broken the power of Italian and Sicilian organized crime—what do they call it there, the Black Hand? The Italian gangsters here hate him.

"Clyde said that Bufalo and Ovarizi had taken off to keep from getting killed. They'd dropped out of sight. He was surprised to find that they'd holed up in the sanitarium. He said he'd like to find out why they were there, but his main source of information was in France at that time. Maybe he could find out something for me on his own."

Robeson stirred impatiently. "What about this shadow your father sees?"

"I'm getting to that. Late last night I got a phone call in my apartment. It was father. He'd escaped, and he . . ."

She stopped. Kenneth turned to see what she was staring at. Then he rose to his feet quickly, pushing the chair to one side.

Von Adlerdreck and his two swarthy companions had returned. The latter had their hands in their coats; it was evident that they held pistols.

3

Von Adlerdreck, his thin handsome features pressed into a smile, approached them. He stopped, bowed slightly, spoke in English with only a slight German accent.

"Your pardon, Miss Burke. Professor Burke has been taken in an ambulance to the sanitarium. But it occurred to me that I owed you an apology for the roughness of my men. I've reprimanded them, and they have promised never to act in such a hasty and rude manner again."

He looked at Robeson. "My sincerest apologies to you, too, young man. You were only being gallant when you interfered. I hope that your injuries are minimal."

Miss Burke said, "I don't think that it was necessary to be so rough. But then father was putting up a fight. I accept your apology."

Robeson said, "Which one of you hit me?"

Von Alderdreck said, "My overzealous assistant, Mr. Bufalo."

He turned and pointed at the slightly taller of the two. Robeson strode past him. Bufalo growled, "Whatcha up to, punk?"

"This." And Robeson delivered a hard right-cross to the battleship-prow chin. Bufalo staggered back, his hands still in his overcoat pockets, and he fell to his knees. Trish said, loudly, "Oh, no!"

Robeson turned away. His fist hurt, and the blow had increased the pain in the back of his head. But he felt satisfied.

Trish screamed. Robeson whirled. Ovarizi had pulled out of his pocket a .45 automatic, a huge, ugly weapon which looked at that moment bigger than a cannon.

Von Adlerdreck shouted, "You fool! Put that away!"

There were about a dozen people in the room. All were silently staring at the group.

Bufalo was up on his feet by now, but he looked as if he still didn't know what had happened.

Ovarizi put the gun back into the pocket. The doctor said, "I suggest you leave now, Mr. . . . ?"

"Kenneth Robeson. And I'm not leaving until I know that Miss Burke is safe."

The German's mouth turned down. But he managed to bring it back up into a facsimile of a smile. "I assure you that I only returned to extend to Miss Burke my regrets for this unfortunate incident. Also to tell her that she can accompany us back to the sanitarium if she wishes. She can stay there with no expense for several days and observe her father. I wish to assure her that he is not being mistreated."

This fellow is too oily, Robeson thought. And he sure doesn't keep good company.

Trish Burke hesitated. She looked as if she wanted some advice from Robeson. Seeing that he wasn't giving any, she said, "Thank you very much, Doctor. I'll take you up on your offer in a couple of days. It'll be a weekend then, and I won't be working. I'm afraid I'd lose my job if I took any more time off."

She smiled. "You know how tough it is to get a job now."

He bowed slightly again, and said, "As you wish," turned on his heel like a soldier, and strode off. Bufalo's eyes had

become unglazed then. He started toward Robeson, snarling silently. Von Alderdreck said something Italian to him in a low voice.

Bufalo said, "I ain't gonna forget this, you punk." But he followed the other two to the elevator doors.

Robeson was shaking with the reaction. He said, "I'll bet those thugs don't have licenses to carry those guns."

He put a hand on her arm and looked into the wide blue eyes. "Listen. Take my advice. Don't go up there alone. There's something rotten about this. It isn't just a matter of a crazy old man."

Trish Burke said, "Why'd you hit him? Not that I mind. I'd like to do the same myself. But why . . ."

Robeson waved his hand. "I had to get my self-respect back. Or maybe I'm just angry at a lot of things, and I took it out on him. I had a good excuse. The thing is, this is too deep for you. You'd better go to the police. Fast."

Trish Burke said, "But I can't get the police interested unless I have something solid to tell them. Will you testify that Ovarizi pulled a gun on you?"

Reluctantly, Robeson said, "Yes. But he can claim it was in self-defense."

He frowned. She was right. The only thing on which the police might take action was the question of weapon licenses. They'd regard her as just a daughter overly concerned about her father, a patient at a respectable sanitarium. He was a penniless pulp-magazine writer—an unrespectable profession—and one who could be charged with battery and assault.

Time was speeding by. Monday morning's meeting with the big shot at S & S was getting nearer every minute. And he still had no series concepts worth considering. Why in hell had he come up here just in time to get involved with this woman, beautiful though she was?

He wanted to leave, but he couldn't. He'd feel like a heel, a coward, if he just walked away from her.

Besides . . . her father's nutty talk about a chemical that could control people's moral behavior! Wasn't that the type of thing he was trying to think of? And wasn't he in the midst of a situation that would make a rattling good story?

Trish said, "I'll call Myra and tell her I'm sick. She won't like it, but I can't just abandon my father because I'm afraid to lose my job."

"Then what?" he said.

She came close enough so he could smell her perfume. It was a very light odor, faint, but it did something powerful to him. Not to mention that beautiful face and huge, imploring blue eyes.

"I have a car. We can go up to Roosville now. They won't suspect we'll be there soon. We can scout around, try to find out what's going on up there."

She had no sense of reality. Maybe she had a touch of insanity, inherited, no doubt. But at the moment he felt as if he was, just by being close to her, receiving some of her determination, her unreasonable resolve to make this a quest of some sort. She was transmitting, and he was receiving. And of course he couldn't receive unless he was on her frequency. In other words, he was as unrealistically romantic as she.

He shrugged and said, "Okay. I'll go."

She didn't squeal with pleasure, but she looked as if she'd like to.

They took the elevators down to the ground floor. Robeson felt the change in his pocket and thought of the three dollars in his wallet. His worldly wealth. If she expected him to pay for her food and the gas for the car, she was going to be shocked. Gallantry only went so far.

They walked four blocks to her car, a rusty 1928 Model A coupe with a rumble seat. On the way he told her something about himself, his boyhood in the Midwest, his sudden resolve to come to New York and write for his living. She looked a little askance at his ambition. It was evident that she had no high opinion of pulp-magazine literature. But she confessed that she'd never read any.

"I suppose it is trash," he said. "Ephemeral stuff that'll be forgotten a month after it's published. But it's a living, and it's a stepping stone to the big league. However, it isn't easy to write for the pulps. You have to have a certain talent for it. Very few can do it. I've sold about a dozen stories, just enough to keep me alive. But I have a chance to make it big now. If I do, the money I make'll give me the leisure to write good stuff. After all, Balzac wrote thrillers in his early days, but he became one of the world's greatest writers."

He was angry with himself for having tried to justify himself.

Why should he appease her snobbery?

They got into the car and shivered in the cold until the motor was warmed up and the heater was going full blast. Trish drove the car down Thirty-Fifth to Broadway, then cut north toward the George Washington Bridge. They were silent during this time, he nursing his wounds over her remarks, she probably thinking about her father.

Then, as they took the highway toward the Catskills, he spoke for the first time.

"We're being followed."

4

He was sure of it, when, five miles further, he told her to pull over onto the shoulder of the road. The big black car slowed, then stopped about four hundred and seventy yards behind them.

"Ten to one it's von Adlerdreck and his gatmen."

She drove back onto the highway again, keeping the beat-up Model A at its top speed, sixty miles an hour. Oil fumes began to fill the interior, and she eased the pressure on the pedal. "It needs a ring and a valve job bad," she said. "But I haven't been able to afford it."

"Who can afford anything nowadays? Keep going. Don't worry. I don't think they'll try anything until after dark, if then. Maybe they just want to see where we go."

"Just what are we going to do?" she said.

"Play it by ear. You're not tone-deaf, are you? Forget about them for the time being. Now, you said you got a phone call from your father. He'd escaped."

"Yes. He wanted me to meet him. He said that von Adlerdreck would be looking for him to go to my place. So I suggested the 86th floor of the Empire State Building. I suppose because I'd been reading an article on its construction when he called. The talk was very short. He was very nervous, he said he'd give me all the details when we got together.

"When I saw him in the restaurant, he insisted that we go outside. He said he didn't want anyone to overhear us. He seemed to think the place was full of spies. And he kept talking about his shadow. Then . . ."

"Just what did he say about the shadow?"

"He said that it was menacing. Savage. It threatened him."

"How could a shadow threaten him?"

"By making terrible faces at him. It had a mouth, and though it couldn't speak, he could lip-read what it said. It said awful things to him. Most of them unspeakable. I mean, they were so bad he couldn't even tell me what they were. Obscene and profane things. So bad they were driving him crazy."

Robeson thought that the professor had the cart before the horse.

"When did this shadow appear?"

"I don't know. Dad was all right one day, and the next day he went crazy. He woke up and there it was, dancing in front of him, grimacing, mouthing those awful words, leaping at him but never touching him. He went to Mr. Biertoss, who suggested he go to a sanitarium. Dad refused, but Mr. Bierstoss phoned Doctor von Adlerdreck anyway. That evening the doctor and those two yeggs showed up and took him away in a straitjacket."

"Yeggs?" Robeson said. "A yegg is a safecracker."

"Oh? Well, gorillas. What's the difference?"

"Bierstoss must've known the doctor," Kenneth said. "I'd say there's a link between the two. But it may not be sinister. Maybe von Adlerdreck was recommended by Bierstoss's doctor."

"Maybe, but I don't believe that's all. Do you?"

"No. What do you know about Bierstoss? Aside from his being an industrialist. What does his company manufacture? What's his background?"

"I don't know much except what father told me in his letter. He came over from Germany in 1920 at the age of thirty. He seems to have had some money then. He purchased a garage and a used-car business. After he'd set up a whole chain of these, he sold it and bought a partnership in a small pharmaceutical firm. He also bought a small publishing house that dealt in religious books. His rise was phenomenal. Five years later he was president of a chain of pharmaceutical stores and some more publishing houses. Even the stock market crash didn't affect his businesses too much."

"What about his politics? And his attitude toward Germany?"

"Dad didn't say anything about those."

They stopped to eat lunch and to gas up. Trish insisted on paying for the food. Robeson didn't object. The big black car had dropped out of sight. That meant nothing. If the doctor was in that car, he knew by now where they were headed. Robeson studied the road map he'd taken from the glove compartment. The doctor could have taken a country road a half a mile back and come back out on the highway two miles northwest of them.

Just before dusk, they pulled into Roosville. This was a village which, according to a sign, had fifty-nine friendly citizens. There was no hotel, but the service-station attendant directed them to Mrs. Doorn's boarding house. Trish turned off the ignition and looked steadily at him. He felt his cheeks flushing.

"I have all my small savings in my purse," she said. "I took it out so I could give it to Dad if I decided to help him hide. I have enough to pay for two rooms—if Mrs. Doorn's charges aren't outrageous—for a couple of days. But I'd like to save as much as I can. So . . . I propose we share a room. We'll tell Mrs. Doorn we're married.

"But I want your word you won't make a pass. I'll tell you now that I'll say no. Maybe, if I'd known you longer, if I were in love . . . I'm no prude but I am sensible. I don't give myself away. You understand?"

He hesitated, looked away, then said, "I'll be honest with you. I don't think I could stand it. It's been a long time, and you're so beautiful."

"Thanks. Okay. If I can manage it, I'll get us separate rooms. We'll say we're brother and sister. Which makes me Patricia Robeson. Here, take the money. It wouldn't look right if I paid."

Mrs. Doorn, a tall, fat, red-faced woman of fifty, accepted their story. She gave Trish a room on the top floor of the three-story house, built when Queen Victoria was still living. Kenneth took a small room in the basement, the cheapest available.

"I go to bed at ten," Mrs. Doorn said. "The key is under the doormat if you intend to stay out late. There isn't anything to do here at night except listen to the radio."

Robeson thought it best not to say that they had business at the Restful Meadows. His feeling that he was on an absurd

quest got even stronger. What, after all, could the two of them do? And why should they be doing anything?

Though they weren't very hungry, they ate dinner at Mrs. Doorn's well-laden table. Kenneth, after his meager diet of hamburgers, hot dogs, and french fries for the last three months, decided that he had an appetite after all. A big thick steak, mashed potatoes with gravy, cranberry sauce, a salad, and a big slice of Dutch apple pie left him feeling happy but logy. It was worth the trip just to eat here. Especially since he wasn't paying for it.

Well, he was footing the bill in a sense. He was giving Trish his time, a commodity a writer couldn't afford to waste. He thought of the typewriter in his crappy apartment, sitting mute and inglorious on a table, waiting for its master's fingers to type out a pulp masterpiece.

While the landlady was cleaning off the table, most of the boarders went into the parlor to listen to the radio. Robeson went to his room for a moment to go to the toilet. He came up into the hallway expecting to meet Trish there. Instead, he found two of the diners. It was evident that they wanted to speak to him.

5

One was a very tall, very skinny man about forty named Bill Homer Smalljack. His long thin nose was very red. He wore very thick spectacles, one lens of which was a supernumerary. Behind it was an obviously glass eye, not even matching the hazel of the good eye.

The other was a middle-aged giant, towering, well muscled, his face as long, narrow, and gloomy as the stereotyped Puritan's. His hawk nose was as red as his companion's. His hands looked as big as quart jugs. In fact, one of them held a jug. He'd been introduced at the table as Hans van Rijnwijk.

Smalljack's profession was digging holes in the ground. Wells, graves, basements, post holes. Van Rijnwijk was a mechanic for the local garage, but he also repaired agricultural machinery, clocks, anything mechanical. Nowadays, a person had to quit specializing to survive.

Smalljack said, "Hans and me run a little business on the side. Give him a sample of the wares, big boy."

Hans, who didn't like to talk, silently removed the cork and handed the jug to Kenneth. He smelled the odor rising from the open neck. His eyes watered.

"Good stuff," Smalljack said. "The best white lightning in New York. I should know. I've tasted it all. Guaranteed, too. And cheap. Go ahead, take a snifter."

"I can't do that," Robeson said. "I don't have much money. I couldn't afford this."

"Sure you can. It's only two-fifty a quart. Even if you don't drink, you can resell it in the city. That'll bring you three times as much on Broadway."

The prospect of making a profit interested Robeson. God knew, he needed the money. But if the car was by some chance inspected by the police . . . oh, what the hell! So he forked over the money to Smalljack, thanked them, and took the jug, wrapped in his coat, to the car. He put it in the rumble seat. While he was doing this, the bootleggers came out of the house. Smalljack winked at him as the two got into a 1932 Packard. Business must be good if they could afford that.

He started back to the house but stopped as Trish Burke came out. After they'd gotten in the Ford, he told her what he'd just done.

"I know it was your money, but it's a good investment."

"Investment, hell," she said. "We'll invest it in our tummies, right now. I need a shot of Dutch courage."

Robeson was pleased, since he had expected her to blow up about it. But he told her to wait until they got out of town. They mustn't be seen by the local sheriff. She drove onto the gravel road that led to Restful Meadows, then stopped on the other side of a wooden covered bridge spanning a wide creek. Robeson got the jug out and offered her the first drink. Though her hands and arms were slender, she handled the heavy jug well, holding it horizontally across her upper right arm.

"Wow! That makes you see stars!"

Kenneth took his turn. The stuff burned his mouth, his tongue, his gullet, his stomach. But it wasn't rotgut. It was just powerful.

Trish took another long draught, then said, "I'm ready to tackle a tiger now."

Robeson decided he'd pass up seconds. His brain was

already beginning to feel numb.

Then they froze. Headlights struck across the bridge, and they could hear a motor. The black-and-white car slowed as it went by them, and they could see a tall-hatted man, Sheriff Huisman, looking at them. But the car speeded up and disappeared around a bend.

Robeson felt his heart resume beating. "We were lucky. He's out after bigger game. Our two dispensers of tabu juice of the corn, I'll bet. You want me to drive?"

"I never feel comfortable when someone else is driving," she said. "I'm just as good as any man behind the wheel and better than most. And I can drink nine out of ten under the table." She added, "In case you were figuring on taking advantage of my drunken condition."

He chuckled. She sure was a pistil. One of those modern liberated women. Maybe he should have registered them as man and wife. No wonder her father didn't want her to go to New York. Even a permissive parent would have worried about her.

The road was dark, the sky being cloudy. The headlight beams showed patches of snow, dry weeds, tall bare trees, ruined choirs. About halfway to the sanitarium, a car passed them going in the opposite direction. It was the sheriff's, going too fast for the road.

"He might be back," Robeson said. "So we ought to park this buggy where it can't be seen."

"Give me some credit for brains."

She was no longer the seemingly helpless woman he'd met on top of the skyscraper. He doubted it was the liquor causing the change. She played roles, and when she was in Rome she did as the Romans did. Or were supposed to do. This tough capable character of hers, though, was probably her real one.

They saw the sanitarium about five minutes before they got there. Lights blazed from and around it. It was obviously set on top of a high hill. When they got to the entrance, they found a pair of iron gates set in a high stone wall. A ditch ran along the walls paralleling the road. A stone bridge crossed the ditch, on the bottom of which was half-frozen water.

Trish stopped the car but left the motor running. "Maybe we should just breeze on in and ask to see my father."

"Then we'd see what they want us to see. That'd be no more

than you saw your last visit. I think we ought to scout around. Maybe we could even get inside the building and waltz off with your father. But if we're caught, we could be charged with kidnapping. Or illegal entry. It isn't that I'm afraid. It's just that I think Falstaff had something when he said discretion is the better part of valor."

"I really have no right to ask you to stick your neck out," she said. "But you did volunteer, and you know there's something rotten about von Adlerdreck and his two mobsters. Why don't we just walk around outside, get the lay of the land, maybe do a Peeping Tom act? Then we can come back to the car for a powwow. After all, we don't necessarily have to take any action tonight."

Robeson agreed. She drove the car into a road which was more two rutted tracks than anything. This cut through a farm across the road from the sanitarium. Trees and bushes lined the wire fence along the acreage. They could conceal the Ford behind them.

Trish drove the car across the muddy field in low gear. Robeson said, "Oh, oh!" He indicated a long black Packard parked by the cover they'd picked out. There seemed to be no one in it.

"It's the bootleggers!"

"The sheriff didn't see it, so it must be invisible from the road," she said.

They left the Ford behind the Packard. They found that the wire fence had been bent open enough to allow them to crawl through.

"Evidently they use this a lot," Kenneth said. "Well, we'll have to be careful we don't run into them."

They jumped across the watery area of the ditch, scrambled up the bank with muddy shoes, went across the road and the stone bridge. As he'd expected, Robeson found that the padlock enclosing two links of the chain around the gates was open. He removed the lock, opened the gates, and the two went inside. He reached in through the steel bars and put the chain back into the large links. A passerby in the dark would think that the lock was shut.

On second thought, he removed the lock and threw it into the darkness alongside the wall. He didn't want to be trapped if the bootleggers closed the lock when they left.

The gravel road wound around the estate, climbed the hill corkscrewlike, and emerged at the front of the huge cubical building. They started down it, then halted.

"Voices! Over there!" Trish said.

6

Somewhere deep in a grove of leafless trees a match was struck. It went out, but the ends of two cigarettes glowed like fireflies.

He took her hand, and they walked into the trees. It was easy to take cover, though the unmelted snow under the branches made slushing sounds. When within earshot, they stopped behind a broad-trunked sycamore.

He counted seven dim figures, all standing close together. There was just enough light to see the silhouette of a jug being passed around.

From the conversation it wasn't difficult to know what was happening. Smalljack and Rijnwijk had come here to sell some of the patients their white mule. The latter had sneaked out of the building to rendezvous here so they could get the forbidden liquor.

If people could get out, unobserved, then they could get back in. Which meant that he and Trish might also enter.

There had been enough time for the exchange of whiskey and money. But the bootleggers were hanging around for the party, accepting the drinks from the people they'd just sold the liquor to. Or, perhaps, the patients had urged them to stay because they wanted the company of outsiders. Whatever the reason, all seven soon moved on, one of them complaining about the cold. This was a woman called "Pat," the only female in the group.

Robeson's face became warm when he heard some of the remarks. They were certainly risque. Trish didn't seem bothered. On the contrary, she giggled.

Robeson considered going up to the building and trying the doors. He presumed that the patients had left by a ground floor exit. It didn't seem likely that they would have come from an upper story window down a string of bed sheets tied together. But the more he listened to them, the less sure he was. They sounded like a crazy bunch.

Which, he told himself, was just what they were. Otherwise, they wouldn't be here.

Trish said, "Shouldn't we be moving on. I'm frozen."

"I don't know. Maybe we ought to follow them. We might overhear something we can use. Also . . . maybe we ought to declare ourselves. They won't turn us in. They can't without exposing their little setup. They might even be willing to help us. In any event, they could tell us something about your father."

Trish didn't think that was a good idea. He argued for a minute, and she finally agreed.

They followed them to a clearing near the wall. In its center was a summer house, a rather large round edifice with a platform extending from the front. Possibly a band played here in warmer weather. A concrete path led from it toward the hill on which the sanitarium stood.

One of the group must have had a key. The door swung open, they trooped in, and the door was shut. Presently he could see a thread of light between a drawn blind and the window ledge. A few minutes later, wood smoke poured from a metal chimney sticking from the side of the house.

He and Trish crept up on the porch, and he placed his ear against the door. There were sounds of low revelry: roars of laughter, fast talking, a sudden scream of delight, or maybe it was protest, from the woman. A radio started blaring the *Maple Leaf Rag*.

Trish was crouching, peeking under the shade. Robeson joined her.

There were Smalljack and van Rijnwijk, still dressed in their overalls and checked shirts. They were consuming their own booze, a testimony to its excellence. Or perhaps they would drink anything.

One of the revelers was even taller than van Rijnwijk. He was about fifty, a hard fifty, broad-shouldered, and he looked as if he might have had an outstanding physique in his youth. He also could have been very handsome once. But dissipation had lined his face, bagged his eyes, and fattened throat and waist. It had also coarsened and reddened his nose. His skin was a sickly yellow and his hair was that sort of brown which youthful red turns into as middle age creeps up. He was chugalugging a jug as the others clapped and cheered him on. Robeson was in awe

at this feat. Anybody who could drink that fiery stuff down gulp after gulp, pint after pint, and not burst into flames, was a phenomenon.

The next to catch his eye was probably the most extraordinary looking person there. He was very short, not more than an inch or two over five feet. In fact, he looked almost as broad as he was tall. His arms hung down almost to his knees, and the face was that of a chimpanzee's: low forehead, the most prominent supraorbital ridges he'd ever seen—they would have put an Australian aborigine's to shame—under which were small rusty eyes, a long upper lip, a receding chin. Though he was about fifty, his shock of hair was rusty red, and a tuft of curly red hair spilled out from the top of his open shirt.

He was engaged in drinking and in arguing with a tall, slim, hawk-faced fellow of the same age, dressed as if for a formal dinner. Robeson couldn't believe it. A tuxedo and an opera hat! He carried a cane, no doubt because of his limp. However, it had another purpose. Robeson saw him twist the gold-colored knot at its top and remove it. He upended the cane, out of which slid three glass vials. While talking loudly and angrily to the apelike man, he uncorked the vials, filled them with corn whiskey, corked them, and slid them into the hollow interior of the cane.

The sixth was an anemic-looking, skinny little fellow with a sour expression. His hair was of a peculiar indeterminate color which Robeson could only describe as "pale." He sat in a corner on a bare wooden folding chair, drinking steadily from a glass.

The last member was the woman, a tall, long-legged woman in a tight, red low-cut dress and very tall high heels. Her stockings were fishnet. She looked as if she were fifty but she could have been younger. Robeson guessed that the lines in her face had been put there, not by the natural aging of Mother Nature, but by hard living. Nevertheless, the bone structure showed that she had been a very good-looking woman in her prime. Her long hair was peroxided. Her bosom was huge, in startling contrast to her waist, which, though ringed by puffy fat, still looked narrow.

When she walked, she had the long stride of the professional burlesque queen. The eyes of the men followed her legs and the

swaying hips when she walked—except those of the pale runt. And the fact that he looked everywhere except where she was showed that he was intensely interested in her. But he didn't want anyone, including himself, to know it.

Ken Robeson, wondering if his plan to question these people was right, despaired. Obviously, they were alcoholics who'd been sent to Restful Meadows by relatives or the lawyers who managed their estates. They'd managed to circumvent the watchdogs of the sanitarium and gotten into contact with the local bootleggers.

They probably wouldn't even know what was going on in the place.

Yet . . . they had to be sober most of the time, even if they didn't like it.

He watched and listened while he tried to make up his mind what to do. The very tall man, whom the others called "Doc," seemed to be of French origin. Though he spoke excellent English, he had a slight Gallic accent. It was obvious that his companions regarded him as a sort of leader. He might be the person to concentrate on.

"Listen, Trish," Robeson said. "These drunks could help us. Or they might think we're just intruders who'll make so much trouble for them that their source of alcohol could be cut off. What do you think?"

Her face was close to his. Her perfume, mixed with the white lightning breathed on him, was intoxicating.

He thought, How lovely she is!

She said, "They can't tell on us without exposing what they've been doing. But maybe von Adlerdreck doesn't care. Maybe he's just running this sanitarium as a coverup, and he could care less if his patients are drinking themselves to death.

"Maybe I'm paranoid. But . . . what he's been doing to my father . . . I think he's more than just a doctor who's concerned about a crazy old man. I don't have any real evidence to back up my feelings. But I'm a pretty good reader of character. I could detect nuances in a voice, in an expression. I know von Adlerdreck's concealing something sinister behind that oily smile. Don't smile. It isn't woman's intuition. It's a fine-honed ability to tell what a man is really thinking. A lot of women have it because they had to develop the ability in order to survive in this man's world."

"I'm crazy to go on just a feeling," he said. "But there is something wrong. I . . ."

He should have been looking into the room instead of at her. The door was flung open, and a man stepped outside.

7

Robeson started to rise. The man, the near-giant, reeled toward him, grabbed his wrist, and started shouting. Robeson tried to back away, but he was held in a grip like a loan shark's. He quit struggling. There was no use antagonizing him and the others.

"We'll go in with you," he said. "If you keep yelling, they'll hear you up there." He gestured at the building on the hill.

For a minute, it was impossible to enter. The apelike man and the slim fellow in the tux tried to get through the doorway at the same time. Jammed together, cursing, they writhed and wriggled, then both fell through together. The big man, still holding on to Robeson, stepped over them into the house. Trish followed them.

Inside, he released his hold and closed the door in the faces of the two. They howled and beat on the door until van Rijnwijk opened it for them. And they fell again, sprawling on the floor.

The woman named Pat screeched with laughter. The others stared silently.

"All right," Doc said, his nose almost meeting Robeson's as he stooped down. "What in hell were you doing? Spying on us?"

Robeson felt the concentration of whiskey in his veins soar as he breathed the man's breath. You could get drunk just by being near this man. His eyes were a peculiar yellow color. Jaundice. This man was dying of liver disease, and yet he was hastening the process by consuming enormous quantities of alcohol.

The two clowns got up from the floor and dusted themselves off. They kept up a firecracker series of insults and curses.

Robeson said, "No, we're not spies. If you'll listen without interruption, I'll tell you who we are and why we're here."

Nothing was to be gained by lying. The truth might be of some help, though these people didn't look as if they would be

much help for anybody. Including themselves.

After he'd finished, there was a long silence. Then the big man said, "Whash, whash . . ." He paused, struggled to get control of his tongue, and spoke more slowly. "What do you want from us? Help against that . . ."

He paused, swallowed the word he'd been about to use, no doubt in deference to Trish, and continued. "Against that medical Attila the Hun, Herr Doktor von Adlerdreck?"

The apish man exploded. "I'm all for it! I tell you, that so-and-so is involved in something crooked! Otherwise, why would he hire two gangsters?"

The lady called Pat said, "Yeah, and I'll tell you something else that's fishy. Eiderduck gets a lot of mail from overseas and from Washington, D.C. Only the letters don't come in envelopes from overseas or Washington. They come inside other envelopes from a New York address."

"Eiderduck?" Robeson said.

"She means Addledrake," the apish man said.

"We call von Adlerdreck a lot of things," the big, dark, yellow-eyed man said. "Some of which ain't fit for young ladies to hear."

He introduced himself as Doctor Marcel Sebastien LeClerc du Bronce du Fauve. He was, he said, a French Canadian of aristocratic descent.

"He ain't a real doctor," Pat said. "He's a chiropractor, a bone bender. He got into trouble because he was too much a ladies' man with his female patients. So he ducked out and hid here. Not that he shouldn't be here. He's a real rummy, just like the rest of us."

"You got a big mouth, Pat," Doc said. "A healer is a doctor, and I healed bodies and broken hearts. Is it my fault that I am temperamentally unable to resist beauty?"

He bowed to Trish and smiled dazzlingly. She backed away, dizzy with the heavy fumes of fermented corn.

The others were introduced. Pat Coningway was just what Ken had guessed. An ex-stripper. But she'd married an old millionaire who'd died a year ago. "He was vigorous for his age, but his heart couldn't take it," she said, looking smug.

The apish man was Anderson Maypole Blidgett, but everyone called him "Jocko." The man in the tux was Ted Scrooch Creeks, Ted to everyone but Jocko, who called him

"Oinks."

Jocko said, grinning at the outraged Creeks, "Oinks is a shyster, an ambulance chaser who got drummed out of the New York Bar Association. I calls him Oinks because he defended a pig rustler in his last case. But he was so bombed the judge threw him in the slammer for contempt of court."

"An out-and-out lie!" Oinks said, waving his cane so close to Jocko's nose he had to step back. "I suffer from diabetes and that morning I had neglected my dosage of insulin. This left me somewhat confused, and the judge refused to accept my defense. He himself was a heavy drinker who had no mercy for those defendants in a similar plight."

"Yeah, tell that to the Marines," Jocko said.

Jocko, it turned out, was a wealthy pharmacist who owned a chain of drugstores. But, as he cheerfully admitted, booze got to be a bigger problem than he could handle. So he'd committed himself to Restful Meadows to dry out. So far, without success.

The anemic squirt with the two bootleggers was Bob Thomas. He'd once been a telephone lineman, but he'd gone into full-time whiskey-making with the other two. He lived in the basement of a private house where he worked on his inventions in his spare time.

"When he's sober, that is," Jocko gleefully said. "Maybe if Lunger Tom laid off the juice, his inventions might work."

Thomas, his colorless eyes blazing, said, "Yeah, you throwback to the missing link, you'd drink too if you'd got caught in a mustard gas attack. What's your excuse?" He began coughing violently but got over the fit when he swallowed more of the white lightning.

"That stuff'll cure what ails you," Smalljack said.

Robeson said, "Well, what about it? Miss Burke and I would like to get her father out of here. But it'll be risky for you, since we don't have a legal leg to stand on."

Doc Fauve lowered his huge bulk into a folding chair, and he took another gargantuan swallow from a jug. Smacking his lips, blinking owlishly, he said, "I don't like that arrogant son of a . . . gun. I'd like to stick it to him. Especially since there is some evidence that he's up to no good."

"Evidence which wouldn't stand up in court," Oinks said, swaying slightly. "But, if we were to capture those letters and

we could find someone who could read German and Italian, we might find that he and his two thugs are engaged in illicit, perhaps even treasonable, activities."

"Treasonable!" Jocko said. "How do you figure that out, Blackstone?"

Oinks hiccuped, then said, "Anyone but a low-browed facsimile of an orang-utang would deduce from what has been reported that von Adlerdreck is an agent of, or at least a sympathizer, with, the Germans. And Ovarizi and Bufalo are agents of, or at least sympathizers with, that strutting jackanapes, Mussolini. It's only a suspicion, I'll admit, a hypothesis, but it certainly warrants investigation. In a sense, though civilians, we are soldiers for our country. All of us here, except for our two young visitors, are veterans who fought in the Big One. I even include Pat, since, as I understand it, she was something of a camp follower and materially contributed to the morale of the doughboys, not to mention any number of officers."

Pat growled, "How'd you like this jug jammed up your . . . ?"

Doc Fauve interrupted sharply. "Hold it, Pat! There's a lady present!"

"Why, you drunken, lecherous quack, you mean I ain't no lady? It'll be a cold day in hell before I let you sweet-talk me again into . . ."

Robeson said, "Please! No quarreling! Now, how about it? Will you help us? If you agree to, then we should make some plans now. And act quickly."

"That a boy, young feller!" Jocko said. "I ain't been in a good brawl since just before I committed myself."

"He doesn't mean we'll bust into the place like a band of Comanches, you microcephalic," the lawyer said. "This will take subtlety, silence, organization."

Doc Fauve said that they should take a vote. Everybody held his hand up. Robeson was surprised that the three bootleggers wanted to join in.

The beanpole, Smalljack, said, "Us three fought against the Kaiser, you know. I was a corporal, Van and Lunger Tom was sergeants. If this kraut is a spy or something, we'd like to get our mitts on him. Ain't that right, boys?"

"Yeah," van Rijnwijk boomed. "Here we fought and got

wounded so we could save the world for democracy. And here's the boche up and back on his feet and making noises again. This time, he ought to be kicked silly so he'll think twice the next time before he goes out to conquer the world."

"I say," said Jocko, "let's storm on up there, kick hell out of the Kraut and them two Sicilians, get the letters, and turn the whole lot over to the feds. Meanwhile, Robeson and the lovely Miss Burke—you're a real peach, kid—can hustle her old man out of here."

This was voted down, since the gangsters were armed and, for all they knew, some of the attendants might be, too.

Everybody downed some more white lightning, including Robeson and Burke. Then the lights were turned out, and they walked toward the big house on the hill. Before they could get out of the trees, they heard automobile motors to their right. They hid behind trees and waited for the cars to come by on the road. But the cars seemed to be staying at the gateway.

Robeson said, "I'll sneak down there and find out what's going on."

Doc, Jocko, and van Rijnwijk said they'd go with him.

"Maybe it's Sheriff Huisman," the latter said. "He's been out looking for us. He's mad at us because we won't kick in more money for protection."

"You mean . . . ?"

"Sure. You think we could operate like we do if we didn't have some official warning us when the Internal Revenue guys are pussyfooting around? I guess we'll have to up the ante to him pretty soon. But we're making him sweat it out."

His three companions kept bumping into trees and crashing through bushes and falling down when they stepped into depressions. Robeson finally called a halt. "You're all too loaded. They'll hear you a mile off. I'll go ahead. You stay here."

"I'll drink to that," Doc said, and he pulled a flask from his coat pocket.

When Ken Robeson got close to the gateway, he saw two long black limousines on the road just inside the walls. The headlights were turned off, and several men were standing by the front right-hand door of the lead automobile. They were looking up at a telephone pole outside the gateway. A man was up there, faintly silhouetted against the light gray sky. Even as

Robeson watched, the last of the wires fell away. The man who'd cut them began to climb down.

Robeson tried to count the number of the party. It was too dark to be accurate, but he estimated that there were twelve.

And then, as someone lit a match to light a cigar, he saw a tough face beneath the brim of a hat. And a tommy gun in the hands of the man standing nearby.

Combining stealth with speed, he turned and made his way back to where the three were. Just as he got to them, he heard the acceleration of motors and the shifting of gears. Through the trees he could see the two vehicles, their lights still out, moving along the road.

"We got company," he said. "Heavily armed troops of some sort. I don't know if they're mobsters or G-men."

They went back to the rest of the group. By then the two limousines had passed the hidden watchers and were climbing the winding road. Robeson told the others what he'd seen.

Trish Burke said, "Then that means we don't have a chance. Unless they're government people making a raid."

"We can only wait here and see what happens," Ken said. "But cheer up. Who knows but what this means that your father'll be sprung very soon?"

At that moment there was a yell. It came from a distance, but even its faintness could not filter out the despair in it.

8

Robeson looked at the building. In its blazing light was a tiny figure running down the hill. Behind it came three others, all shouting.

By now the two limousines were out of sight beyond the curve of the hill.

Trish started forward, crying, "Father!"

Robeson grabbed her arm and swung her around. "Don't let them know we're down here!" He turned to the others. "Duck behind the trees! Get ready to jump Adlerdreck and the Gold Dust Twins. But be careful! They're armed. Rijnwijk, why don't one of you get the car? Have it ready for us."

Van Rijnwijk, swaying, said, "Well, I dunno. We can't all gesh . . . get in our car. Need another."

Robeson said, "Trish, you take off with him and bring your

car, too!"

"What! And leave my father! I can't, I have to find out what's going to happen to him!"

He could understand her reluctance, though he thought it was ill-advised. He said, "Jocko, what about you? Would you take her keys and drive the car to the gateway entrance?"

"Not me, kid! I ain't gonna run away when there's a good fight coming up! Oh, boy!" He rubbed his big, hairy-backed hands together and hopped up and down like a chimpanzee working himself into a battle frenzy.

Robeson got Trish to open her handbag so he could remove the keys. He offered them to the lawyer, Creeks, who shook his head. "No' me. I like a brawl as much as that monkey there. Anyway, he'd say I was chicken if I took off."

All the men refused on the grounds that they'd be thought cowardly if they left now. Besides, as Doc said, they were spoiling to get their hands on Adlerdreck.

Then van Rijnwijk refused to go on the same grounds.

"Whyn't you go?"

"I will, but I can't drive more than one car at a time!" Robeson cried. "Don't any of you have any sense at all!"

"I do!" the ex-stripper cried. Theshe dimb bozosh ain't go' the shenshe they was born with—if any. Gi' . . . give me the keysh!"

Robeson doubted that she could even find the car, let alone drive it. But she was a last hope. He handed her the keys to the Ford. She immediately dropped them and was then down on all fours groping for them. Lunger Tom, the pale, sour runt, said, "Okay. I'll bring the . . . hic! . . . limouzhine. I got some shenshe, and nobody'sh gonna call me chicken. No' . . . not after I got gashed . . . gassed . . . in the Big One. Gi' muh the keysh to Trish'sh . . . Triss's . . . car."

But he began coughing violently, and Doc Fauve and Smalljack jumped on him, covering his mouth so the approaching quartet wouldn't hear them. He kicked out, catching Rijnwijk in the groin. The big man howled in pain, let loose of Thomas, and writhed on the ground. Jocko leaped upon him and clamped his hand over Rijnwijk's mouth. Then he howled and danced around holding his hand which the big man had bitten.

Robeson threw his hands up in the air.

Doc Fauve said, "Shomebody's gotta shtraighten em out. All thish noise."

His big right fist cracked three times, and Thomas, van Rijnwijk, and Blidgett were laid out and snoring. Robeson almost went amok then. They needed every man available to overwhelm the three pursuers of Burke, and all of a sudden they were reduced to six, two of them women.

He looked up the hill. The professor was still going strong, almost at the road at the foot of the hill. The others were about ninety feet behind him.

Then he saw the first of the big black limousines come around the corner of the house and pull to a stop in front of it. Men with tommy guns and shotguns piled out of it while the second vehicle stopped behind the first. One of the men must have looked down the hill. He pointed, and the others turned to look. One had a flashlight which he directed toward the four running men.

One of the men from the limousines, evidently the leader, waved his arms and screamed orders. Four men ran into the building, their guns ready. The others plunged on down the hill.

By then Professor Burke was heading toward the woods, wheezing like an asthmatic mule.

"Quick! Drag these guys under the trees!" Ken Robeson said. "Then get ready to jump on the Doc and his buddies!"

"Doc?" Fauve said, swaying. "Whash you wanna jump on me and my buddiesh for?"

"Doctor von Altereddrake!" Robeson said. "Holy cow! You got me doing it! I mean, Adlerdreck and his thugs!"

"Oh! Well, okay. Lishen, Robeshon, don' worry. I'm a chiropractor. I may be deshpished in the medical profeshion, but I know what I'm doing. Thoshe quacksh are jealoush of ush chiropractorsh. Don' worry about me taking care of thoshe guysh! I know all about presshure pointsh on the human body!"

Robeson had already dragged van Rijnwijk's heavy bulk under the branches of a nearby tree. Pat and Trish, he saw, were carrying off the light body of Lunger Tom. He straightened and said, "What do you mean? Pressure points?"

Doc's gigantic body loomed above him, swaying like the Empire State Building in a high wind. A big hand came down

and its thumb pressed on his neck.

"Like thish, shee? I probe, I find the nekshush—nexus—of nerve shentersh here, I pressh, and . . ."

9

Kenneth Robeson wasn't unconscious very long. But in the short period Professor Burke had reached them. He must have been startled to find a body—Robeson's—on the cold ground and above it a gigantic menacing figure weaving back and forth. Probably mumbling about the prejudices and persecutions of the medical profession and the pressure points of the human nervous system.

Though he didn't know what had happened while he was out, Robeson could reconstruct it. Burke had veered to one side, but von Adlerdreck and his two colleagues, following him closely, had rammed into Doc Fauve. All three had fallen.

He supposed this was so—he was still in the supposing stage because his wits hadn't all rallied to him yet—since the sanitarium head and Bufalo and Ovarizi were just getting up off the ground.

Then two figures—Pat and Trish—flew out of the darkness. Trish's handbag thudded against Ovarizi's temple. He went down. The long-legged, high-stepping, high-kicking Patricia Coningway—she must have thought she was on the stage—kicked high. The point of her shoe caught Bufalo under the chin. He emitted a glugging sound, and went down.

The tall blond von Adlerdreck didn't even see what had occurred behind him. He was running off into the darkness, shouting something unintelligible.

Robeson got to his feet. Doc Fauve rose a few seconds later. Very dignifiedly, he said, "Offisher, I wassh jusht crosshing the shtreet, with the light, mind you, when thish truck . . ."

He stopped, took a quick look around, and said, somewhat embarrassedly, "What happened?"

At that moment Jocko, muttering something about "Mabel," got up. He stood for a few seconds, crouching, his knuckles on the ground, exactly like a gorilla aroused from sleep. He growled, "Where are they? I'll kill 'em!"

Robeson, restraining his anger, said, "Drag them under the trees!"

Too late. Ovarizi and Bufalo leaped up and staggered off. It was evident from the way they kept running into the trees that they were still dazed. Since they were armed, Robeson decided not to go after them.

Van Rijnwijk, Thomas, and Jocko, all groaning, got to their feet. At that moment, Robeson heard feet thudding. There were so many, it sounded like a buffalo stampede. Before he and the others could hide, they were invaded. Men poked guns at them in the illumination of two flashlights.

Robeson could not see for a moment or so. Then the blinding beam was directed toward the surrounding trees. The two women were not visible. Either they'd fled or were concealed behind tree trunks.

Now he could see the leader. He was medium-sized though muscular, clad in a gray cloth coat with a gray fur collar. His head was bare, allowing Robeson to see a shock of polar-bear white hair and a middle-aged face that would have been handsome if it weren't for its total lack of expression. It looked like the mask of a dead man. Or the features of a man playing dead. Since Robeson was very close to the man, he could distinguish the color of the eyes. The gray of Arctic ice-fields. But under the pale, washed-out flatness was a blaze as if a natural-gas leak has caught fire under the polar icecap.

Robeson recognized him from the photographs and the descriptions in many newspaper and magazine articles.

"Ricardo Bensoni!" he gasped.

"You said it, punk!"

The dead lips didn't move. It was as if Bensoni were a ventriloquist who projected his voice. In fact, the words seemed to come from the open, but still, mouth of a huge guy standing like a wooden dummy by him.

So this was "Il Vendicativo." "The Avengeful." The story was that his wife and daughter had disappeared, and Dito "Finger" Sporcizio's mob was blamed. Dito's protests of his innocence did him no good. Bensoni and his gang had wiped out every member of Sporzicio's organization, including some kids who ran numbers. Then Bensoni had taken over the dead ganglord's territory.

A few months later, a juvenile street gang had made the mistake of stealing the hubcaps from Bensoni's armored Cadillac. Bensoni had burned them out of their basement headquarters

and machine-gunned the survivors as, their clothes on fire, they ran into the street. The next day, crime dropped 86 percent in Brooklyn.

One of Bensoni's uncles, who ran a grocery store in the Bronx, was beaten up because he refused to pay for "protection" by Affamato Porco's thugs. Bensoni wiped that gang out.

The police knew who had committed these crimes but couldn't prove it. Only last month Bensoni had been shocked to find out that Sporcizio had been innocent after all. Bensoni's wife had run off with a used-car salesman, taking her child with her. They were last seen boarding a ship in Los Angeles bound for Brazil.

The huge man was Hidtkot Schmidt, chiefly noted for his ability to get past electrical security systems. And now Robeson saw another infamous member of the mob, McMurdoro, "The Murderer." He was a tall Scot with hands almost as big as van Rijnwijk's.

Bensoni did not have the prejudice of Sicilian mobsters against non-Sicilians. He hired only the best help, and if the man wasn't from the Old Country, he did not care.

Il Vendicativo spoke softly to Robeson, asking him who he was and what he was doing here. Robeson was too deep in a state of shock to think of a lie. He told Bensoni the truth.

"If you're giving it to me straight, you have nothing to worry about," the wax-mask-faced man said. "Some people say I got a mean streak, but that's a lie. I'm not vengeful. I just see to it that justice is done."

He turned to Schmidt and McMurdoro. "Get Burke. Don't hurt him. Don't knock off Ovarizi and Bufalo if you can help it. I want to put some questions to them."

A chill ran over Robeson at these words. He could imagine Bensoni's type of inquisition.

All of the gang except a tall, skinny colored man ran into the woods to do Bensoni's bidding. The Negro held a tommy on the prisoners.

Bensoni started to say something but stopped. A wild yell came from the woods, followed by the booming of .45 automatics and the chatter of submachine guns.

10

"You bums stay here!" Bensoni snarled without moving his lips. "Otherwise, I blow your heads off!"

He and the Negro ran off into the trees. Robeson called softly, "Trish! Pat! You out there?"

A scream soared above him and through the branches, riding even over the gunfire. It was a woman's voice filled with terror. And it seemed to come from the direction where all the noisy action was.

Robeson ran toward it, shouting, "Where are you, Trish?" Behind him was a thunder of feet, the others stumbling after him. He went perhaps a hundred yards, then dived into the cold, hard ground as streaks of fire shot off the night and bullets wheeled above his head, smacked into tree trunks, and pattered in the soil around him. Behind him was a heavy thump, his followers hitting the dirt at the same time as if they were a trained ballet group.

The firing stopped. A car motor roared, and tires squealed. Raising his head, he got a glimpse of headlights moving away from him. They flashed on the steel gates and then they disappeared. From the sound of the motor, the car was going full speed toward Roosville.

There was some loud cursing near the gate. Then Bensoni's voice rose. "That does it! #%$&**! Burke got kidnapped! Right in front of our eyes, under our noses! †=%&*@¢#!"

Robeson called out. "Hey, Bensoni! Are the women okay?"

"Yeah! It was on account of them we quit shooting! That #$%&@¢†=&!X Bierstoss used them as shields!"

Bierstoss! Who . . . ? Then Robeson remembered what Trish Burke had told him. Bierstoss was the industrialist who'd financed the professor's experiments. The man who'd paid von Adlerdreck to take care of him. He must've driven up just in time to get the professor. What was he doing here?

"Can we come in?" Robeson called.

"Okay. But with your hands up and slowly."

Evidently Bensoni didn't trust anybody. Robeson didn't blame him. The kind of life he led, he couldn't afford to trust his own wife. *Especially* her.

He got up, then stood still as Bufalo's voice cut through the night. "Hey, Bensoni! A truce! We . . ."

The rest was cut off as the second limousine, occupied by the four men who'd entered the building, roared up. Il Vendicativo told them to hold their fire, and he said, "Okay, what is it, Chips?"

"I was just wondering if we ain't after the same thing. For the same people. How about a truce so's we can talk?"

At that moment someone touched Robeson on the shoulder. Startled, he whirled, ready to strike out. But it was Trish Burke.

She said, her voice trembling, "Oh, Ken! That man drove off with my father! Where's he taking him?"

Robeson didn't know. He shushed her so that he could hear the powwow. However, there wasn't going to be any.

Bensoni ordered his men into the two cars. As he got in, he called, "Chips! You and Eggs! You keep out of this if you know what's healthy for you! Got me?"

The lead car started out with the wheels turning in the gravel, firing stones right and left. The second car followed, tommy barrels bristling from the windows.

Robeson figured that the gangsters were going after Bierstoss and his captive—if Burke had been taken along involuntarily.

Von Adlerdreck and his two attendants suddenly emerged from the bushes on the far side of the driveway. They ran up the hill, evidently making for the garage by the big building.

Ken Robeson grabbed Trish's hand and pulled her after him as he ran for their car. Behind them came the sound of stampede again, the patients and the moonshiners taking off after them, none probably knowing why. When, breathless, he and Trish got to the Model A in the farmer's field, the rest piled into the big Packard. All but Doc Fauve. He got onto the running board of the Ford and shouted through the closed window.

"There isn't any room for me there! I'll ride here so I can be your lookout! We're not going to miss out on the excitement! Tally ho!"

Robeson thought he was nuts, but if Doc wanted to stand out there and freeze, it was okay with him. The cold should sober him up, though he'd be lucky if he didn't get pneumonia.

Then, as Trish backed the car toward the farmer's road, a figure ran toward them. Crouching, its long arms dangling,

bounding in a curious run, it looked like a chimpanzee. Trish straightened the car out on the road and started forward. Shouting, Jocko leaped on the running board, opened the door, and got in.

"They threw me out!" he said bitterly. "That lewd shyster Oinks got kind of familiar with Pat, and he blamed it on me. Wait until I get my mitts on him. I'll tear the wings off that legal eagle!"

There was an explosion, and everybody tried to duck. Robeson banged his head on the dashboard, and the pain in it, which had disappeared during the recent frenzy, came back. Trish said, "That wasn't a shot! My right front tire blew!"

The car was stuck in the gateway to the wire fence. The Packard stopped behind them, and everybody tumbled out. There wasn't time to put on the spare, which was, in any event, as bald as the one just punctured. Smalljack said he'd push the Ford out of the way with his car. Then they should all get into his car. There was some argument between Pat Coningway and Jocko while Robeson and Trish danced with impatience. Finally, Jocko, unable to convince Pat that he wasn't the culprit, said he'd promise to keep his paws off her. By then the Ford had been pushed over into the ditch on the other side of the highway. They started to get into the Packard. Jocko took advantage of Oinks's unprotected rear and kicked it hard.

That started another brawl. The lawyer swung his cane at Jocko, missed, and slammed it across van Rijnwijk's shoulder. The huge fellow struck Oinks on the shoulder with his great fist.

By the time peace had been restored, and they were all jammed uncomfortably into the car, some on top of others, they saw headlights coming out of the sanitarium driveway. They'd wasted so much time, the doctor and his cohorts had gotten a head start.

Within forty seconds, they were rocketing down the road, the rear lights of von Adlerdreck's car about a quarter-mile ahead. Robeson was never to forget that wild, reckless, dangerous, stomach-squeezing, tire-screeching ride. Smalljack drove like a drunken maniac. Maybe he wasn't crazy, but he certainly was intoxicated. He took the Packard at the sharp turn into Roosville beautifully, however. It only turned around three times while negotiating the curve, it didn't roll

over once, and it ended up pointing in the right direction.

It tore through the village of dark houses with rustic sleepers inside. Robeson wondered where Sheriff Huisman was. Fifteen minutes later, he found out. By then their car was only a few yards behind the doctor's. And less than a quarter-mile ahead of it was a red flashing light on the roof of the sheriff's car and the faint wail of a siren lifted toward them.

"Huisman must be chasing Bensoni's gang!" Smalljack said. Holding on to the wheel with one hand, he lifted a jug with the other and drank. Then he passed it through the window to Doc Fauve, who was standing now on the running board of the Packard. Doc drank deeply and passed the jug back to Smalljack, who passed it to the ex-stripper.

She began to drink, then stopped, and, swearing, rammed the bottom of the jug hard against Jocko's forehead.

"You keep your hands off me!"

The pharmacist said, indignantly, "Honest to God, Pat, I never touched you. It's that sneaky ambulance-chaser."

"I can vouch for that," said Trish, who was sitting on Robeson's lap. "I know it wasn't Oinks because Jocko's been trying to feel my leg!"

Jocko swore that he was innocent. He claimed it was Lunger Tom, who was seated next to Trish. Lunger Tom got mad and took a poke at Jocko. Oinks began laughing but Jocko's hand closed around his throat. Van Rijnwijk, in the front seat, turned and roared, "No more of that! How in hell can Homer here drive with you bunch of stupid jerks rousting around back there?"

Smalljack said, icily, "I told you never to call me Homer, Van. It's Bill, and don't you forget that!"

For a while there was comparative peace. For some minutes, Robeson could even close his eyes and enjoy having Trish Burke on his lap. Would that this were so in a less disturbing situation. Would he ever get her on his lap again?

The big question, though, was: Would they survive this ride? A dozen times, swinging around sharp curves, the right wheels had gone off onto the shoulder. Once, they skidded sidewise, and this time Robeson was sure they'd turn over. But Smalljack straightened the vehicle out.

Robeson wanted to ask how fast they were going, but he was afraid to.

After an hour and a half, which seemed like five hours, they roared through a police roadblock. This had been set up at the junction of the county road with the state highway. But Bierstoss had taken the narrow opening between two cars and thundered on through. So did Bensoni's limousines, the sheriff's Plymouth, and von Adlerdreck's. And, emulating them, so did Smalljack.

Presently, there were five State Police cars, lights flashing, sirens screaming, behind them.

After Robeson got his breath back—it had been caught somewhere below his lungs—he shouted, "Why don't we stop and explain the situation to the police?"

"Are you crazy?" Lunger Tom squeaked. "We got all this moonshine, and there's distilling equipment in the truck, not to mention two rifles, a sawed-off shotgun, and a couple of hot gats."

Robeson shut his eyes again. He couldn't bear to look. He could hear Jocko and Oinks quarreling again. The lawyer was angry because he'd just found out that his swing at Jocko with the cane had broken the glass vials inside it. When he'd unscrewed the gold knob, the liquor had run over his arm and his shirtfront and soaked his pants. Jocko was laughing like crazy, then a sharp sound exploded in Robeson's ears.

He opened his eyes. Jocko was howling with pain and holding his cheek.

Trish said, "Keep your hairy paws off of me!"

"It was an accident, an accident, I swear!" Jocko said.

He hunkered down on the floor, jammed between Thomas's legs.

"See! I'll keep my hands in my pockets!"

"Good!" Oinks said, and he poured the rest of the booze in the cane over Jocko's head.

Robeson expected that the police would set up a roadblock at the George Washington Bridge. But there wasn't any. And the crazy caravan continued at seventy miles an hour down Broadway, then over to Fifth Avenue, with whistles blowing, tires screaming, horns blaring, pedestrians and angry car drivers shouting. And violent bumps as the Packard sometimes detoured traffic and went over curbs and down the sidewalk, Smalljack pushing in on the horn button, it blaring, and Doc Fauve, on the running board, waving wildly with one

hand for the pedestrians to dive out of the way.

Then, a block from Thirty-fourth, what Robeson had been praying for happened. The gas tank ran dry.

Smalljack smoothly put the gear into neutral and the car rolled for another block.

Robeson looked out the window. They were right back where they'd started from: the Empire State Building.

11

Bierstoss's Lincoln was parked with its left wheels on the sidewalk. Just behind were Bensoni's two Cadillacs. And entirely on the sidewalk, its front smashed against the side of the restaurant at the corner, was von Adlerdreck's Cadillac. He never did see the sheriff.

All the vehicles were unoccupied.

Doc Fauve, his yellow complexion blue from the cold, was running up—no, shambling—toward the entrance to the building. Trish opened the door and slid out from Robeson's lap.

In the distance came the dismal sound of sirens. The State Police, and the city police who'd joined them, would arrive inside a minute.

Robeson got out. He wanted to tell Trish they should stay here and tell the police what had happened. Otherwise, they were as likely to be shot by the cops as by the gangsters. But Trish was running toward the doors to the skyscraper. He found himself also running, though he told himself that the smart thing to do was to stay put. However, he couldn't let her venture by herself into that place which would soon be no-man's-land.

The lobby was brightly lit. Some kind of festivity was being held; big signs, ribbons, decorations, booths all over the place. The attendants, however, were not in a festive mood at the moment. They were running this way and that, screaming, yelling, diving under the counters of the booths, heading toward the exits, taking protection behind the many stone pillars.

A stench of cordite hung in the air, and one pillar was chipped where bullets had struck. No one seemed to be hurt, though.

Robeson saw Trish going into an elevator. He ran after her

but the doors closed in front of him. Trish didn't seem to hear his pleas to keep the doors open.

He grabbed a man by the arm. "Those guys who were shooting? Where'd they go?"

The man, pale, trembling, pointed upward. Robeson took another elevator.

But only to the second floor. Swearing at himself for not keeping a cooler hand, he watched the dials over the doors. Trish's elevator was one of the two expresses, already past the 52nd floor. She didn't know any more than he did about Bierstoss's destination. She was just going up in a frantic, desperate search. But maybe she wasn't so foolish. Maybe she thought that Bierstoss would, in his panic, go as high as possible. He could be operating on the fugitive's instinct, one inherited from ape ancestors. Get as high on the tree as possible.

He went down the stairs to the lobby. By then it was full of state troopers and New York's finest. They didn't seem to know what to do; they were milling around or questioning people. He took the other express elevator which fortunately wasn't being used. It would go to the 80th floor, as high as any elevator could go in one stretch. When he got out, he went down the hall and hopped over the chain put up to keep visitors out. Then he took the elevator that would carry him all the way to the 86th floor. Nobody stopped it because nobody was around.

But plenty of people had been here recently. There were cigar butts, cigarette stubs, a chewing gum wrapper, and a broken whiskey jug just outside the elevator doors.

When the doors opened, Robeson started to stick his head cautiously out of the exit. He didn't hear anything, but that meant nothing. There might be many men lying silently in wait for all hell to bust loose.

Then, a screaming, arm-flailing, leg-kicking, wild-eyed tousle-haired apparition appeared. It seemed to come from nowhere, but its destination was certain. It struck Robeson, drove him back against the back of the cage, and almost bore him under. He grabbed the crazed man—Professor Burke—and he tried to shout sense into him. No use. The man kept on attacking him, at the same time screaming, "My shadow! My shadow! Keep it away from me!"

His face was scratched and his nose was hurting where it had

been struck and Robeson angrily picked up the thin man and shook him. "Pipe down! There isn't any shadow!"

Then he hurled the professor against the wall, and the man, sobbing and moaning, crumpled. Robeson stepped forward to punch the button. He'd take this maniac down to the ground floor, tell the police his story, and let them handle it from there on. Much as he wanted to find out where Trish was, he knew that the logical way was to let the cops do it.

But Doc Fauve's big dissipatedly handsome face, its normal, if unhealthy, yellow hue restored, appeared. He seemed to have sobered up somewhat.

"Robeson? You got him, huh? Listen, von Eiderduck and his Gold Dust Twins're cornered by Bensoni's men. The former are outside on the observation platform. The latter're inside, waiting until they can get a shot at the former. Or is it the former is the latter and vice versa?"

He frowned, then said, "Never mind. What does matter is that Bierstoss has got the young lady, and he's in the top room of the dirigible mooring mast."

"Where are your buddies?" Robeson said.

"We're in the hallway outside the elevators and behind the concession counters. We got Bensoni's men at a standstill."

"With what?"

"With our weapons, of course. Didn't you see Lunger Tom and Smalljack get them out of the trunk?"

"No. How'd Professor Burke get here?"

The near-giant scratched his head. "I don't know. Must've broken loose and nobody shot him because he's the key to the whole mess. One thing he's good at. That's escaping."

"How'd Bierstoss get hold of Trish?"

"Who knows? Somehow, during the confusion, he got hold of her but the professor took off."

Robeson said, "Is Bierstoss armed?"

"Is Roosevelt a Democrat? Sure he is. I got a glimpse of him. He's got two .45 automatics."

"I'm going to take this poor devil down," Robeson said. "The cops can handle it from there."

Doc Fauve came into the cage. He was carrying a gallon jug, and he proceeded to lighten its weight with four or five swallows.

"Yeah? Well, me and the boys, we're going up the elevator

into the mooring mast. And we're going to rescue the damsel from the dragon."

"You'll get her killed!" Robeson said. "You guys are too bombed to know what you're doing. You can't go charging in there. He'll open fire the moment the elevator doors open! You'll be massacred!"

Doc Fauve offered the jug to Robeson, who shook his head.

"Yeah? Maybe so! But we're going to do it anyway. Listen, buddy, there's none of us worth a damn. We all had good prospects; we could have been something. Decent, respectable, giving something to others, our relatives, families, the community. Instead, we peed it all away. We're all drunks, von Addledrake's patients and the moonshiners. And up there is someone who might be something, a real nice girl who got into a situation she isn't responsible for. We've talk about this among us, and we figure we can atone for what we've done, our wasted life, if we can rescue the girl from that villain, Bierstoss!"

Doc Fauve sat down on the floor and drank some more moonshine. Robeson said, "It's alcohol that's talking. It got you into this mess. One final act of redemption, huh? Nonsense! You'll get slaughtered, and Trish will get killed, and all because your booze-soaked brains and your whiskey-rotten conscience have told you you're no good, but you can redeem yourselves by throwing yourselves away. You understand?"

Doc Fauve began weeping. "You don't understand! We're trying to make up for what we've done!"

"If you were sober and aching for drink, you wouldn't be doing this," Robeson said. "It's strange how alcohol carries the seeds of its own . . ."

At that moment a voice bellowed out. Bensoni's.

"Von Adlerdreck! Ovarizi! Bufalo! We know who you are! We got the goods on you! Listen! This has gone far enough! We've been working at cross-purposes! I didn't want to have to tell you this, but there's no way out!

"Listen, I just found out about you last night. I mean, I found out who you and your buddies were and what you were up to! So come on in, you three, and we'll put our heads together and see if we can work something out without these civilians making trouble! How about it?"

Robeson could hear a voice muffled by the glass windows on the 86th floor. But he thought he heard von Adlerdreck say something about not knowing if Bensoni was lying to him.

Doc Fauve got up. He was no longer crying. He said, "What's that gangster talking about?"

The professor quit whimpering, and he tried to get up on his feet. Robeson pressed him back down.

"I don't know. This has been a very confusing night."

Doc Fauve bellowed, "You guys! Come here! We're going on up and rescue Miss Burke!"

The others appeared and crowded into the cage. Robeson wanted to get out; but the press of bodies prevented him. He said, "Damn it! All right! I'll go with you! But this is idiotic! Bierstoss will murder us!"

"He can't get us all!" Jocko shouted. He punched the button and the cage shot up. "One of us'll get him! Here, Robeson, you look scared! Have a shot of Dutch courage!"

Ken Robeson shook his head. "You damn fools! If you start blazing away the moment the doors open, you're just as likely to shoot Trish!"

"Yes," the lawyer said. "But at least we'll have vengeance! Bierstoss isn't going to escape!"

The cage stopped. The doors, whispering, began to open. The tall, skinny Smalljack and the apelike Jocko held revolvers. Van Rijnwijk had the sawed-off shotgun. Little Thomas, who was coughing, waved the deer rifle around. Pat Coningway had a knife in her hand.

Robeson said, "Where'd you get that?"

"I keep it in a garter sheath," she said, smiling. "That's to defend my virtue."

"Yeah," Jocko said. "This is the only time she ever pulled it out. And her virtue ain't at stake. How about that?"

"How'd you like this shoved up between your glutei maximi?" Pat said. Jocko broke up, bending over with uncontrollable laughter, slapping his knee, and then "accidentally" ramming his elbow into Oinks's ribs.

Oinks yelled with wrath and grabbed Jocko by the throat. "You Pithecanthropus not-so-erectus! I'll squeeze your throat until your brains pop out! If, that is, you have anything in your skull except a vacuum to squeeze out!"

The doors opened. Smalljack's revolver exploded. Van Ri-

jnwijk's shotgun boomed. Pat, screaming like a Valkyrie, tried to dash forward, her little blade extended. Unfortunately, Doc Fauve was in her path, and the point sank into his back. He yelled and threw his hands out, one knocking Thomas out and the other rendering van Rijnwijk half-unconscious. Jocko's revolver went boom!-boom!-boom! as his eyes popped under the pressure of Oinks's fingers. Fortunately, it was pointed upward, and its bullets smashed harmlessly through the ceiling of the cage.

Later, Robeson was to think how extremely fortuitous it was that Trish Burke wasn't standing before the elevator doors. But she was off to one side, looking down at Bierstoss. He was a short, pudgy man lying on his back, his mouth open, his eyes closed.

His forehead was streaked with red. Trish held a .45 automatic pistol by the butt. She was waiting for him to recover consciousness.

But for the moment, she was frozen with shock at the bellow of shotgun and crack of revolver.

The cage was emptied, its occupants spilling out, most of them falling flat on their faces. Robeson went to Trish. "Are you all right?"

"Yes," she said, lowering the hand holding the Luger. "I grabbed him where . . ." She seemed reluctant to say the exact words. After all, she was a lady. "I mean, . . . you know . . . and while he was writhing on the floor, I grabbed his gun from the floor . . . he'd dropped it because he was in such pain, and I hit him on the head with it."

Swaying, pale, she looked at him with enormous blue eyes. "How's father? Is he safe?"

Robeson jerked a thumb at the elevator cage. "I think so."

Trish's eyes got even wider, a feat he would not have thought possible.

"But . . . the elevator! It's gone!"

Robeson turned. The doors were closed. Somebody, maybe the professor, maybe a person on the 86th floor, had punched its button.

As he stared, too stupefied from all that had happened to react swiftly, the doors opened. And there, in the cage, was the white-haired, expressionless Bensoni. With him were von Adlerdreck, Ovarizi, Bufalo, Schmidt, MacMurdoro, the

colored man, and a dozen others. All had weapons, tommies, .45 automatics, some revolvers. One man was even holding a grenade.

Bensoni stepped out into the room. He said, in his emotionless, robotlike voice, "Well, this is quite a mess, isn't it?"

He put his hand inside his gray flannel jacket and pulled out a gray wallet. He flipped it open. Robeson got a flash of a badge.

"You're all under arrest!"

12

Kenneth Robeson sat typing in his one-room apartment. He'd been writing since morning, stopping only for obligations of Nature, including a three-hour sleep. By now he not only had the continuing characters, themes, and permanent locales of the series worked out in detail, he had half-written the first novel.

His fingers were flying, the keys spewing out golden words of high adventure and low comedy, when someone banged at his door. Impatiently, he rose and went to the door. He didn't want to be interrupted by anybody, not even by Trish Burke.

He flung the door open and looked up at the yellow face and eyes of Doc Fauve. The near-giant looked even sicker. In his hand was a quart bottle, not of moonshine, but of Duggan's Dew of Kirkintilloch. At sight of that Robeson lost his cross expression. He was only a moderate drinker, but this brand of scotch was his favorite liquor. He hadn't been able to afford it for a long time.

"I know you're busy," Doc said. "But I'd like to have a few minutes. This is a sort of farewell visit. A couple of snorts, and I'll be off. But I'll leave the bottle behind as a memento mori."

Ken felt a shock travel through him. Fauve didn't expect to live much longer, and he'd come here so Ken Robeson could pay his premortem respects. And he was paying his way with the gift of scotch.

"Come on in," Robeson said. "Sit down."

He got two chipped coffee mugs and half-filled each. Doc, sitting on the worn and torn overstuffed chair, raised his mug. "Here's success to you in your career. And a wish that you and

the young lady hit it off well."

Ken sipped at the delicious, heady liquor. Doc Fauve said, "Our bootlegger friends have had to close down their local stills. Sheriff Huisman is mad because Bensoni and Bufalo and the feds and God knows how many other agencies put the lid on everything. The word is mum. Nothing ever happened. He can't even talk about the affair, let alone arrest anybody. But he did find and destroy our friends' booze-making equipment. So they're bringing in stuff from Canada until the heat dies off. Lunger Tom slipped me a couple of cases of Duggan's yesterday."

He hadn't taken his greatcoat off. Now he opened it and revealed two more bottles of the priceless stuff in specially made pockets. He removed these and put them on the floor.

"These are yours, too. Whenever you take a drink, think of me. And the other guys, including Pat."

Robeson felt a little embarrassed at the references to Doc's coming demise. He said, "Listen, I'll think of you, of the whole bunch, every time I write a story in the series."

"Yeah. I'm glad you told me about it. I'm tickled. All the boys, and Pat, too, are tickled. It's a sort of immortality, you know.

"But whoever would have thought the other night that things'd turn out the way they did? Bierstoss was a German agent, planted years ago so he could operate as a respectable manufacturer and pillar of the church. And so here comes Professor Burke and his secret chemical formula. Burke thinks the chemical can force people to act morally. Bierstoss sees it as a great thing to make people sort of brain slaves. The formula could be modified, he hopes, to make people think as the German state wants them to think. Of course, he doesn't tell Burke this.

"But Burke goes crazy, poor old devil. The chemical injection brings up all the evil thoughts and repressed desires that are in even the most moral of people. So he sees his subconscious projected as a savage shadow which threatens his inner being. He can't endure it, and he goes insane.

"Bierstoss is upset by this. But he figures that maybe the effect can be used after all. All it needs is experimentation. There's plenty of human guinea pigs available to the Germans. So he sends Burke to Adlerdreck, who's a federal agent posing

as a German sympathizer. Bierstoss thinks von Adlerdreck can get the formula out of Burke. Burke hadn't told Bierstoss what it was; he carried it in his head. But that head was all mixed up. So von Adlerdreck was supposed to catch Burke in a sane moment and get it from him, even if he had to use torture.

"Von Adlerdreck pretended to go along with Bierstoss so he could get a line on everybody in Bierstoss's organization. Including his tie-ups with the secret Italian Fascist cells. He used Ovarizi and Bufalo, who were also double agents."

Robeson laughed. "And Bensoni was another double agent working for another secret federal agency. Like Ovarizi and Bufalo, he'd established himself as a genuine gangster. But he didn't know the doctor and his two cronies were also Uncle Sam's employees."

Doc Fauve lost his smile for a moment. He shook his head. "Yeah. That Bensoni! He got lost in his role. It's all right to knock off rival gangs. But to murder a juvenile street gang just because they stole the hubcaps off his car. The man's a psychopath."

"That he is," Robeson said. "Still, that gang was mugging old ladies and beating up store owners if they didn't come across with protection money."

"I heard he's locked up in a mental hospital now," Doc Fauve said. "Though that may be just a story to account for his disappearance. He had to drop out of sight once his cover was blown."

Robeson nodded. Bensoni had been furious, but he had to tell everybody involved just who he was and what he'd been doing. First, he'd extracted a promise of silence from the people in the mooring-mast floor. Everybody agreed, especially after Bensoni had threatened to throw them in jail on trumped-up charges if they didn't keep their mouths shut. Then, while the elevator was kept from operating, so the police would be held off for a few minutes, Bensoni had revealed all that needed to be known.

Robeson had asked him if the story of his wife's running off with a used-car salesman was a fake, too. Bensoni had looked as if he were going to strike Robeson, and he'd told him that was none of his business.

Doc Fauve emptied his cup and poured in an even more generous portion. "Ah, the stuff that kills!" he said. "I'm glad

to see you don't overindulge, my boy. Don't ever do it. It wrecks the brain, the belly, the kidneys, the liver, and isn't too good for the heart. And it causes financial distress, breaks up marriages and friendships, strews its golden path with cripples and corpses. Demon Rum and John Barleycorn! Thy names are Satan! Thy grip is legion! I campaigned for Prohibition, I know, and I'm a member of the WCTU. So much for a weak will and a lust to commit slow suicide!"

Robeson didn't want to get into a long drunken-maudlin scene. He said, "I'll have to get back to work soon. But first, let me tell you what I've done. I got a great concept for the series. It's about a sort of superman who, with his five aides, battles the forces of evil. He's one of the richest men in the world, young and handsome, absurdly knowledgeable, moral, and dedicated. He's been raised by scientists who've taught him all they know, which is about everything except women. He invents all sorts of things to benefit mankind and a lot of gadgets to help him in his battle against crime.

"His headquarters are on the 86th floor of a mid-Manhattan skyscraper."

Fauve raised his eyebrows. "There's only one building high enough to have an 86th floor. And that's the observation floor. Nobody lives there."

"Sure. But how many, including native New Yorkers, know that? Anyway, this is fiction, and I take poetic license."

"So, what's the name of our superhero?"

"Doc Savage. *Fauve* means a wild beast in French. That made me think of Savage. Catchy, isn't it? Has a nice ring—and Savage is also known as the Man of Bronze. In fact, that's the title of the story I'm writing. Doc is called this because his skin is a golden-bronze derived from long exposure to tropical suns. His hair is bronze, too."

Fauve laughed. "Unlike my yellow pigment, huh?"

"Well, one of your family names is du Bronce. That gave me the idea for the bronze aspect."

"And Doc Savage's eyes?"

"Yellow. No, don't laugh. Not bilious yellow, begging your pardon, but golden. Magnetic whirlpools of molten gold."

"You could have named your hero Sauvage. French for savage."

"No offense, Doc, but all the major leads in this series will

have to have English names. The big boy at S & S says the readers don't like the good guys to have foreign names. It's okay to use Irish or Scottish names, but English names are surefire. It's the Anglo-Saxon complex.

"So, Hans van Rijnwijk becomes John Renwick. He was only a sergeant in real life, but in this series he's a colonel. The same with the other aides of Doc. They're brigadier-generals, majors, et cetera. And van Rijnwijk is promoted from a garage mechanic to one of the world's greatest engineers.

"Anderson Maypole Blidgett, 'Jocko,' a pharmacist, becomes Andrew Blodgett Mayfair, 'Monk,' one of the world's greatest industrial chemists. And so on with the others. You get the idea."

"What models do Patricia Coningway and Patricia Burke provide?"

"Well, I'll combine them, an ex-stripper and a bookkeeper for a beauty salon chain, into Patricia Savage, Doc's lovely young cousin. She'll come into the series later. She'll own and operate her own very posh beauty salon, and she'll be a scrapper who's always getting into trouble. A real Amazon but feminine. She ought to appeal to the adolescents who'll constitute the bulk of the readers.

"There'll be a lot of science in the series. Pseudo-science, rather. And the stories and the characters'll be bigger than life. A lot of the locales will be in far-off, exotic places. This is the Depression, Doc. The readers don't want grim stuff that'll just remind them of their sorry lot. If they're going to part with a hard-earned dime for a story, they'll only do it for something that takes them into the golden realms of fantasy. Where they can identify for a couple of hours with men and women who're rich, who fight successfully against the evils which make so many people feel helpless, powerless to battle."

"Sounds like a splendid idea," Doc Fauve said. "I wish I was going to be around long enough to see myself! Oh, well, the others ought to live long enough to read some of the series. If they can stay sober long enough to read them.

"But what about this Ricardo Bensoni, Il Vendicativo? Since you've turned sick alcoholics and small-time rural moonshiners into heroes, what about Bensoni? You could use your inside-out magic on him and his associates, transmute their lead into gold."

"I've thought about that. If this series peters out eventually, I could start a new one. The hero could be Richard Benson, the Avenger. Gangsters do away with his wife and daughter in a vast, malevolent plot. Benson's hair turns white and his facial muscles become paralyzed from the shock. He vows to avenge the deaths of his loved ones, and he does. This gets him into the business of fighting crime—he's independently wealthy—and he forms Justice, Incorporated, an illegal but highly effective tool for laying low the great criminals of this nation.

"I might even use that Negro aide of Bensoni's as a model. But he won't be the type you usually find in pulp fiction, the 'hush ma mouf, feets-get-going' comical type. He'll be college-educated, speak excellent English, and be a genuine contributor to Justice, Inc. I don't know if the reader will accept this type of black, but by the time I get the *Avenger* series going, maybe readers' attitudes will've changed. We'll see."

Doc Fauve raised his mug. "I like your transmutations."

"They're such stuff as dreams are made on."

Doc drank, then said, "A slight paraphrase of Shakespeare's *The Tempest*, a line from Shakespeare's *The Tempest*, act four."

He refilled the mug and raised it again.

"And this is such drams as stiffs are made on."

Ken Robeson winced, and said, "Well, it's time for you to go back to your world and me to mine."

THE 1940's COME ALIVE!

Meet **Schlomo Raven**, private eye, raconteur and three-feet of fabulous talent. With a rep to rival Spade and Marlowe, the diminutive detective takes on two of the biggest jobs of his career—the kidnapping of the 4 famous Farx Brothers comedy team—and the mysterious murder of a stagehand behind the scenes at an all-black musical version of *Citizen Kane*!

CHANDLER

The legendary graphic story artist and writer *Steranko* returns with a full-color thriller. Set in New York, 1940, Red Tide pits hard-boiled dick **Chandler** against a phantom murderer. An anti-heroic gumshoe in the atmosphere of seamy New York, **Chandler** has already been acclaimed as a classic of graphic story art. Over 200 illustrations compose a tense and intricate collage of the *film noire* and *Black Mask* conventions.

AFTERWORD

A few notes here for those of you still with us.

First, some acknowledgements: A big *thank you* to Shel Dorf, Rich Butner and the Board of Directors of the San Diego Comic Convention for our work on *Weird Heroes* and *Fiction Illustrated*. This convention, an annual affair, is one of the best run and most entertaining in the country. The award, a marvelous surprise, is deeply appreciated.

Another *merci* to the folks at *Comic Media* in England who also saw fit to acknowledge us with a *Special Recognition* vote. To receive such notice from a country where the books are only sporadically available is most encouraging.

Finally, a notice to those of you who are interested in a career in comic art. *The Joe Kubert School*, run by one of the medium's most talented storytellers, is an established institution with a specialized curriculum in comics and art. For further information, you can write to The Joe Kubert School, Box 777, Dover, New Jersey 07801.

Looking back on eight volumes of *Weird Heroes*, four anthologies and four novels, gives us perspective on the place of illustrated fantasy in the mass-market milieu. I think it is safe to say that there has been some innovation here, some exciting design and some truly memorable characters. I hope you, as our paid audience, have enjoyed at least some small part of what we have done. Our newer talents are some of the best in the fantasy field. Writers like Mike Reaves and Art Cover have long, interesting careers ahead.

The illustrated book is in the process of re-acceptance. *The Hobbitt* and *Ragtime* are prominent examples of a renaissance in graphics-oriented publication. Both have had deluxe editions released after the 'regular' book. Fantasy is particularly suited to the illustrated form. We at B.P.V.P. will be continuing to experiment with graphic fiction in collaboration with such writers as Roger Zelazny and Theodore Sturgeon. We welcome your ideas, thoughts and suggestions. As mass communications takes on an increasingly visual nature, the role of the graphic storyteller will continue to grow.

The medium needs an emotional response from its readers. The way to most immediately effect a change in the composition of the form is to get involved yourself. Communicate—either with your own mind, an audience or other individuals interested in the future of the graphic story.

Weird Heroes is an experiment. There are many others. Don't miss out on the opportunity to develop approaches of your own.

For the science fiction readers who purchase our books, I hope the series has expanded in some small way your concept of what a 'regular' paperback can be.

It's been a pleasure to be involved with an adventure like *Weird Heroes*. On behalf of our writers and artists, I'd like to thank you for joining us, too.

Byron Preiss
a cool summer night
New York, 1977